Sue Gee was born in 1947 and spent her early childhood on a farm in Devon and in a Leicestershire village. She worked in book and magazine publishing before going freelance as a writer and editor in 1983. This is her fourth novel. She lives with her family in London.

Her previous novel, *The Last Guests of the Season* is also available in Arrow paperbacks.

'Sue Gee explores the fascinating relationships that bind people together set against the uncertain and often worrying changes in Eastern Europe . . . A book that deals with difficult issues and one that tugs at the heart strings'
Lincolnshire Echo

'. . . a sensitive and intelligent stylist . . . *Letters From Prague* is an evocative tale that performs a delicate balancing act between the literary novel and more romantic genres'
Barry Forshaw, North London News

ALSO BY SUE GEE

Keeping Secrets
Spring Will Be Ours
The Last Guests of the Season

LETTERS FROM PRAGUE

Sue Gee

ARROW

The Forbidden Room by Helga Schubert (Luchterand, 1982)
is as yet untranslated into English. I am pleased
to acknowledge the quotation from it as coming from
Berlin, The Dispossessed City by Michael Simmons
(Hamish Hamilton, 1988).

First published in 1994

1 3 5 7 9 10 8 6 4 2

First published in the United Kingdom in 1994
by Century, Random House UK Limited

This edition is published by Arrow in 1995,
Random House UK, 20 Vauxhall Bridge Road, London SW1V 2SA

Random House Australia (Pty) Limited
20 Alfred Street, Milsons Point, Sydney,
New South Wales 2061, Australia

Random House New Zealand Limited
18 Poland Road, Glenfield
Auckland 10, New Zealand

Random House South Africa (Pty) Limited
PO Box 337, Bergvlei, South Africa

Random House UK Limited Reg. No. 954009

A CIP catalogue record for this book
is available from the British Library

ISBN 0 09 927451 5

Printed and bound in Great Britain by
Cox & Wyman Ltd, Reading, Berkshire

To Jamie

And to the memory of my brave and lovely mother

LONDON

The scale of world events

I

On a wet night in April, 1969, Harriet Pickering sat in the striped armchair by her bedroom window, reading a letter from Prague. The envelope was of thin, poor-quality paper, and bruised with postmarks: others had opened the envelope before her, and resealed it with a line of cheap glue. Harriet, who had been waiting for this letter since last autumn, coming home day after day from school to deepening disappointment, felt a shiver of distaste.

She pictured a poky room in a border station, a single light bulb, a desk piled high; she pictured a small fat man with drink on his breath, reaching for his paper knife, slitting and slitting, as if he were gutting dead fish, exposing brave words – *I am well, and hope you are also* – and scoring through braver – *You will understand that things are rather difficult now* – with thick black pen. Snowflakes fell through the darkness on to the railway track; a train drew into the station; a boy came into the poky room with a sack and snow on his shoulders.

The small fat censor shovelled the heaps and heaps of envelopes filled with absence and deprivation – *we all miss you, and hope to see you again one day* – into the sack and pulled open the drawer of his desk. He unscrewed the bottle inside it. The boy flung the sack to the back of a carriage; the train was shunted into a siding, and sat there for weeks.

Was this what had happened to Harriet's letter? She looked again at the front of the envelope, with her name and address in hesitant Biroed capitals: Miss Harriet Pickering, 143, Thackeray Gardens, Kensington, London W8, Anglická. She looked again at the letter, where he had written his own address: ulice Klimentská 6, Byt 8, Žižkov, Praha.

Apartment 8. Stone stairs inside a rambling tenement. An echoing stairwell, a roomy old apartment divided and subdivided, a wood-burning stove and a dark wall hung with tapestries. Or perhaps that was all wrong. Perhaps he lived in a concrete block on the outskirts of the city, with unmade roads around it and a broken lift within. There was a tiny kitchen where condensation streamed down ill-fitting windows; a strip of bedroom where he slept and studied, and wrote to her.

9

He had written! How could she have doubted him?

Kochana Harriet, Vesele vanoce . . .

Harriet got up from the striped armchair and went to her bureau. A poster was pinned to the wall above it; the bureau was open and strewn with essays; there were textbooks on top of it, pages marked with strips of paper; more textbooks lay on the floor – Milton and Molière and A.J.P. Taylor, A-level English and French and History, none of which seemed at this moment to matter much. She took from one of the pigeonholes the small blue phrase book and dictionary Karel had bought for her last August, from W.H. Smith in Regent Street, near the vegetarian restaurant where they were both working.

'Now,' he said, as they came out on to the crowded pavement, 'we talk more easier.'

'Easily,' said Harriet, slipping the phrase book out of its paper bag. 'Thank you.'

It was five o'clock, and they were both going in for the evening shift, he in the kitchen, washing up, and she behind the counter, serving parsnip soup. Normally given to polite impatience with arrogance or dithering in the queue, Harriet found herself these days smiling radiantly at elderly ladies peering at chick peas, charming those who changed their minds about stuffed mushrooms. She smiled at the ticket collector at Oxford Circus on her way in, and at the one at High Street Kensington on her way back; she smiled, these days, at everyone. Now she smiled at Karel, and looked up 'lovely' and 'day', bumping into a tourist with a backpack.

They made to cross and she stepped out too early, the number 12 bus roaring past her, lifting her summer skirt. He took her arm.

'You are crazy, stay by my side.'

They walked hand in hand through the narrow streets leading behind Liberty's to the restaurant. Earlier, they had met and had lunch in the basement bedsit Karel had rented in a house just off the Earls Court Road. The house was given over entirely to bedsits. Enormous Australians thundered down the stairs, collected mail from plywood boxes fastened to the wall and shouted to each other as they banged the front door shut. Beneath, looking out on to dustbins and railings, Karel's room had cracks in the ceiling and a carpet pockmarked with cigarette burns from a previous tenant, a small desperate Irishman who had left without paying the rent. The room also had a Baby Belling on a shelf, a scratched table with two folding chairs, a cheap chest of drawers and a gas fire. Pushed up against the wall between door and window was a narrow bed, covered in greying candlewick. Harriet, on her third visit, had replaced this with Indian cotton, and put roses in a coffee jar on the table.

'Is better,' said Karel, who had cleaned the windows and was stuffing the candlewick bedspread into the chest of drawers. He turned to look. 'Thank you.'

'My pleasure,' said Harriet. 'Where's the Hoover?'

There was no Hoover, but a squeaking Ewbank in a cupboard in the hall with one or two mournful-looking dusters and a floormop. Harriet ran the Ewbank over the cigarette burns and picked up a certain amount of fluff.

'I try before,' said Karel, making tea in glasses. 'Is very old, that thing.' He dropped slices of lemon into the glasses and set them on the table by the roses.

'Poor old thing,' said Harriet, and put the sweeper back in the cupboard. When she returned to the room she saw that Karel had opened the window: now the glass was clean the dustbins beyond didn't seem to matter quite so much. Footsteps went past; morning sun, heralding another baking day, made its way down the basement steps and shone on to the roses. They sat at the table, drinking their lemon tea.

'In Czechoslovakia,' said Karel, lighting a Marlboro cigarette, 'there is no Hoover. Everything is old brush and – ' he flicked out the match and made a gesture. 'What you call this?'

'Dustpan?' said Harriet, looking at Karel's long, beautifully made fingers, and the fortunate cigarette, resting between his lips.

'Dustpin,' said Karel, inhaling deeply. 'My grandmother is sweeping carpet with dustpin since I am a little boy.'

Harriet thought of Karel as a little boy and felt her heart turn over.

'In this country,' he continued, having been here some five or six weeks, 'everyone is materialism.'

'Materialistic. Not everyone.'

'In my country we are fighting for the essentials. For liberty to meet and make discussions, to move without the police spies, to – ' he made another gesture.

'To write?'

'To write, yes, but also – ' He picked up his *A–Z* and gave out multiple copies in rapid motion.

'To publish,' said Harriet, illuminated.

'To publish, yes.' He drew again on the cigarette.

'But things are easier now?' she asked, with vague memories of intermittent news items earlier in the year, of nice Mr Dubcek and his unassuming manner, his modest smile. A few months ago, Czechoslovakia had been just another country. A few months ago she had never even met Karel.

Never even met him!

'They are easier,' he was saying. 'But how long? We are exciting and also fearful.'

Harriet finished her tea. 'I must go, soon. I'm on at one today.'

Morning sun fell past the jar of roses and on to the Indian cotton bedspread, dusty pink and blue.

Karel stubbed out the Marlboro cigarette. 'Now you work, I study. This evening I wash up all alone.'

Harriet thought of the crowded kitchens, the heavy wooden chopping boards and clouds of steam, the people coming and going as Karel stood in his jeans and white T-shirt before the enormous sink. People came and went with trays, but he thought of himself as alone, just because she wasn't there.

'We must rearrange our shifts,' she said.

'Must what?' He looked at her, laughing.

'We must have the same shift,' she said slowly and clearly. 'Sorry. Anyway, I'll see you on Friday.' She got to her feet. Friday. Two and a half days!

Footsteps pounded down the stairs above them, someone bellowed, 'Okay, that's cool,' and the front door slammed. A little puff of plaster dust fell on to the bed from one of the cracks in the ceiling. Harriet brushed it off on her way to the door.

'Bye, then,' she said.

Karel had picked up the empty glasses of tea, whose slices of lemon lay brown and bloated at the bottom. He put them on the shelf beside the Baby Belling, and said, turning, 'You make my room nicely and then you go.'

Harriet looked at him. He was wearing a navy blue sweater over his white T-shirt, which showed at a slender neck. Above it his thin, suntanned face and curly dark hair were more beautiful than ever. He leaned against the wall and smiled at her, and she smiled back, realising suddenly: I shall never forget this moment. A shabby room, a hot summer street outside, Karel looking at me, holding out his hand.

Well. So this is love. So simple, so complete.

They lay upon the Indian bedspread and gazed into each other's eyes. Karel's were hazel, with interesting little flecks; Harriet's were grey, terribly ordinary, she knew, but in looking into his she did not feel ordinary.

'Harriet,' he said slowly, stroking her hair.

'Yes,' she said, and felt herself on the threshold of a journey, which began with the expression in his eyes, and ended – where would it end?

'My beautiful Harriet.' He gathered her close.

'There must be many beautiful girls in Czechoslovakia,' she murmured wistfully.

'That is true.'

She buried her face in his neck, thinking of them all.

'But none of them called Harriet.' Karel drew away, so that he could look at her again. 'Never I think I will meet someone like you.'

'Nor me.' She closed her eyes on all this happiness.

Above them the doorbell rang with a vengeance: gigantic feet came thundering down the stairs. The door was opened to enthusiastic greetings and closed as if to keep out armies. Another little puff of plaster came floating down through the sunlight, on to their feet.

'I must go,' said Harriet.

He kissed her hand. 'I wait for Friday.'

'Me, too.'

He saw her to the door; she walked down the road to the tube in a dream.

Now, as they were approaching the restaurant hand in hand, she felt, still, as if such joy could not be quite real – even if it felt, also, as if it were the only real thing that had ever happened to her. Late afternoon sun and shadow barred the pavement; it seemed that only now did the pigeons murmuring on the ledges of Carnaby Street shop windows, and the screech of taxis in Regent Street have any meaning. She had lived in London all her life: Karel had brought it alive.

The tables by the restaurant windows were already occupied: people meeting early, after work, sat drinking herb tea from heavy stoneware cups, making their way through oat and apricot slices. She and Karel walked through the double glass doors as if they, too, were customers, and went through the restaurant to the back.

'I'll see you at supper,' she said, reaching for the hessian apron on her peg. Another girl on the shift, already in her apron, came past them in the narrow corridor, and they greeted each other. Then Karel lifted Harriet's hand to his lips in a gesture which felt as though it said everything – you are mine, I shall see you soon – and disappeared through the swing doors into the kitchen. Harriet brushed her hair, hung up her bag on the peg and went out to the counter, thinking: I have everything I ever wanted. Please may it last for ever.

And it wasn't until the following morning, coming down late to breakfast in Thackeray Gardens, still in her nightdress and not quite awake, that she realised, seeing the faces of her parents and brother as they sat listening to the news, that nothing could last for ever, and that falling in love, which had seemed to encompass everything, was, in the scale of world events, only a little thing really. That evening, in the drawing room, she turned on the television; her family joined her and they all stood in silence: watching the tanks crawl through the beautiful streets of Prague, where people stood numbly: watching Czechoslovakia fall.

2

They stood on the Continental platform at Victoria station and waited for the train to Dover. It was four o'clock on an afternoon in autumn. All through August London had baked, the grass in Hyde Park and Kensington Gardens parched and brown, the air dry, the pavements dusty. Now it was a little cooler, the platform and empty track lit by a sun which felt melancholy and pale, even though it was still only just September.

It felt melancholy, but it would have done so today whatever the season. Ten weeks ago Karel had arrived in England. It was eight weeks since Harriet had walked into the restaurant kitchen, put down a trayful of stoneware plates next to the new washer-up and realised, with each returning trayful, how much she liked the look of him. It was three weeks since the Russian tanks had crossed the Czechoslovakian border, and during that time the look of Karel had changed.

Harriet had seen pounds drop off his lean frame overnight. She had seen fury and despair in a face which until now had been filled with interest and humour and affection. She had watched him watching the television in her parents' drawing room, smoking in a house where no one smoked, swearing in English and Czech in a house where no one, on the whole, ever swore, as modest, slant-eyed Mr Dubcek disappeared.

There were frightening rumours. Harriet made Karel endless cups of coffee and paced up and down the kitchen while the kettle came to the boil. What was he going to do?

This was what he was going to do. They stood on the platform, not touching or talking, waiting for the train. From Dover Karel would cross the Channel to Ostend; once there he would travel with his rucksack halfway across Europe: through Rotterdam, West Berlin, East Berlin, Dresden, crossing the heavily guarded German border and coming, at last, to Prague. A different city from the one he had left, full of hope: a city now under occupation, filled with resentment and fear.

'What else can I do?' he had asked her, packing his things in the Earls Court basement.

You could stay with me, thought Harriet bleakly, but she knew it was not possible. There was his family, his mother in tears on the telephone, on the single occasion he had managed to get through; there were all his friends, active in a crisis he could only watch on a foreign television. There was the expression in his eyes, his withdrawal from everything here: from the restaurant, from the bedsit, with its Indian bedspread and fading flowers; from her. Prague was his home, and home, at such a time, was everything.

'Of course you must go,' she told him, and folded the bedspread and put it in a carrier bag to take home. Then: 'Karel? You have this. Please.'

He took the bag and looked inside and smiled. It seemed such a long time since she'd seen that smile.

'Keep it,' she said. 'Go on.'

He nodded, raising her hand to his lips. 'I keep and remember Harriet.'

They kissed, then, their first proper kiss for weeks, standing in the middle of the denuded room, oblivious to Australians overhead; oblivious, it felt for a while, to everything. But love, as Harriet rediscovered most sorrowfully then, cannot, in such circumstances, be allowed to cast a country to oblivion, and anyway had not been spoken of. Not really. They drew apart, and finished packing.

And now they stood on the Continental platform, and now the train was coming.

It drew to a halt, doors opened, travellers returned. Harriet watched couples reunited, families gathering up children and suitcases and going along to the barrier; she watched Karel, scanning the carriages as they walked down through the crowds to the front, looking for a seat: already, it seemed, a long way away from her.

They found a corner in a smoking compartment, facing the front, with a table. Karel stowed his rucksack in the rack overhead, Harriet clenched her hands in the pockets of her denim jacket and willed herself not to cry. He turned and looked at her; she burst into tears.

'No, no,' he said, his face full of concern. 'Please.'

People pushed past them; she sank into the seat opposite his. He leaned across the table and stroked her hair without speaking. She covered her face, and tried to stop.

'Excuse me? Are these seats taken?'

She stopped. A healthy American couple in their fifties beamed down on them.

'Please. No one.' Karel was indicating that the adjoining seats were free; healthy American suitcases were swung up on to the rack.

'You have a cold?' the woman enquired kindly of Harriet, as she wiped her eyes.

For the first time in her life, but not the last, Harriet was rude to a total stranger.

'I'm crying,' she said coldly. 'Can't you tell the difference?'

'Gee, I – '

'Come on,' she said to Karel, all at once filled with anger: at America, at Russia, at the world. She got to her foot. 'We can't say goodbye here.' She pushed blindly past the woman, past everyone, and out on to the platform again, not turning to see if he had followed.

He had followed. For a moment her anger included him, too, for leaving; then he put his arms round her and drew her close.

'Fierce,' he said, and she could tell that he was smiling. 'I did not know you are so fierce.'

'Nor me,' she said, kissing his denim jacket, bought with savings from the restaurant after sending money home.

Further along the platform a whistle blew. They clung to each other, doors slammed. The whistle blew again; they kissed for the last time.

'Bon voyage,' said Harriet, and then, with wavering recall from last night's session with the dictionary, she struggled to say it in Czech.

'*Dobra*. Very good.'

Then Karel got back on the train again, and stood at the open window of the door. Beneath his dark hair his face was pale; he felt for a cigarette.

'Good luck,' said Harriet, bravely. 'Good luck, good luck.'

He nodded, lighting up, flicking away the match.

The last door slammed, the train began to move.

'Write to me,' she said quickly, walking alongside. 'Write and tell me everything.' She could see the Americans, smiling at her through the grimy window. Fools. Kind fools. They overtook her, the train was gathering speed.

'Write!' she said again, breaking into a run.

'Yes, yes.' He was leaning out of the window, cigarette held in graceful fingers.

People were waving all along the platform; there were other heads at other windows.

'Goodbye!' called Harriet, waving too. 'Goodbye, goodbye!'

'*Sbohem!*' he called back to her. '*Sbohem*, Harriet!'

The carriages creaked and the train went faster. Then it was gone.

Rain fell steadily on to the pavements of Thackeray Gardens, on to the bare trees and iron railings bordering the pleasant square of lawn and shrubs and hard-pruned roses in the middle. It splashed on to Harriet's windowsill and against the curtained window, and she hardly heard it, curled up once again in the striped armchair with her letter, her small blue dictionary.

Dear Harriet, Vesele vanoće! Happy Christmas! I send you best wishes for the new year and I hope you are well . . .

He had written to wish her a happy Christmas, and the letter had only just arrived. He had written in November, ten weeks after saying goodbye.

Ten weeks before Jan Palach's suicide.

Harriet looked across at the poster above her bureau. The blown-up black-and-white face of a young man looked out at her; beneath were his name, and the date of his death. On 16 January, 1969, he, a young student, had stepped out into Wenceslas Square, in the heart of Prague, and poured petrol all over his clothes. He had lit a match.

He had died five days later, on 21 January, in agony, in protest.

But not in vain, thought Harriet, looking at his photograph. Surely not in vain.

The poster came from Athena, in Oxford Street: it would not be on sale in Prague, though Palach's name would be on everyone's lips. Where had Karel been, when the match was lit? Had he gone running to Wenceslas Square?

London seems a very long way from me now. Since my return life has been –

Something was crossed out here, and she could not understand what followed. It had taken her fifteen minutes to get this far, and the phrase book was not much help, not really. It was full of requests for the bill, the doctor, the chambermaid. What had life been for Karel? What was he trying to tell her?

I am living with my parents once more; it is – something crossed out –

good to be with them again, but – here the small fat censor of Harriet's imagination had been at work, with a vile black pen. She felt despairing. All these months and months of waiting, of giving up hope, and there was barely a line on the thin single page which she could understand. Why hadn't he written in English? Wasn't it safe?

I hope to study law again one day, but at present I am working as a porter. It is – again, the black pen. Harriet was close to tears. It was hardly worth having, this stiff, formal letter, with its careful crossings-out by Karel and the vicious deletions made by the censor. Then she thought of all the letterless mornings and afternoons she had endured, all the nights when she had gone to sleep with her arms round her pillow, hoping to dream of Karel, and she lifted the page to her lips. Of course it was worth having!

She looked at it again, scanning the Biroed words for a phrase, a particular phrase, which had never been used by either of them, in either language. *Miluji vás.* I love you.

It wasn't there. The letter ended as if to anyone:

I hope you will have time to write to me one day. I think of you. Karel.

Well, almost anyone. He thought of her. In the midst of such difficult days, he thought.

Harriet got up. She folded the letter and slipped it back in its cheap, grubby envelope and put it into her bureau pigeonhole. She looked at the pile of essays on the open flap, at Milton and Molière and *The Origins of World War II*, all heaped up on the floor.

She thought of her expensive school, with its view of Kensington Gardens, its library, its gleaming laboratory and airy polished hall, where a list of head girls was painted in gold on a wooden board on the wall. At the end of this summer, when she had left, her own name would be added: Harriet Pickering, 1968–69.

She went to the window and drew back the curtains; she stood looking out at the rain, falling through the neon halos of street lamps, drenching the well-laid lawn in the square, dripping off the trees, just in bud, and off the iron railings. Hundreds of miles away, behind the Iron Curtain, Karel was thinking of her. He was working for a pittance, unable to write, or study, unable to plan his life.

Perhaps he had stopped thinking of her by now: it was months since he wrote that letter. Perhaps he had given up hope of hearing from her, perhaps he thought she'd forgotten.

Forgotten!

I shall write to you, Karel, thought Harriet, leaning against the window pane. I shall write, and send parcels, and keep on writing. She closed her eyes and saw him in the shabby Earls Court bedsit, his thin suntanned face alight with affection and hope. She felt his arms go round her, drawing her close. She saw the ugly monstrous tanks, parting the weeping crowds on the streets of his city, the blank bemused faces of the young Russian soldiers, looking about them.

One day, we shall be together again, she thought. One day I shall see you again, Karel.

3

They stood outside the buffet near the Continental platform, having an argument: Harriet Pickering, tall, dark, furious, and her daughter Marsha Pickering, ten next birthday, tall for her age, dark hair cut in a bob, adamant.

Marsha was wearing blue-striped shorts, bright pink sweatshirt and trainers, every item new, chosen by her last Saturday and bought by Harriet for the journey. Beside them were two suitcases; each, in addition, carried a shoulder bag. Between them was the cause of the argument, just produced from Marsha's bag: small, white, pink-eyed and sleek, at present washing himself vigorously in her hands after his confinement. He was supposed to be in his nice airy cage, staying round the corner with Marsha's friend Ruby, who had been given a quantity of mouse food, mouse bedding and mouse instructions.

It was half-past ten on a cloudy morning in August, 1993, and their train went in twenty-five minutes. Harriet's parents, who had come to see them off, knew better than to intervene. Her father looked at the headlines, her mother looked at her watch.

Marsha said: 'If he doesn't come, I'm not coming.'

'You have no choice.'

'I'll scream at the barrier,' said Marsha. 'I'll scream and say you're abducting me. I'll ring up Childline. And the RSPCA.'

'Look,' said Harriet, and drew a breath.

'Look,' said Marsha fondly. 'Isn't he sweet?'

Victor, for it was he, was bent over his right haunch, parting the fur with small, exquisite pink fingers and examining it with interest. Small mouse droppings fell through Marsha's fingers.

'What,' demanded Harriet, 'do you suppose we are going to do with him? How can we possibly take a mouse all that way?'

'How,' demanded Marsha, 'can we possibly leave him now? What are you going to do, abandon him on the station? Let him starve?'

Victor finished with the right haunch and returned to his face, running his hands all over at top speed, cleaning his handsome whiskers.

'He could live with the pigeons,' said Harriet weakly. 'He could have quite a nice life.'

For a moment there was a lull, as mother and daughter, each endowed with vivid imagination, pictured Victor, with small brown suitcase, setting up house with a benevolent pigeon family, living comfortably on crusts and burger buns, an interesting change from his usual well-monitored fare of rodent mix and grated vegetables; meeting, perhaps, another mouse. Marsha, with a rush of feeling, saw mouse babies, all in a nest; Harriet, whose vision of the bliss of motherhood had been tempered by the experience of living with Marsha, saw Victoria Station overrun with grey and white vermin. She saw poison being laid, and Victor eating it.

'When,' she demanded, 'did you go and get him from Ruby?'

'This morning. While you were paying the milkman, and I had one last skateboard round the block, remember?'

Harriet remembered. She said, with real conviction: 'Marsha, if I can't trust you, we're done for.'

'I know.' Marsha was stroking Victor's long sleek back as he ran up her arm. 'But I couldn't leave him. I'm sorry.'

They had spent the best part of ten minutes engaged in all this, and Harriet was dying for a coffee. They could get one on the train, but probably not for a while, and anyway it was nice to take one on with you, so you could avoid the first rush down the corridor, and settle down and relax.

With a nine-year old. And a mouse. All the way to Prague.

Harriet drew breath. 'I'm sorry, too,' she said. 'He's not coming.' She turned to her parents. 'Help?'

They came to the rescue.

'Darling.' Marsha's grandmother addressed her coaxingly.

Marsha looked mulish. 'What?'

'Please may we have him? Just until you come home? He'd be such good company when we'll be missing you both.'

'I'll miss *him*,' said Marsha. 'Anyway, you've got Thomas. He'll eat him, I know it.'

'I know,' said her grandfather. 'I've the very idea.'

'What?'

'He can come to the office. He can sit on my desk and entertain me while I do my sums. He can help.'

'He needs cleaning out – '

'I'll clean him out. I'll enjoy it. Much better than doing sums.'

'With what?' asked Harriet. 'You need sawdust, bedding, he has to have a dish, food, water bottle – honestly Marsha, this really is too bad. Poor Grandpa.'

'I've got all those things,' said Marsha calmly. 'They're all in my suitcase.'

Harriet looked at her. 'Then you'd better get them out again, sharpish. And what on earth are we going to put him in now?'

Everyone thought, as Marsha bent to unzip her bursting bag.

'A burger box?' suggested her grandmother.

Harriet looked at her gratefully.

'Brilliant,' said Marsha, removing mouse equipment from amongst pyjamas and sweatshirts. 'Can we get them to punch airholes in it?'

'We'd better get a move on,' said Harriet's father.

Some minutes later they emerged from the buffet with a carton of orange juice, coffee in a polystyrene beaker and Victor in a polystyrene burger box, scrabbling. People were moving steadily through the barrier. They made for it, hotfoot.

'Thank you,' said Harriet, hugging her parents. 'Whatever would I do without you?'

'Have a wonderful time.' Her father patted her shoulder. 'Give our love to Hugh and Susanna.'

'I wanted them to see Victor,' said Marsha.

'Never mind, darling.' Her grandmother gently took the box. 'Thank you so much for letting us borrow him. It'll do Grandpa the world of good.'

Marsha looked at the box. Beside them, the queue for the train moved faster.

'Come on,' said Harriet quickly. 'Come on, or we're done for.'

They all made their way down the platform. Reserved seats were waiting in Carriage D.

'Promise me something,' said Harriet, as they settled themselves, and looked out to where her parents were waiting, holding the box with encouraging expressions.

'What?'

'Don't ever lie to me again.'

'I didn't lie.'

'Deceive, then. You know what I mean.'

'OK.'

'And for the rest of the journey you do as you're told, OK?'

Marsha hesitated.

'Please?' said Harriet. She felt for her passport. Their passport: hers, with Marsha's photograph inside it, so no one could ever take her away. It had always, almost since the beginning, been just the two of them.

'Don't keep on about it,' said Marsha. 'I'll try.'

They both knew it was touch and go.

Their seats were opposite each other by the window of a No Smoking compartment; their luggage was stowed away above them. Harriet carefully removed the lid of the polystyrene beaker and let the smell of British Rail coffee waft with a little wreath of steam towards her. She sat back, waiting for it to cool, watching the compartment fill with travellers. Vast nylon rucksacks on aluminium frames were heaved about in the corridor, children ripped open packets of crisps and asked when they would get there; childless couples opened their books. Beside them, two clean Dutch students were settling into their seats.

Since the end of term at the comprehensive school where she tried to teach, and at the primary school where Marsha was supposed to learn, Harriet had been ironing, packing, organising the departure of one lodger and the arrival of another, cancelling papers and milk. She had risen this morning at half-past six. Now she let the surrounding activity wash over her. Opposite, Marsha was pulling a sorry face. She'd be all right once they got moving.

Last-minute passengers were panting up to the doors. Harriet, drinking her coffee, barely took them in. She forgot about Marsha, forgot about the mouse. She saw an afternoon in autumn, twenty-five years ago, two figures on the same platform, both in denim jackets; she saw them cling to each other and kiss; she saw, as the last door now slammed to, Karel, at the window in the corridor, leaning out with his cigarette, and she running alongside as the train began to move, waving and waving.

'We write! We write!'

And they had written: the polished bureau which had stood once in the bedroom of her parents' house in Kensington stood now in the sitting room of her own house in Shepherd's Bush, and had in its second drawer a wooden box of letters. Each was written on thin cheap paper, each one worn from being unfolded and folded again, read and re-read.

Thank you for writing, I was pleased to hear from you . . .
I am sorry not to have written, but things have been . . .
I am afraid that – something crossed out – *All is well, but unfortunately*
– something crossed out –
I am afraid that it has been a long time since I wrote to you . . .
I am afraid that it is difficult for me to write to you at present . . .
I am afraid . . .
I am afraid . . .

Then they had stopped. The last worn letter in the box was dated
March 1971. Harriet had read it with her dictionary-phrase book,
sitting at the plain, light wood desk of her university study bedroom.
Her life had changed: A-levels long distant, first-year history exams
behind her, new people all around her. One, in particular, she liked the
look of, as she had liked the look of Karel. Reading his letter, trying, yet
again, to guess what lay behind the formal phrases, he seemed far from
her in a way which she knew in her heart was due not only to absence,
or distance, but her own preoccupations. He was fading. She had
thought that would never happen, but she knew, if she were honest,
that it was so.

And what, she thought then, folding the letter, and putting it back in
its envelope, was the point of anything if one could not be honest?

There was a knock at the door.

'Harriet? We're off – you ready?'

'Coming!'

She put on her long dark Julie Christie coat and left the room,
leaving the letter on the desk, leaving that part of her life behind her,
running down the corridor to catch up with her friends.

Weeks later, feeling almost as though it were a task, she wrote,
briefly:

*Since it is so hard for us to communicate, perhaps it is better that we do
not try, though I shall always remember you with affection and hope that
all is well with you . . .*

She dropped the letter into the campus box next morning, on her way
to a lecture, posting it with a card to her brother, who was working for
his O-levels. And then, hurrying across the windswept grass and
tarmac to the lecture theatre, she forgot about Karel.

*

25

The whistle blew, the train began to move.

'We're off!' said Marsha, waving to her grandparents.

'We're off.' Harriet smiled at her, and at them, waving back, standing near to each other, solid and kind.

'Goodbye, goodbye.'

The train swung round the bend in the track. 'All right?' she asked.

'Not yet.' Marsha sat down again.

'When will you be all right?'

'When we get to Brussels. When we see Uncle Hugh and Susanna.' She unwrapped the straw on her carton of orange juice and began to drink.

'Yes, I'm looking forward to seeing them, too.'

In truth, Harriet was a little apprehensive. Did merchant banker brothers really welcome impoverished teacher sisters? Would Susanna, a banker's daughter who did not, apparently, work, and with whom she had, surely, little in common, find showing them round the city a chore? Despite the fact that she had married her brother, and invited Marsha to be her bridesmaid, Harriet felt she hardly knew Susanna.

Marsha had been a pleased but somewhat astonished bridesmaid. She had never been to such an event in her life, and was unlikely to do so again, Harriet's friends being, on the whole, either resolutely unwed; partnered without formalities; or succumbing only as the children grew older, their grandparents sadder, slipping off to the Register Office in the lunch hour and holding a drunken party that evening.

'So make the most of it,' Harriet told her daughter, twirling before the mirror of her grandmother's bedroom, in full-skirted cream silk with a dusty rose sash. It wasn't a church wedding, but Susanna had said she wanted the chance to dress up, and to dress Marsha up, and Marsha, uncertain at first, had, in the end, enjoyed unheard-of outings to Liberty's.

From downstairs came the muted exclamations of aunts, arriving, followed by uncles, clearing their throats.

Marsha regarded herself in the full-length mirror. 'I look amazing!'

'You do look nice,' said Harriet. Was this pretty child, with gleaming hair and satin pumps, really the one who spent most of her time in secondhand dungarees and trainers, refusing to do things? She held out a coronet of tiny cream silk flowers, with ribbons at the back. 'Let's put this on now.' The gleaming head bent obediently; Harriet settled the coronet in place, smoothed out the pair of cream ribbons. Together, mother and daughter regarded the reflection, and hugged each other. 'Perfect. Perfect!'

'I wish I could be bridesmaid every day,' said Marsha, and ran to open the door, running along the landing calling out 'Granny! Granny! Look at me now!'

And Harriet, following, stopped to look in the mirror once more, and saw there someone else who looked different: a tall dark woman usually in jeans, usually in a hurry, dressed now in midnight-blue linen, with a slender string of pearls, and lipstick, going to her brother's wedding, by herself, watching her daughter be bridesmaid, by herself.

So. There had been all that – the arrival at Chelsea Town Hall, the flowers, the photographers; Susanna in sandwashed silk and heavenly cut-away shoes; Marsha, grave and exquisite; the smiles, the tears, the signing of the register; the reception – too many speeches, too much champagne; the waving goodbye, goodbye. Hugh and Susanna, a banker and a banker's daughter, meeting in Brussels: he, even then, beginning to look middle-aged, but with such a dear, kind face; she all fair hair, slender hands, cool charm, smiling and waving as they climbed into the waiting car in a cloud of confetti, and drove away. For a honeymoon in Tuscany, then back to Brussels.

Since then, almost four years ago, they'd seen each other only once, when Hugh and Susanna came over for her father's seventieth birthday, when the house, as for the wedding, had been full of visiting relatives, with little opportunity for real conversation. Susanna, in any case, had seemed – Harriet was not sure if she had misinterpreted this – to avoid real conversation. And watching, once, over a crowded lunch table, Harriet had the sense that things between her and Hugh were not, somehow, quite right. Or perhaps she had imagined it.

Well. Hugh had sounded welcoming enough in his letter, and it was only the first lap of the journey. It gave them a good reason for seeing Brussels, and then they'd be back by themselves.

The track was straight again, the train picking up speed. They passed small brick houses crammed together; tower blocks rose beyond them. Karel, travelling along this track twenty-five years ago, would have looked out on to much the same view, give or take a tower block. Harriet, reading history at university, had almost forgotten Karel, but she had kept his letters.

She kept other letters, too. The second drawer of the polished bureau held those from Marsha's father, who had, as Karel never had, told Harriet that he loved her, but who had, when it came to it, loved her not quite enough.

Late on a Saturday afternoon one mid-November, when Marsha, at almost three months, was screaming with colic, her baby legs drawn up and her scarlet face contorted, her father told Harriet he was just going out to the shops. It was 1983, and Harriet, like many women of her generation, was trying to do everything: have a baby, run a house, go back to work and entertain on Saturdays. They were entertaining tonight: two couples who had not yet thought about babies, who showed no more than polite interest in Martin and Harriet's baby, and who were certainly not interested in having her appear during supper, let alone be breastfed in front of them.

Harriet, exhausted, dreading the evening, pacing up and down the knocked-through sitting room of the terraced house in Shepherd's Bush with screaming Marsha, barely noticed Martin had gone. He was a good cook, he was cooking tonight: she assumed he had forgotten cardamoms, or cumin or turmeric, none of which went well with breastfeeding, though she could hardly expect their guests to enjoy Weetabix and banana or slices of ham with mashed potato, which was what, in her heart, she felt like. She didn't really care what ingredient Martin had forgotten, she didn't care about anything except how to stop Marsha crying, and she barely heard the front door close, though she did feel, not for the first time, a rising resentment that it was usually she who did the pacing.

Some forty minutes later, with Marsha, at last, asleep in her basket – about, Harriet knew, to wake and start screaming again, as she did every evening – she went, almost shaking with tiredness, into the kitchen. Martin had been making preparations. There was a bunch of supermarket coriander, a china bowl with eggs in it, a bottle of red wine and a chopping board put ready, with a sharp Sabatier knife, to chop the meat which Harriet dimly recalled was in the fridge with a large carton of sour cream. None of these things looked as though it had anything to do with her, or her life as it had become since Marsha's arrival.

There was also a note, with her name on it, propped up against a box of wild rice. She put on the kettle and looked at it, as if from some distance.

She took it back to the sitting room. The light was fading. She read the note, and then she read it again, sinking on to the sofa from Heal's which she and Martin had chosen together, long before Marsha was thought of.

I am sorry . . . this is not . . . I cannot . . . I never wanted . . . you know I never wanted . . . you are better off without . . . I am sorry . . . goodbye . . . goodbye . . .

It had grown dark. Beyond the uncurtained doors at the end of the room the little square of West London garden was invisible. In her basket, Marsha was stirring, beginning to draw her legs up, screwing up her baby face with pain. Harriet, on the Heal's sofa, cried and cried.

She had largely – not quite – forgotten Karel at university: there had been many times since when she had thought of him. She had thought of him whenever Czechoslovakia was in the news again: in 1973, the year after she left with a good degree, when an amnesty was granted to those Czechs who had remained abroad after the Russian invasion. Forty thousand exiles returned, then, hoping for better times. She thought of him in 1977, when hundreds of intellectuals signed Charter 77, the manifesto of human rights, and a new wave of arrests and imprisonments began. Was Karel among the signatories? Had he, too, been arrested? She pictured him, long and dark and beautiful, brutally woken from sleep – on his own? With his wife? His lover? – by a bang on the door and harsh, implacable voices; driven away, as Dubcek had been driven away.

Never I think I will meet someone like you, Harriet . . .

In the summer of 1981, she sat watching programmes about the strikes and unrest in Poland, about Solidarity and Lech Walesa: all this was in the neighbouring country, and might spread. There were more arrests in Czechoslovakia. Again, she wondered: was he safe? Had they come for him in the night?

Harriet, sobbing on the Heal's sofa as Marsha, in her basket, began to wail, remembered Karel's departure and cried even harder. The only men she had ever loved, and both had abandoned her. But Karel had a reason, a real reason, and besides, they were both so young.

And so in love, she thought brokenly, picking up her baby.

It had grown even darker; people were coming to supper. In tears, Harriet made a phone call, and asked for another to be made, explaining about babies, and colic, and tiredness, sensing a mixture of concern and impatience at the other end.

Who cared? They were his friends, not hers. Childless accountants. Is that what Martin wanted to be? She hated them all.

In tears she went into the kitchen, and swept every last item of dinner-party fare into the swingbin. Marsha continued to scream.

At last, as every evening, she stopped, and Harriet fed her. She changed her and watched her fall at last like a stone in a well into a deep, real sleep; she took herself into a hot bath and afterwards, in her dressing gown, she ate slices of ham and bread and butter. Then she went to bed and fell asleep too, her baby beside her, both waking in the night to cry again.

Gradually, they recovered. Marsha, on the dot of three months, gave up colic, as the clinic had said she would. Harriet, finding herself with a transformed baby – smiling, cooing, feeding well – stopped crying quite so much. Christmas was miserable, spent with her family, trying to be brave. New Year was worse, spent with a friend she'd made in the NCT class, whose husband had not abandoned her, and who was radiant. Marsha's father, as Harriet had begun to think of Martin, severing painfully his connection with herself, sent a letter. He would arrange for a monthly sum, a standing order.

Well. That was something. No. That was the least he could do.

Harriet, back at work, with Marsha at a childminder, typed out a four-line announcement, and photocopied it in the school office.

Harriet Pickering announces the end of her marriage to Martin Rivers. She and Marsha Pickering will continue to live at their present address until further notice and look forward to seeing you there.

She posted a copy to all her friends, she put up a copy in the staffroom. And then, because she had to, and because she had a baby, she got on with her life.

*

Marsha went to nursery school. She went to primary school. Harriet changed jobs, moving to a school closer to Marsha's. She became, in due course, head of the history department; she became, somebody told her, rather intimidating. She and Marsha had lodgers, they had friends; they had, on the whole, a well-run and enjoyable life: two strong-willed individuals who battled in the mornings and made it up in the afternoons, collapsing at the end of school with tea and television, curling up with a book at bedtime. There were people in and out of the house. It was, said Marsha, a nice house.

There was not, however, a man in Harriet's life. Nor, for a long time, wary and angry, did she wish for one. When that changed, and she did begin to wish, there seemed to be no one who was both desirable and free. There was certainly no one, among those few men with whom she went to the cinema, to the park with Marsha or even, occasionally and discreetly, to bed, for whom she felt it might be worth disrupting the settled existence she and her daughter had now established.

Some of the energy which might have been given to a man went, rather more usefully, she felt, into local politics, community issues, national campaigns. It was the Eighties, and a lot of money was being made by a certain kind of person. It was not, on the whole, being made by the parents of Harriet's pupils, many of whom were facing unemployment. Her department budget was being cut with every term. She spent a great deal of time in meetings, on marches, writing angry letters.

Now and then, in discussions with friends, or in rare quiet moments on her own, she reflected on the political progress of her life: from privileged, privately educated accountant's daughter to radical teacher, campaigning member of the Labour Party. She retained much affection for her parents, but she dissociated herself from her background and their politics, refusing, in particular, to send her daughter anywhere but the local school.

Sometimes she tried to connect the person she was now with the girl who had watched the Russian tanks invade Czechoslovakia. She reflected that to be a socialist in Britain, where the class divide grew in some ways ever wider, did not mean identifying with Russian imperialism. She reflected on something she had heard at university from a lecturer she had much liked the look of, who had told them, in a seminar, about a badge worn by Communist Party members in Britain after the Hungarian invasion of 1956, when she had been only five.

I think, therefore I see.

Well, yes, that was right. She tried to be clear-sighted.

She tried, too, to give Marsha a sense of the world.

In Marsha's bedroom there stood on top of the bookshelves an illuminated globe. There was also a map on the wall. Sometimes Harriet tested her on seas, or capital cities; she told her about the Berlin Wall, which meant there was a capital city divided. She told her about the Iron Curtain, and once or twice, as their fingers moved eastward over Europe, reaching Czechoslovakia: 'I used to know someone from here. He lived in Prague, the capital – here, see? It's supposed to be beautiful.'

Marsha yawned. Harriet put the globe back on the bookshelf and kissed her goodnight. She stood in the doorway, looking at patchwork Europe, shining down; at the pointer, marking Prague.

'Will we ever go there?' asked Marsha, pulling her lion pyjama case down beside her.

'I shouldn't think so,' said Harriet, hearing Annie the lodger come in downstairs.

'Because of the Iron Curtain?'

'Yes. Goodnight.'

Hugh and Susanna were married in the summer of 1989. That autumn, Europe changed for ever. On a grey November Saturday, Harriet and Marsha and Annie the lodger sat on the worn Heal's sofa watching the Berlin Wall come down.

Within a fortnight they were watching a demonstration of two hundred thousand people in Prague, snow falling on Wenceslas Square, bells ringing, a government, without a shot being fired, giving in at last. Harriet found herself searching, with every close-up of every face, for a particular face, thin, dark-haired, older. She could not find it, but she could not tear herself away.

Then, at Christmas, the cameras swung to Romania. Harriet and Marsha, spending Christmas in Kensington, sat with her parents and various aunts, watching the demonstration, a very different one, before the presidential palace. They saw the dawning realisation on Ceaucescu's face: the angry crowd, the helicopters on the palace roof, the trial, the execution. Harriet did not like Marsha watching this, and was glad of the distraction of presents.

At the end of Boxing Day they drove home across a deserted

London. Next day, they watched a tumultuous Prague, as Dubcek, smiling, triumphant, older, came out on to the balcony of the National Museum, waving to the thousands ringing bells in the square below. Harriet wept.

'Why are you crying?' asked Marsha. 'I hate it when you cry.'

'I'm sorry,' said Harriet, drying her eyes, giving her a hug. 'I just can't help it.'

It's a great circle, she thought later, having a glass of brandy by the fire, amongst the Christmas cards, as Marsha fell asleep upstairs. Dubcek had fallen, been taken away and humiliated, and now he was back: although once that seemed impossible it now seemed inevitable.

Perhaps other things, also, had possibilities.

The fire had burned low, the lights on the tree in the corner shone like white stars. I don't know, thought Harriet: perhaps one day we might, after all, make a journey to Prague.

She got up and went to the bureau; one or two Christmas cards slipped as she opened the second drawer. She took out the little box of letters and sat by the fire again, reading them through for the first time in over twenty years, those long-distant phrases which seemed to her now not formal and stiff but uncertain, apprehensive.

I am afraid it is not possible . . . I am afraid . . . I am afraid . . .

What had happened to him? Was he, with everyone else in Prague, out in the Square beneath the balcony, ringing a handbell in the snow? She looked at the address, the Biroed capitals. Ulice Klimentská 6, Byt 8, Žižkow, Praha. Was it possible, after all these years, that he lived there still?

I shall go and find out, she thought, with sudden resolve. I shall make the journey he made, next summer, with Marsha. We shall travel by train, through a different Europe, and one day –

Well. In maturity, she thought, finishing the brandy, one must, I suppose, qualify one's dreams. Still. You never know. Perhaps, one day, I shall see you again, Karel.

BRUSSELS

Villette and the House of the Swan

I

Fine rain swept the rooftops. The doors to the bedroom balcony were open a little, and now and then opaque net curtains, affording privacy from the apartments opposite, were disturbed by a current of cool air. Harriet, in a room of many mirrors, in a spacious apartment in a foreign city, had almost finished unpacking.

She opened the doors of a walnut wardrobe and put in their luggage – worn canvas, mother; tough nylon, daughter. Both articles looked unequal to the place in which they now found themselves: within a fine piece of furniture in a spare room larger than Harriet's sitting room; in a fourth-floor apartment in one of the sleekest residential quarters of Brussels. Her clothes, neatly folded and put away, looked, here, similarly unequal to the task of being Hugh's sister, let alone Susanna's sister-in-law. Harriet knew very well how to be Marsha's mother, but that was in London, where her life, so busy and organised, seemed overnight to have become incommunicable.

She closed the wardrobe doors with a click. She put her striped sponge bag next to the washbasin, shaped like a shell, washed her face and brushed her teeth, and then, with no other task to occupy her, stood in the middle of the pale grey carpet, looking uncertainly about her.

It was a long time since Harriet had felt uncertain. In the years since her husband's departure she had learned more self-reliance than perhaps she might have chosen to, but it had become a part of her. She was a competent head of department at school, a competent if exasperated mother, a sensible landlady to her lodgers: students who came and went, given clean sheets on Saturdays and instructions to keep the noise down. Harriet had a life in London which felt, on the whole, rather full.

It was full. There were, naturally, wet weekends when she and Marsha quarrelled, when Marsha retired to her room in sulks and Harriet stood in the hall in despair, staring at loose flaps of wallpaper and scuffed skirting boards, wondering what she had done to deserve all this. But at such moments she had recourse to the telephone, to her friend Fanny, two streets away, whom she had met on the Labour Party street stall just before the 1987 election, and who could generally be counted on for a cheering glass or two while the children played. She had recourse to Robin, her deputy head of department, who had a pretty wit and a season ticket to the National Film Theatre. There were her parents, who enjoyed being Marsha's grandparents – making, indeed, a rather better job of caring for her than they had of their own children. There were any number of people in London, and, furthermore, there was work itself, which despite mounting heaps of paper and frustration at the National Curriculum, still gave satisfaction. It certainly gave little time to think, to dwell.

Harriet, now, found herself dwelling: on the prospect of a good few days in the company of a brother whose life could not be more different from her own and a sister-in-law of whom that was also true, and who felt, still, something of an unknown quantity.

Their reunion at the Gare du Nord had been warm but hesitant. A kiss, enquiries after parents and the journey, luggage put into the waiting car; and then a muted drive through the afternoon rain: along the Rue Royale and past the great Parc du Bruxelles and the Palace.

The windscreen wipers went back and forth. Amongst the drooping, rain-soaked flags of EC member states, and the EC flag with its circle of stars, the Belgian tricolour hung sombrely, looped up with broad black ribbons. Leaning against the Palace railings the cellophane wrapping of thousands of flowers glistened and dripped.

'Of course,' said Harriet, after a moment. 'Baudouin has died.'

'Who?' asked Marsha from the back.

'The king.' Susanna looked at her in the mirror. 'Last week the city came to a standstill. People were weeping in the street.'

Harriet shook her head. 'No one in England knows much about him. It was on the news, of course, but – '

'He was loved,' said Susanna. 'He was a shy man, but he was hard-working and represented something solid, and lasting – the Belgians have had so many changes of government since the war, I couldn't tell you how many. And he did a lot to unite the country – ' She indicated a street sign in Flemish and French. 'Hugh will tell you more about it all, if you're interested. Anyway, it was sad. You'll see black ribbons everywhere, not just on the flag – people hung them over their balconies. . . . Look, there's one above that pharmacy.'

They looked at a heavy fall of black over elaborate wrought iron.

A city in mourning, thought Harriet, who had watched the news like everyone else, but who had not quite been able to anticipate how disorienting and excluding it might feel to arrive in such a place, greeted by a member of the family who in truth she barely knew.

'Did you have a ribbon?' Marsha asked Susanna.

'Yes, but more for respect, and form, if you know what I mean. We've taken it down now.'

They drew up at traffic lights, and Marsha went quiet, Harriet sensing her sudden exhaustion. It was left to her to comment on expensive shops and restaurants, on the well-dressed women walking on generous pavements, pausing at plate-glass windows, discreet arcades. She asked Susanna one or two questions about her life here; Susanna gave one or two answers, revealing little. Harriet, feeling her way, gave up.

At the Place du Grand Sablon, they turned off into a quiet side street, drawing up outside an apartment block. They paid the taxi driver; a porter came out to help with the luggage. Thick carpets, a lift ascending in silky silence, the doors to other apartments solid, and firmly closed. There was this generously proportioned room, to which Susanna had shown them, inviting them to unwind and unpack before tea; there was a sudden quiet, a sense of displacement amongst strangers which Harriet, standing now in the middle of the pale grey carpet, found completely unnerving.

Marsha was having a shower. From the kitchen at the far end of the apartment Harriet could hear the chink of china. She went to the low buttoned chair where she had put down her capacious shoulder bag, and from it withdrew a small wooden box and a notebook.

The box she put on her bedside table. All those letters, all those years ago. In these new and unfamiliar surroundings, the box looked as out of place as she felt herself to be, but it also felt comforting, a link with London and with her past.

However.

Karel had not answered the letter she had written to him last autumn, to his old address, in which she had announced her intention of travelling to Prague.

It is so many years since we met –
I am not sure if you will remember me –
I have a daughter, now –

39

I am thinking of bringing her for a holiday next summer –
And you? What of your own life? I should so like to hear –

Without a reply, should she be making this journey? Doubt assailed her. She sat on the low buttoned chair, turning the pages of her notebook.

The notebook was thick and black, its corners tipped in Chinese red. She had bought it at the newsagent's at the end of their road one Saturday afternoon last winter, taking it home with a pile of books from the library: histories and guides and biographies. She had piled them up on her desk in the sitting room, and spent, thereafter, many winter evenings of discovery. The notebook was filled with a summary of all her reading: with dates, with the names of monuments, churches, bridges; with quotations. To the teacher of history which Harriet had become to her very bones this marshalling of facts was deeply satisfying. And now, turning the pages, she rediscovered a little of herself, and her purpose.

This journey was worth making for its own sake. She had realised that on those long winter evenings, curled up with her books on the sofa, or making notes at her desk, absorbed in the lives of the dead.

In Brussels, impoverished lacemakers worked cold fingers to the bone, coughing in damp, ill-lit cellars, where the thread was less likely to break.

In Brussels, on the run from the civil police in Paris, Marx took rooms on the Grand Place, and then a poor little house in the suburbs. Here, his dear wife Jenny had more babies, and he and Engels, visiting from England, became the nucleus of a small community of German political exiles. The *Communist Manifesto* was written here, rolling off the printing press in 1848, when capital cities all over Europe were in revolutionary uproar.

And in Brussels, a few years earlier, Charlotte Brontë had suffered the anguish of unrequited love.

Harriet stopped reading through her notes and leaned back in the chair, yawning. The cool current of air through the balcony doors disturbed the fine net curtains; she closed her eyes. All those books, and notebooks, all those months ago. Much of what she had written she had already forgotten, but knowledge, in any case, paled beside imagination: as a historian, seeking to interpret and reinterpret the past, she had always known that.

And now, tired from her journey and on the threshold of sleep, imagination took hold, and Charlotte, small and downcast, filled with loneliness and longing, returned to the Pensionnat Heger from her afternoon walk. She drew her cloak around her against the wind, dreaming of her Professor, of a look, a word, a smile.

She slipped inside the front door, her heart pounding, and moved, oh so quietly – was he here? Was he coming? Was that his footstep, crossing the hall? – towards the stairs. Younger pupils descended, giggling; they stopped at the sight of their mouselike English acquaintance, hands to their mouths, nodding politely, stepping aside as she crept past. Up in her room Charlotte removed her bonnet, her cloak, laying them on the narrow iron bed, pressing her hands to her face. After a while, she crossed to the gabled window. She stood looking out at the rooftops, slate-grey beneath gathering cloud. Was this how she had imagined it all, planning it out with Emily in the Parsonage dining room? She had not imagined such pain, such longing.

In 1843 Charlotte returned to Haworth and the moors. She wrote long, impassioned letters to Professor Heger, receiving no reply.

I suppose animals kept in cages, and so scantily fed as to be always on the verge of famine, await their food as I awaited a letter . . .

Years later, renaming the city Villette, she poured her remembered suffering into the fine and disturbing novel in which Lucy Snowe, impoverished and friendless, took a teaching post in a girls' school in Brussels, falling in love with its handsome English doctor. Her feelings were not returned; in the long summer vacation when the school was empty, she was driven by loneliness to the borders of breakdown and despair. One wet evening she crept into the cold and sombre refuge of a Catholic church. Bells rang; she was almost fainting –

'*Mon père, je suis Protestante . . .* '

The current of air at the open windows was cool and fresh. There was no sound, where a sound had been. Harriet, waking, realised that the rain had stopped. She rose from her chair, and went out on to the balcony. Ivy, shining and wet, trailed along the wrought-iron railing. Wet geraniums stood in clay pots in a corner; a fuchsia dripped. Harriet stood surveying the street below, the elegant houses opposite, waiting for Marsha's return from the shower, and Susanna's summons for tea.

The houses opposite were like this house: neoclassical, graceful; stone façades supporting slender pilasters. Susanna was a slender pilaster: decorative, but incapable of bearing weight. Was that true? What was it, over a crowded birthday lunch in her parents' dining room, which had felt, somehow, not quite right? Had Harriet imagined it, or had Susanna, today, been deliberate in deflecting questions about herself as they drove, from the station, along the Boulevard St Lazare? The Jardin Botanique should be pointed out, of course, but even so.

Balconies hung on the houses opposite; at the same level as Harriet, net curtains obscured another life. No, not quite: a shadowy figure moved past them. So. Who was at home in the afternoon, alone in a silent apartment? Who was somebody waiting for, nerves on edge at the discreet buzz of the intercom? Charlotte Brontë had suffered and wept, but Brussels in 1993 did not, so far, feel like a city for romantic assignation. Still. You never knew. For a moment, Harriet wondered: how does Susanna spend her days? Her afternoons? And then, surprising herself at her own intensity: if she hurts Hugh, I shall never forgive her.

She leaned on the balcony, looking down at the to and fro of traffic. She had not quite got her bearings here, but she knew that not far away in the south-west stood the Palais de Justice and, sprawling in its magnificent shadow, the impoverished, densely populated district of the Marolles. Tomorrow was for exploration, and settling in – and perhaps, in a day or two, she might also find her bearings in relation to her brother's marriage. She brushed shining water from the curve of the balcony railing. Please, she thought, again surprising herself: don't let this one go wrong.

A sound behind her: she turned, seeing Marsha with wet hair, a towel wrapped round her, dropping her clothes on the bed.

'Susanna says tea in a few minutes – when we're ready.' She came up beside Harriet in bare feet.

'You'll catch your death.'

'No, I won't.'

Marsha looked down at the street, Harriet saw a gooseflesh chill run all along her arms, and drew her to her, rubbing them warm. Below them, gleaming cars slid past.

'It's terribly posh,' said Marsha.

'Isn't it? Everything. How was the shower?'

'The bathroom's posher than Granny's, even. There's millions of bottles and things.'

'Lotions and potions.' Harriet continued to rub bare arms. 'Are you all right?'

Marsha nodded, but didn't answer. She probably didn't know. Children were powerless, taken hither and thither to meet this person and that. Marsha was rooted and outgoing at home; these surroundings – such space, such a carpet, such gilded mirrors – had silenced her. And Harriet, suddenly, saw Hugh, two years younger than Marsha was now, sent off to boarding-school, silenced.

Bells chimed the half-hour; Marsha shivered.

'Come and get dressed. Susanna will be wondering where we've got to.'

'Where have we got to?' Marsha asked, dropping the towel to the floor and pulling her knickers and socks on.

This is what comes of being an only child, thought Harriet: all that adult conversation. There aren't many nine-year-olds who'd answer like that, and be so accurate.

Marsha pulled on jeans and sweatshirt; she laced up her trainers.

'Let's do your hair.' Harriet pulled a brush through the damp dark pageboy, the thick soft fringe. Mirrored mothers and daughters did the same. 'Tonight we'll see Hugh again. You look a bit like him at the moment.'

'How?'

'A bit lost. That's how he used to look, when he came home from boarding-school. He used to sit in the dining room and talk to himself.'

'What about?'

Harriet put down the brush. It was a long time since she had thought about those distant, well-run holidays, with outings to Kensington Gardens, and children in for tea. She had forgotten what she now could see so clearly: a child whose companions in a chilly Northumberland dormitory were scattered all over the country when term ended; a child who knew no one in London, who came home to his family and took a week to rediscover how to talk to them, when there was no one else to talk to.

She saw the gradual unwinding, relaxing, always polite but not so rigid, and then the build-up to silence again, as the end of the holidays drew near. At intervals in this interlude, Hugh sat with his back to the open door of the dining room, a dark room, with family portraits, a window hung with heavy curtains, a view to a London garden. He sat at the long, polished table; his legs in long socks swung beneath it; his

43

fingers drummed. He was talking: Harriet, stopping in the corridor, could hear him. Not the words, but the tone. He was confiding – even at ten or eleven, sheltered Harriet was aware of this, as Marsha, more precocious, assuredly would be, too. Confiding what? To whom? She stood in the corridor, pressed back against the wall: listening, eavesdropping, guilty. Once, she coughed. The monotone stopped, the drumming on the table ceased. He turned, she fled.

Even as children, they could not confront each other.

'What did he talk about?' Marsha was asking again.

They moved towards the bedroom door; she turned the china doorknob, painted with birds. 'That's pretty.'

'I never knew,' said Harriet. 'Perhaps it's best not to mention it.'

'Why?'

Pretty well everything was mentioned at home.

'Oh – '

They were out in another corridor now, carpeted in deep blue wool, with runners in coffee and cream. The walls were hung with pale paper; watercolours hung at intervals, at just the right height. Susanna, in linen trousers, was coming towards them.

'Well done.' She smiled at Marsha. 'You look nice. Shower all right?'

'Fine, thanks. I like all the bottles and things.'

'I should have told you to help yourself. There's a jar of oatmeal, did you see that? You can put it in your bath, if you choose a bath next time.'

'*Oatmeal?*'

'It's all rather a far cry from home,' said Harriet, as they followed Susanna towards an open door, recalling, perched on the corner of the bath at home, an almost empty bottle of Safeway's bubblebath. The bottle disappeared as they entered the drawing room: so large that it had been made, effectively, into two rooms – one by the marble fireplace, where piped sofas and chairs stood before a screen in *petit point*, and one to the right, a similar arrangement, but made in relation to crammed bookshelves: a peaceful reading corner.

Marsha immediately made for the corner.

'Help yourself,' Susanna said again, then added, 'Only I'm afraid there's almost nothing there you'd like. It's all rather grown-up.'

'Oh.' Used to a house overflowing with Puffins and the books of Harriet's childhood, Marsha stopped for a moment, disappointment visible.

'You've brought plenty of books with you,' said Harriet. 'Come on, come and have tea. Yes?' She looked at Susanna enquiringly, seeing on the low table by the fireplace a well-laid tray.

'Yes.' Susanna gestured Harriet to an armchair, sat herself before the table and lifted a blue and gold teapot which would not have looked out of place in the V&A. Marsha, in the corner, hovered before the bookshelves. Harriet looked about her.

There were doors to a balcony here, too, opened to let in the last of the afternoon light. Light fell on a round table, placed in a corner, with a chair. On the table a book, a glass vase, a few white roses. One or two petals had fallen on to the dark mahogany. Table, light and fading flowers: it belonged on the cover of an Anita Brookner novel, but Harriet, though she registered this, was also taken, instantly, to another table, brown and cheap, a coffee jar of roses, morning sun coming through a basement window. Karel, sitting on a junk-shop chair, lit a Marlboro cigarette and sipped tea from a thick glass mug, with a slice of lemon.

Never I think I will meet someone like you, Harriet . . .

And there had never been anyone else like Karel. In adulthood, with a daughter, it felt almost shaming to be thinking this still, but it was the truth.

So. This is love. So simple, so complete.

Nothing had been simple since then. There had been interest, and liking, and even, with Marsha's father, love, but look what had happened to love. There had been desire; but there had never, actually, been quite that sense of innocent belonging. And probably, if the truth were told, there never would be now. Harriet was no longer innocent, and who knew, if she found him at all, what kind of man she might meet in Prague?

Susanna passed wafery sandwiches, papery pâtisserie dusted with icing. Marsha abandoned the bookshelves and began to tuck in, much as though she were tucking in at McDonald's.

'You must be starving,' said Susanna.

'I am. This is yummy.' Marsha inhaled some of the icing, and began to cough, and could not stop. Flakes of fine pastry flew across the room.

Susanna rose; Harriet banged Marsha on the back; her eyes streamed.

'I'll get you some water – ' Susanna hurried from the room and returned with a glass. 'Here.'

Marsha sipped gratefully, and wiped her eyes. 'Thanks.' Pastry flakes lay all over the sofa; she brushed them on the carpet and then, getting up to brush more off her sweatshirt, trod them all in.

'Marsha,' said Harriet, wondering that pastry could be, in such immaculate surroundings, so visible, so loud. At home, the house was well run, and Marsha was taught to be tidy, but even so – there was always clutter, and something that needed clearing up, or mending. Here –

'Sorry,' said Marsha, moving to sit down again, and knocked a cup and saucer flying. A pool of fine scented tea sank into the carpet and settled down.

'Marsha!'

'Sorry, sorry.' Marsha, visibly distressed, sank back on to the sofa. 'It's like *Granny's*,' she blurted out. 'Everything's so *special*!'

'Susanna,' said Harriet, rising, 'I'm sorry, she's tired, we've been travelling since – '

'I know, I know, please, it's quite all right.' Susanna was leaving the room again, hurrying in search of a cloth. 'Please,' she said again over her shoulder, 'just leave it – it really doesn't – '

Marsha and Harriet looked at each other.

'Don't be cross.'

'I'm not, I know how you feel.' Harriet picked up tea leaves, one by one, and dropped them into a saucer. 'But you shouldn't have said that, even so.' Rising, she took in what before she had somehow not quite taken in: Susanna's portrait, hung above the fireplace, gazing out of the frame – not at her, but beyond her, refusing to meet the observer's eye.

'Marsha,' she said quietly, as footsteps returned along the corridor, 'don't worry about it, just be careful, that's all.'

Susanna was back in the room, with a cloth and a bottle of something. She smiled at Marsha, who blushed.

'I didn't mean it,' she mumbled. 'Sorry.'

Harriet was moved to put an arm round her; Marsha, scarlet, shrugged it off.

Susanna knelt down upon the carpet, and did not speak, rubbing gently until the stain had gone, leaving only damp wool, which she brushed with long, well-cared-for fingers. How long was it since she had had to go down on her knees and clean up anything?

'There.' She rose, smiling again at them both. 'I've fixed it, and now we forget about it. And please don't say sorry, Marsha: you're right. A grown-up place can be terribly prim.'

'It's beautiful,' said Marsha uncertainly.

'Well. Who'd like more tea? Or have we done tea for today?'

'I think we've done it,' said Harriet, realising, with relief, that she liked Susanna. 'Thank you for being so nice.'

'Not at all. And in that case – ' Susanna stood there, damp cloth and bottle of something incongruous against pale shirt and linen trousers. 'I'll get rid of this and then we can talk about your visit. I've got lots of books and maps – is there anything you particularly want to see?'

'I want to see Hugh,' said Marsha.

'Of course you do.'

Tea was cleared; books and maps were spread upon the table by the bookshelves. They looked at pictures of the cathedral, of markets, museums, parks with lakes, and waited for the sound of a key in the lock.

'Hugh.' She held out her arms.

'Harriet.' He kissed her, once on each cheek. No hug: a greeting as to a dinner-party guest, as Susanna had greeted them. But with warmth, undeniably, and when he drew away to look at her he still looked like Hugh. Medium height, compact – well, perhaps just a bit of thickening round chin and middle; close-cut curly hair receding from a clear, intelligent forehead; kind brown eyes. In his well-cut suit, and blue silk tie, he looked, it had to be said, what he was: a Eurocrat, a bit – oh, dear – of a fat cat. But Hugh, still, in that smile.

'God, it's nice to see you.'

'You, too. Where's my favourite niece?'

Marsha, suddenly shy, had retreated from hall to drawing room.

'Marsha?' He strode towards the open door. 'Come out, come out, wherever you are.'

She came, giggling. He held out his hand, very formal; she took it, and shook it, and he picked her up and hugged her.

'What a weight. What a *weight*!' He staggered into the drawing room, and dropped her on to a sofa. Marsha jumped up again, knocking the coffee table.

'Careful!' said Harriet, following. 'Careful, *please*!'

'Especially now,' said Susanna, behind her. There was a shivering chink: Harriet, turning, saw a tray with champagne, fresh orange juice, tulip glasses. 'Oh, how lovely.'

47

'But of course.' Susanna set the tray down on the table, and Marsha, setting herself to rights, told Hugh, 'I knocked tea everywhere before you got here.'

'Did you, now?' He was straightening his tie. 'Please – let me.' He picked up the bottle and peeled away the foil; he unscrewed the wire –

'Susanna? Have you a glass?'

She held it ready. They waited, watching the cork's slow rise –

'There!' It flew across the room towards the bookshelves. He filled the glass, more glasses; they raised them. All, it felt clear, were suddenly filled with warmth and goodwill.

'To you. Welcome.'

'To you. It's lovely to be here.'

'Shouldn't this child be drinking milk, or something?'

'*Milk*?' Marsha sipped again. 'Ugh. Ow. There's bubbles all up my nose.'

Susanna poured fresh orange juice into a fresh glass. 'Here.'

'Thanks.'

They made themselves comfortable, they began to talk. Susanna had closed the balcony doors against the approach of evening; even though it was August, the air, before she did so, had begun to feel perceptibly cooler, and the room, because the apartment faced so directly on to other buildings, had begun to darken. After a while, she rose, and turned on the lamps: light shone through green shades, falling in pools on tables and the arms of armchairs and bookshelves, and on Susanna's face, as she sat down again, sinking gracefully against cushions in the corner of the sofa by the *petit point* screen, beneath her portrait.

There was a lull. Hugh stopped asking Harriet about her work and Marsha, with initial coaxing, began to tell him about her school. Soon, with enthusiasm, she was relating a fearsome history of personality clashes.

Harriet looked up at the portrait and back at Susanna. She was watching Hugh and Marsha; she seemed relaxed, happy to listen.

And yet – every now and then there passed across her face an expression which Harriet could not quite understand but which gave her, once again, that sense of things being not quite as they should be.

Susanna, in the portrait, wore sleeveless silk and was set against an indeterminate background of short, painterly brush strokes, in ochre and green. The whole of the painting was done in this manner – soft, informal, intimate, even, as if whoever painted her had known her well.

And yet – all this was belied by the gaze beyond the painter, beyond whoever would stand and look, and seek to know her. Perhaps the painter, too, had seen what Harriet, looking back at the original, saw now: a fleeting preoccupation, quickly covered as she felt her sister-in-law's eyes upon her, and smiled, coming back to the room again.

'I thought we'd eat early tonight – after your journey, and with Marsha here. About seven-thirty – would that suit you?'

'Of course. Then we can be fresh for tomorrow.'

'Yes,' said Hugh. 'But tomorrow night I'm afraid we shan't be just us – well, I don't know if "afraid" is right, but it does feel nice to be *en famille*, doesn't it?'

'Very,' said Harriet, aware of Marsha's adoring look at him as he rose to refill their glasses. 'What's happening tomorrow?'

'Believe it or not – ' he was holding the bottle above her glass, 'someone I knew at school is coming to dinner.'

'How extraordinary. Thank you.' Harriet lifted a newly foaming glass to her lips. 'Who's that? Did we ever meet him?'

'Did you ever meet anyone from school?' Hugh was refilling Susanna's glass: their hands touched briefly, and he turned back to Harriet. 'Chap called Christopher Pritchard, who interestingly enough has some kind of East European connection, as we do.' He smiled at her. 'Everyone seems to, these days.'

'Yes,' said Harriet, recalling a letter whose contents she had skimmed. 'Remind me what yours is.'

He sat down again. 'You're making your journey, we're in a joint venture with the European Bank – financing a clean-up job on a power station in northern Bohemia. I haven't been there, yet, but it's near the Krušne Hory mountains – along the German–Czech border.'

'And what are you doing exactly?'

'Lending the money for a desulphurioation unit. Trying to help do something about the fact that Bohemia has some of the worst acid rain pollution in Eastern Europe.'

'We've done pollution at school,' said Marsha.

'Have you, now? Do you know anything about lignite?'

She frowned. 'No. But I know about acid rain.'

'Well, then, you might be interested in this. Bohemia's power stations run on stuff called lignite – that's brown coal to you and me; it gives out grisly amounts of sulphur. You have to burn more of it than ordinary coal, so that makes it worse. And the countryside in that part

49

of Czechoslovakia – the Czech Republic, as it is now – is choking to death. Fish dying in rivers, trees all bare, the air too thick to be safe for children so they have to stay indoors in winter, sometimes. So we're lending money for this unit to take the sulphur out, and help reduce pollution. Does that meet with your approval?'

'Yes,' said Marsha. 'It sounds good. I could do a project.'

'And this schoolfriend of yours?' asked Harriet. 'What's his connection?'

'He wasn't exactly a friend – it seems extraordinary that he's resurfaced. I think he must have come across my name through common contacts – or perhaps he looked me up somewhere, I'm not sure.' Hugh raised his glass again. 'Cheers once more.'

'Cheers,' said Harriet, realising that the 'somewhere' Christopher Pritchard might have used to look up his old contemporary could well have been *Who's Who*. Hugh was modest, but he was making his mark – and how was it possible to connect, now, this charming and quietly successful man, with his lovely wife and elegant apartment, with the lonely child who had kept everything stiffly laced in behind perfect manners; whom Harriet used to come upon, muttering to himself in an empty dining room?

'Anyway,' Hugh was saying. 'Pritchard seems to be acting as some sort of east–west middleman – I'm not quite sure about his field. He has a background in the City, but he didn't say much about that. Funnily enough, his name rang a bell in that connection, too, when he called, but I can't place it. Too many names to remember in my old age. But he's a bit of a one-man band these days, I gather – office somewhere out in the suburbs, been here only a few months. Couldn't quite get the picture, but no doubt I'll hear more. He seemed keen to renew our acquaintance, and it seemed a reasonable idea to invite him over while you're here. He might even be useful to you. Is that all right?'

'Of course. An interesting diversion. And did you like the sound of him, after all these years?'

Hugh thought. 'Not sure. The last time we saw each other was in '66. I can't say I cared for him much.'

'Why?' asked Susanna from across the room.

He shrugged. 'I don't know. He was a bit of a bully in those days.'

'*Was* he?' Marsha was all ears. 'We talk about bullies at school, in social education. What did he do?'

But Hugh did not elaborate, and Harriet sensed that he did not want to be pushed. What in childhood had been deep reserve had developed, as he grew older, into deep discretion – a quality which had no doubt done much to earn him trust and respect among the bankers of Brussels, but was possibly not always easy to live with. Still. Was not a sister allowed to know a little?

'I hope,' she said thoughtfully, drinking, 'that this chap did not bully you.'

Hugh shrugged again, and who knew just what he meant by that? 'I kept out of his way. But people used to have an eye on him, I think. Especially where younger boys were concerned.'

'You mean . . . ' she hesitated, and broke off. Who knew what Hugh himself might have got involved in, amongst that community of boys?

Marsha was fully focused now. 'Are you talking about child abuse?'

Hugh's and Susanna's mouths both fell visibly open. Harriet laughed.

'Sorry. This is precocious only child in 1993.'

'This is my niece!'

'Come off it.' And she suddenly switched from long-ago concerns about her little brother to her life as it was lived now, in multi-cultural London, with a daughter she was bringing up to be confident and direct. Her earlier sense of uncertainty and displacement fell away: she was no longer intimidated by these surroundings but was making her own mark.

'I suppose,' she said clearly, 'it must seem bizarre when you don't yet have children of your own, but London kids are streetwise now, you know – they have to be. I mean, I try to protect Marsha from growing up too fast, but it's rather a losing battle. And if that's the case, I'd rather we talked about things – wouldn't I, Marsha? – so that she knows how to cope – '

She heard her voice, no doubt all the stronger for a couple of glasses of champagne on an empty stomach, ring out into a deafening silence.

'Well, of course,' Hugh said smoothly, 'you're talking to the uninitiated. You're right – what would we know? It just seems rather a far cry from our own protected childhood, doesn't it?'

'It does,' said Harriet, trying to cover her own confusion, thinking, as she looked at the rise of bubbles within her glass, breaking on the surface: but how protected were you, Hugh? Any kind of abuse might have been done to you in that distant and expensive place.

'Supper,' said Susanna, rising rather quickly. 'I'll just go and see how it's getting on . . .'

'Can I help?' asked Harriet. 'You've been doing everything.'

'It's fine, I enjoy it. I'll call you in a few minutes.'

And she went gracefully from the room. The linen trousers had been replaced by a skirt in the finest cotton, a dusty jade, with a loose cream shirt tucked into the narrow waist. She's perfect, thought Harriet, watching her. She's perfect. What has gone wrong?

'On formal occasions,' said Hugh, leading them along the corridor, 'we eat in there. When it's just us, we use the kitchen.'

'Good,' said Harriet, looking in at 'there': a dining room hung with striped wallpaper and containing a table intended for twelve. It looked like nothing so much as the dining room in her parents' house, as if Hugh and Susanna had skipped a generation and landed, effortlessly, with the accoutrements of late middle age. Again, for an instant, following her brother, she saw him murmuring at the long mahogany table of their childhood, and then they were all in the kitchen, assembling round something much less formal and quite charming: print cloth, china candlesticks; basket in the centre heaped with fresh rolls, butter imprinted with oak leaves.

Marsha sank happily into her chair and took a roll from a solicitous uncle. Susanna served soup from a pottery tureen. They began to talk of parents, in Kensington and Wiltshire; of life in retirement – useful committees, private views and dedication to the garden. Such talk felt cementing and, in still strange surroundings, comforting, so that when they turned to plans for the week it did feel as if they would be setting out on excursions as a family, known and secure.

'And tomorrow the bully's coming,' said Marsha, tucking into a warming casserole.

'Marsha,' said Harriet.

'What?'

'Hugh didn't say he was a bully *now* . . .'

'Hugh wishes he hadn't said a word,' said Hugh, with a forkful of beef. 'Niece please forget. He's probably charming.'

'He might still be horrible.'

'Beware, Marsha,' said Susanna, thawing now, Harriet could see: no longer the dutiful hostess but relaxed, genuinely pleased they were there. 'Someone might say unkind things about you, one day.'

'Impossible,' Marsha said calmly. 'I'm a Sabbath child.'

'So you are,' said Hugh, and there was a pause, as he and Harriet, in different ways, recalled that summer Sunday, nearly a decade ago, when Marsha, after a long struggle, had made her entrance into the world, and Martin had rung Harriet's family to tell them. Hugh had been living in London, then: he had kept a brotherly distance from an over-emotional mother, and arrived on the Tuesday, with a pile of novels for Harriet to read while breastfeeding.

'Thank you,' said Harriet, bemusedly, looking at them from the frontiers of another country. Marsha, scarlet from overheating, slept in the crook of her arm. Hugh bent over her, and his face took on an expression which Harriet had never seen there – had not, indeed, seen even on the face of Marsha's father. Not quite like that.

'She's – gosh. Isn't she – '

'Isn't she?'

In the weeks of colic and screaming that followed, Harriet had barely opened a newspaper, never mind a book. In the winter after Martin's departure the pile of novels had, however, proved comforting – like Hugh.

'See much of Martin?' Hugh asked casually now.

Harriet frowned. 'You know I don't.' Perhaps, from her earlier remarks about openness, he thought it all right to mention him in front of Marsha. It was, at home. Not here, not at the start of a holiday.

'My dad might as well not exist,' said Marsha, yawning.

'I don't know if that's quite true,' said Harriet.

'Yes it is.'

'Salad?' asked Susanna. 'Has everyone had enough?'

'Salad would be great. Thank you. Marsha – eat something, please, don't just fiddle about.'

Marsha yawned again.

'She's done for,' said Hugh. 'Look at her.'

'You can get down if you like,' Susanna said kindly.

She shook her head. 'I'm not a bit tired.'

But she was, after pudding, persuaded to retire.

Harriet kissed her as she lay beneath the thick blue eiderdown. The balcony curtains were drawn and a lamp between the beds shone softly through parchment-coloured silk.

'Nice evening? Everything all right?'

'Mmm. Are you going to be long?'

'No. I'm tired too.' She kissed her again, wondering about Martin, and Marsha's relationship with him. 'Do you really feel – ' She began, and stopped. It was late. She wasn't up to it.

'Feel what?'

'Nothing. Goodnight.'

'Night.' Marsha turned over, heavy-eyed. 'Leave the light on.'

Harriet rejoined the others. They sat over coffee in the drawing room.

'She's a very nice child,' said Hugh, sipping from a white and gold cup. 'You've done well with her.'

'Thank you. She loves being here – she loves being with you.'

'Sorry if I blundered, earlier on. About her father.'

'It's okay.'

'There hasn't been anyone – '

'No. Not serious, anyway. Of course – ' she held out her cup for Susanna to refill. 'Thanks. Of course, there's always my Czech chap. Remember him?'

'Yes. You're not really going all that way just for – '

'No. No – I'm going for its own sake. For Marsha's pleasure and education. And my own. Still – you never know.' And at the prospect of this unknown future she saw again Karel's lean, vital face, and smiled, despite herself. After all. After all these years of keeping the show on the road, and doing right by Marsha, it might be nice to strike a blow for romance.

'We'll see,' she said, and found herself yawning, too.

They kissed goodnight with affection.

Harriet was tired, but she could not sleep. On the other side of the bedside lamp, switched off now, Marsha was sunk into the pillows, an arm in red and white spotted pyjamas flung out across the eiderdown, her breathing steady. Harriet lay listening, and thinking. From beyond the curtained balcony came the muted sound of traffic. From somewhere outside her door came the sounds of an apartment being put to rights for the night: doors closed quietly, considerately; footsteps along thick carpet, a tap run; another door opened and closed. Then silence.

Harriet could not sleep. The ferry made its progress across the Channel, and gulls shrieked in its wake. The train pulled out of Ostend station, gathering speed in the rain. There was a family reunion in a foreign city.

Here Charlotte Brontë had suffered and wept. Tomorrow they would visit the house where Marx had taken rooms. Harriet thought about her black-bound notebook, tipped in Chinese red. *Brussels*, she had written, and page after page of facts. Lacemakers/convents/the Belgian Congo. Invasion / capitulation / resistance / Jews in hiding. Architects and designers. Horta and art nouveau. Surrealist painters: Magritte had trained in Brussels; so had Paul Delvaux.

Harriet lay in the darkness and silence of her brother's apartment and revisited the iconography of these painters: Magritte's faceless men in bowler hats, the body of his faceless mother, covered in a sheet, lifted from her suicide in the river at Charleroi. She saw Delvaux's long-haired, wide-eyed, naked women, drifting after dark through deserted city streets: moonlight shone pale and still on broken buildings; somewhere a train breathed through the night.

Beginning to drift towards sleep at last, Harriet took these images with her, into her dreams, so that when, in the small hours, she woke, suddenly, unable to think where she was, she did not know if it was one of these sexual, somnambulic creatures whose cries had woken her or whether, somewhere in the dark apartment, she had heard Susanna: weeping, weeping.

The morning was bright and fresh. By just after ten, Harriet, Marsha and Susanna were walking over the cobblestones in the Grand Place, breathing in the scent of carnations, late summer roses, blowsy stock in soft, mothy shades of lavender, dusty pink and cream. The flowers lay in boxes or stood in cool metal buckets, presided over by women in headscarves. A waiter moved through an open-air café on the far side, smoothing heavy white cloths, straightening up and yawning. There were one or two people drinking coffee, and a middle-aged man with a jacket round his shoulders sat smoking and reading the paper, but it was early still, with few people about, the shops empty and inviting. In places, in the shade, the pavements were still wet from the cleaning lorry which moved through the streets with brushes and a sprinkler, leaving them spotless.

Harriet, in what Victor Hugo had once called the loveliest city square in Europe, looked up at the richly decorated façades, Gothic and baroque, of the houses all around them, gilded blues and greens and greys, elaborate gables rising in harmony to the morning sky, and despite the anxious moments of the night she felt her heart lift. She was on holiday, for the first time in a long while, and what yesterday, standing in the spacious bedroom, had seemed uncertain and unsettling, now felt light and carefree.

Beside her, Marsha and Susanna briefly touched each other, stepping out of the way of an ice-cream cart. They smiled at each other, and their hands fell back to their sides.

Harriet observed them, noting their obvious affection, grown from the memory of a wedding four years ago and the acquaintanceship of a few hours. Susanna, this morning, looked at ease, relaxed. She was wearing her linen trousers, with an open-necked shirt and a pale blue sweater; a fine gold chain was round her neck, and tiny stud earrings showed when she pushed back shining hair. Surely this picture from *Vogue* could not have been overheard weeping in the small hours: it was hard to imagine Susanna weeping at any hour, so perfect had her control seemed yesterday, so composed did she seem today.

'In the Middle Ages,' Harriet told Marsha, as they walked over the cobbles, 'this place was a marsh. Then it was drained, and became the market of Brussels. All these heavenly buildings went up, blasted to bits at the end of the seventeenth century by Louis XIV. It was rebuilt extraordinarily quickly – by powerful tradespeople, dedicated to the glory of commerce.'

'And to God,' said Susanna. 'Look at that spire.'

They craned their necks.

'That's the Hotel de Ville,' said Harriet, who had seen pictures.

'It is.' Susanna touched Marsha's shoulder. 'The Town Hall, to you. See the figure right at the top? The weathervane?'

Marsha leaned back, shading her eyes. 'No. Yes. I think so.'

'That's the archangel Michael. He fought the devil and won, and now he keeps watch over the city.'

'Gosh,' said Marsha politely.

Elaborately decorated with sculpture, the building stretched almost half the width of the south side of the square.

'I think we should see inside, don't you?' Susanna asked Harriet. 'There are tapestries – they're rather wonderful.'

'Yes, I've read about them.'

Susanna smiled. 'You've read about everything.'

'I wanted to get the most out of it. I almost felt I'd been here.' Harriet looked about her. It had grown warmer, and the square looked bright – almost, already, too bright. Neither the Grand Place nor the Hotel, nor any of the streets through which they had walked to get here was, in reality, quite as she had imagined: she felt as though, like Alice through the looking-glass, she had strayed from within the pages of a book and found herself looking at the mirror image of what had, before, been the only reality. Did these soaring buildings feel in some ways less substantial than those she had carried in her head? Well – yes, they did. And thinking this, as the others, ahead of her, entered the foyer, she was surprised to feel, again, a moment of uncertainty and unease, and, as yesterday, found herself thinking of Lucy Snowe, enduring the loneliness of the empty school, the empty city, during the long vacation.

She followed Susanna inside.

The main entrance led to an interior courtyard, where fountains played. Marsha's face lit up.

'Just what we needed.' Susanna watched her run her hands through the water. 'You'd better not do that,' she said after a minute. 'Everyone's terribly proper here. I think we'd better look for a guide.'

Marsha was disappointed. 'Can't we just wander round by ourselves?'

'I'm afraid not.' People were assembling in a corner. 'That lot's German. There must be – yes.' They joined an English group at the entrance to the city council chambers, and wandered from room to stately room, gazing at the substantial desks of burgomasters, at eighteenth-century panelled ceilings, triumphant flourishes of lamps, noble bookcases, marble busts on marble plinths, paintings of the city. They stood before great tapestries in dull crimson and gold, where saints' heads fell at the stroke of a sword, and sweet-faced musicians raised trumpets to their lips.

Tall windows overlooked a garden; there was the murmur of voices, footsteps on polished floors. Marsha, growing restless, detached herself from the adults and went across to one of the windows: she stood looking out at formal flowerbeds, running a finger up and down the glass. Harriet turned to Susanna, to suggest they moved on, and found she was no longer at her side but standing before a tapestry in a shadowy far corner, gazing up at it, her back to everyone. Distance and detachment hung about her like a shroud: Harriet, sensing this, did not approach her, but followed her gaze.

The tapestry was large and complex: maidens, musicians and dancers at court, narrow-haunched hounds at rest. Susanna was looking at a detail: Harriet moved closer, and saw two lovers touch. She, in faded cream and blue, raised her face to his; he, in dusty green and gold, lifted her hand to his lips. Their profiled faces were long and fine and concave – in-bred, over-bred, delicate faces, her hair drawn back from a high forehead, taken in a hood, his curling gracefully to a collar. Their eyes met, their lips curved in a hesitant smile: *I have watched you and watched you: at last you are mine* . . .

Susanna was weeping. Harriet froze in consternation. Across the room, light from the tall window washed the polished floor and Marsha slid a finger up and down the glass. Heads in the guided groups of tourists turned at the squeak.

'Stop it,' said Harriet, automatically, and Susanna wiped at the corners of her eyes, her body quite still, save for her long pale fingers brushing the slow-moving tears, over and over, as if she were simply smoothing away a wrinkle with face cream, as if the tears simply happened to be there, a natural phenomenon quite unconnected with how she might be feeling, what she might be thinking.

What might she be thinking?

'Mum? Can we go now?'

Marsha had stopped squeaking along the glass and was looking at her mother.

'In a minute,' said Harriet. 'Can you just – '

What could Marsha do?

A door led out to the garden.

'Go on,' Harriet told her. 'You go out in the fresh air. I'll be with you in a minute.'

Marsha stepped through the open door and made her way along a gravel path bordered by lavender, hung about with bees. The garden was small, with beds of standard roses set in the grass and espaliered fruit trees trained against a brick wall facing south. Seats were placed here and there. Birdsong and the faint scent of grass and lavender came through the door, fastened back with a hook. A security guard yawned, and looked about him.

Susanna continued to wipe the outer corners of her eyes in the repetitive stroking movement which put Harriet suddenly in mind of a bear in a bear pit: the head swinging back and forth, back and forth, an inverted arc of boredom and despair. Her back was resolutely turned to Harriet, who realised that she dare not move for fear of showing her distress.

Harriet approached her. She touched her arm. Susanna shut her eyes, and shook her head. Other people came to admire the tapestry.

'Susanna,' said Harriet quietly. 'Let's go outside.'

Tears fell on the polished floor.

Their guide had marshalled the group around him: he began to describe the tapestry, commissioned from a convent in Liège. He pointed out the dancers and the dance, announcing, Harriet was dimly aware, that an early-music quartet would be playing the great hall later in the week. He pointed to the lovers, to their delicate glance of desire. It was thought they were portraits of the son of the house and his betrothed bride, who died, aged seventeen, in childbed.

The tourists murmured. Susanna looked at the floor and wept. Harriet put her arm round her and shepherded her across the room and out through the door to the garden. Two seats were occupied by couples; Marsha, on the third, was swinging her legs, contentedly stripping stalks of lavender.

'I'm so sorry,' said Susanna brokenly. She fumbled for her bag, for the clasp. 'Don't take any notice.'

'Don't be ridiculous.'

Marsha had looked up and seen the tears. She frowned. Harriet made an incoherent gesture. Susanna had found a handkerchief. Her shoulders shook. Marsha slid off the seat and scrunched on the gravel towards them.

'What's the matter?' The scent of lavender clung to her: she put out a hand towards Susanna and withdrew it again. 'Why don't you come and sit down?'

They made their way to the garden seat. Little birds hopped about in the fruit trees, and pecked at ripening pears. A bumble bee sailed past on a current of air. It could not have been a more beautiful morning.

'Have you got a headache?' Marsha asked.

'Sort of – ' Susanna blew her nose and wiped her eyes.

'Smell this.' Marsha held out a lavender stalk; Susanna sniffed, and tried to smile.

'Lavender's blue, dilly-dilly . . . ' Marsha, who had quite a sweet voice when she put her mind to it, began to sing, trying to comfort.

'Lavender's green.

When I am king, dilly-dilly,

You shall be queen.'

Susanna covered her face and sobbed. Harriet and Marsha looked at each other. Harriet wanted to ask Marsha to leave them alone, but felt that was unfair; she did not know, herself, whether to go or stay. Not since she had wept on Victoria station, saying goodbye to Karel all those years ago, had she known anyone cry like this: uncontrollably, in the middle of the morning, in a public place. What should she do?

Marsha got off the seat and touched the purse that hung round her neck. 'I'm going to look at the postcards. I'll come back in a little while.'

Harriet, in familiar London, would have issued automatic instructions: come straight back, don't talk to any strangers, don't spend all your money, be sensible – Here, in a foreign city, an unknown public building, she simply nodded in gratitude. Marsha was already sensible, she'd be okay for a bit. 'Don't be too long.'

'I won't.' And she left them, entering the tall doors to the gallery with a smile to the attendant, poised and grown-up, as Harriet turned back to Susanna.

'What can I do for you? How can I help?'

Susanna, at last, stopped crying. She blew her nose again and wiped her eyes and she sat beside Harriet looking straight ahead: at the well-cut grass, the well-trained fruit trees. Water poured from the mouth of a small bronze lion head, set in the wall, into a shallow basin; a sparrow flew down and alighted; it began to bathe, busy and contented.

'Tell me,' said Harriet, watching the bird. 'Tell me what's wrong.'

Susanna said slowly, 'I've been like this all my life.'

Harriet felt a prickle of apprehension, as if a door were opening into a dark room which someone had once told her about but which she had never entered. She could hear her mother, and people like her mother, say briskly, 'Don't be ridiculous, what are you talking about, this is all out of proportion.' She knew that what she would most like now would be to get up, look for Marsha and take the morning back, warm and ordinary, a mother and daughter with time to themselves, for once: relaxed, enjoying each other's company. She knew that this pleasant and desirable state of affairs was, for the moment, quite unreclaimable. Who was Susanna? What had gone wrong?

She started to say: 'You always seem so – ' and stopped. There was a silence. 'Go on,' she said. 'Tell me.'

Susanna said: 'That's the whole point, isn't it? I always seem so – '

Yes, and I sensed it almost as soon as I arrived, thought Harriet; perhaps even before then: that how you seem and who you are don't begin to come together, are most disturbingly at odds. 'Go on,' she said again. 'I'm listening.'

Susanna said nothing. People came and went through the tall glass doors: relaxed, enjoying a holiday. They felt, to Harriet, just for a moment, like alien beings.

Susanna said: 'We should go and look for Marsha.'

'No, we shouldn't. She'll be fine.'

'She's lovely. You're very lucky.'

'I know.' Of course, Harriet heard her mother saying, over the flower arrangements, of course, if they had children there'd be none of this nonsense, there wouldn't be time –

'Please,' she said to the still, sad figure beside her. 'Tell me. What do you mean, you've been like this all your life?'

Susanna shrugged. 'Do you know about depression?'

'Not really. No, I don't think so. Not in the way you mean.'

'No.' Susanna's slender foot, in a narrow shoe, with a narrow chain,

61

moved slowly across the gravel, up and down. 'It's hard to explain. It's nice of you to listen.'

'Of course I'll listen. I want to get to know you.'

She shook her head. 'You wouldn't if you knew what I'm really like.'

Harriet thought: that's how depressed people think, isn't it? That they're worthless. She remembered a very young teacher at school, ages ago, doing her probationary year. She, come to think of it, wept in the morning, in a public place. In the staff lavatory, actually, during the break. She locked herself in, and came out smiling, saying she was fine. It wasn't just the pressure of school, they discovered later, it was much more than that.

Susanna said: 'People die of it. They hate themselves so much they do themselves in.'

'Oh, Susanna, please. You don't feel like that, do you?'

'Sometimes. It comes and goes. I was free for a while, and then – ' The ball of the narrow foot pressed into the gravel, moving from side to side.

'And then – '

Susanna drew a long breath. 'Everything seemed to change when I met Hugh. He was everything I needed, but – '

This is it, thought Harriet, recalling the intensity of her feelings yesterday afternoon, when she had stood on the balcony, wet from the afternoon rain, and dreaded hearing what she was about to hear.

'But what?'

'But we can't have children,' said Susanna. 'That does seem cruel.' And shook her head slowly, slowly, a bear in a cage, as Marsha came out again, through the gallery doors, approaching them with a paper bag full of postcards, smiling, asking: 'Are you feeling better now?'

After that, it was not possible to talk any more. Susanna went to the loo to wash, and Marsha questioned Harriet, who refused to be drawn. 'She's just feeling a bit low, that's all.'

'But *why*?'

'I don't really know, we didn't have time to go into it – I expect she'll feel better soon.'

They waited out in the flagstoned hall, which was beginning to fill with more groups, more guides, and when Susanna rejoined them she was almost as she had been yesterday: smiling, in charge. Her face was pale and her eyes were still swollen, but brushed hair and lipstick drew attention away from this, and as her bag bumped the arm of an elderly man with a stick she apologised with as much poise and charm as if she were running the place. Which perhaps she should be, thought Harriet, observing. She's clever and creative – you can see that by the way she runs the apartment. Shouldn't she be doing more than cooking Hugh's meals and making everything nice?

Susanna touched Marsha's arm. 'Drink? Ice-cream? Both?'

'Are you all right?' Marsha asked gravely.

'Yes, I'm fine now, thanks. I don't know why I – ' She was shepherding them out, into the sunshine; she put on dark glasses.

'Have you got PMT?' asked Marsha. 'Mum's awful when she's got it.'

'Thanks,' said Harriet.

'Or perhaps it was just too much culture.' Susanna led them over the cobbles. 'Let's have a break.'

They sat at a table laid with a white cloth, waiting for a waiter.

'What are we going to do next?' asked Marsha, fiddling with a bowl of sugar lumps.

'What would you like to do?' Susanna caught the waiter's eye.

They had coffee, and complimentary chocolate, dark and rich. Marsha had ice-cream; they planned the rest of the day.

'I must see Marx's house,' said Harriet.

Marsha yawned.

'We're meeting Hugh for lunch, remember.'

She brightened.

'Behind all this,' said Susanna, gesturing at the square, 'is what's called the Ilôt Sacré – it's a warren of narrow little streets, you'll like it, Marsha, it's full of nice shops and things. We'll have a wander there, and then meet up with Hugh. And this afternoon – shall we see how we feel? There's Tintin in the Comic Museum, there's the Toone Museum, that's a puppet place, there's the park and the Royal Palace . . .'

Marsha dropped a sugar lump into her ice-cream and moved it about. 'I'd like to see Tintin.'

'Fine. And then we'll go home.'

'And then the bully's coming.'

'Marsha . . .'

'Sorry.' She spooned up the sugar lump, covered in strawberry ice, and ate it with relish. A light breeze lifted the corners of the tablecloth. They paid the bill, left a tip, and walked towards Marx's house.

'At least I think that's it.' Susanna was pointing towards a house a few doors down from the Hotel de Ville. She pushed up her glasses, pushed back her hair. 'Can you see a swan? Above a doorway?'

'I think so.' Harriet peered. She looked at Susanna. 'Sure you're okay?'

'Sure.'

'What about tonight – it won't be too much for you?'

She shrugged. 'I'm used to it.'

'To being nice when you're feeling awful.'

'Well . . .'

'Were you feeling awful yesterday? When we arrived? Were you dreading it?'

'Stop it. I love having you here.'

Marsha was trailing behind them; Susanna put out a hand. 'Can you see a white plaster swan over there?'

'No.' She was squinting against the sun, growing brighter. '*I* need dark glasses.'

'We'll get you some.'

They made their way through the flower stalls; they stood before the house, a restaurant now, with plate glass, an open door, *La Maison du Cygne* flowed in gold across the glass; they craned their necks to look at the swan in the lintel, craning his. Inside, a young waitress was moving amongst the tables, setting out silver, and vases of summer flowers.

'What do you know about Karl Marx?' Susanna asked Marsha. 'Anything?'

'I've seen his grave, it's in Highgate cemetery. We went one weekend, and it rained.'

'Oh, dear.'

'It was okay.'

'It was, wasn't it?' said Harriet, who had initiated this outing. Here, in the bright morning sunshine of a summer's day in Brussels, she recalled them, walking along damp paths between overgrown graves, one Sunday afternoon last autumn. Leaves drifted from the trees; from somewhere nearby came the voices of people clearing weeds and brambles and overgrown ivy from amongst the crowded headstones; there was the sound of a rake, of shears. They came to a neater, better-tended area, where the grass was cut. A dark head loomed high up before them. It began to rain.

'That's him,' said Harriet, putting up her umbrella.

'He's *huge*.'

They drew near; they stood amongst other umbrellas, a handful of foreign visitors, looking up at waves of bronze hair, and bushy beard, and brows above a deep-set gaze. The plinth was a pale granite lettered in black. KARL MARX 1818–1883. WORKERS OF THE WORLD UNITE.

'He changed the world,' said Harriet. The rain fell harder, people walked away.

'How?'

'By thinking. By writing.' Harriet watched rainwater trickle down the great bronze features. Pigeons flew by, making for the trees. 'He had a vision of a world where everyone was equal – where working people had control over their own lives. It was a great vision but it went wrong. That's why we had the Iron Curtain – remember? That's why my friend Karel went back to Czechoslovakia.' It was pouring now. 'Let's go.'

They walked back along the path, holding the umbrella.

'He's got a nice face,' said Marsha.

'Yes. And he lived in London for years and years – longer than anywhere else, I think. He and his family were very poor, but he went to the British Museum every day and wrote and wrote. Before that he was always on the run.'

'Why?'

'Because governments thought he was dangerous. He was. He fled from Berlin to Paris, and from Paris to Brussels, and from Brussels to London. He died here. When we go to Brussels next summer, we'll see the house where he stayed.'

'Oh.' Marsha dropped hands and jumped over a puddle.

'Did you understand any of all that?' Harriet asked her.

'Not really. Can we go and have tea now?'

That was last autumn, and here they were now, in the city where the *Communist Manifesto* had been written, a prosperous and expensive city, Western Europe's head office, a monument to capitalism. Harriet stepped back and looked at the upper windows. Which had been Marx's rooms?

Heavy footsteps climbed a narrow flight of stairs, a key was pulled from a pocket with a hole in it, a door unlocked. Inside, a table was spread with papers, a bed unmade. The windows needed washing, the floor was dusty. He didn't notice. He stood looking out of the window, absently surveying the flower market, the songbirds in their cages.

Behind him, Engels stacked up pages of notes, and poured out grainy coffee.

Was that how it had been?

Laughter came from inside the restaurant. Harriet saw Susanna turn away from the doorway.

'We're meeting Hugh at half-past twelve,' she said composedly. 'Shall we go?'

Marsha had begun to stray. They recaptured her from outside a window of cashmere sweaters and recrossed the Place, which by now was full of tourists. Susanna led them into the maze of the Ilôt Sacré.

The air was warm, the little streets were crowded. Rock music throbbed from small boutiques, shoppers with glossy carrier bags pushed in and out of doorways. People meeting for lunch caught sight of each other and waved and called; the smell of good food was everywhere. At two minutes before half-past twelve Susanna indicated the restaurant where they were meeting Hugh: they found him ready and waiting at a table in the window. This organised punctuality seemed to say everything about their lives: it was hard to imagine that either might ever be late for the other, or, indeed, for anyone, despite Susanna's revelation of her inner battle. Perhaps it was all the more important, with an inner battle, to keep everything just so.

Hugh rose to greet them. They kissed, they sat, they looked at the menu.

'Gosh,' said Marsha.

'Quite,' said Harriet.

Hugh, sitting next to Marsha, smiled at them in avuncular and brotherly fashion respectively. His gaze fell upon Susanna, studying the entrées. Harriet saw his flicker of concern, his noting of her paleness, her eyes still swollen. Was their life together always like this? When had Hugh discovered Susanna's true nature? Perhaps it had been kept at bay in the early days. 'It comes and goes,' she had said this morning, scraping her foot up and down on the gravel path.

Perhaps children would have made it better. Perhaps children would have made it worse.

I shall take her aside, thought Harriet, seeing Hugh's almost imperceptible flicker of disappointment, Susanna's strained little smile of reassurance. I shall get to the bottom of this. She returned her own gaze to the menu, wondering at the burden they were carrying.

*

66

Mobiles of Captain Haddock and Professor Calculus, Tintin in boots and brave little Snowy moved gently in the air conditioning; the Thompson twins glared beneath their bowler hats. The walls were lined with frame upon neat frame of wild adventure: together, Tintin and Snowy outwitted villains in Egypt, in China, in South America and Tibet. They got lost in the world of the Incas, shot off in space suits to the moon. The galleries were full of happy people, reliving childhoods brightened by –

'*The dagger has gone! Look, it was here on the table . . .*'

'*It's growing dark now. We'll camp for the night, Snowy, and make a fresh start in the morning . . .*'

'*Rameses II, go back at once to the place where you saw the eyes . . . Go!*'

Steam trains thundered towards helpless victims, feathered chieftains scowled, chauffeurs stepped back in alarm, approached by armed men in masks. A torchbeam pierced dense shrubbery beyond a shuttered mansion, sleek limousines slid in and out of the frame.

'*Mr Tintin? I'm the head of World Vaudeville Inc., and I'm signing you up for one thousand dollars a week. And here's my cheque for five thousand dollars expenses . . .*'

'He was a genius,' said Susanna. Footsteps came and went on the polished boards; someone was laughing aloud.

'He was also a right-wing bastard.' Harriet stepped back from framed first-edition pages of *Tintin in the Land of the Soviets*. That had been Hergé's first, in 1930.

'He was of his time.'

'He may have been a collaborator.'

'There were quite a few collaborators under the occupation here.'

'That doesn't excuse it.' Harriet paused before pictures of full-lipped Negroes, behaving idiotically. 'He was a racist.'

'He was of his time,' Susanna said again.

'He only died ten years ago.'

'Where's Marsha? I'm surprised she's allowed to read him.'

'I believe in confronting issues, not in censorship,' said Harriet primly. An enormously fat blonde singer in a tight green dress hit a top note, her eyes closed in rapture; Tintin and Calculus covered their ears, Snowy hid beneath the table. 'He was a misogynist. The only time a woman makes an appearance, and she hardly ever does, it's to make an ass of herself.'

'Oh, well.'

'What do you mean, oh well? Don't you care?'

'Not at the moment. I'm coming up to a high.'

Harriet looked at her.

'What do you mean?'

'I'm feeling a bit better. I'm feeling better!' Susanna stepped forward and kissed her.

Harriet was bemused. 'How come?'

She shrugged. 'Who knows? Perhaps it's having you here – perhaps it's getting it out of my system this morning – perhaps it's having an argument with you.'

'I should hardly call this little exchange an argument.'

'It's something, though, isn't it? An exchange. I dared to disagree.'

'Don't you usually?'

Susanna shook her head, and her whole face looked different now: lit up, open, engaged. 'I'm a diplomat. The perfect Brussels wife.'

'Even in 1993?' asked Harriet. She hesitated. 'Don't . . . don't most of them work? I can't understand why you – '

'Where's Marsha?' Susanna demanded. 'Where on earth has she got to now?'

They looked along the gallery, they walked through to the next. Marsha was bent over a glass cabinet, giggling. She looked up and saw them.

'I like the swearing best.'

'What?'

'Captain Haddock.'

'Blistering barnacles,' said Susanna.

'**!@!!**?' said Marsha, after a fashion.

They fell about.

No one, after Tintin, felt like visiting anything else. They went home by tram, not talking much, listening to the hum of the wheels on the rails, looking out contentedly at neat little parks, well-kept squares, elaborate statuary.

At just after five they let themselves into the silent apartment which yesterday had felt so unsettling and unfamiliar. Susanna opened the balcony windows; Marsha flopped on to the sofa.

'Have a rest,' said Susanna. 'Have a sandwich.'

She had both, half-watching Belgian television in a corner of the drawing room, setting up little models of Tintin and his companions, bought in the museum shop, on the table in front of her. Harriet had a shower, and went to help Susanna, who was chopping vegetables in the kitchen, listening to the radio.

'Les événements en Bosnia-Hercogovine aujourd'hui ont passé une nouvelle état . . .'

The last time Harriet had listened to French radio had been in the summer of 1967, when she had spent the month of August with a family in Nantes, before going up to the Sixth. The family had been kind, and she had been homesick, helping to look after two little boys, sorting their clothes out, taking them to the park, sitting over endless lunches of pâté and salad, listening to the news while they played with pellets of fresh baguette, and kicked each other under the table.

'Moi, je n'aime pas Harriet . . .'

'Moi n'en plus . . .'

'Ding-dong. Les ouvriers de Renault aujourd'hui déclarent . . .'

It had broadened her vocabulary, the purpose of the visit, but it had not been French she had required the following summer, when she and Karel spent long afternoons in the Earls Court basement room. Now, sipping tea, looking at Susanna deftly slicing aubergines and courgettes, sweeping them into a pan where garlic and onion sizzled in oil, she said, 'I suppose you must be completely fluent.'

Susanna turned down the flame. She seemed, once again, rather tense. 'Pretty much.'

'Could you use it? I mean for work . . .'

She snipped at rosemary and thyme, growing in pots on the windowsill, catching the last of the sun. 'Brussels is crawling with interpreters and translators – it's very highly paid and very competitive. Sometimes I don't feel up to it . . .' The herbs went into the sizzling pan, she stirred it all round with a wooden spatula.

'President Clinton disait ce matin que les Etats-Unis sont encore préparé d'utiliser des armes si c'est nécessaire . . .'

'The UN doesn't seem to be doing a very good job,' said Harriet, listening, picturing the fall of American bombs on mountain strongholds.

Susanna shook her head. 'It's almost impossible . . . ' She ground in sea salt and black pepper.

Harriet, half-watching, half-listening, said, 'We haven't talked about any of this, have we? I've just been a tourist all day. In London I think about it more.'

'Of course. You're on holiday here.'

'Yes, but – ' She finished her tea, and sat thinking. 'I imagined that once I'd crossed the Channel it would all be upon me – well, I suppose it will be, as we travel. I feel hermetically sealed from world events here somehow, even though Brussels is a sort of nerve centre – '

'It's half-asleep. Like me.' Susanna gave one last stir, turned the flame right down, and looked in the fridge. She took out tomatoes and mushrooms in plastic boxes, and peeled off the cellophane. 'I find it difficult to concentrate on the news. Hugh has an update every fifteen minutes – if Clinton sneezes it's on the office screen before he's got his handkerchief out, but I – of course I try to keep up with things, but sometimes – '

Harriet looked at hard red clean tomatoes, spotless white mushrooms. Like them, the kitchen was immaculate, pale grey worktops and cupboard doors without a finger mark, plates shining, every cup on its hook.

She thought: You don't work, and it's too much of an effort to take in the news. If I had not begun, today, to understand you, I should be dismissing you. And I only begin to understand because you dropped your guard – uncontrollably, in a way most people hardly ever do.

How often did that happen? What did most people make of Susanna? Who did she talk to? Who were her friends?

She said: 'Susanna, do you mind if I ask you – ' and then there were sounds from out in the corridor: a key in the lock, the door opening. They heard Marsha, running out excitedly, and Hugh's voice, and another voice, and more than one briefcase dropping to the floor. They looked at each other.

'Oh.' Susanna frowned. 'He's brought this man – he's already with him. I thought – '

Then Hugh was in the kitchen, which all at once felt small and cramped, and full of dolls' furniture, as he – looking also much smaller, with a subdued Marsha beside him – introduced the man who was having this effect on everything.

'Susanna, my wife – Christopher Pritchard – my sister, Harriet Pickering – Marsha, my niece.'

Christopher Pritchard held out an enormous hand to each of them, and even his smile seemed loud. He was six foot two, perhaps even taller; he was overweight; he wore a creased linen jacket and trousers which also looked in need of a press. Dark straight hair flopped across a broad forehead; his skin was open-pored, with a faint sheen of sweat, a shadow of stubble. A narrow crimson tie was loose at the neck: he loosened it further, revealing to Harriet's critical gaze a missing button.

'Okay if I smoke?'

'Of course . . . ' Susanna opened a cupboard and passed him an ashtray; Hugh was getting out cans of beer from the fridge.

'Mind, darling – ' He gestured to Marsha, who shrank. She moved behind the counter where Susanna had been chopping and made a face at Harriet. Harriet looked away.

'Well,' said Christopher Pritchard, inhaling deeply, 'it's good to be here and meet you all. I've been looking forward to this.' He coughed, and flicked ash into the ashtray. Some of it missed.

Hugh handed Christopher can and glass. 'Nice to see you again, too. Harriet, what will you have? Shall we go and – '

'Yes,' said Susanna, somewhat to the air. 'Why don't you all go and have a drink while I – ' She gestured at the vegetables, the room. 'And I must change . . .'

'Must you?' asked Christopher Pritchard. 'You look pretty good to me.'

She gave a careful smile. 'That's kind of you, but – '

'I think,' said Hugh, moving towards the door with a tray, 'I think we'll go through, shall we, Christopher?'

Christopher inhaled, dropping the lighter back in his crumpled pocket. 'Sure.' He looked at Harriet. 'You joining us?'

'Yes,' she said, ignoring Marsha's wild grimacing. 'I'll just give Susanna a hand for a minute.'

'Okay, good.' He put an enormous arm round Hugh's shoulder. 'We'll leave the ladies to it while we catch up, then.'

'We're not *ladies*,' Marsha blurted out with scorn.

'So-rry.' He flicked ash somewhere. Marsha flushed. 'You're a bit of a little madam, aren't you?'

There was another, ghastly silence, as Harriet felt these phrases land in the room and roll around on the floor like marbles. She wanted to grind them underfoot.

'What's a *madam*?' Marsha demanded.

'Marsha – ' Hugh's, Susanna's and Harriet's voices, in tones ranging from the soothing to the severe, descended in unison upon her head. She hung it, scarlet-faced and furious.

'It's okay.' Hugh patted her shoulder. 'Go and get a Coke or something from the fridge. Now. Christopher.' He led him firmly from the room.

'Must just go to the bog,' said Christopher, as the door swung to behind him.

They looked at each other.

'He's awful,' hissed Marsha. 'He's *awful*.'

'Have a drink,' said Susanna, passing her, as suggested, a Coke from the fridge.

Marsha tore at the aluminium ring and tipped the can up into a glass. 'Sexist,' she muttered, drinking. 'He's sexist and horrible.' Bubbles went up her nose and she sneezed. Ash from the ashtray flew into the air. She pushed it violently away. 'A bully. And he *smokes*.'

'All right, all right.' Harriet removed the ashtray and swept its contents into the bin. She felt completely at home, she realised, doing this: extraordinary how being one day ahead of a new arrival could anchor you. Particularly an arrival such as Christopher had proved to be. Marsha was right: he was pretty awful. She straightened up, wondering if he had this effect on everyone. If so – She said, 'Even if you don't like him, you can't behave like that, it's terribly rude.'

'*He* was rude.'

Harriet gave up.

'I don't think he meant to be,' said Susanna. The last of the vegetables and herbs had gone into the pan; she wiped the chopping board and returned it to its place on the worktop, leaned against it, pushing her hair back. 'I think perhaps he's just a bit shy – '

'Oh, *sure*.' Marsha rolled her eyes to the heavens, as Harriet, recalling ancient Flanders and Swann songs played on their first gramophone when she and Hugh were small, suddenly heard herself sing:

'He's shy, he's shy,

He's really terribly shy . . .'

Marsha, who knew this one, joined in, so that when Hugh pushed the door open, coming back for nuts, he found the two of them in stitches, Susanna watching in amusement. He looked from one to the other, smiling; he took packets of cashews and pistachios out of the drawer.

'Hey,' said Marsha, 'can I have some? We only have peanuts at home.'

He tossed her a packet. 'Share the joke?' he asked mildly, tipping them into a bowl.

Harriet thought: He's probably pleased to see Susanna relaxing. So am I. She felt a wave of affection for both of them saying: 'Nothing, just – ' and nodded towards the open door, the absent Christopher.

Hugh said, *sotto voce*: 'I shouldn't take too much notice, I think he's just a bit shy.'

They held their sides.

Supper, at Marsha's request, was to be in the dining room. Susanna, heaping broken meringue, frozen raspberries, redcurrants and cream into layers in a snow-white bowl, reminded her that they only ever used it for formal dinners.

'But you're not going to have one of them while we're here, are you?' Marsha licked a finger and pressed up crumbs of meringue from the worktop.

'No, thank God.' The last spoonful of cream dropped into the bowl; Susanna slid it into the fridge. 'You'll be ill,' said Harriet, seeing Marsha lick the spoon. 'We've been eating all day.'

'And walking.' Marsha held the spoon under the tap, and turned it on, too hard. Water fanned into the spoon and sprayed everywhere. 'Help. Sorry.' She turned it off. 'Please,' she said to Susanna, brushing her wet T-shirt. 'It looks so special in there, we never have meals anywhere like that at home.'

'Oh, all right, if it makes you happy. Christopher can be the excuse.'

'And we can lay the table,' said Harriet. 'You go and join the men.'

'Yes, I must. But don't worry, I'll do the table, I know where everything is.'

Harriet protested. Susanna insisted. They should go to the drawing room; she'd join them in a few minutes. They did as they were told. She's powerful, thought Harriet, taking Marsha down the corridor, with a bottle of wine, hearing Susanna, in the dining room, slide open drawers. She falls apart but she never lets go of the reins. Are all her guests made impotent? What happens on other people's territory?

She led Marsha into the drawing room: the men rose.

Christopher, his back to the open balcony doors, glass and cigarette in hand, looked as though he had unwound a little. The sheen of sweat had gone, he had brushed his hair, and standing here now, in the context of this beautiful, well-arranged room, he looked less disorderly than raffishly eccentric. Actually, she realised, greeting the two of them, he had presence, and not just because of his size. It was hard to know yet what qualities might redeem his earlier crassness, but she sensed, suddenly, that they might be there.

73

Marsha made straight for Hugh's side. Harriet, not wishing to line up in a row of three opposite Christopher, but feeling, just for a moment, socially disconnected, found herself hovering.

'Please,' said Christopher, gesturing to the sofa. She went to sit beside him. He stubbed out his cigarette, which was only half smoked, and drained his glass.

'We've been reliving the distant past,' Hugh told her.

'Is this wise?'

'Rather enjoyable.' Christopher shifted on the sofa, crossing his legs. 'Not many people I'm in touch with now with whom I can share my memories of those happy days.'

'Were they happy?'

He shrugged. 'There were moments. We survived.'

'Made us the men we are today,' said Hugh drily, refilling his glass.

'Quite.' Christopher lit another cigarette, and Harriet noticed a tremor in his hand as he did so, and leaned back. Inhaling deeply, he looked up for a moment at Susanna's portrait – pale hair, bare arms, silk dress – at the softness of the brush strokes, the remoteness of the gaze.

'That's rather fine.' He went on smoking, and looking. 'Who's the painter?'

'A friend.'

'Mmm.' He looked back at Hugh.

Hugh made a gesture towards the bowl of nuts: Marsha leaned forward beside him, and helped herself.

'Are you married?' she asked Christopher abruptly.

'Marsha . . . ' Harriet gave her a look.

'Divorced,' said Christopher flatly, drinking.

Marsha looked into the bowl again, embarrassed. She fingered the nuts, picking out pistachios.

'Not a problem,' he said easily, kindly, even. 'And I'm sorry if I got up your nose just now – in the kitchen. Had a long hot day at the office.'

She blushed. 'It doesn't matter.'

'Tell me about your school. What's it like?'

'It's nice.'

'A far cry from what we had, I can tell you that,' said Hugh. 'Sounds like a holiday camp.'

Marsha kicked him with a trainered foot.

'Much prep?' asked Christopher.

She looked blank.

'Homework.'

'Oh. No, not really.'

'What do you do after school?'

'See my friends.'

'Lucky you. Remember prep, Hugh? Remember those quiet hours under eagle eyes in the Upper Fourth? The scratch of the nib and the rumble of the half-starved stomach?'

'How could I forget?'

Harriet noted Christopher's phrasing, which was pleasing, and pictured, as she drank, high windows, bent heads, legs in grey socks swinging beneath the desk, footsteps over the floorboards to sharpen a pencil. The sounds of boys down at the cricket nets drifted in through an open window; church bells rang across the moors. There was all that. It was ordered, it was peaceful, it was what her parents must have envisaged and hoped for, and it had, no doubt, contained such nourishing hours. It had also, she felt certain, contained times as painful and lonely, in their way, as anything Lucy Snowe had experienced during the long vacation in Villette. And she saw, as Hugh refilled her glass, and she listened to their exchange of groans and laughter at the names of particular masters, particular boys, one boy waiting for another on a darkened stairway, pulling him into an empty classroom, closing the door.

And then?

He was a bit of a bully, Hugh had said lightly of Christopher, and shrugged when asked if he himself had been a victim. Looking at the two of them now, reacquainting themselves with the past and with each other, it was hard to believe that their relationship had ever been one in which Hugh had not been in control. He was the host, he was the well-mannered listener. He was also rich and successful, and no one coming upon them now, seeing him laughing, pouring drinks, smiling with affection at his niece, would make a connection with a distant, disturbed little boy who did not know how to talk to people. He had found his place in the world.

And his wife wept in public places, and they could not have children.

'Supper,' said Susanna, appearing in the doorway. She had changed into a pale green dress; dull pewter earrings shone softly, like shells, beneath her hair.

Christopher rose.

They smiled at each other.

No, thought Harriet, all of a sudden. No, please no.

They made their way to the dining room.

In the last of the evening light at the window, the polished table shone. This room was at the back, on the darker side of the building.

'Hugh tells me you're en route to Prague,' said Christopher, breaking his roll into pieces. He helped himself to a quantity of butter. 'Summer hols?'

'Yes,' said Harriet briskly.

'Been there before?'

'No, never, but – '

'Wonderful city. A dream. Crawling with tourists now, of course, as no doubt you know. Most visited city in Europe – ruining the place. All eating McDonalds and patronising the massage parlours. Like the Czechs. Still, why not? After forty years of being told what they couldn't have, people should be given what they want. And if that's trash and junk food and pornography, too bad, don't you think? Hope I'm not putting you off. Have you got any connections? Know anyone there?'

'Well – sort of.' She was treading carefully, unwilling to share anything of herself with this man.

Christopher held out his glass to Hugh, who was settling everyone in with an opened bottle. 'Thanks.' He turned to Harriet again. 'You must let me give you a few tips – I know Prague pretty well by now, I'm beginning to make a bit of an impact.'

'Doing what, exactly? Hugh's told me a little, but – '

'Selling.' He took a mouthful of roll. 'I'm a born salesman, I'm afraid.'

'Why should you be afraid?'

'Just that you look a bit high-minded.'

Harriet ignored this. 'What do you sell?'

'Pretty well anything. In the more desperate moments of my youth it was encyclopaedias. In London I was a commodity broker for quite a while, with a special interest in Eastern Europe.'

'Oh?'

'Speculating on futures in Yugoslavian bauxite and Bulgarian tomato juice, that sort of thing. Yugoslavia's not exactly the place to do business now, of course, poor bastards, and anyway – I got my fingers

76

burned, in ways we won't go into.' He was talking compulsively, hurriedly – as if, she realised, he really wasn't quite used to conversations with women. Or perhaps that was nonsense, perhaps he always steamrollered on in this way.

He took a mouthful of cucumber soup, disturbing a gentle pool of cream and chopped chives.

'So, I came here, and set up my own show, using the old contacts. But I specialise a bit now – raw materials for paints and plastics, mostly. Polymers, resins. Buy here, sell there, or vice versa – they need practically anything I can get them, I'm delighted to say. I'm a pragmatist, only too happy to give people what they want. Mind you, competition's pretty fierce – the whole of Western Europe has its mitts in Eastern Europe these days, doesn't it? Do you know anyone who isn't opening up a branch in Bratislava?'

'I don't know anyone who's opening up a branch anywhere,' said Harriet, carefully tipping her shallow soup plate away from her, and keeping half an eye on Marsha. 'I don't know if that says more about the recession or my limited acquaintance with the world of commerce.'

'No doubt the latter. I told you, you look high-minded. What do you do?'

'Teach.'

'Bad luck.'

'It's not so bad.'

'Isn't it? What sort of school?'

'A large west London comprehensive. I'm the head of history.'

'God, how frightful.'

Harriet put down her soup spoon and looked at him.

'Sorry,' he said. 'Only joking. Must be a bit dreary, though, isn't it?'

'No more dreary,' she said tartly, 'than selling tins of paint, or whatever it is you do.'

'Touché.' Christopher had finished his soup. He licked a finger and pressed up crumbs of roll from his plate.

'I hope,' said Hugh, with mild authority, from the top of the table, 'that there is no disharmony among my guests.' He turned to Susanna. 'That was delicious.'

'Certainly was,' said Christopher, and raised his glass. He smiled once again at Susanna, who looked away. 'And what do you do, if it's not impolite to ask. Quite eclipse the rest of us, I imagine.'

'I look after Hugh.' She gathered the soup bowls.

'Lucky Hugh.' He turned back to Harriet, as Susanna gave Marsha the bowls to take to the kitchen. 'Go on, then, tell me about your school. You mustn't take me too seriously, you know, I'm just a loudmouth out of my depth in these gracious surroundings. I'm sure what you do is admirable.'

'It's a job,' said Harriet. 'I happen to believe in it, and fortunately I also enjoy it, though of course it's difficult, much of the time. The climate in education these days makes for a lot of stress, as I'm sure you know – I mean with the National Curriculum, the tests, the lack of resources – ' She could feel herself getting into her stride.

'Best thing to happen for years', said Christopher. 'We've been turning out a generation of semi-literate, half-baked, unskilled and unemployable lost causes. High time schools were licked into shape.'

'And what,' Harriet asked him, twisting her napkin, quite carried away by the force of her reaction, 'did your privileged education do for you? Is that what has equipped you to sell plastic to the other half?'

'Harriet – ' Hugh was turning his knife over, frowning, inasmuch as Hugh ever seemed to frown, or express displeasure. 'It's not as though you didn't have a good education yourself, is it? Why are you getting so hot under the collar?'

'A good education is supposed to make you aware. I'm riding my political horse,' she said, realising it was quite a while since, on a social occasion, she had had need to. Like-minded colleagues and friends surrounded her life in London: no one, except perhaps her parents, would speak as Christopher had just spoken, at this polished, middle-aged table, in this clean, expensive city. She thought of her friend Jo, on long afternoons in the art room, leaning over the shoulders of her painting group, where Winston, who had learning difficulties, and roamed the playground in the dinner hour, looking for trouble, was here completely absorbed in the still life set out before them. She thought of the hours spent in curriculum meetings, of the cuts in the budget: in art room materials, books and stationery, in visits to places of interest, provision for special needs.

She recalled, as Hugh refilled their glasses, a march, on which she had taken Marsha: hundreds of union members gathering beneath umbrellas in Trafalgar Square; the forest of placards; the slow moving off and gathering pace as the six-deep column made its way down Whitehall, past the river. The rain stopped, people began chanting: *Tories out, Tories out, Tories out, out, out! Ban the tests, ban the tests, ban the tests, tests, tests!* Riverboats hooted, the sun came out. They moved into the heart of Westminster: traffic slowed and tourists stared. A detachment, whom Harriet and Marsha, right in the middle, could not see, took a petition to the offices of the Department of Education, a little group of people in raincoats walking purposefully through narrow streets behind the Cathedral. They were cheered on their reappearance: the marchers moved through Parliament Square and into the Methodist Hall. Marsha ate from her lunchbox. Harriet was one of the speakers.

She said now: 'I've been a socialist all my life.'

'More fool you,' said Christopher.'

'I beg your pardon?'

'Come, come,' said Hugh.

Susanna and Marsha reappeared, with dishes. They set down lamb, piping ratatouille, rice with coriander and toasted almonds. Susanna served ratatouille on silvery grey plates, passing them round.

'Do help yourselves to rice ... ' She noticed the silence. 'Is everything all right?'

'We're having a crisis,' said Harriet, recovering herself by an effort of will, and regretting her words immediately. How was Susanna on social crises? Did guests often quarrel at her dinner table?

'Oh?' Susanna looked at her, and then at Hugh.

'My fault entirely,' said Christopher smoothly, and smiled at Susanna across the table. 'I can't resist getting a rise, and Harriet seems to rise so very satisfactorily. You just press the button and she's off.'

Harriet felt herself go scarlet. She bit back the words, 'How dare you – ' just as Marsha, between Hugh and Susanna, said with indignation, '*Don't* talk about my mother like that!'

As in the kitchen, earlier, a horrified silence fell, but this time Harriet, moved by her daughter's loyalty, moved straight to her defence.

'Okay, Marsha. Thanks, it's okay, let's just – '

There was another silence.

Christopher said: 'I can see I shall have to watch it. My apologies.'

Hugh said: 'You were always rather – ' and stopped.

The two men looked at each other. There was a different kind of silence.

'Rather what?' Marsha asked hotly.

'Nothing,' said Hugh, and then, in his more familiar tones,

avuncular and kindly, 'Why don't we just talk about the weather for a bit?'

'Is that of interest to anyone?' asked Harriet, still on her mettle, trying to calm down.

'Yes.' Susanna spoke with surprising authority. 'I think the weather has a real function on occasion. I don't know exactly what you were discussing – '

'Politics,' said Christopher. 'Always a mistake.'

'But central to character,' said Harriet, and then: 'Oh, all right, I'll stop. Marsha – eat up, it's all right now.'

'Yesterday it rained,' said Hugh.

'And today the sun shone brightly,' Harriet said gamely, doing her best.

'And it was ever thus,' said Susanna, with a smile to the table of such charm, such all-inclusive warmth and gentle humour that Harriet thought: She's not just beautiful, she's irresistible. She glanced at Christopher, as she picked up her knife and fork and felt again a flicker of unease – no longer for herself, but for Susanna, at whom he was gazing.

It grew darker: Susanna lit candles. They went on to talk – neutrally, carefully, gradually relaxing – of the city, its blend of charm and formal elegance.

'There is the other side,' said Hugh, over pudding, as Marsha yawned. 'Tomorrow you must visit the Marolles.'

'There's always another side.' Harriet took a spoonful of raspberries. She had read about this overcrowded district, as about much else. 'So. Tomorrow we go slumming.'

'I might join you,' said Christopher. 'I'm rather good at slumming.' He smiled at Susanna, and finished his meringue. 'That is, of course, if I'm invited.'

Marsha looked down at her bowl. Hugh suggested they talk about it later, over coffee. There was so much to see and to do, and they weren't here for long –

'Absolutely,' said Christopher. 'Just a thought.'

Beyond the windows bruise-coloured clouds were gathering; reflections of the candle flames shone deep in the glassy surface of the table.

'Mind if I smoke?' he asked, feeling in his pocket.

Nobody said that they did. He leaned forward, and again Harriet noticed the tremor in his hand as he drew the candlestick towards him a little, a cigarette between his lips. Flame and tobacco met; his eyes met Susanna's; again, she looked away.

'They're sexy as hell and they kill you,' he said, inhaling hard.

In the uneasy laughter which followed, Harriet's mind was full. Marsha should go to bed. Christopher should go home. Where was his home? In the midst of these thoughts, which felt anxious and disordered, she was unexpectedly assailed by the memory of Karel, unpeeling the cellophane wrapper from a packet of Marlboro, the thin gold strip between his finger and thumb, the lid flipped open, a cigarette withdrawn. She saw these things with the clarity of a film, watched in a darkened cinema: Karel lighting up, leaning back, inhaling, looking at her across the varnished table. In her summer dress, on the other side of the table, she rested bare arms and looked back at him, absolutely still. The sun shone through the open window; above them, on the pavement, people went to and fro.

I shall never love anyone else ...

For all that twenty-five years had passed, for all that Harriet had been hurt, and grown up, and grown wiser, she still thought now, as people began to get up, and leave the table: he was wonderful. He was brave and committed and rare.

She felt Christopher's heavy presence beside her, smoking still as they left the room – so loud, so disruptive, intrusive: a man adrift. She saw Karel's long brown fingers close on a western cigarette, inhaling not with coarseness but with grace, and she thought: you put all the rest in the shade.

What had become of him? Where was he now?

Marsha was sent to bed: she was dropping.

'Sleep tight,' said Christopher, as she left the drawing room. 'Make sure the bugs don't bite.'

She gave him a thin smile.

'What time are you coming to bed?' she asked Harriet, as they made their way down the corridor.

'Soon. When Christopher's gone.'

'He's not going to come with us tomorrow, is he?'

'Ssh, I shouldn't think so.'

She sat on the twin bed, watching Marsha undress, and pull on her red spotted pyjamas. She stood at the basin, brushing her teeth; dark hair, bare feet, pre-adolescent thinness and straightness – a reed, a fawn. She looked vulnerable, very much a child, but she also was fiery and fierce, they had all seen that tonight. For a moment Harriet wondered whether to take issue with her: one had to learn to control oneself in social situations, no matter how provoked; she herself had often failed to, whereas Susanna –

Whereas Susanna wept, when she could no longer keep herself under clamps.

And anyway, Marsha had been right. Touchingly loyal.

'Come here,' she said, when the brushing and spitting had stopped, and the toothbrush – very blue, very new – and been put back in the mug.

Marsha crossed the pale grey carpet and sat on her lap. They rested their heads against each other, and rocked. Marsha's slender foot brushed the carpet; she buried her face in her mother's neck.

'You were great,' said Harriet. 'Thank you.'

'Marsha this and Marsha that,' she murmured. 'You're always trying to stop me saying things.'

'I know. I'm sorry.'

'*You* say things. *You* get cross.'

'I know.'

Marsha drew back, and looked at her. 'Why was Susanna crying?'

'I don't really know, not exactly.'

Marsha's foot went slowly across the carpet: bare toes, grey wool, over and over. 'They haven't got children,' she said.

'No.'

'Is that why?'

'What a grown-up person you are. Perhaps. I don't know.'

You wouldn't like me if you got to know me – I've been like this all my life . . .

'Come on,' she said, patting Marsha's back. 'Bedtime. It's been a long day.'

'Full of interest and activity,' said Marsha wryly, clambering beneath the covers.

'Indeed. Precocious child.' Harriet bent to kiss her. From along the corridor came the rise and fall of voices, the chink of coffee cups, Christopher's laugh, too loud. 'Sleep tight.'

'Don't let the bugs bite,' mimicked Marsha. 'Ugh.' She made a face, pulled down the pillow, and closed her eyes.

Harriet switched out the light and left her.

In the drawing room, Susanna, next to the *petit point* screen, offered coffee from the green and gold tray before her. Christopher was sharing the sofa, albeit at a distance; an arm was stretched out along its back towards her.

'I'm about to hit the road,' he told Harriet.

'Oh?' She took a tiny cup and sat next to Hugh, stirring with an exquisite little spoon. 'Which road do you hit? I can't remember where you said you – '

'I didn't.'

Harriet went on stirring, seeing in her mind's eye her well-worn map of the city. The blue vein of the Canal de Charleroi ran down the western side; the east held the Parc de Bruxelles, divided by long straight paths laid out like the arms of compasses, a lake's circle of blue at the head. Compasses – one of the symbols, she had read somewhere, of the Freemasons. Right in the heart of the city.

Where, between east and west, was Christopher living? Looking at him as she sipped her coffee, and took from a silver dish a chocolate, offered by Hugh, she wondered: is he the kind of man whom the Masons might invite to join them? Is he rich? Discreetly powerful? Willing to swear an oath, to keep a secret? To keep it unto death?

He had moved his arm from the back of the sofa; he leaned forward, eating the chocolate. His jacket was rumpled, his tie swung against the overweight chest, his hair could have done with a wash. There were all these things, and his manner, to reckon against him, and yet, as she had done earlier in the evening, before their confrontation, she recognised, albeit unwillingly, a kind of attraction, as he leaned back again, and looked her full in the eyes.

No. He was a maverick, a self-seeker – a bully? – not to be trusted. No, she thought, looking away from his gaze, with its curious mixture of insolence, humour and directness: he isn't the Mason type.

And then, with a prickle of gooseflesh: no, but Hugh is.

Christopher set down his coffee cup. He brushed crumbs of chocolate from over-large hands. He said, 'You won't have heard of my neck of the woods. I've taken rooms, as in better educated times they used to say, in a quaint little suburb beyond the Gard du Nord. Convenient for the office. You must come and see the office, it's rather nice.' He rose, running his hands down his thighs. 'I must be off.'

They got to their feet; there were smiles, a general exodus, expressions of gratitude and enjoyment. No one said anything more about the next day's excursion: out in the corridor there was an exchange of kisses, as Hugh held open the apartment door. Recalling many an evening in her parents' house as she grew up, Harriet had time to wonder, as Christopher and Susanna brushed each other's faces – once, twice – if there were any social hiccup which the English were not capable of smoothing over with this gesture. And then Christopher was turning towards her, looking down at her, full in the face.

'Goodbye to the opposition.' And this time his expression was so full of humorous irony that she could not help but smile back, as he took a step towards her, and put a heavy hand on her shoulder. Harriet was tall, but he was so very much taller that she, as Susanna had been, was forced to reach up as he bent for the social kiss – once, twice.

'Sorry if I was crass.'

'Perhaps I over-reacted.'

As quite often in London, at her parents' house, the end of an evening, with the prospect of freedom, created its own warmth and good mood; the most irksome guest might be viewed, on the way to the front door, with a certain affection. And she watched Hugh and Christopher shake hands warmly, with expressions of pleasure at their renewed acquaintance.

'We'll be in touch again.'

'Very good.'

They moved out on to the landing, waiting for the lift.

'Shall I come down to see you out?'

'No, no, I'll be fine.' A last word of thanks. The lift came, the door closed behind him; he was gone.

'Phew.'

'Actually he wasn't so bad.' That was Susanna.

Hugh looked at her. He put an arm round her. They made their way into the kitchen, yawning. Harriet followed, feeling two things at once: the pleasure of being, at the end of an evening, part of a family, with people to talk to, over a nightcap; and the sadness of being out on a limb, of not being part of a couple. In London, where family lives were complex and various, this feeling was swiftly dealt with by the relief of not having to endure or deal with the marital unhappinesses she from time to time witnessed amongst her friends. Here, even though she had been given an insight into real unhappiness, she was, after all, on her own with Marsha, who was asleep.

Hugh and Susanna warmly included her in their conversation – talking, it seemed in retrospect, about anything except Christopher Pritchard – as they put things into cupboards and dishwasher, brought through the coffee tray and offered a brandy. But still. She could not help but be conscious, as they sat round the table, that when this conviviality was over Hugh and Susanna would, in whatever state of harmony or disharmony, go to bed together, and she would go to bed alone.

3

Courtyard opened into courtyard; the streets were full of people, the air full of music, tenement balconies hung with washing. The underclass of the city lived here; this, too, was the immigrant quarter, populated by guest workers from Turkey and North Africa.

So far, Harriet and Marsha had been shown privilege, prosperity, architectural grace. It had felt first alienating, then alluring – Marsha, after a couple of days, had lost all awe of her surroundings, bathing freely, this morning, with Susanna's oatmeal pack, munching from a dazzling array of cereals in the kitchen and generally moving about the apartment as though she had lived here for years. Harriet, having coffee with Susanna before they set out, had heard her humming as she came out of the bathroom, with its porcelain doorknob and handpainted tiles. She and Susanna had smiled at each other, pouring more coffee, planning the day.

'Are you sure you feel up to all this traipsing about?' Harriet asked her, lifting a blue and white cup.

'Of course. I like showing you things.' Susanna pushed back her hair. She was pale this morning, and looked tired, but hers had been the footsteps Harriet heard first on waking, moving about the kitchen.

'How did you sleep?' she asked her, putting the cup down.

'Fine, thanks.'

Harriet wondered, but did not ask. There was quite a lot she wanted to ask about, but not first thing in the morning. They left soon after the arrival of the cleaning-lady, who greeted Marsha in Flemish.

Marsha frowned. 'Sorry?'

'Good morning,' Susanna translated. 'I am very pleased to meet you.'

'And what do I say?'

Susanna told her. Marsha struggled. The women nodded kindly, putting on her apron. They closed the apartment door on the soothing sound of the vacuum cleaner.

So. There was all that.

And now there were unwashed children in cheap clothing, kicking a ball about a courtyard. There were black faces on the crowded streets, and black music throbbing from open windows; strings of vests and faded jeans hung out to dry. It was very hot. Mediterranean women in pinafores sat on cheap wooden chairs outside dark doorways, keeping an eye on the children, peeling vegetables. Scrawny cats with coats full of dust rolled over in sunny corners, dogs lifted their legs in the gutter and nosed amongst piles of plastic rubbish. Nineteenth-century buildings which looked, from the street, to be in reasonable repair, were revealed in the rear courtyards to be neglected and rundown, even dangerous. Window frames rotted, peeling distemper showed bulging brickwork, balconies were rusting. Unlit stairways wound up into darkness and stank, even at the entrance, of urine; every now and then the air was heavy, too, with the unmistakable smell of dope.

Harriet drew Marsha to her side as someone in a hurry came racing down a flight of stone steps and out into the sunlight: a man in his twenties, in torn jeans and a cut-away vest, bag slung over his shoulder. He stopped at the entrance to light a cigarette, threw down the match and moved swiftly past them, out across the courtyard and on to the crowded pavement. A window was flung open, a woman leaned out and yelled after him, then slammed it shut again. Various children were crying. Harriet took Marsha's hand.

Marsha shook her off. 'It's too hot.'

They wandered, with Susanna, out on to the street again, passing a dimly lit bar, chip stalls and kiosks. Students on bicycles wheeled in and out of traffic, almost at a standstill; they came to a crossroads, and smelt something different.

'Fish?' asked Marsha.

'Mussels,' said Susanna, indicating a stall on the corner. A girl in frayed shorts and long, untidy hair had parked her bike and was dipping into a plastic container with her boyfriend. Lemon juice ran down their fingers, they picked out soft flesh from open shells, dropping them, empty, into a litter bin.

'Mussels from Brussels.' Marsha was watching uncertainly.

'Quite. Want to try some?'

She shook her head.

'Oh, go on. It's almost a national dish. And delicious.'

They all had some, standing on the pavement by the litter bin, stepping out of the way of swerving bicycles with violent bells, getting hot. This was Indian summer weather, quite unlike the rainy day of their arrival. Sweat ran down the backs of their necks; the mussels were tangy and rich.

Marsha licked her fingers. 'I feel foreign.'

They wandered on, Susanna asking about other holidays, other trips abroad. There had not been many. Harriet and Martin, before his abrupt departure, had talked of taking their baby with them everywhere. In the end, on her own, Harriet had taken her to Brittany once, with her old friend Dido, from university days. That was when Marsha was three, and it had been a success in its way, with carefree days on the beach and evenings over a bottle, letting their hair down while Marsha slept.

'I wish I had a child,' said Dido, whose men, like Martin, had proved unreliable.

'It can be a bit of a strain,' said Harriet.

It had been, then, working and doing it all on her own. Holidays were required to be undemanding weeks with other families on the domestic and familiar English coastline. And anyway –

'I don't think of this as a trip,' she said to Susanna. 'It's a journey.'

'Of course it is.' Susanna changed her bag to the other shoulder, moving slowly in the heat, still rather pale.

And here was someone else who craved a child, and who knew what else besides, and Harriet must find the right moment to listen.

On the Place du Jeu de Balle there was a flea market. The best time to come here was early morning, when the stalls were being set up; Harriet, when Susanna had told her about this, had pictured damp cobbles, grey light, the banging of trestles and tables, bread and hot coffee. There were no cobbles and no grey light, and in the mid-morning heat the stalls were laid out beneath awnings. Much of the best had gone. They moved into the shady aisles, picking up flowery plates and putting them down again. There were racks of coats and jackets, rows of old shoes; plastic Mannekin Pis dolls; there were secondhand books, a stall of LPs.

'This looks more like it.'

Harriet stood flicking through peeling record sleeves in cardboard boxes. Well-worn Tchaikovsky, Mendelssohn and Brahms, played by unfamiliar orchestras, rested against jazz, against rock, against Sixties pop.

'Hey – '

Françoise Hardy pouted at her from beneath a heavy fringe, eyes thick with liner.

'Remember her?'

'A bit before my time.'

'Yes, I suppose it would be.' Harriet began to hum, then to sing. 'Tous les garcons et les filles de mon âge/se promenent dans les rues deux par deux . . .'

Marsha looked at her. 'What?'

'Everyone has a lover but me,' said Harriet. 'In essence.' And then regretted it, as Marsha, frowning, turned away, wandering on to the T-shirts on the next stall. Lovers were not on the agenda in mother and daughter discussions. Harriet, as far as Marsha was concerned, had friends who were men, and had once had a husband, who'd left her. That was quite enough for now. Her precocity, and their discussions about other people's domestic arrangements – adopted children, neglected children, divorce, contentment – had never included a direct look at her and Harriet's arrangement, or the possibility of change. Harriet had tried, wanting to air it; Marsha had resolutely refused to discuss it – knowing, it seemed, what was good for her.

'You know you can ask me things,' Harriet would say from time to time, as they finished their supper.

'Okay.' And Marsha got down from the table, and asked nothing.

'Do you remember this?' Harriet asked Susanna now, turning the LP over. 'I used to listen to her mooning about like a loony, all through '66.'

Susanna shook her head. 'You're a different generation.'

'Come come.'

'Ten years.'

'God, is it really? Let's sit down.'

Trees bordered the square; tables stood in a corner, in the shade, outside a café. Marsha was beside them again, touching her purse.

'That's kind.' Susanna admired the purse. 'But drinks are a fortune here.'

'It doesn't matter. You've done nice things for us. And I'm really thirsty after the mussels.'

'Well. We'll see.'

They made their way to the café: doors wide open, a dark interior, invitingly cool. Marsha took their orders, and went inside.

'She's wonderful.'

'She likes you.'

They sat at a table on slatted chairs.

Harriet said: 'It would be nice to have a talk.' She took a packet of sugar out of the bowl before her, and fiddled with it, suddenly shy. Should she, however gently, be confronting Susanna in this way? She looked up. 'Would it?'

Susanna looked away. 'Perhaps.'

The packet of sugar slid between Harriet's fingers.

'How are you this morning?'

'All right. Better than yesterday morning.' Susanna leaned back in her chair. 'Yesterday was an aberration – I'm sorry. ' She smiled at Harriet. 'You were very kind.'

'I didn't do anything. When you say an aberration – you mean to cry like that, in the mornings, or to cry in front of someone else?'

'In front of someone else.' She made a gesture, coolly dismissive. 'Please don't worry about it, Harriet, it's just how I am.' Footsteps came out of the café towards them. 'Here's Marsha.'

'The drinks will be here in a minute.' Marsha sat down beside them, and looked about her. A family two or three tables away were tucking into enormous ices: a mother in bright pink skirt and top, a large balding father, two large boys. The father said something: the boys burst out laughing, chocolate ice-cream was dropped from a spoon down a T-shirt. Everyone groaned. 'Boys are so *messy*,' said Marsha.

'What's it like at school?' asked Susanna. 'Do you play with the boys?'

'Not if I can help it.' Marsha rested her arms on the table: looking, this morning, completely in control. The nerves which had attended their arrival, making her as clumsy as anyone, were clearly forgotten. Harriet did not remind her.

'But do you feel at ease with them?' Susanna was asking. 'I mean – when I was your age, boys were alien beings.'

'They are alien beings,' said Marsha. 'That's the point.'

Their drinks arrived in tall glasses. The boy scraping ice-cream off his front made a remark; the balding father guffawed.

Marsha shrank. 'He's worse than Christopher Thingy.'

'Did you really dislike him?'

'I really disliked him.' She sipped at her Coke through a straw.

Watching her, Harriet thought: I could be in trouble one day. If Karel and I . . . If someone else and I . . . If she took against him, what would I do?

In the Little Church of the Carmelites, the organist was playing Bach.

Harriet, Susanna and Marsha, seeking refuge from further walking in the heat, had crossed the Boulevard Waterloo and came in through the door from a side street near the Place Louise. They made their way quietly to empty seats by a pillar.

'It's nice,' Marsha whispered, as they sat down, and she looked about her, at smooth, cool, creamy white walls, high windows, worn flagstones, full pews.

'It's packed.'

'It's a concert,' Susanna whispered 'Ssh,' and closed her eyes.

You could hardly exclude people more effectively, but in some ways this, with the whispering, seemed a rather intimate thing to do: nothing dramatic, like weeping, but something which nonetheless you might allow yourself only with people you trusted. And Harriet, on the other side of Marsha, felt briefly as though she had stepped just over the threshold into a room from which she was, indeed, normally excluded, but where she was for a few moments permitted to observe something private. She looked over her daughter's dark head at Susanna's fine features, at her pale thin-skinnedness, and soft fair hair, as though she were in the doorway of a bedroom, where a woman rested alone upon white pillows, waiting – for what? To sleep? To be woken?

Bach took possession of the church, and its congregation. Harriet leaned back, closing her own eyes, and let the music possess her, too. And as last night, watching Hugh and Susanna move about their kitchen when Christopher Pritchard had gone, she allowed herself to bring to the surface what at home she pushed most resolutely away. The organ rose and fell and she thought once again of Lucy Snowe, driven to the edge of breakdown during the endless weeks of an empty summer, creeping, one wet evening, into the sanctuary of a Catholic church. Bells rang; she was almost fainting.

'*Mon père, je suis Protestante . . .*'

I said, I was perishing for want of a word of advice or an accent of comfort. I had been living for some weeks quite alone; I had been ill . . .

Bach came to his conclusion. There was silence, then a respectable applause, steady as rain, a murmur of conversation. After a while, people got up to go. Harriet and the others sat watching them.

'They record these concerts sometimes,' said Susanna. 'For the radio. I come here quite often – it's a bit like going to St John's, Smith Square, except that doesn't feel at all like a church when you go there, does it?'

'I can't remember – I haven't been there since I was a child,' said Harriet, returning. 'The last time we were near Smith Square was on a march, wasn't it, Marsha?'

'What?'

'Never mind. Shall we look round?'

She shook her head. 'I like sitting here.'

'So do I,' said Susanna. 'People have been sitting here since the Middle Ages. What's the rush?'

So they stayed, as the pews gradually emptied, leaving the statutory old women in black, heads bowed, hands trembling. Tourists wandered along the aisles, and up to the altar rail; a young man in his twenties, with the face of a Modigliani, long, narrow-eyed, intense, moved from station to station of the Cross.

'Why don't we go to church?' Marsha asked Harriet.

'Oh, God.'

Susanna looked at them both. 'Why don't you?'

'Do you?'

'No.' She hesitated. 'But when I was younger, I wanted to be a nun.'

'Did you?' Marsha regarded her in fascination.

'Lots of young women think like that.' Harriet, her fleeting sadness briskly put aside, spoke as she might during one of their conversations at home, after supper: with adult authority, clear about what Marsha should know. 'It's just a phase.'

'Did *you* want to be a nun?' Marsha asked her.

'No. Never. I was much too engaged with the world.' She looked at Susanna. 'But for you – '

'I took it rather seriously. For a while. Anyway. As you say, it's a phase.'

'You didn't go to a convent school.'

'No. I just read things, and hid away. My engagement with the world has never been very secure.' Susanna spoke lightly, but it was clear she was serious. The church was emptying; the sound of departing footsteps on stone, and their own conversation, floated into the quietness.

And now is the moment, thought Harriet, but Marsha is here. Marsha is always here, and in the evenings there is Hugh, or a visitor, and when shall we talk? Perhaps she doesn't want to, perhaps she really doesn't. But –

'I think I'd like to be a nun,' said Marsha.

'You don't know anything about it.'

Marsha turned to her, in a spasm of irritation. 'Why are you so bossy?'

'I – ' Harriet, long used to mother and daughter confrontations, was on the whole used to having public ones only in front of people she knew well – other mothers, other single parents whose children drove them, at times, to the edge. Also, she had been enjoying Marsha's affection and loyalty in recent days, and had forgotten how it felt to be spoken to like that. Especially here. Especially now. She floundered; she was hurt. 'I –'

Marsha turned back to Susanna. 'Tell me about it.'

'You have to be strong.' Susanna made a gesture. 'I should have been hopeless. Some people think of it as escape, and repression, but actually I think it can be full of purpose. It requires limitless reserves of generosity and discipline. I think it's admirable.'

Marsha was silent, and who knew how much of all that she had understood, or how much Susanna had cared if she understood? She had been talking for herself. And Harriet, listening, thought: this woman has missed her vocation. Not to be a nun, or not necessarily, but to be directed, to be fired by something. She's lost: her life is nowhere.

Early afternoon sunlight streamed through high windows. Marsha said: 'I'm strong.' She shifted in the pew. 'I think.'

Susanna regarded her. 'Yes, I should think you probably are. No doubt it comes from your mother.'

'She's a bossy boots,' said Marsha, but leaned against Harriet briefly. 'Sorry, Mum.'

Harriet patted her. 'It's okay.' She stretched, partly out of genuine need to, partly as distraction from a disconcertingly powerful rush of maternal affection. I'm at her feet, she thought, bewildered. She has the power to crush me utterly – how have I not realised that? And if I were to lose her –

She rose. 'I have to move. What shall we do?'

'There's a particular kind of convent in Belgium,' said Susanna, getting to her feet. 'I expect you've read it all up.'

'The Béguines.'

'I knew you would have done. Yes.'

'The what?' Marsha was following her out of the pew.

'An order of women who live as a sisterhood but without vows. They have power to return to the world.' She looked at Harriet. 'Yes?'

'You would know better than I, but yes, that's how I understand it. Dating from the fourteenth century.'

'Possibly. It's the convents which remain here. They're extraordinarily lovely – airy and quiet. Would you like to visit one?'

'Yes. It was on my list, anyway.'

'I'm sure.' They were out in the aisle; they wandered between the pillars, looking around them. The young man with the Modigliani face had gone; the organist, with only a handful of listeners left, began to play again, softly, something gentle and high. They stopped to listen. Every now and then the door swung open, as somebody left, or somebody else arrived; they walked on, looking at tombs and plaques and wall hangings.

'More tapestries,' said Harriet, adding quickly, not wishing to take Susanna into whatever painful territory had made her weep before the last one: 'The other thing about the Béguinages, of course, was that the women were exploited by the cloth merchants. Isn't that right? They wove to the glory of God, all through the fifteenth century, and the merchants made a fortune.'

'Yes. Like the lacemakers, except that they were worse off – no protective convent, just their own homes, or some miserable cellar.'

'The convents sound perfect,' said Harriet, as they completed their tour, and came, once again, to the heavy oak door. 'I mean in principle. Sanctuary, sisterhood, power to leave when you choose.'

Susanna was opening the door, and did not answer.

Outside, the pavement was hot and the sun was dazzling. Streets and buildings were bleached and deserted, outlined here and there by tall black railings. Convent colours, broken now and then by a brimming windowbox. They put on their sunglasses, and wondered what to do.

'I'm hungry,' said Marsha. 'I'm thirsty.'

'We all are.' Harriet looked about her, wishing for a hat.

'Lunch,' said Susanna, 'and I know just where to have it.'

She led them through the sleepy afternoon heat to a pleasing, surprising flight of steps down into a little park. Mothers watched prams beneath the trees, lovers strolled hand in hand along the paths.

'I'm *hot*.'

'Keep walking.'

Ahead, a lake was shimmering. Beyond, a white-painted café beckoned from the shade. It suited their requirements exactly.

*

94

The heart of Brussels, the capital of Europe, was shaped like a heart. Broad boulevards enclosed it; fine avenues led out from it: towards Laken, in the north; the Bois de Cambre and the Forest of Brussels to the south-east; Anderlecht in the south-west. These, and other outlying districts, were inviting, but could not, within the space of a few days, all be visited, any more than Harriet could expect to visit everything on her list in the centre, especially with Marsha to consider, and especially in this heat.

But the heat passed, that day an exception to those which followed: manageably cooler, with a breeze; and the heart of the city – served through it was by buses, blue and yellow trams and a metro whose art nouveau entrances, and platforms filled with murals and sculpture, meant that travelling on it was full of delights and surprises – was, like Amsterdam, small enough to make walking pleasurable. It was a place full of charm, full of parks and gardens and graceful, well-kept buildings; for the next two or three days it was – for Harriet, at least, and she tried to make it so for Marsha – full of interest.

Sustained now and then by paper cones of *frites*, sold at kiosks everywhere, they wandered through crowded street markets and gazed in the windows of antique shops near the Place du Grand Sablon. They spent a whole morning in the Royal Art Museums, buying postcards of Brueghel, Van Eyck, Ensor and Magritte, writing a select few home at the table of a café in the Parc du Bruxelles, where that evening they sat in deckchairs listening to a concert. The next morning, exhausted, they spent at home, but went out to stand, at noon, amongst the pigeons in the precincts of the Cathedral of St Michel and St Gudule, listening to a joyous and intricate carillon of bells.

The streets were full of tourists, from whom they pretended they were distant and different, even though such differences were, truth to tell, largely indistinguishable. Harriet felt that she probably bought less and thought more, and ventured as much to Susanna, in light-hearted vein, as they walked slowly home that afternoon.

'You're a snob,' said Susanna. 'A terrible snob.'

'Just clear-sighted.'

'And so modest, too.'

They walked on companionably, passing the plate glass and pillars of a tiered arcade of shops. Lace and crystal, leather and cashmere, beribboned boxes of chocolates – perhaps it was the effect of too much sightseeing, but Harriet felt, for the first time since their arrival, a mixture of satiety and distaste. The city was charming, well ordered and full of variety, but it also felt somehow unreal – not as it had done the morning after their arrival, when she had stood in the Grand Place and tried to get her bearings, but simply too pretty, too expensive, too pleased with itself. The capital of Europe, with mountains of butter and mountains of paper, issuing directives, bossing everyone about. Like me, she thought, feeling a sudden puritanical desire for the strict routine of work, a day's accomplishments ticked off, a supper earned. This was no good: clearly she had become stuck in her ways, unable to relax and take pleasure in freedom. Or perhaps it really was, when you were so used to running your own show, difficult always to be the guest.

These newly critical feelings were partly confirmed and partly alleviated next morning, when they visited Hugh in his office. Situated in the solidly substantial streets of the upper city, not far from the parliament building and amidst the offices of ministries and insurance companies, Hugh's bank was all gold lettering, white-painted stone, wrought-iron railings alongside shallow steps.

'Gosh,' said Marsha.

They had taken a tram up here, as Hugh did every morning, and walked the last few hundred yards. It had rained in the night, but the morning was fine, the streets almost edibly clean, windowboxes stuffed with ivy and petunia. Men in suits came in and out of doorways, purposeful women in narrow shoes swung slender briefcases and hailed taxis with a finger. The brisk part of Harriet responded to all this, as they stood looking at the smooth exterior of Elbridge & Rowinski; she glanced at Susanna, who had been here often, whose background, indeed, was in this world, but who did not work.

'Shall we go in?'

They went through double doors fastened open, crossing a threshold of matting and brass on to a sage green carpet, and were greeted by a commissionaire.

'Good morning, Mrs Pickering.' He smiled at Susanna, and at Marsha, beside her. 'Your husband's expecting you? I'll tell him you're here.'

Susanna's hand rested on Marsha's shoulder; she looked a little on edge, as though she were not simply accompanied by her visiting niece, but needed to be anchored by her, and their relationship. Following, as the commissionaire buzzed an intercom, Harriet glanced to the right, where closed glass doors showed young men in shirt sleeves at dark designer desks, leaning back to talk into trim white telephones, chucking screwed-up faxes into a bin.

'Hugh's on the fifth floor,' said Susanna, and led them both to a lift even more silkily silent than the one in their apartment building.

They came out on to a hushed sunny landing, carpeted in grey and lit by tall sash windows at either end. Passages and discreetly labelled doors led off it; the lift gave a ting and descended, empty.

'Well,' said Harriet, taking in the view of rooftops beyond the gleaming windows, the rinsed morning sky.

'Here you are,' said Hugh, coming out through double swing doors. He kissed them all. 'I meant to be here to greet you.'

'You were, almost.'

'But not quite. A phone call from Paris. Anyway, come through.'

He ushered them along a corridor, hung with framed posters – not the over-familiar Impressionists you might see in any London office, Harriet noted, but decent contemporary prints – to more swing doors, and an open-plan office. Harriet's immediate impression here was that Hugh, in the midst of much activity, carried immense authority. There were more young men like those downstairs, and quite a few women; none looked older than twenty-five and they had about them an air of sharp brightness against which Hugh, some twenty years older, felt solid and wise and much more interesting. She was somewhat taken aback by the force of this realisation, and then he was introducing them all, in a sweeping gesture, and people were turning from their computer screens and smiling. Clocks on the wall gave London, New York and Tokyo time, which intrigued Marsha; boards were chalked with prices and commodities; telephones rang, a fax machine whirred, there was the smell of good coffee.

'Come and see where I am.' Hugh led them away from all this into one of a number of much smaller offices on the perimeter. 'So.' He moved to sit in a swing chair behind an enormous desk where his computer stood. 'What can I do for you? You have come to see the bank because – '

'Because we want to see where you work, silly.' Marsha was picking up a paperweight from the corner of the desk.

'Oh, is that what it is? I thought you had come for a *loan*.' He pressed his fingers together and looked at them gravely.

'Can I sit there?' she asked.

'Certainly not.'

She picked up the paperweight and made as if to throw it at him. He ducked behind the desk.

'Spare me, spare me, I have a wife, six children – '

'No, you haven't.' Marsha walked round the desk and tugged at his buried head. 'Move,' she ordered. 'Move, or you die.'

He moved, cowering, to crouch behind the chair where Harriet sat observing this exchange with a mixture of delight and sadness. How had Marsha survived for so long without a father, or father figure, to order about in this way? Close as she and Marsha were, their life together had not, for a long time, allowed for play.

Marsha sat herself down in the swing chair and swung. She swung back again, picked up the phone. 'Paris, please. Thank you. Yes. Hello? I should like to – ' she hesitated. 'I want to – ' She stopped, and put the phone down, demanding: 'What *do* you do?'

They all laughed, but Harriet, turning to share her amusement with Susanna, saw in her face as she stood with her back to the window, a fleeting but unmistakable shadow.

'Good question,' Hugh was saying to Marsha. 'Lend terrifying amounts of money is the answer.'

'Can I have some?'

'Do you wish to make polymers in Bulgaria? To convert feedstock in the Ukraine? Would you like to stop acid rain in Bohemia?'

'I'd like to stop acid rain,' said Marsha, whose class project on pollution had lasted the whole of the previous autumn term, and who had irritated Harriet, against her better nature, by ferreting about in the kitchen separating the rubbish into three different piles and demanding trips to dumps and bottle banks.

'Well, then. You are now the President of the Bank of Bohemia. We shall lend you the necessary, and you will guarantee to repay us within the next ten years, putting up half of Bohemia as a guarantee. Is that clear?'

Marsha nodded uncertainly.

'This is in fact what you were talking about the other night, isn't it?' said Harriet. 'Financing the desulphurisation unit – is that right?'

'Exactly. We were talking about it the evening Christopher Pritchard came to supper, I think. He seems to have gone to earth, by the way. So. Enough of all this. Susanna has heard me droning on about work too often, haven't you, darling?'

She smiled, looking preoccupied. 'It's all right.'

'No, it isn't, it's as boring as old boots.' He looked at Marsha, who was turning the paperweight over. 'All I can say to you, dear niece, is that if you continue in this high-handed manner, you will most assuredly be running a bank by the time you're eighteen.'

'Good,' said Marsha, and then, as the telephone rang, 'I bet you that's Christopher Pritchard.'

'Why on earth should it be?' Hugh reached for the receiver. 'Hugh Pickering. Good heavens, how extraordinary, we were just talking about you.'

'Told you,' said Marsha, getting out of the chair as he moved towards it.

'Why?' asked Harriet, holding a hand out towards her.

She shrugged, and came to stand beside her. 'Just had a feeling.'

They waited, listening: Harriet and Marsha engaged with each other, Hugh talking to Christopher, and Susanna, her back to the window and the summer-morning sky, fingering her wristwatch, watching them all, set apart.

'Actually, I've got the family here,' Hugh was saying. 'Just showing them round, we'll have a bit of lunch . . . oh, at the Cockatrice, I should think, round the corner; then – ' he glanced down at an open diary 'then I'm in a meeting. So I'm afraid today's not really on, unless – ' He raised his eyebrows at them all.

'No,' mouthed Marsha elaborately. 'No, please no.'

Hugh covered the telephone. Harriet covered her mouth. Her back against the window, Susanna was absolutely still.

'Another time,' said Hugh. 'Give me a ring? Or I'll phone you? Very good. Nice to hear from you. Yes, I will. Bye.'

He put down the phone and Marsha gave a sigh of relief.

'He's not *that* bad,' Hugh said mildly.

'He is. I don't want to have lunch with him, anyway.'

'Well, you're not going to. Now, then. Is there anything else you want to organise while you're here?'

She looked round the room, so curiously bare after all the activity in the outer office, its walls hung with a couple of watercolours, the gleaming window giving them the city. There was the computer, a bookcase in a corner, a table with copies of *The Economist* and *Financial Times*. Other than that –

'I don't know,' she said. 'What do children do in offices?'

Hugh got up from his desk. 'Dear Marsha, don't sound so sad. Sometimes I wonder what grown-ups do. How about sending a fax?'

'Yes! Who to?'

'Grandpa? In London? I send faxes to his office sometimes.'

'What do you say?' They were walking towards the door.

'Oh – what is the price of oil this morning, and what have you got in your sandwiches?' He opened the glass-panelled door to the outer office and held it for her, courteous and grave.

'Don't be silly.'

'I'm perfectly serious. What are you going to say?'

'I'll ask him about Victor.'

'Who?'

'My mouse.'

'I didn't know you had a mouse.'

'I don't know if I still have.'

He followed her through to the buzz, laughing.

'Give Grandpa my love,' called Harriet.

'Will do.'

The door swung to behind them. She turned back to Susanna, saying, 'That was a nice idea.'

Susanna was looking beyond her, into the office. 'Yes.' She turned to the window, where clouds sailed slowly by, and said carefully, 'I think it'll be fine for the rest of the day now, don't you?'

'Probably.' Harriet picked up the paperweight, a heavy glass sphere with a small flat base to rest on. Within its transparent solidity the parts of a clock were suspended, as if in air: cogs, small brass wheels, a coiled spring. She turned it over, feeling its cool heaviness, watching Susanna watching the sky.

She said: 'Only two more days. You've done such a lot for us – it'll feel very strange travelling on without you.'

Susanna nodded. 'We'll miss you.'

There was a silence. The glass-panelled door sealed the office away: there was only, through the open window, the muted sound of traffic from the street below, and the sight of the drifting clouds.

Harriet ran her fingers over the smooth curve of the paperweight, looking at Susanna's profile, so clear; at her expression, so remote.

'Susanna?'

'Yes?'

She turned; their eyes met.

'I should so like to get to know you better. Before we leave.'

'We have got to know each other better.'

'Yes, but – ' Harriet rested the paperweight on the desk again, observing the separate parts – a slender pair of black pointed hands, a scattering of minute brass screws – frozen, still. She said: 'I'm fearful of prying. I just want you to feel you can talk to me if you need to. I shan't say it again.'

'Now is not the moment.'

'It never is.'

'No.'

'Do you mind if I ask: is it painful for you, being with Marsha? Seeing her with Hugh?'

'Yes. But I've always – ' She lifted her hands to her head, and clasped it – briefly, but as if she couldn't help herself, as if she were trying to hold everything in place. 'Never mind,' she said quietly, shaking her head, her eyes closed. 'Never mind, never mind, never mind, never mind – '

'Susanna – ' Harriet rose from her chair. 'Forgive me.'

Susanna's hands went over her face. 'Stop it. Please. They'll be back in a minute.' She drew a deep breath, lowered her hands and looked at her, smiling decidedly. 'There. Let's leave it, okay?'

Behind them the door swung open.

'We did it!' said Marsha. '*And* he replied. He says Victor's missing us, but he's eating well. Look.'

She waved a sheet of fax paper under Harriet's nose.

'I wish I were eating well,' said Hugh, following. 'Who's for lunch?'

The clouds were thickening as they came out of the building: it no longer looked as though the day were set fair, and as they set off down the street, Hugh in the lead, it felt cooler, too. He turned to reach out a hand for Susanna, saying to the others, 'It's not far, this place, just round the block.'

'Is it posh?' Marsha asked hopefully, leaving Harriet's side.

'Very.' He held out a hand for her, too, but she moved to disengage Susanna's, so that she was between them, a hand each.

'Now I've got both of you.' She swung their arms.

And Harriet, walking a pace or two behind, so as not to take up the whole pavement, observed the three of them, close and relaxed, looking, to passers-by, like a neat little family: two plus one, quite content.

An expensive-looking man in a hurry brushed past her, bumping her arm without apology.

'Excuse you,' she said sharply, but he had gone, unheeding. As yesterday, passing the shopping arcade, with its calfskin bags and cashmere cardigans, she felt a shiver of distaste. There were too many people here earning too much money, and perhaps that included her brother. This was not just the self-styled capital of Europe but of European capitalism itself, and for all that Hugh's projects sounded useful and right-thinking there was a part of her which felt firmly: and so they jolly well should be.

The street was beginning to fill with people looking for lunch – more expensive food, more consumption. She had had enough. I shall be glad to be on the train to Berlin with a packet of sandwiches, she thought, as they rounded the corner, and then, seeing Marsha looking happily from Hugh to Susanna, and Susanna's affectionate glance in return, felt chastened. There was no less sorrow here than anywhere else: that could not, in the quietness of Hugh's office, have been made more plain.

Our way lay through some of the best streets of Villette, streets brightly lit, and far more lively now than at high noon. How brilliant seemed the shops! How glad, gay, and abundant flowed the tide of life along the broad pavement! While I looked, the thought of the Rue Fossette came across me – of the walled-in garden and school-house, and of the dark, vast 'classes' where, as at this very hour, it was my wont to wander all solitary, gazing at the stars through the high, blindless windows . . .

Is it Susanna, or is it myself? thought Harriet, surprising herself. Which of us, all solitary, is wandering in that walled-in place?

A few drops of rain began to fall. Ahead, the others quickened their pace, Hugh turning to call to her: 'It's on the next corner, okay?'

Harriet followed the tide of life along the broad pavement, catching up with them as they reached the glass door of a restaurant hung with pink awnings. On the glass a gold creature was painted, a twisting serpent with malevolent gaze.

'The Cockatrice.' Hugh told Marsha, holding open the door, and then, to Harriet, 'Sorry – you've been rather left behind.'

'I have been with my thoughts,' she told him primly.

'And what were they?' asked a voice behind them, and they turned to see Christopher Pritchard, who made an inclination, saying, 'Sorry, couldn't resist it. This is on me.'

*

'The thing is,' he told them, as they settled themselves bemusedly at a corner table, 'that I thought I might not see you all again for an age, and I didn't like the idea of venturing to the interior without a return of hospitality.'

'Which interior are you venturing to?' Hugh asked him, picking up the menu.

'The east dear fellow, always the east. Now, then.' He ran his eyes over the wine list. 'Who'd like what?' A waitress hovered, young and superior. 'Probably doing her PhD.' He gave her a breezy smile. 'Can you bear to take an order?'

'Monsieur?' She observed him from the heights.

Under the table, Marsha gave Harriet a kick. Harriet winced, and frowned at her.

'Something wrong?' asked Christopher. 'Susanna – what will you have?'

She shook her head, looking at him quickly, then away. 'I don't really drink at lunchtime, thanks.'

'Oh, surely – '

They established, with difficulty, that none of them drank at lunchtime. Hugh compromised with a beer; Christopher, with a great show of reluctance, ordered juice and mineral water.

'So. Cheers. Cheers when it comes, anyway. And what shall we all have to eat?'

Eyes down, they perused the menu with the utmost concentration, aiming for something light but sustaining, fending off persuasion towards the rich and heavy. In the end, after a certain amount of argy-bargy, smoothed over by Hugh, they settled on fish, received their drinks, and sat back, politely raising glasses.

'Cheers again.'

'Cheers.'

'So. What have you all been up to?'

This, thought Harriet, at her most acid, was the kind of question guaranteed to kill all conversation dead. Who should answer first? What had they been up to? Tricks? No good? Ho ho ho. And then, seeing a flicker – just a flicker – of discomfiture in his heavy face, as he looked round the table, she thought: but what a very critical person I am. Do I really need to pick up on his every intonation? No wonder Marsha reacted so strongly against him: she gets it all from me, and how is her passage through the world to be tolerable, if she cannot learn to tolerate?

'Susanna has been showing us Brussels,' she said with a smile.

Susanna made a deprecating gesture. 'Some of it.'

'I wish I had had such a guide when I first got here. Ah. Nibbles.'

They described, over a dish of crudités, something of the past few days: markets and churches and galleries and music in the park.

'No low life?' asked Christopher. 'No dives?'

'Certainly not,' said Hugh.

'What's a dive?' Marsha was munching on a radish.

'A graceful plunge into a swimming pool.'

'Ha ha.'

Dishes were distantly delivered by the waitress. They shook out sugar pink napkins.

'This really is terribly kind of you,' said Hugh, deftly slicing along the backbone of his trout.

'My pleasure. As I said, I wanted to catch you all before – '

'Yes. Where are you – '

'Prague,' said Christopher Pritchard, helping himself to potatoes. 'Prague, of course. Where else?'

Outside, it had begun to rain. Drops fell against the window panes and trickled down the golden cockatrice; people hurried past beneath umbrellas. Inside, the restaurant had darkened; art nouveau lamps with pale pink opaline shades were switched on by the manager. A couple pushed open the door and came in laughing and wet.

'M'sieur-dame?' He went to receive them, taking their umbrella.

Harriet said, carefully, studying her fish, 'You didn't tell us you were going to Prague.'

'When I came to dinner? Didn't know, then. Thought it might be Budapest. Thought I might be here for the duration. Yesterday a phone call from a useful contact. So – I'm off in a couple of days. Looking forward to it.' He raised a forkful of plaice to his lips, saying to Harriet: 'We should meet up. When did you say you'd be there?'

Harriet was conscious of her family's eyes most consciously averted, and of Marsha's desperate, silent signals coming across the airwaves as she picked up her glass of mineral water and watched the little bubbles rise gently within it to break on the surface.

'I don't think I did,' she said slowly, and there was no way in which her obvious withholding of any more than that could be interpreted as anything but rude.

For a moment there was a silence. Conversation from other tables, the splash outside of traffic through the rain, people making a dash for it – all sounded, within this horribly awkward pause, like dinner gongs.

Then Christopher said pleasantly: 'Well. Perhaps we'll bump into each other.' And then, picking up a small silver boat of caper sauce: 'Can I offer anyone this?'

Hugh came to the rescue, as always, taking the dish and changing the subject, as Harriet, drinking her sparkling water, felt herself blush to the roots. A discussion began between the men – contracts, negotiations, financial backing, plant – from which, in any circumstances, she would have switched off. She let the blush fade, not looking at anyone, then raised her head, smiling distantly at Marsha, and glancing at Susanna, to share the moment.

Susanna was not eating, and now she came to think of it, Harriet realised that she hardly ever did. She cooked, she presented and served most beautifully, but she did not, actually, eat. She toyed with, she picked, she pushed to one side. And what was she doing now?

She was looking at Christopher Pritchard.

And Christopher, as though he felt her gaze upon him, turned from his conversation with Hugh and returned that look – only for a moment, with not a word spoken between them, but it was clear to Harriet (and surely, surely to Hugh?) that for those few seconds, for both of them, all else ceased to exist.

The moment passed, the meal ended. Outside, they stood beneath dripping pink awnings, saying their goodbyes. The rain had stopped as they had coffee; puddles shone, the sky cleared, and afternoon traffic sent up sprays of water.

Across the street from the Cockatrice a man in a good grey suit came down the steps of a white house and turned to wave to a woman at the window, touching his hand to his lips. The woman nodded, returning the gesture; she pushed up the window and leaned out, watching him go.

Harriet turned from this scene, and rested her hand on Marsha's shoulder. She said goodbye to Christopher Pritchard, who did not, on this occasion, move forward to kiss her, but nodded to both of them, with a smile. He shook Hugh's hand, and he kissed Susanna – lightly, a brush on the cheek, once, twice. He said he hoped they'd all see each other again on his return, and they all thanked him, again, for the lunch, and then he was gone, walking away up the wet street towards a tree-lined boulevard, not looking back.

Hugh put his hand beneath Susanna's arm. He shepherded his family from beneath the dripping awnings, and along the pavement, keeping them out of the way of a passing taxi. People went to and fro; Harriet and Marsha fell back, allowing them room. They held hands, walking behind the others, and Marsha, who had been silent through most of lunch, began to talk again, asking what they were going to do now, and what they would do tomorrow, and what time their train went on Sunday. Harriet made perfunctory answers, watching the last of the clouds ahead drift away, and a watery sun appear; watching Hugh and Susanna, arm in arm, looking now and then in shop windows: seeming, from this distance, so companionable and close.

He moved on, and I followed him, through the darkness and the small, soaking rain. The boulevard was all deserted, its path miry, the water dripping from the trees; the park was as black as midnight. In the double gloom of trees and fog, I could not see my guide; I could only follow his tread. Not the least fear had I: I believe I would have followed that frank tread, through continual night, to the world's end . . .

Is it me, thought Harriet, late in the night: is it me, or is it Susanna?

The bedroom was dark, the apartment quiet. She sat by the balcony window, whose long fine curtains let in a little of the light from the street lamps below, touching the walnut wardrobe, the pale carpet, the bed across the room where Marsha lay sleeping. In ten years they had been separated for two or three nights at a time – no more, and not often. My dear companion, Harriet thought, watching the stillness of the form beneath the bedclothes, hearing the light high breath.

Is it me, or is it Susanna? It is such a long time since I endured separation and parting: in different ways, on different occasions, I have endured it twice. I am alone, still, though Marsha, for all these years, has been my solace. Susanna has a husband, but is childless, and grieving, and neurotic. I fear for her, and for Hugh, and their future. What kind of separation is she enduring now?

She leaned back in the armchair, closing her eyes; listening for the opening of a door, footsteps along the corridor, a woman smothering sobs.

There were none of these sounds: only from outside came footsteps along the street, returning to other apartment buildings, the slam of a taxi door, a distant plane.

Christopher Pritchard was flying to Prague.

Harriet, in the darkened room, relived the moment in the Cockatrice when she had seen that look pass between him and Susanna, excluding everyone. She relived a number of moments in the days since her arrival: his entry into the apartment kitchen – so large, so overpowering, so hard to like; their argument at the dinner table, and Susanna's gentle deflection of their mutual irritation; his looking up at her portrait above the fireplace; Harriet's own recognition of his presence – and yes, somewhere within that boorish, off-putting manner, the attraction he held for her. She saw Hugh, pouring drinks, making easy conversation about his work, making Marsha laugh, and she saw Susanna, the morning after their arrival, weeping before the delicate glance between lovers on the tapestry in the Hotel de Ville.

I have watched you, and watched you: at last you are mine . . .

Who was watching and waiting for whom? Who in this city was destined – like Charlotte Brontë, like Lucy Snowe – to suffer the anguish of unrequited love?

It was Saturday, their last full day. In the morning, Hugh had to go into the office; Harriet, Marsha and Susanna took the metro out to Anderlecht, to visit the Béguine convent.

'Is that all right?' Susanna had asked them at breakfast. 'I think you'd enjoy it, but I don't want to inflict – '

'We'd enjoy it,' said Harriet, buttering a croissant.

'The funny kind of nuns.' Marsha was dipping her croissant in a bowl of hot chocolate.

'Yes. You won't be bored?'

She shook her head, leaning over the bowl. 'I wish we had breakfast like this at home.' She took a mouthful, quickly, before it all fell apart.

Hugh rose to go. 'I'll see you at lunchtime, and we'll walk along the canal; would you like that?'

They made their arrangements; Harriet, on impulse, followed him out to the hall.

'Hugh?'

'Yes?' He was pulling on his jacket, feeling in the pocket for keys.

'It's just – ' She felt suddenly shy. 'Just that we haven't really had time to ourselves. And we'll be gone tomorrow – '

'Is there anything special – '

'No.' She hesitated. 'It just feels strange, to spend all this time with

Susanna, but not you. I mean, she's been so good to us, but you and I – '

He had found the keys and picked up his briefcase. 'Well. Let's try and have a talk this afternoon, shall we?'

'Thanks.' She reached out and kissed him, touching the smooth, well-shaven cheek with her lips, smelling the subtle scent of expensive soap. Then he was opening the door of the apartment, saying he must be off, and she rejoined the others – feeling, she realised, better than she had done for days.

And now the three of them, this familiar little company so used, by now, to spending time together, came out of the metro at Saint-Guidon, and walked through clean, half-empty streets towards the convent. It was after ten, but the atmosphere, as Marsha said, felt more like Sunday than Saturday: few morning shoppers and few tourists, just a handful of early visitors to the nearby church and the museum of Erasmus House. Susanna led them past the church on the Place de la Vaillance, and into a little square. The morning air was light and cool; a bell began to ring.

'That's it.'

She nodded towards a dark door, half open, set beneath an arch in a medieval wall; they followed her across, and as she fully pushed open the door Harriet felt as though she were stepping into a Dutch painting: a door opening into a courtyard; flagstones; a woman in a silent room beyond; the sound of a bell. But this woman was not the serving girl of a Vermeer, nor, dressed in a dull blue satin, was she playing upon the lute or virginals. She was a nun, a middle-aged woman in black and white, bent over her book, who looked up at their approach and smiled calmly. They greeted each other and walked on, Susanna leading them through room after small quiet room, where heavy oak furniture stood against whitewashed walls.

'It's lovely,' said Marsha. 'I'd like to live here.'

Susanna put her arm round her. 'I'm glad you like it.'

'Now I see why you wanted to become a nun.'

'Well – ' Susanna released her. 'You want all sorts of things when you're young.'

And when you are older, too, thought Harriet, listening. She turned from the contemplation of a tall white candle set in an alcove beneath a painting of the Ascension. What, or who, do you want now, Susanna?

It was afternoon. Hugh and Harriet walked along the waterfront of the

Canal de Charleroi. The air was warm, and the sky was hazy; people were lingering over coffee outside cafés on the boulevard running alongside, sitting on benches on the broad pavement overlooking the water. There were bookstalls, one or two news-stands; a few leaves drifted from the trees and fell. It reminded Harriet a bit of the South Bank, of walks along the Thames after a movie at the National Film Theatre, and she said so.

'Your London is so different from how mine used to be,' said Hugh. 'You do interesting things.'

'You must have visited the NFT.'

'Perhaps I did.' Hugh stepped out of the way of a cyclist. 'Mostly I made money: very dull.'

'I don't think of you as dull. Or as one of Thatcher's children.'

'No. Even so – that's what I am, I suppose. Enough of one to come here and live as I do.'

'But with a heart,' said Harriet, thinking of good causes in Bohemia. She put her arm through his. 'You do have a heart.'

'Somewhere.' He patted her wrist.

Susanna and Marsha were far behind them: deliberately so.

'I want to talk to my brother,' Harriet told them, outside the café where they'd had lunch. 'I want to re-establish our unique relationship: is that okay?'

Everyone laughed, and everyone knew she was serious.

'Marsha and I will linger outside shop windows,' said Susanna. 'We might even shop.' A light breeze stirred her hair; she held out her hand. 'Come on, niece. Let us enjoy the last hours of our own unique relationship.'

They made their arrangements to meet. Tonight, their last night, they were going to the theatre. Then Susanna took Marsha's hand and led her away. And once more Harriet wondered at the manner in which Susanna's inner turbulence was so successfully kept hidden: no one, seeing her and Marsha now, so contented in each other's company, would imagine the solitary weeping, the sudden breaking down in public, the look of desire at a man who was not her husband. Everything, it seemed, was façade.

And Hugh?

'Tell me about your life,' she said to him, leaning her head on his shoulder. 'Talk to me.'

He smiled down at her. 'I have talked.'

'No, you haven't. Not in the way I mean.' She raised her head and looked at him. On the broad stretch of the canal boats were going by, drawing up at the quay across the water. Pleasure boats, cargo boats, leaving and returning. Gulls wheeled in the hazy air above them.

'Are you happy?' Harriet asked.

There was a silence. Leaves scrunched beneath their feet.

'With reservations, yes.' He patted her wrist again; lightly, keeping things light. 'I've been happy having you two here.'

'We've loved it, too. It's been wonderful for Marsha.'

'Does she see – forgive me. We all have our boundaries – I know you don't like talking about it. But does she see her father at all?'

'Sometimes. She finds it difficult – she doesn't say so, but she does. It's like old-fashioned ideas about visiting children in hospital: they get upset when you leave, so you shouldn't see them. Better to let them settle down and get on with it. I think there's something to be said for all that.'

'And it's not as if she has childhood memories. Of him being with you both at home, I mean.'

'No.' There was another silence, in which Harriet revisited some of her own childhood memories. She said: 'When you were little, I felt that I couldn't get near you.' And then, after a pause, 'Now we're grown up, I realise how much you mean to me.'

'What a nice thing to say.'

'It's true. I've realised it since coming here. Amongst other things.'

'What things?' He was looking down at her again: she smiled, then withdrew her arm from his. To broach certain subjects needed distance. They walked on, passing other people.

She said: 'You're right. We all have our boundaries. I don't like to intrude.'

'Then don't,' said Hugh gently. 'Some things are better left unsaid. Quite a lot of things, really.'

'You and Susanna – '

'Susanna and I are all right.'

Are you sure? thought Harriet, walking slowly. Do I misread everything?

'We can't have children,' he said, after a while. 'I expect she's told you.'

'Yes. I'm so sorry – '

'She grieves. We both grieve about it. But – ' He spread his hands. 'Some things have to be borne. In time we'll come to terms with it.'

'That's brave.'

A shrug. 'There's not much else one can do.'

'Adopt?' she said cautiously.

'Susanna doesn't want to – she doesn't feel confident, now, that she'd be a good mother. I suppose she's lost her nerve, or something. She – ' He stopped. 'I think that's enough about it now. And anyway: we have Marsha. Haven't you been clever?'

'That's a nice thing to say. Thank you.'

'Well. It's true. She's great for all of us, isn't she?'

'Yes. It was hard when she was little, but now – I suppose we're on a bit of a plateau at the moment. Pretty companionable.'

'Good.' He looked about him. 'We seem to have come quite a long way.'

Harriet looked up. A bridge crossed the water ahead of them, broad and carrying traffic. Riverboats hooted – another reminder of London, which felt, at the moment, so distant. And soon they would be in another city. Berlin, she thought, with a shiver of apprehension. No brother there, no spacious apartment. Just she and Marsha, amongst East and West living uneasily together. Berlin – a different and divided city when Karel had been travelling through it, so urgently, so full of anger and fear – could be tough.

They came to a bench; they sat down.

'So,' said Hugh, in much the same tone as he had greeted Marsha, on their visit to his office. 'Was there anything else?'

Harriet smiled at the tone, and sat thinking.

Some things are better left unsaid. Quite a lot of things, really –

It was true.

'Christopher Pritchard,' she ventured, and he frowned.

'What about him?'

She took a deep breath. 'What did he do to you at school? Did he harm you?'

'No. He did nothing. For all I know he did nothing to anyone else, either – nothing serious, anyway. He just had a reputation.'

'And – ' She was willing herself to get it right, not to disturb calm waters. 'He didn't – '

'Didn't what?'

Didn't know Susanna before, she wanted to say. Did not meet her in secret, without your knowledge; does not meet her in secret now.

She shook her head. Much too dangerous.

'Mmm?'

'Nothing. Forget it.'

'What will you do if you run into Pritchard in Prague?'

'God knows – I hope we shan't. Marsha can't bear him, as you know.'

And what about me? What do I think of this man? I think I'm well shot of him, that's what I think.

'And when you get there,' Hugh asked her, 'how are you going to find your Karel chap?'

'Go to his old apartment, and take it from there.'

'A needle in a haystack. After twenty-five years.'

'I know. Do you think I'm barmy?'

'I think you're romantic and adventurous. And barmy.'

'You do remember him?'

'A bit. I remember the invasion, and all that. He was a nice chap?'

'The love of my life,' she said slowly.

'Are you serious?'

'I don't know.'

'Well. I wish you luck.'

'Thank you.'

'So.' They watched two children run up and down, called by their parents. 'So. Anything else?'

'Just one more thing,' she said, remembering the dinner, the tension, her sudden speculation. 'But this *will* sound mad.'

'How intriguing.'

She turned on the bench to look him full in the eye. 'I had a sudden wild thought, once, when I looked at the map here. You know in the park – '

'There are lots of parks.'

'The Parc de Bruxelles. Where the Palace is. The lake and the paths – they form the Masonic compasses, don't they?'

For a moment Hugh looked bemused. 'Er – yes. Yes, I think I knew that.'

'Well, it just made me think, that's all. About you. You're very powerful now – '

'I wouldn't say very.'

'I would. In comparison with quite a lot of people. You're rich and successful, and influential – '

'Come come. What are you getting at?'

'Just – you're not, are you?'

'Not what?'

'A Mason.'

He laughed at her. 'What do you think?'

'I don't know. I realised it was possible.'

'And?'

'And I didn't like it.'

'Well,' said Hugh, and his foot moved, for a moment or two, up and down along the pavement, much as Susanna, weeping in that little garden, had moved hers over the gravel: a repetition, a distraction, a gesture almost unconscious, but imperative. 'Well – if I were, do you think I'd tell you?'

Harriet looked at him: at the moving foot, and at his face, so dear and so familiar.

We all have our boundaries –

And secrets; and vows.

'No,' she said, after a while. 'No, you couldn't.'

'Quite. But I'm not, I assure you.' The foot stopped, he gave her a smile. 'Believe me?'

'I think so.'

'Good.' His arm went round her; she leaned once more against him. 'What a thought. What a lot of thoughts you have. Have we dealt with the issues of the day?'

'I think so.'

'Shall we walk on?'

'In a minute. It's nice sitting down for a bit.'

'Yes.'

They stayed there, talking about nothing very much after that – train times, the morning's arrangements – looking out over the water, at the boats, leaving and returning.

The train went at half-past ten next morning, from the Gare du Midi. It had a German engine, and carriages from Belgium and Austria.

'How do you know?' Marsha asked Hugh, as he put down their bags on the platform.

'I know all sorts of things. And I like trains.'

'So do I.' She looked at this one, raised, like the one from Ostend, high off the rails. 'I feel excited now.'

'The prospect of departure from kith and kin means nothing, I suppose.'

'What?'

'Come on,' said Harriet, who had been putting their tickets back in her shoulder bag. 'Carriage F. Three along.'

They found it, and climbed on, looking for their seats in the open gangway. Marsha was disappointed.

'It's modern. It's all clean.'

'What do you want, the Orient Express? Here we are.' Hugh stowed away the bags.

'Where's Susanna?'

'Right behind you.' Susanna touched Harriet's arm. Last night, after the theatre, she had looked drawn and tired, and had gone to bed, full of apologies, almost as soon as they got home. This morning she had risen early and set out a wonderful breakfast.

'All my favourite things,' said Marsha, looking at cherries, heaped-up croissants, jams, vanilla yoghurt, a honeycomb.

'Tuck in, then.' Susanna poured her a bowl of hot chocolate.

'She won't have room for lunch,' said Hugh, joining them.

'Oh, yes I will.' Marsha broke up her croissant and reached for the honeycomb. 'I love train food.'

'We're taking sandwiches and fruit,' said Harriet, drinking her coffee.

'*What?*'

'Ssh. If you behave yourself there might be a little visit to the buffet at some point.'

'There'd better be.'

Harriet reached for the bowl of cherries. 'This is so nice, Susanna. When you visit us in London I'll do it for you.'

Susanna smiled, seeming better this morning.

And now, looking up and down the carpeted gangway, at other passengers settling themselves, spreading out Belgian Sunday papers on the tables before them, she said: 'I wish I were coming too.'

'So do I,' said Harriet, kissing her, but it wasn't true. The truth was that she was longing, suddenly, for time to herself: time to look out of the window and think, to read her book – providing Marsha read hers – and to do what she wanted. Yesterday's nervousness at the prospect of knowing no one in Berlin had vanished, at least for now. How refreshing: to be in charge of her life again.

Hugh was looking at his watch. 'We're in good time.'

'Yes.' She stood aside to let someone by. 'You don't have to stay – I mean, if you don't want to . . .'

'Oh, sure,' said Marsha, who had taken her book out and put it on the table. 'Sure. We're going to say goodbye and they're going to leave us without waving us off or anything, and just *go*. Honestly.'

Everyone laughed.

'Well,' said Hugh, as a door slammed. 'There's a good few minutes. What shall we do?'

'Sit down,' Marsha ordered. 'Sit down with us – ' She looked at Harriet. 'Or are these seats next to us taken?'

'They're reserved,' said Harriet, and as she spoke an enormous German appeared in the gangway, with an enormous wife. There followed some stepping aside, and general kerfuffle with cases, and Hugh said, 'Let's go back to the platform.'

They made their way out there, began their goodbyes.

'It's been – '

'We'll miss you – '

'Thank you for everything – '

'Write to us – '

Hugh picked up Marsha, and staggered.

'What a *weight*.'

'You can talk.' She hugged and kissed him.

Harriet looked at this scene, and she looked at Susanna, standing apart. She went over and kissed her, again, with real affection.

'It's nice, having a sister.'

'It is.'

'I hope everything – I hope you – '

'Thank you.' Susanna turned to the others.

A whistle blew, on another platform. Everyone jumped.

'Hugh,' said Harriet, moving towards him.

They hugged, for the first time in years. No formal kiss on the cheek, as he'd given her when they arrived, but a real embrace.

'You're a darling,' she said. 'I'm so glad I've got you.'

'Likewise.' He patted her shoulder.

And then their own whistle blew, and they climbed back on again. Doors slammed: they settled themselves with the enormous Germans, and looked out of the window at Hugh and Susanna, standing next to each other, not touching. They waved, and the train began to move.

'Goodbye, goodbye!'

The carriage swayed, they went faster. Hugh and Susanna were moving alongside, trying to keep pace. They waved again, laughing as

Hugh made a marathon runner's face, doubled up in exhaustion, and then the train had really picked up speed, and then they were gone.

'What time do we get to Berlin?'
'Just after six. I'm going to gather my thoughts for a minute, okay?'
'Okay.'

Harriet leaned back, and looked out of the window. They were moving into the suburbs: life on a Sunday morning went past. She watched windows being opened, windowboxes watered; people collecting the papers, greeting each other at the church door. Cars were washed and grass was cut and lovers slept late behind drawn curtains. They went faster, they travelled through woods. Opposite, Marsha, too, was quiet. Harriet closed her eyes, making the most of it.

She let her mind drift over the days in Brussels: over conversations, revelations, things – so many things – left unsaid. She moved through Hugh and Susanna's spacious, sad apartment, and she moved through the city, revisiting streets, galleries, churches, parks. She saw the lovely merchant houses on the Grand Place, and the House of the Swan, where Marx had taken rooms. For a moment, remembering that, she remembered the rainy afternoon of their arrival, feeling so strange and unsettled, falling asleep in a low buttoned chair over her notebook –

Marx, almost forty, unpublished, expelled from France.

Charlotte, not yet thirty, craving the reciprocation of passion. An invisible person, a writer, going home to the moors to write and die.

Revolution.

A secluded life.

I seemed to hold two lives – the life of thought and that of reality . . .

The outer and the inner; and which, thought Harriet, as the train went faster, is the more important?

She thought of Germany, and of public, politically passionate women – Rose Luxemburg, Ulrike Meinhof, Petra Kelly – meeting their violent ends. She saw the divided city of Berlin, the wall down and a river of refugees from the Eastern Bloc pouring across the border.

She thought of the city she had left, where Marx, working late into the night, had written the *Communist Manifesto*. She saw Charlotte, hurrying back to her school for young ladies, craving a look, a word, and she saw Susanna, privileged, desperate, pacing, weeping, locking herself away.

And where, on that scale of public and private, am I, she wondered.

116

I am a single parent, caring for a child, leading a useful working life. I have, now, no passionate engagement with anyone. Where does my destiny lie?

She thought of Karel, whose choice had been unequivocally political: to go back, to resist.

A velvet revolution in the snow.

'Mum?'

Harriet returned to her daughter as though from another country.

'Hello, there. Yes.'

'I thought you were asleep. I'm going to the loo.' She nodded towards the sign at the end of the carriage.

'Okay.'

She watched Marsha struggle past the Germans and move down the gangway, and then she looked through the window again. They were out in the country. Flat, harvested fields lay cropped and golden, the weather was fine. She glanced at her watch. Three hours and a bit to Cologne.

They read, they went to the buffet for drinks, they played pocket Scrabble and talked. They had lunch: the sandwiches and fruit Harriet had brought and a bar of Belgian chocolate. They stood out in the corridor, watching the landscape change, growing hillier, and wooded, then making a descent into the great Rhine valley. Vineyards stretched away to the horizon; clouds sailed above castles on distant hilltops. Marsha was entranced.

They followed the line of the river, mighty and broad. Oceangoing vessels headed slowly northwards, to the coalfields of the Ruhr and the North Sea; they came in with billowing chimneys, to dock at Cologne. The train slowed, approaching the outskirts: they looked out at factories, office blocks, the twin spires of the cathedral.

'I wish we could get out.' Marsha's face was pressed to the glass as they drew into the station.

'I know.' But people were getting on and off, and Harriet drew her away, and back to their seats. They'd be moving again in a minute.

They crossed the river, looking down on to more ships, and smaller vessels, everything busy and sunlit, and then they were picking up speed and Marsha, in Harriet's corner now, began to yawn and stretch. She leaned against the head-rest, she slept.

Harriet sat reading, feeling free. After a while, she thought she might go to the buffet, taking her book, and enjoy a peaceful coffee; she looked at the German couple opposite. He, too, had fallen asleep and was snoring lightly; she was knitting, and glanced up as Harriet rose. In her broken German Harriet indicated her intention and the woman nodded and smiled towards Marsha. She would keep an eye.

Harriet moved along the aisle and along to the next compartment. One or two people were getting up, moving ahead of her, and one or two more came back, carrying luggage or cups. The train swayed, rounding a bend. She held on to a seat, and moved on, coming at length to the buffet entrance, and the bar. A small queue waited: a family, two middle-aged women, a man on his own.

The man was tall, and heavily built, holding a briefcase, feeling for change with the other hand. He nodded to the barman and took a can of beer with an upturned glass and as he moved away somebody came towards him, trying to get past, and he stepped aside, clumsily, apologising to the two women. Harriet now could see his face, and it was too late to pretend that she hadn't, or that she wasn't there, as Christopher Pritchard frowned in surprised recognition, and came towards her.

BERLIN

In the Hotel Scheiber

I

In 1945 Berlin, a devastated city, was salvaged by women. Tap tap. Tap tap tap. In print wraparound pinafores, hair in turbans to protect it from the dust, they moved through the ruins, picking up the pieces, chipping away with trowels at broken bricks and old cement, piling the bricks up four by four, neat stacks between bombed-out houses, on the corners of obliterated streets. Tap tap, chip chip chip, four by four, so. One hundred million tons of rubble. Brandt, looking back on those eerie, postwar days, described Berlin as a no man's land on the edge of the world, every little garden a graveyard.

'Elise? We're stopping for lunch.'

The voices of the *Trümmerfrauen*, the rubble women, the tap of their trowels, broke the silence. They did it for extra rations, and they did it because there were hardly any men left to do anything. They were dead, they were missing, they were on crutches.

Houses, department stores, familiar corner shops, once-crowded cafés and bars had been blown to bits. Whole districts were without gas, electricity, sewage, water. The Tiergarten, Prussian hunting and pleasure grounds, all lakes and woodland and light and air, crossed by a great boulevard rolling towards the Brandenburg Gate, was a sea of mud and uprooted trees. Those trees still standing, blackened and scarred, were hacked down for firewood as winter approached. As winter approached, people were still living in cellars: overcrowded, insanitary, cold, a breeding ground for disease. Streams of refugees poured westwards, and were held in bleak transit camps, huddled over their bundles, waiting for transport. Shivering queues stretched to soup kitchens out in the street, fires burned, smoke rose from the ruins.

Tap tap. Chip chip chip.

Red flags flew, then the city was quartered: Russian in the east, the Allied British, American and French sectors in the west. Europe had become two continents: an Iron Curtain came down between them. Later, a wall went up. Then it came down again – every last graffiti-sprayed bit of it.

Bang bang. Chip chip chip.

'My first thought was: I'm the one who has been walled in. They have built a wall around me.'

Harriet, in the buffet car, gazed out of the window at forested hillsides and felt those words, as if in a dream, take hold of her. They came from an untranslated novel, *The Forbidden Room*, written over a decade ago by Helga Schubert. A writer Harriet had never heard of, until she came across her one evening last winter in a history of Berlin.

She had put the book down on a pile of books – all that reading, all that preparation – and let the stark, frightened sentences sink into her. She wrote them down, in the thick black notebook tipped in Chinese red, got up, and put some more coal on. She went to the kitchen for coffee and stood leaning against the worktop, thinking: I'll remember those words when I get there, when I walk where the wall used to be. Then the kettle came to the boil, and the phone rang, and she forgot them.

Now, as Marsha slept in their own carriage, and Christopher Pritchard, sitting unwelcomely opposite at the table, put down his glass of beer and lit another cigarette, they came back –

I'm the one who has been walled in . . .

Cologne was far behind them, Berlin lay hours ahead. Of course, thought Harriet, looking out at the blue-green, densely planted firs, hearing Christopher's heavy inhalation of smoke: that is the essence, the heart of how it must have felt. Not just a city, but a room, a life.

Christopher blew smoke towards her; she waved it away. He apologised. He said: 'I do find this extraordinary.'

'Yes,' said Harriet, turning from the window with reluctance. Her peaceful, thoughtful journey had been snatched away. 'I thought you were flying to Prague.'

'I didn't say so.'

'I assumed – '

'I assumed you were. Why aren't you?'

'Why aren't you?' she countered, unwilling to be drawn.

He drew on his cigarette again. 'I could say it's because I like train journeys, but the truth is partly that I have business en route in Berlin and Dresden, and partly that I can't afford to fly. Things are a bit tight at the moment.'

'Oh.' Harriet recalled the Cockatrice, the lunch, the insistence: 'This is on me.' She recalled the credit card with which he had paid, and recalled, too, the look exchanged with Susanna. She said, unable to resist unleashing some of her fears then, and resentment now: 'I thought things were going well for you.'

'They are, on the whole.' He sounded defensive, equally irritated. 'It's just at the moment, that's all.'

'I'm sorry,' she said distantly, and another silence fell.

The train hummed smoothly along the track. Like Marsha, she had been disappointed at how modern and clean it all was. She had wanted to reclaim everything she had imagined about Karel's journey, twenty-five years ago: doors slamming shut on smoke-filled compartments, a cheap *couchette* whose dull red vinyl seats were marked with cigarette burns, a crowded corridor with an attendant making tea in glasses in an ill-lit cubbyhole. Instead, there was this air-conditioned gleaming white interior with clean upholstery, fresh-brewed coffee, almost soundless progress. 'Proof,' as the brochure from the German Tourist Office had informed her, 'that the transport problems of today and tomorrow can be solved by intelligent and purposeful planning.' All that remained of Harriet's imagined journey was the smoke from Christopher Pritchard's cigarette – allowable only in the buffet – which was making her cough.

'Sorry,' he said, and stubbed it out. He drained his glass of beer and tried again. 'What about you? How come you're not flying direct?'

She felt nervousness and tension unfurl within her, as if she had been caught at Customs, concealing her real purpose. She fiddled with her spoon. 'I like trains. I like being able to see where I'm going.' She could feel him looking at her intently.

He said: 'I get the feeling there's more to it than that, but I'm not going to pry. Even though it might seem that fate had placed us not just on the same route but the same train. Don't you find that remarkable?'

'Yes,' she said brusquely. 'I've already said so,' and turned again to the window. The afternoon sun was beginning to sink towards the hills; the shadows of slow-moving clouds passed over the fir trees. It would be evening when they arrived in Berlin. As yesterday, when she had been talking to Hugh, walking along the canal, she had now a moment of real apprehension. How foolish to arrive in an unknown city as darkness fell, a woman and child with no one to meet or escort them as they looked for their hotel. She could feel Christopher's eyes upon her, watching her carefully averted face. The afternoon sun was taken by one of the clouds; the hills became sombre and still.

'Harriet?'

'Yes?' Her tone was as light as she could make it, but she knew it sounded strained.

'What's the matter?'

'Nothing.'

She thought: I sound like Susanna, this isn't like me, I must pull myself together –

She turned to say: I must go and see if Marsha's okay, I've left her too long, and of course I'm perfectly all right, why ever shouldn't I –

She saw him looking at her with genuine concern, and interest, and a gleam of humour.

He said: 'I really do infuriate you, don't I?'

'I wouldn't say that – '

'You wouldn't, but you do. With every gesture, every word you cast in my direction, ever since we met. You couldn't make it clearer. I'm sorry I'm on your train, and I'm sorry I exist, but that's how it is. Shall we try to make the best of it?' And then he smiled at her, a warm, direct smile which after those melancholy moments looking out at the brooding forest did feel cheering. She smiled back.

'That's better,' he said. 'You look almost presentable now. Should we go and check on your daughter?'

What was this 'we'?

'I'll go,' said Harriet. 'I'm sure she's all right.'

'Like her mother.' He looked at her quizzically, and she rose, ignoring the look.

'I'll be back in a few minutes.'

'I'll try and wait.'

This time she laughed.

'Steady on,' said Christopher.

She found Marsha as she had left her, leaning against the head-rest, hair falling across her face, breathing in the light, almost imperceptible fashion of childhood. When did your breathing start to slow down, grow heavy? When you were troubled, perhaps. Marsha, sleeping peacefully, her hands in her lap, could not have looked further from sadness or distress. Across the table the large German woman looked up from her magazine and smiled, showing bad teeth. Beside her, the husband snored, lolling.

Harriet said again in her broken German: 'I am in the buffet car. If my daughter wakes – '

The woman nodded. She would tell her.

Harriet made her way back. Two businessmen were drinking at the bar. She looked along the carriage to the table where Christopher was sitting, his back to her, looking out of the window; wanting to get a new sense of this man, unchallenged by him and unobserved. So far she had seen him only in the company of others, finding him on both occasions intrusive, insensitive, overbearing. That, too, was how Marsha had experienced him. And yet – standing now in the lit-up little bar, with its shining glasses and rich smell of beer and coffee, fresh bread and sausage, she recalled other feelings about him: her realisation, as he rose to greet her in Hugh and Susanna's drawing room, that this could be someone of real presence – not overbearing, but simply powerful. She remembered once again his look across the table at Susanna in the restaurant: so intent, so serious, so full of desire. What had her own feelings been at that moment? Unease and astonishment. Fear for her brother, but more than that. Fear for herself, at being excluded?

He would take and hold my hand two minutes; he would touch my cheek with his lips for the first, last, only time . . .

Beside her the two men in suits laughed loudly, much as Christopher sometimes laughed: to fill a silence. Harriet moved away from them, and a little towards him, so that, in profile, she could see his face. He was smoking again, looking out of the window, where the view had changed: no longer the high forested hills, but farmland, rolling and open, dotted with neat red-roofed houses and barns. A poster for a prosperous land. The sun came out and the sun went in again, and Harriet stood watching this huge, heavy man, his expression, in repose, distant and withdrawn as he drew on his cigarette; sensing his loneliness and strength.

They sat over their empty glass and coffee cup, and he said it was a good thing it was Sunday, and the train uncrowded, or they'd have had to move and give someone else their table. He asked if he could get her another coffee, and she said no, she was fine, and then changed her mind. She sat at the table and watched him standing amongst the handful of other passengers at the bar, towering over them as the white-coated attendant poured from a steaming glass jug. She realised she was enjoying this moment, cherishing it even: watching him and waiting for his return, being looked after, having things done for her. She remembered how in the last days in Brussels she had imagined this journey; independent and free, in charge. Well. There was plenty of time.

He turned from the bar and came back to her, guarding the cup with his left hand from the slight tremor in his right, which threatened to spill the coffee everywhere. Have I noticed that before? she wondered, and remembered that she had: when he raised his glass, when he reached across a table for something – a bottle, a dish – it wasn't there always but sometimes it was, causing one thing to knock against another, a moment quickly glossed over.

He looked up and saw her, watching, and gave her a smile which this time was suddenly awkward. Harriet thought: he's afraid – of me, of this moment – and then: so am I – oh, I don't want this.

He had reached the table; he put down the coffee and some of it spilt in the saucer and he sat down, spilling some more, and looked at her.

'Well,' he said slowly. 'Here we are again.'

There was another silence. Someone moved past them; beyond the window the clouds grew denser, broken every now and then by a struggling sun, touching a barn, a slow-moving tractor in a distant field, a line of poplars. A few drops of rain fell against the glass, then trickled away to nothing. They passed a canal, and two people cycling alongside, followed by a dog, some kind of terrier. Then they were gone.

Christopher said: 'I probably shouldn't say this, but beneath the hostilities I do feel we have a kind of understanding. Do you feel that?'

Harriet turned her coffee spoon over and over. DEUTSCHES BUNDESBAHN was imprinted in small deep letters all along the back.

'Perhaps.' She raised her head and looked at him, at the dark hair in need of a trim, the open-pored skin, large features, ordinary mouth. An ordinary face, in fact, but –

He said: 'This is, as it were, a sentimental journey. For you, I mean.'

'I suppose so.'

'Retracing footsteps? You said you'd never been to Prague.'

'I haven't, but . . . I know someone there. Well, I used to. It's a very long time ago.'

'Most sentimental journeys begin a long time ago.' He looked at her ringless fingers. 'You're not married.'

'Divorced. That's also a long time ago.' She hesitated. 'You – '

'I'm also divorced, I think I told you. Like my parents – yea, into the second generation. Most people these days have split up, don't you find?'

She was about to say, 'Hugh and Susanna – ' and then stopped abruptly, saying instead, 'How long were you married?'

'Not long. I don't want to talk about it now.'

'Sorry.'

'A while. Perhaps another time.'

'Okay.' And she took the conversation back to what was manageable. 'Tell me about Berlin.'

'There used to be a wall there, and now there isn't.'

She looked at his deadpan expression and began to laugh. 'I want to go and see it. Where it was.'

'Of course. Everyone does. Beware of counterfeit bits of it – they'll rip you off as soon as look at you on the stalls round Checkpoint Charlie.'

'How will I know what's real?'

'How, indeed? I've been asking myself that all my life.'

'Ha ha. How shall I really tell?'

'Well – perhaps you'll allow me to show you.'

They looked at each other and then away.

'You know the joke,' he said, 'about this unified city?'

'What?'

'*East to West*: "We are one people." *West to East*: "So are we."'

This time Harriet did laugh. 'Where are you staying?' she asked him, fiddling with a packet of sugar. 'What are you doing in Berlin, anyway?'

'Leave that thing alone, why don't you?' he said, and took the packet from her, dropping it back in the bowl between them. 'Sugar's bad for you. Like cigarettes.' He lit another, carefully blowing the smoke away from her. 'I have one or two business contacts, manufacturers from west Berlin who've bought up cheap factory premises out in the eastern suburbs. And I stay in a place called Prenzlauer Berg, if that means anything, which it probably doesn't. It's in the north-east – full of character, feels a bit pre-war, like me. The wall used to run right past it. Before '89, they flew white ribbons from their car aerials to show they'd applied for visas. Now, like most of the East, it's changing by the hour.' He pulled out a card from his inside pocket and scribbled a number on the back. 'What we should do is meet up, so I can show you around a bit.' He passed her the card. 'Give me a ring. What about you – where are you staying?'

Harriet hesitated, thinking of Marsha's reaction to all this.

'I'm sorry,' he said at once. 'I'm rushing you, aren't I? I always put my foot in it.'

'No, you don't.' She felt in her bag and pulled out her wallet, searching in her notebook for the address of their hotel, booked through the German Tourist Office last month. 'It's in Schöneberg,' she said, copying it down on a page at the back of the notebook. 'The Hotel Kloster.'

'The Hotel Kloster I know not, but Schöneberg's a good place to stay – lots of visitors end up there. It's down in the south; a bit rundown, but interesting: full of Turks and nightlife. Thanks.' He took the page she had torn out, and folded it carefully into his wallet. There was something about the way he did this which she found touching. 'And what are you doing to do when you get there?'

She spread her hands. 'Look around, explore, get the feel. What does one do in a strange city? I've read quite a bit . . .'

'I can imagine.'

'Don't you read?'

'Not if I can help it.' He smiled at her. 'Isn't that the worst thing you ever heard in your life?'

'Shut up.' She smiled back at him, beginning, now, to relax, and then she became aware of something needing her attention and looked up to see Marsha, her face flushed from sleep, coming down the aisle towards them. She was frowning, trying to see who her mother was talking to. Then she saw, and her face fell.

The landscape became open and flat: low land, the German plain, dotted with lakes and crisscrossed by rivers – the Rhine, the Elbe, the Weser, the Spree, which flowed through Berlin – all following the northwards slope towards the Baltic or the North Sea. It had grown much darker, rain was falling steadily now, and the small town stations they passed through at speed were lit up with neon strips along the platform, so that the rain on the windows briefly shone. The lights in the train, too, had been switched on, and people in the bar were drinking spirits, as if to fortify themselves for the city.

Harriet and Marsha had left Christopher there, and returned to their own carriage. Marsha had pulled on a raspberry-coloured cardigan over her white T-shirt and striped dungarees. She sat with it pulled close round her, hunched up in the corner, watching the rain, not speaking.

'Please,' said Harriet, for the third time.

Marsha did not answer. Her hair fell across her face; she pushed it back impatiently, then rummaged in an outer pocket of her holdall, producing, after studied exasperation, a tortoiseshell hairslide. This she fastened in on the offending side, and leaned back again against the window, chin in her hand. She looked casually exquisite – Harriet thought that perhaps she had, undetected, suddenly grown in Brussels, as children were supposed to do in the summer holidays, under adult attention. Well, she had certainly had plenty of that. She tried once more, venturing: 'You look very nice.' No response. She gave up, and looked at her watch.

Half an hour. Again, she felt her stomach churning, but now it was from feelings more complicated than simply the prospect of the unknown. She had envisaged herself and Marsha, alone in the city: that had its own anxieties – possible loneliness, possible dangers. Now, there was the possibility of an unlooked-for companion, someone who knew the realities of Berlin, while she knew only a little history; someone about whom she was still ambivalent, or at least uncertain, whom she hardly, in any case, knew; and the prospect of getting to know him was, it was clear, about to be blighted.

'I don't want him anywhere *near* us,' Marsha had hissed as they left him queueing up at the bar. 'How dare he come too?' Harriet ushered her onwards. 'Don't *push*!'

'I'm not pushing. Behave yourself.'

And the sulks began. Six hours away from Hugh and Susanna's soothing generosity and they had relapsed into the kind of atmosphere usually reserved for the direst of wet weekends in London, when all Marsha's schoolfriends had something to do and Harriet, two-thirds through the term, had a mountain of marking.

Now what?

The train slowed; she looked past her daughter and saw a sign flash past. Potsdam. They really were almost there: she saw the lights of the town – shop windows, tower blocks, street lamps – and then they were rounding a bend and passing a great stretch of water, the Wannsee, before moving into the suburbs. They slowed, stopped for signals, moved on. She said:

'We come into Zoo Station. That's where we get off.'

'I know,' said Marsha. 'You told me.'

'Marsha – '

'What?'

'Please don't be so difficult.'

'I'm not, I'm just saying you told me, that's all.'

Movement behind them. Christopher, bearing his luggage. He said: 'Another ten minutes or so. We come into Zoo Station. I expect you know.'

'Yes,' said Harriet, and as Marsha turned exaggeratedly back to the window she thought: actually, I wish he'd just go away, I can't be doing with all this, we were quite all right as we were.

Bahnhof Zoo. The train drew in under a great glass roof and for a moment, as they looked out of the windows, Marsha forgot to sulk.

'We're really high up!'

They were. The station was set storeys above street level, and even through the rain and the lights of the platform they could see, far to their right below them, the buildings of the Berlin Zoo, the landscaped gardens, stretching away.

'Can we go there?'

'If you like.'

The engine stopped, the doors were opening. They heaved their luggage out on to the platform, listening to announcements in unfamiliar German. The train emptied: everyone seemed to know where they were going. Christopher found a trolley, and loaded it up; they made their way to the ticket barrier, and came out on to the concourse: florists, lingerie and chocolate shops were closed but lit up; an *Imbiss* kiosk sold coffee and *Wurst*. Everything looked clean and well-kept: Harriet remarked on it, as they took the escalator to street level.

'It's a different story down here, I can tell you.' Christopher kicked in his bag as someone came past them.

'What do you mean?'

They reached the bottom, and stepped off into another open area which did, at once, feel different: dingier, with a sour smell in the air. He nodded towards a rear entrance. 'Not the kind of place to hang around – it's full of down-and-outs and drug pushers.'

Marsha looked at him scornfully. 'What do you mean, down-and-outs? They might just be homeless, like in London.'

'Marsha – '

'Like mother, like daughter.' Christopher was feeling in his pocket: he fished out coins. 'I have to make a couple of calls, check on my hotel and all that, so I'll say goodbye.' He nodded towards a cluster of phone boxes. 'You all right for cash? There's a money exchange over the road, in the Europa Centre. Not far from the Kaiser-Wilhelm church. It's a bit grim round there, too.'

'We're fine, thanks. Hugh organised all that.'

'I'm sure. Well . . .'

They both hesitated. Harriet looked out through the front entrance towards the U-Bahn sign. She must find a map. She looked back at Christopher.

'I'm here for a few days,' he said. 'You've got my number. If you need anything – '

'Thanks.' Harriet was aware of Marsha, stony-faced, as they smiled at each other. He came forward, put a hand on her shoulder; they kissed on both cheeks.

'Have a good time.'

'And you.'

He shrugged. 'I'll be working. Wheeling and dealing. Wheeling, anyway.' He nodded to Marsha, who was fiddling with the strap of her holdall. 'I shall follow your career in social work with interest.' Then he picked up his cases and walked away.

'Thank God for that,' said Marsha.

Rain fell from a heavy sky on to high-rise buildings and soaking pavements; unfamiliar makes of small car, which Harriet dimly guessed were Trabants from the east, screeched in and out of dense traffic; a bright yellow bus with its wipers going hooted impatiently at a couple of jaywalkers at the lights. Everything looked bright and wet and fast and foreign – the shop fronts, the neon signs, the hurrying people beneath umbrellas – and as Harriet and Marsha stood sheltering at the station entrance, trying to take it all in, someone touched Harriet's arm, and spoke in German.

'Hast du Wechselgeld?'

'What?'

She turned to see a young man with matted hair and yellow-grey skin, holding out his hand. He wore black – the kind of loose, dirty, sweatshirt fabric Harriet was used to seeing on the neo-punk beggars in

131

London, stretched out on the pavement with their dogs on a string and their rings through their noses, holding out a hand, as he was. But the beggars in London never frightened her: they were undemanding, unaggressive, familiar – she quite often gave them change, coming out of the supermarket or the bank. This young man's face was hard, insistent. She clutched at her bag.

'Du Wechselgeld,' he said again.

'Mum?' said Marsha.

'It's okay.' She turned quickly away from him. 'Come on.' He tugged at her sleeve; she yanked it back and grabbed Marsha's hand. 'Come on!' They ran through the rain, panting with the luggage, towards the U-Bahn, and down into the subway. Harriet scanned the queue at the ticket office, the people idling round a news-stand: did the *Polizei* hang about down here? Was there, somewhere, a friendly face? She turned round cautiously, looking up the steps. He had gone.

'Mum?'

'It's okay,' she said again. 'Let's have a look at the map.' She was shaking as they stood by the wall between the ticket booths, gazing at the unfamiliar grid.

'What did he want?'

'Only money.' Her fingers travelled south-west, trembling. She took a breath. 'Here we are ... two stops to Nollendorfplatz, then change. Think we can manage that?'

Marsha took her arm and hugged it. 'Are you all right?'

'Yes, I think so.' Harriet drew another breath. 'You?'

She nodded, burying her face in her mother's sleeve.

'Come on.' Harriet stroked the glossy hair. 'Your hairslide's coming undone.' She clipped it back again. 'There.'

Marsha mumbled: 'I'm sorry.'

'Thank you. Let's go.' They picked up their bags and looked about them for the right line. 'The thing is,' said Harriet, as they followed a sign, 'in London I'd be able to cope with that. I wouldn't like it, but I'd cope. But here – ' she stopped. No point in making a meal of their situation, as they travelled to an unknown hotel.

'Sorry,' said Marsha again.

'See what Christopher Pritchard meant? It is a bit tough here.'

Silence.

'He's not *so* bad.' They were walking through an arm of the subway, following the flow. Ahead, they could hear a guitar, and somebody singing.

132

'Like London,' said Marsha, cheering up.

'Like London.' Harriet shifted her bag to the other hand. 'Now, which is our platform?'

When they came out of the station at Bayerischer Platz they found the sky emptied of rain. The station was on a tree-lined road running through a square: Schöneberg was a residential district. A few blocks away to the north-east, off Nollendorfplatz, stood the house where Christopher Isherwood had lived in the years before the war, the Weimar years of cabaret and hunger, where he had written *Goodbye to Berlin*. Here, in an area bombed to bits in the war and rebuilt in the Fifties and Sixties, Turkish workers had settled, opening shops and cafés alongside streets of middle-class housing. Harriet looked about her, and looked at her map.

'I'm cold,' said Marsha.

'Darling, I'm sorry. You should be wearing your jacket.'

They dug it out of her holdall and zipped it up. 'That's better. Now then . . .' She turned the map in her hands. 'North-west across the square – come on.'

Carrying their bags, they walked beneath dripping trees, past tall houses whose bells and labels by the door indicated an endless division into flats and bedsits. Sunday evening hung in the air: they looked into windows where people were ironing, watching television, reading the papers. They came into their own street, which at once felt different: faster, more alive. Late-night shops had fruit and vegetable stalls out on the pavement; there were cafés, traffic, the neon signs of hotels.

'Which one's ours?'

'The Kloster. Can you see it?'

'No. I'm hungry.'

'Okay, okay.'

A group of young men came noisily towards them, carrying beer cans. Harriet put her hand on Marsha's arm; they stepped aside.

The Hotel Kloster, when they came to it, looked what it was: cheap, which was why Harriet had chosen it. Probably much too cheap, and she should have booked a pension, and why hadn't she? Because she had wanted something different for each city, when she had planned this journey: family in Brussels, a hotel in Berlin, a pension room in Prague, where hotel rooms now were astronomical.

So. Here they were. They carried their bags up shallow steps towards glass doors which needed cleaning. Beyond them, a girl with peroxided hair, hooped earrings and black nail varnish sat at a desk turning the pages of a magazine. The hall was lit by a neon strip and had brown flock wallpaper; television blared from a lounge. They crossed the carpet to the desk and coughed.

'Guten Tag.' The peroxided girl looked up, unsmiling.

'We have booked a room,' said Harriet, and produced her confirmation slip.

The girl consulted the register, pushed it across for signature, reached for a key from a rack behind her. Harriet, signing, saw the magazine she had been reading, and hoped that Marsha hadn't. She took the key; the girl nodded towards stairs behind her. They were on the third floor, breakfast was between seven and nine. The girl went back to her magazine, sighing as the telephone rang beside her.

Harriet and Marsha climbed narrow stairs lit by a time switch.

'All right?' Harriet pressed the switch on the second-floor landing, just to be sure.

'Yes,' said Marsha uncertainly. A lavatory flushed and a man came out; he nodded to them and disappeared into a bedroom. The doors to all the rooms were fire doors: solid, ugly, unpanelled. Apart from the man, they saw no one, and could no longer hear the television from downstairs. The silence peculiar to hotel landings – everything going on behind closed doors, between strangers – followed them up to the third floor. What have I done? thought Harriet. What on earth are we doing here?

'Thirty-four,' said Marsha, behind her. 'That's us.'

'Well done.'

They went in, putting the light on.

Twin beds with dull green covers took up most of the room, set at right angles to the door. A shiny wardrobe stood by the window; a basin was opposite. There was a cheap wooden cabinet between the beds, a list of fire regulations pinned on the wall. That was it.

'Well,' said Harriet. 'At least it's clean.'

Marsha crossed the narrow space between the foot of the beds and the wardrobe and looked out of the window. Harriet turned back the covers. Marsha returned and sank on to a bed.

'It's awful,' she said miserably. 'It's awful.'

'Oh, come on,' said Harriet, knowing it was. 'It's not that bad.'

'I hate it. I wish we'd never come.'

'Oh, Marsha, please – '

'Please what? Why on earth did you choose this place?'

'It's cheap,' said Harriet. 'It's cheap. We can't afford to go splashing out – ' She trailed off under Marsha's reproachful gaze.

'Why couldn't we have stayed in Brussels? I loved it. We don't *know* anyone here.'

Harriet tried to rally. She opened her mouth for a lecture – adaptability, readiness for different circumstances when travelling, kindness to tired mothers. She closed it again, feeling dreadful. Poor little girl.

'And I'm *hungry*.'

'I know. So am I.' She went over, and gave her a hug. 'I'll tell you what we'll do. We'll wash and brush up and go out for supper. I'll take you to a café and we'll have something hot and come back and have a good night's rest, and in the morning it'll all look nicer, I promise.' Silence. 'It usually does.'

And it had better, she thought, as Marsha, somewhat comforted, got off the bed and went downstairs to the lavatory. She crossed to the window, and stood looking down on to the street, so bright and busy, so strange, so far from home.

Well. This was something of how Karel must have felt: on his arrival in London, and on his departure, returning to an occupied city – alienated, distanced, afraid.

The sky was darkening. Harriet stood watching the traffic lights change, and the cars move off beneath them; she watched the revolving lights of a nightclub sign, further along, and she had, all at once, such a powerful memory, of such a different place: of a wet spring evening twenty-four years ago, and she curled up in the striped armchair by her bedroom window, reading – struggling to read – a letter from Prague. That was where this journey had begun. The letters were all in her suitcase, in their wooden box.

And surely, she thought now, leaning against the glass, I cannot be doing all this for nothing. Surely, when we get to Prague, I shall find – what shall I find?

She turned from the window, hearing Marsha's step on the stairs.

2

'You have no idea how much darkness there is in Berlin during the winter,' wrote Rosa Luxemburg, coming home to her rooms in Cranach Strasse, from walks beneath bare trees in the Tiergarten. 'How I long for sunshine.'

When Marx died, Rosa Luxemburg was twelve. She came to Berlin when she was twenty-seven. It was 1898 and she, the daughter of Polish Jews, educated in Warsaw and Zurich, had taken German citizenship through a marriage of convenience to a socialist émigré in Basle. Turn-of-the-century Berlin was in nationalist, expansionist mood. Rosa, a revolutionary, an independent spirit, collaborated with a radical lawyer, Karl Liebknecht, on a wing of the German Socialist Party. War was in the air. As the new century advanced, Rosa organised demonstrations, on Sunday afternoons.

On 1 August, 1914, the Kaiser addressed a crowd of a hundred thousand from a balcony on the Royal Palace. The country was at war with Russia.

'I no longer know parties,' he declared, his voice filled with emotion. 'I know only Germans . . .'

The crowd roared.

Troops, troop trains, music, flowers, waving girls.

Rosa and Karl published an open letter denouncing an imperialist conflict. They formed the Spartacist League: socialists opposed to the war.

The euphoric mood of the city changed. There were power cuts, rations, rising prices, curfews. Rosa wrote: 'Gone are the patriotic street demonstrations . . . No longer do we see laughing faces from train windows . . .'

She and Karl were arrested on charges of conspiracy.

He was sent to bury the dead on the Russian front, she to a cell in Spandau prison. She smuggled out letters, calling for revolution.

By the time Karl returned, war casualties were mounting; Berlin was sustained by a black market. In May, 1916, he addressed thousands on an anti-war demonstration in Potsdamer-Platz. He was rearrested.

Waves of strikes were staged in his support. In January 1917 almost half a million stopped work. The police were everywhere, the city on the brink of civil war.

In October, Liebknecht was released. By now, the Kaiser was a distant figurehead, all power in the hands of the generals. On 9 November he fled with his family to Belgium in a dramatic abdication; that day, Liebknecht proclaimed a socialist republic from the balcony of the Palace. Rosa, released, was convinced that a revolution throughout Germany, not just in Berlin, was needed to overthrow capitalism.

In January 1919 street violence gripped the city. The right-wing *Freikorps* struck: Rosa and Karl were arrested and murdered. Her body was thrown in to the icy waters of the Landwehr Kanal, flowing past the winter-bare trees of the Tiergarten.

The dining room of the Hotel Kloster was gloomy, and largely occupied by silent men in suits, but among them an elderly American couple smiled from their table and wished Harriet and Marsha good morning – cheered, it was obvious, by the presence of a child. They had a granddaughter just about the same age – how old might Marsha be, exactly? She told them she was almost ten.

'And you're having your birthday here in Berlin? My, that's exciting.'

Marsha, with a polite smile, gave her attention to the table, gazing at plates of cold sausage, smooth, milk-white cheeses, dark bread in a basket.

'It's like lunch.'

There were little plastic pots of jam, a steaming pot of coffee.

'Tuck in,' said Harriet, pouring. 'Make the most of it.' She drank, and looked at her guidebook, planning the day.

Later, when they went out, the weather was windy and bright. They stood at a bus stop on Grünewald Strasse, feeling better. Racing clouds streamed through a light, high sky and the bus, which came soon, was a cheerful yellow. They sat on the top deck as they rode through the city, travelling north. Harriet told Marsha a little about the rubble women, a little about Rosa: her passion and vision, her brutal, tragic end.

Marsha half listened, looking down out of the window, on to the traffic, the to and fro on the pavements, the wind in the summery trees.

*

Knowledge pales beside imagination, Harriet had always known that, but imagination can deceive and disappoint. There is much to be said for the solid reassurance of facts.

So, The Tiergarten. Harriet knew, from the map, and from one or two tourist brochure photographs, something of what its scale must be. But such a poetic name had nonetheless evoked for her, in London, trees, tears, water, walks in winter – a winter garden, indeed, with all its austere, seductive melancholy: frost on hard-pruned roses, ice on the pond, the crunch of feet on damp gravel.

It was not like that. They were here in late summer, and the Tiergarten was vast: acres of wooded parkland in the centre of the city which did, indeed, contain much water – bordered by the winding ribbons of the Spree to the north, and the Landwehr Kanal to the south, with great stretches of lake between – but was also crossed by roads, and speeding traffic, no more a quiet winter garden than Hyde Park.

Bisecting it from west to east, from Ernst Reuter Platz to the mighty Brandenburg Gate, ran the boulevard along which Prussian huntsmen had sounded their horns, where their carriages had taken the air. Charlottenburg Chaussee, it was called then. In the 1930s, when Hitler came to power, it became the East-West Axis, a favourite place for Nazi processions and torchlit rallies; in the Battle of Berlin it was bombed to pieces. Now it had another name, commemorating the summer's day in 1953 when impoverished workers throughout East Germany came out on strike. The Soviet forces moved in swiftly: in the riots that followed, four hundred people died.

In their memory, the boulevard became Strasse 17 Juni, and forty years later, on a bright August morning, Hariet and Marsha were walking up from the south side of the Tiergarten towards it, alongside the canal. Behind them was Cornelius Bridge, and the little sculpture commemorating Rosa Luxemburg.

'There's a demonstration in her memory every year,' Harriet told Marsha. 'On the day of her death. She was a communist, she followed Marx, but she believed in freedom and free speech and individual rights. She helped the wall come down, in a way – people put up her words on banners.'

Leaves blew into the water; ahead were boating lakes, to their left the Zoo, on Hardenbergplatz.

'Can we go?' asked Marsha, hearing shrieks and roars.

'What about for your birthday? Anyway, I thought you didn't approve of zoos.'

'I don't, but – ' She trailed off, watching a family walking ahead of them: two sisters, perhaps six and eight; a little boy of about three, let out of his pushchair, darting. His sisters moved quickly towards him as he neared the water's edge; behind them, the parents kept an eye, walking arm in arm. Squawks and trumpetings came from the zoo as they drew near; a balloon seller stood at the gate.

You don't approve, but you need something for children, Harriet thought, looking at Marsha looking at this little scene. Something more your size, to settle you down in a strange city.

She said: 'Have I been going on at you? Too much history?'

Marsha took her hand. They were together again. 'A bit. I mean it is interesting, sometimes, the rubble women and things, but – '

'I know. I'm sorry, I'll shut up. We'll go to the zoo if you'd really like to.'

She said she would really like to; they went through an entrance like a pagoda, paying through the nose.

A zoo is a zoo, at least in Europe, the contentment or despair of its inhabitants dependent on much the same factors in London, Paris or Berlin. This one was spacious, and well laid out, and some of the cages seemed too small and some seemed tolerable. Marsha, anyway, enjoyed it. She and Harriet wandered in and out of the ape house, peered at bushbabies in the nocturnal rooms, enjoyed the penguins. It reminded Harriet of weekends when Marsha was little, and had not learned to disapprove of things: when it had been enough to be together and enjoy a park, a playground, a Sunday afternoon at the zoo.

'Look at him – oh, Mum, quick, do look.'

They gazed at a vulture, hunched on his perch, lifting and examining scaly grey feet, each horny toe. When he had finished, he stretched out huge clipped wings, flapped and refolded them, and fell asleep.

'Had enough for one day.'

'He's bored,' said Marsha, more accurately, and then, 'I do hope Victor's all right.'

'I'm sure he is.'

There was a crowded playground: she broke into a run. And for twenty minutes or more Harriet sat on a bench in the sun, watching her clamber and swing amongst dozens of German schoolchildren, enjoying their summer holidays. It was over a week since Marsha had been with other children. In Brussels, once the ice had melted, that had not seemed to matter at all – she was too busy making the most of Hugh and Susanna. Now, without family, it began to feel as though it might be too much for her. Had she been foolish? Harriet asked herself again. Planning the journey in London it had felt essential to visit Berlin *en route*. Karel had passed through here, crossing the 'anti-Fascist protection wall', a border observed by armed guards in watchtowers, patrolled by dogs: a place of death which had always been, for her, a potent symbol of what had made him go back to Prague and leave her. Now that wall was down, bringing in its wake governments all over Eastern Europe. Berlin, with its violent history, such a passionately beating heart at the heart of the continent, was reunited.

Well, in theory, anyway.

We are one people.

So are we.

There were, of course, a lot more people in Berlin than Berliners, in Germany than Germans. The papers at home this year had been full of the violence meted out to foreign workers and asylum seekers, of the rise to power of disaffected thugs, Hitler's inheritors, bred in poverty, growing up to a jobless future in the East. What was it really like, the place which for most of her life had been 'over there'? Perhaps it smacked of voyeurism – the western tourist eyeing up drab streets and grey estates, moving, with a sigh of relief, back to a smart hotel in the Kurfürstendamm? Well – whatever it smacked of, she wanted to go. And anyway, they weren't exactly staying in a smart hotel.

'Mum! Mum!'

Marsha was perched at the very top of a climbing frame, a pyramid of steel and bright blue rigging where children swarmed. She waved, pretended to fall and then, as Harriet leapt up, resumed her position, scratching under her arms like a monkey, making horrible faces.

'Very funny!' Harriet sat down again, relieved. They had done the right thing in spending the morning here, no question. Marsha was now engaged in monkey business with a boy about the same age, chasing him up and down the rigging, making awful noises. He was dark and lean – not unlike how a younger version of Karel might have looked; not unlike Marsha herself, in fact – he could have been her brother.

Harriet did not allow herself to pursue this thought. She sat in the sunshine watching them play, watching gulls wheel above them, looking down for scraps. It was beginning to get hot. What about the rest of the day? She had planned to take a bus through the Tiergarten down to the Brandenburg Gate, and to walk through to the avenue Unter den Linden beyond it, crossing the old boundary of the wall, going east, going east – a metaphorical further step along her journey.

But perhaps that was all too much for the first day: perhaps she should postpone it, and keep things simple and untiring. And perhaps, in any case, she should think again about Christopher's offer to show her these places himself. She felt in her shoulder bag, pulled out her wallet, and his card.

Christopher Pritchard, Marketing Consultant. An office address in Brussels, phone and fax numbers. Marketing Consultant. In the 1990s they covered a multitude of sins, those little words, usually redundancy. Is that what had happened to him in London, or was it, as it had felt when he mentioned it so casually over dinner at Hugh and Susanna's, something more?

Getting my fingers burned – what might that mean?

She turned the card over. Hotel Scheiber, Prenzlauer Berg. The address and phone number were written in bold fountain pen – a good hand, product of an expensive education. A nice hand, actually, it had to be said. And he was nicer than he had at first appeared. He would make a good companion, showing her round the city.

And Marsha would hate it.

'Hi.' She dropped on the bench beside her. 'What are we going to do now?'

'I was just wondering.' Harriet looked at her pink cheeks, and general air of cheerful ordinariness. 'What do you feel like?'

Marsha shrugged. 'I don't know.' Somewhere a church bell was chiming midday; from beyond the Zoo gates to the south came the roar of traffic. She leaned against Harriet's shoulder. 'What do you think Hugh and Susanna are doing now?'

Harriet put her arm round her. 'I expect Hugh's in his office, don't you, probably on the phone, thinking about lunch . . .'

Marsha smiled. 'What about Susanna?'

'Good question.' Harriet thought of her, alone in that lovely apartment, without work, without a child, and felt, as always, both chilled and full of sympathy. Who knew, if she herself were in such a position, how she might feel, or how she might fill her days? I must talk to Christopher about her, she thought. Is that going to be possible?

'I don't know,' she said to Marsha. 'Perhaps she's shopping, or meeting someone for lunch . . .' It sounded like the life of a woman from decades ago, the kind of woman Marsha knew nothing about, really, amidst the busy, purposeful lives of her mother's friends. Nonetheless, it was a fact that Marsha had rarely warmed to one of her mother's friends so quickly. Perhaps it was simply because Susanna was Hugh's wife, and therefore family, but it had felt more than that. Perhaps Marsha knew she filled a gap, as Hugh filled a gap for her.

'Are you missing them?' she asked.

'A bit. It's okay.'

'Why don't we send them a card? And then the rest of the day –' Harriet outlined her original plans. She said cautiously: 'But I did think, as Christopher Pritchard knows Berlin, and is staying in the east, perhaps we might ask him to – '

Marsha gave her a look. 'We were going to do it all on our own before,' she said. 'Weren't we? Before we met him?'

'Yes.'

'Well, then. Don't be so wet.' She got off the bench. 'Can we buy a card from the shop? I want to send Hugh an animal.'

Harriet followed meekly.

In the end, they spent the rest of the day getting hot. Marsha said she wanted to wander – just look about a bit, round here, and not take in too much at once. They bought cards, and some overpriced bread and *Wurst* from a stall, and walked back through the Zoo munching it, coming out near the station where they'd arrived last night. As then, the roads around felt fast and furious. They crossed to the top of the Kurfürstendamm, by the Kaiser-Wilhelm-Gedächtniskirche, with its ruined, bombed-out spire.

'Why don't they mend it?'

'I think it's left like that deliberately – so people don't forget the war.'

A tower block of shimmering glass, a shopping centre, was grafted on to the northern side of the church. At the foot of this bizarre conjunction sprawled post-punk adolescents, much as in Piccadilly Circus. They wore grubby dark clothes, earrings in ears and noses; an air of apathy and aggression hung about them. As often in London, Harriet realised that few of them were much older than her pupils; here, she wondered how many of them were from the east, coming up in hope of a quick touch from well-heeled westerners and tourists. Hard to blame them, but after yesterday evening's encounter outside the station she still felt uneasy, with Marsha to protect, and walked with relief on to the main thoroughfare.

This relief was short-lived. Spring, or late autumn, with plenty of money, were probably what was needed to enjoy the Ku'damm, with its endless shops and bars and hotels. Now, the midday heat was powerful, with a clamminess which slowed them down. Petrol fumes rose from the traffic, and the pavements were crowded with shoppers and tourists. Music blared from hot boutiques, the smell of fast food hung in the air; everyone looked indifferent, or in a hurry.

'Oh, God.' Harriet bumped into a hard-faced woman hung about with glossy carrier bags and apologised, moving on. 'This isn't much fun.'

'I'm thirsty.' Marsha was looking at a kiosk offering violently coloured fizzy drinks.

'Those look foul.'

'It's *hot*.'

'I know it is.'

They walked on, gazing at the windows of department stores. Businessmen hurried from hotel lobbies, office blocks claimed the skyline.

'Can't we stop?'

They should, thought Harriet, have stayed right where they were, on a bench in the sun in the Tiergarten, watching the boats on the lake, taking a boat out, even, taking their time. Poor Marsha – how could you expect a child to enjoy trailing round foreign cities, with heat and history lectures and no one to play with?

If Harriet had followed this train of thought much further she might herself, just then, have succumbed to exhausted misery. As it was, she saw, when they reached a corner, a shady side street, and a café with tables set out upon it. They made a beeline.

And sitting over iced coffee and the tallest glass of ice-filled lemonade Marsha had ever seen, writing postcards to London and Brussels – *Just arrived, all is well, thank you for everything* – they both calmed down.

'We must be sensible,' said Harriet, draining her glass. 'We must take it bit by bit.'

Marsha completed a row of kisses to Brussels. 'You're telling *me*?'

For a while they sat watching the world go by.

'What do you want to do for your birthday?'

Marsha shook her head. 'I don't know. I've never had a birthday in Berlin.'

'Darling.' Harriet leaned across and kissed her.

'We should really have had it in Brussels, shouldn't we? With our family. *That* wasn't very well planned, was it?'

'I – ' Harriet floundered. It was true.

'Especially,' Marsha went on, 'as I haven't got a brother or sister.'

'Oh, Marsha – '

'Or a father,' she concluded flatly.

Harriet drew a breath. 'We've talked about all this – '

'Not for a long time.'

It was true.

'Go on,' said Harriet, and waited.

'Go on, what? It's just a fact, isn't it? I'm an only child, I'm almost ten, and my father might as well not exist. He never writes, I never see him, I don't suppose he even knows I'm here.' She looked at Harriet. 'Does he?'

'I – no.' Harriet tried to take Marsha's hand; Marsha withdrew it. Harriet said hesitantly, 'I didn't think it worried you . . .'

'Well, it does. It does at the moment, anyway.' She looked away. 'Being ten is supposed to be special . . .'

'Oh, Marsha.' Harriet felt quite helpless. 'I'm so terribly sorry.'

'It's okay.' Marsha's foot beneath the table swung back and forth; she turned her postcard over and over.

Harriet sat watching her, holding herself back from more words, another gesture. It obviously wasn't okay. Another child might have been in tears by now, but Marsha so rarely cried. Perhaps that was a bad thing. Perhaps Harriet hadn't allowed her to cry enough, or to talk about Martin enough – useless, abandoning, selfish Martin, she thought with a wave of anger, having given him so little thought for so long.

The foot, after a while, stopped swinging, and the postcard lay back on the table. Harriet said carefully: 'We can talk about it again. Now, or whenever. Whatever you want.'

Marsha shook her head. 'Let's leave it.'

'Would you like something else to drink?'

'No, thanks.'

'Shall we go back to the hotel? We could have a rest, and change, and go out for a look round, find somewhere nice for supper . . . Or would you like to eat in the same place as last night?'

Last night's place had been a Turkish café two blocks along from the hotel where they'd eaten kebabs and pitta, much as if they were in London, because that was what Marsha had wanted: something she knew. Now, she said:

'I think I feel a bit like you do sometimes, at the end of term. I'm tired and I don't know.'

'I know the feeling exactly. Let's go and have a rest and take it from there. And Marsha – '

'What?'

'You're wonderful.'

'I know.'

By the time they got back to the Hotel Kloster the sun was going down. The street, after the newness of everything else in the day, had a known quality about it which felt pleasing.

'Let's have a shower, and a rest,' said Harriet, 'and then go out and explore.'

The glass doors of the hotel were open now, and late afternoon sunlight fell on to the floral carpet. A different girl was at the desk: she had long dark hair and smiled at them, and when Harriet asked for their key she turned to the metal pigeonholes above the key rack and said there was a message.

Harriet took the envelope, recognising the writing at once:

Greetings from the east. An interesting choice of hotel. I'm chez moi this evening; give me a ring if you like. Hope all's well. C.P.

They took a yellow double-decker through the Tiergarten, travelling along the Strasse des 17 Juni towards the Brandenburg Gate. The morning was clear and bright, and the park stretching away on either side of them beyond the trees was full of tourists and students on holiday, taking the sun in deckchairs or wandering along the little tributaries of the Spree. There were statues – to Bismarck, to Wagner and Goethe and to the lesser known, but Harriet forbore from pointing them out to Marsha, who knew none of them, and who was, in any case, accompanying her with a show of reluctance.

'I've told you a million times – I don't like him.'

'You have,' said Harriet. 'You most certainly have. And all I can say is that I didn't like him either, at first, but I think perhaps I misjudged him, and I can't see what's wrong with letting him show us round a bit.'

This was over breakfast, where Harriet, who last night had waited until Marsha was asleep before phoning Christopher, had broken the news.

'He says there's a swimming pool near his hotel. Would you like that?'

'I don't particularly want to go swimming with him.'

'He says he thinks we might like his hotel – it's small and old-fashioned, and apparently there's a hotel cat.' Harriet paused. 'Apparently she's had kittens.'

Marsha was making a sandwich from slices of sausage and cheese in alternate layers. She balanced a slice of sausage studiedly on top.

'How many?'

'Three.'

'Did he say what colour?'

'That I didn't ask, I'm afraid. We can find out when we get there.'

'*If* we get there.'

Well, they were on their way. Ahead, beneath a bright blue sky, was the Brandenburg Gate. Harriet felt, on seeing it, much as she supposed tourists seeing the Tower of London might feel: it was real, and she was really here. Extraordinary. Revolutionaries had assembled beneath it in the turmoil of 1848, and Marx had rushed back from Brussels to join them. Here, Rosa Luxemburg and Karl Liebknecht had addressed huge crowds; here, in the mid-1930s, were the torchlit Nazi rallies. And here, on 9 November 1989, just beyond the massive columns, people had stood six deep on the top of the wall, laughing and cheering in the winter sunshine, looking across to the other side, and she, on a grey afternoon in London, had sat watching it all on television: the crowds, the red flags fluttering in the last days of a divided city, students in jeans and anoraks smoking, waving to the cameras, clambering up on each other's shoulders, feet scraping the graffiti.

My first thought was: I'm the one who has been walled in ...

'Look,' she said to Marsha now. 'We saw that on television, when you were six.'

'Saw what?'

'The Brandenburg Gate.'

But Marsha did not remember, how could she; though she did, when reminded, recall Annie, their lodger that winter, with whom they had watched all these events. Annie soon afterwards had left, to go and live with Dominic, her new black boyfriend, in his house in Dalston Lane. A lot of their lodgers did that: they drank Harriet's coffee at her kitchen table, they babysat Marsha, who grew fond of them, and then they departed – for college, or boyfriends, or girlfriends, leaving post to be forwarded and things in drawers which they phoned about, and said they'd come back for, and usually didn't. Harriet had a black bag full of such items, stuffed into the cupboard on the landing, which got in the way and sometimes made her cross. She was also intermittently cross about the fact that no sooner had someone settled in and got to be part of the furniture than they were gone, leaving Marsha with a renewed sense that most people in the house, including fathers, were transient.

How were fathers this morning? After yesterday's controlled outburst Harrriet had gone to bed thinking that Marsha had put up with enough in her ten years, and borne up well, and should in future have her wishes taken more seriously into account – which might include Harriet asking about, rather than announce, plans for holidays, birthdays and so on. This resolution, however, had not prevented her this morning from making sure that today was spent as she herself wished to spend it. The truth of it is, she thought now, looking at Marsha's sleek dark head by the window, that we both have wills of iron. It is probably what has seen us through, and I suppose one day it might be what divides us. But not yet – please not yet.

Beyond the dark head she could see, far to their left, the towering buildings of the Reichstag, but refrained from pointing it out, just saying casually, as the bus drove on through the Gate, 'Hitler made speeches here, too.'

'Oh.' Hitler was within Marsha's ken – she had watched him making speeches in wartime newsreels shown in a television series last year, and he had made an impression. Indeed, he was probably more real to her than many more recent figures, with the exception of Nelson Mandela, on whom, on his release from prison, her class had done a project. But she did not ask any more, and Harriet let her alone, as they passed beneath the roof and crossed an unmarked line where the wall had run. They were out on Unter den Linden.

'Beneath the lime trees' – as the Tiergarten had spoken to Harriet in London of winter trees and frozen water, so these words had evoked for her an atmosphere, an era: summer afternoon on the boulevard, the rustle of leaves, the clip-clop of hooves, wheels turning, hats raised, parasols prettily concealing blushes, as the Prussian aristocracy took the air. Was it possible, as the traffic of the 1990s swept along, to imagine this still?

Well, yes, it was, and closing her eyes for a moment, continuing her running inner dialogue between fact and fiction, present and past, Harriet thought: the past means more, history means more – all sorts of imagined scenes mean more to me, much of the time, than my own life. Can this be true? This, surely, is Susanna talking.

'Mum?'

'Yes. Sorry.' She opened her eyes again.

'You okay?'

'Of course.' She looked out at the long straight rows of trees, hundreds replanted after the war, as the neoclassical façades of the buildings beyond had, in the 1960s, been restored. Here they were in the East, a place always pictured as bleak and drab, and it felt quite possible to step back for a moment, as she had done, into the pleasing lines of the nineteenth century. Berlin, bombed to pieces during the war, its bricks retrieved and stacked by the *Trümmerfrauen* in their turbans and pinafores, had been remade into a smart new city in the West – as they had seen yesterday, on the Ku'damm – and restored to its Prussian grandeur in the East: a policy designed to give the newly

Russian-occupied sector a sense of continuity, even as the Iron Curtain came down. It was not so everywhere, of course: desolate concrete estates and tower blocks lay beyond: though how many of them, Harriet wondered, could be so much worse than their counterparts in London?

They were crossing Friedrichstrasse; ahead, at the far end of the avenue, elaborate statuary adorned the Schlossbrücke over the Spree. In the Sixties and Seventies people had drowned in the Spree, swimming across in desperate escape attempts from the east by night. This Harriet did tell Marsha, and to this she did listen attentively, as how could you not, picturing the darkness, the gasp of cold, the silent frantic swimming; then lights, shouts on the wall, shots, and the swirling gush of blood into the water.

'That's horrible.'

They got off the bus in Marx-Engels Platz, wandering with others to look at a hideous bronze monument surrounded by steel pillars.

'No one's scratched things on Marx in Highgate,' said Marsha. 'He looks better there, doesn't he?'

'He does.'

Oppression, revolution, corruption, disillusion: was the cycle of history ever different? Harriet stood looking up at the vandalised figures of men whose vision, as she had told Marsha that wet afternoon in the cemetery, had changed the world.

And now the world had changed again, and it was nationalism, not internationalism, which was devouring and dismembering continents. East and West Germany had been reunited, but Czechoslovakia was now two states, the Soviet Union in sixteen republics, Yugoslavia in ruins.

We are one people.

So are we.

Harriet and Marsha walked along Karl Liebknecht Strasse, craning their necks to look up at the TV transmitter rising two hundred metres to a needle-sharp point towards the summer clouds above Alexanderplatz.

'You can go up there,' Harriet said. 'Like the Post Office Tower, only more so.'

'Shall we go up there?'

'We might.'

Days before the wall came down, thousands had crammed into this concrete square, part of a city-wide demonstration; now, bus routes to East and West converged beneath the S-Bahn line, which ran overhead beneath a canopied roof, and in the shelter of the high-rises all around dozens of little stalls, unheard of a few years ago, did a brisk trade in cheap jeans and flashy T-shirts.

They wandered through to the U-Bahn, locating the crowded train to Senefelder Platz.

'Nearly there,' said Harriet, as they found two seats, and got out her map again, looking for Christopher's street.

Prenzlauer Berg was set on a hill, a nineteenth-century urban working-class district of tenements and factories. In the war it was fiercely fought over, but not demolished: much remained standing, although many of the buildings were still scarred with bullet holes. Even before the wall came down, it had become a quarter of East Berlin frequented by artists and intellectuals, with a rich café life. Now, it had been discovered. Harriet, getting off the U-Bahn with Marsha and crossing the square into Kollwitz Strasse, was soon aware of being in quite a different atmosphere, a heady mix of pre-war and postmodern which diverted even Marsha from complaint as they walked.

Cobbled streets were lined with decaying tenements, through whose dark entrances they glimpsed overgrown courtyards, peeling paintwork, unlit stone stairways. Narrow-fronted shops, cafés and bistros were crammed up against each other; the pavements were crowded and it was growing hot again, though the height of the buildings and the narrowness of the streets meant that many were in shadow. They passed cramped galleries painted in stark white or electric pink and green; beneath paintings and film posters, sagging sofas on bare floorboards were occupied by twenty-year-olds with white hair and dark glasses, smoking and staring into space. Students in wire-rimmed spectacles sat over soup in tiny cafés, reading the papers; young men in earrings and sleeveless T-shirts hung over dimly lit bars.

Harriet and Marsha walked on to Husmanstrasse.

'It's like a film set,' said Harriet.

It was. They were in a perfectly restored and preserved nineteenth-century street of stately façaded, five-storey buildings with curving wrought-iron balconies and tall windows on the upper floors, antique shops at street level.

'It's like Brussels,' said Marsha.

'This bit is, you're right.'

'It's nice round here.'

'I'm glad you like it.'

They turned off into a network of back streets. And I like it too, thought Harriet, as they looked for Christopher Pritchard's hotel, passing bars, a bookshop, a café painted green. How clever of him to stay here.

'There aren't any hotels in this street,' said Marsha, looking up and down.

'There must be one. He said it was small but he thought we'd like it – it's called the Hotel Scheiber.'

'What's the hotel cat called?'

'Good question. Puss.'

'What's puss in German?'

'Kottelet. Cutlet. I don't know. I think he said the hotel had shutters – look, that must be it.'

A small painted sign by an open door announced it: a narrow-fronted three-storey house on the other side of the street, with faded blue shutters and worn doorstep. They waited for a battered Trabant to pass, then crossed over, and walked inside. There was no one about in the little hall – 'But it's nicer than ours,' said Marsha, observing a desk, a fabric-shaded lamp, pigeonholes in polished wood on the wall behind.

'It is.'

Worn rugs lay on the uneven floor; there were pictures; it felt more like a family house than a hotel – well, that was no doubt what it was, a hotel-pension, just the kind of place they should be staying in. A half-open door to the right revealed tables laid with white cloths, a stuffed bird in a dusty case on a sideboard, amidst bottles and decanters. At the back of the hall was another door, with a window through which they could glimpse a passage and light beyond.

'Well, come on,' said Marsha. 'Let's ring the bell or something.'

'Why don't you ring it?' Harriet nodded towards a little brass dome on the desk, with a protruding knob in the centre.

'That's not a bell.'

'It's a pinger. Go on, ping it.' She demonstrated with the flat of the hand on the air. Marsha looked doubtful, crossed to the desk and struck. A pleasing single note sounded in the quiet hall. She smiled; they waited. She struck it again.

The door at the back swung open: a large man in a white apron came through it. He was balding and jowly and comfortable looking; he greeted them in pleasant apologetic tones, and Harriet explained their call.

'Herr Pritchard? He is expecting you, he is out on business but will be back within – ' he glanced at the clock on the wall ' – within half an hour. Please.' He gestured towards the half-open door, the dusty bird. 'You will take some coffee? Something to eat?'

Marsha was nudging Harriet's elbow. 'Ask him about the *kittens*.'

But Harriet, whose German had just about equipped her to understand the conversation so far, could not remember the word for kitten, and shook her head.

The proprietor looked at them enquiringly.

'Go *on*.'

'Herr Pritchard mentioned a cat . . . ' said Harriet feebly. 'With – er – little cats.'

'Ah, yes! She has three.' He looked at Marsha kindly, and put his hands four or five inches apart. 'Three kleinen Meizen. Just so big. You would like to see them?'

Marsha needed no translation: her face lit up. 'Come on!'

'Marsha . . .'

But the proprietor was holding open the door to the passage, gesturing to them to go through. They saw light at the far end, a doorway, a flagstoned garden where the summer's last geraniums stood in the sun.

And thus it was that when Christopher Pritchard returned, he found Harriet drinking coffee on a hard wooden chair beneath a little apple tree, and Marsha sitting cross-legged on the ground beside her, with a lapful of assorted kittens. The mother cat, a marmalade, sat on a low brick wall, observing through half-shut eyes.

'What a pretty sight.'

Harriet jumped, and turned, spilling coffee.

'*Careful*,' said Marsha, edging away.

'Sorry. Hello.'

'Hello.' For a moment Christopher stood there, filling the doorway. He had had his hair cut; he looked well. He was beside her, kissing her lightly on each cheek, looking down at Marsha. 'Are they behaving themselves?'

'Of course.' She held up the smallest, a tabby with white socks. 'This is my favourite.'

'The runt.' He bent down, extending a large finger, and tapped it on the nose. The kitten blinked and shrank; Marsha drew back.

'What's a runt?'

'The one most in need of care and protection,' said Harriet.

'Or drowning.' Christopher got to his feet again.

'*What*?'

'He's joking.' Harriet moved her chair: the garden, like the kitchen in Brussels, seemed to have halved in size since his arrival. 'Aren't you?' she asked him.

'What do you think?'

'I don't think that's funny.' Marsha, cradling the kitten to her cheek, looked at Harriet crossly. 'They won't really drown him, will they?'

'Sorry,' said Christopher, loosening his tie. 'Wrong foot as usual, start again. How are you both?'

'We're all the better for being here,' said Harriet, putting her cup down. She shaded her eyes to look up at him. 'It's very nice – we've been making unfavourable comparisons with our own hotel, I'm afraid.'

'Yes, I can imagine. Sorry – shouldn't say that.' He sat on the low wall beside the mother cat, rubbing her face. For a moment she let him, then leapt down towards her kittens again.

'What were you doing there, anyway?' Harriet asked him. 'It's quite a stretch.'

'I had a meeting nearby. And also, of course, I was curious to see how you were getting on. How have you been getting on?'

'Okay, thanks. We've probably tried to see a bit too much in a hurry, you know what it's like – ' She told him about yesterday – the Zoo, the Tiergarten and the Ku'damm in the heat, and today's long walk along to Alexanderplatz.

Christopher listened, running his thumb along a little groove in the wall.

'You must be exhausted. And it's all very large-scale and public, where you've been.' He nodded towards Marsha, watching the kittens, who were suckling now as their mother stretched out in the sun. 'Isn't it a bit much for her?'

'Probably.' Harriet might have felt defensive, but the warmth of the courtyard and the sleepy contentment of the cat made it difficult.

153

'That's why it's nice to be here – quite unexpected. How did you find this place?'

'The proprietor's nephew is a business contact. Dieter Scheiber, a nice man. They're an interesting family, the Scheibers, they've hung on to this hotel for three generations. It was badly damaged in the war, like everything else, and then of course it was nationalised. When I came here in '88 it was a rundown dump, but of course it was cheap, which is why I used it.'

Harriet looked at him. 'I didn't realise you'd been coming here for so long.'

He made a gesture: does it all need explaining? 'Passing through. Looking about. That's another story. Anyway, ever since the war old grandfather Scheiber had held on to the title, and before he died he passed it on to his son Ernst – that's who you've met, he's running it now. In 1990 he was able to produce the papers. There was a lot of kerfuffle, but in the end he was able to reclaim the place and he's been restoring it ever since, bringing in family furniture again, putting it right. He's doing a good job, don't you think?'

'I do. It's lovely. And what about the nephew? Dieter. You're still in touch?'

'Absolutely. I've just been to see him.' He pulled out his cigarettes and lit up. Again, Harriet noticed the slight but perceptible tremor. 'Until '89 Dieter was managing a section of a nationalised factory on the outskirts of Marzahn. That's a few miles further east. Godforsaken place – grim before '89 and pretty grim now.'

'Would you take me there? I really want to see – '

He hesitated. 'I'm not sure about that. Not much fun for Marsha, for a start.'

'Well. Tell me about it, anyway.'

'I've said – grim. Cheap 1970s housing, high-rise misery. Unemployment, rising crime, drugs. Desolation city.' He inhaled deeply. 'But in early 1990 Dieter saw the chance of a break. He got in touch with an old family friend in the West, chap called Steffen Wilkendorf. That's who I was seeing yesterday. Dieter persuaded him to invest in the factory, try to make a go of private enterprise. Wilkendorf & Scheiber – they make paints and industrial dyes: for textiles and stuff. It's still early days, but they haven't gone under yet. Dieter's the man at the workface, and since I managed to help them out a bit in Bohemia I get a discount here at the hotel. So that's handy.'

'Hugh's investing in Bohemia,' said Harriet thoughtfully.

Christopher looked away for a minute. 'That's right. He's financing a desulphurisation unit, isn't he? But Wilkendorf & Scheiber are small fry, nothing on Hugh's scale. Anyway – ' Ash fell to the ground; he rubbed at it with his foot. 'Can I get you another coffee?'

'No, no, I'm fine, thanks.'

'I think I might go and get a beer.'

'Of course.' She watched him go back into the house and sat thinking. Christopher talked like someone who knew his way around – he clearly did know his way around, he'd been coming to Berlin for years. He was, it would seem, doing well. Then why the shoestring trip on the train, the constant references to being short of money – needing a cheap hotel in the Eighties, needing a discount now?

'Mum,' said Marsha. 'I'm starving.'

'Even after that enormous breakfast?'

'That was hours ago.'

Harriet looked at her watch. So it was.

'I'm hungry, too.' Christopher had returned, and was stubbing his cigarette out on the wall. He flicked it away to a corner and Marsha watched with distaste. He saw her expression and laughed. 'Nice people don't do that.' She looked away in embarrassment. 'Oh, come on, I'm only teasing. Let's go in and see what they can do for us.'

Marsha looked at Harriet. 'Can't we eat out here?'

'Marsha – '

'We could do,' said Christopher, and they did. Herr Scheiber put a cloth on a table beneath the apple tree. He brought out a platter of cheeses, a basket of rye bread, a bowl of fruit. He gave Marsha a Coke, and Christopher another beer and Harriet a small carafe of wine, and they sat eating and drinking and watching cat and kittens fall asleep in the sun. It could hardly have been more delightful, and Harriet said so, adding, with a glass of wine inside her and in an unthinking moment, that in two days' time it was Marsha's birthday.

'Is it really?' Christopher reached for the cheeses. 'In that case we must celebrate. How old will you be, Marsha?'

'Ten,' said Marsha, and gazed fixedly at the kittens.

Harriet kicked herself.

Christopher said: 'I'm sorry, how presumptuous of me. I'm sure you have your own plans . . . ' He dug his knife into a drooling piece of Brie. 'Who'd like a bit of this?'

The moment passed; it grew hotter. Even in the dappled shade of the apple tree sweat trickled down Christopher's forehead. He wiped it away, and leaned back against his chair, where his jacket was hung. He was wearing a short-sleeved shirt, a pale striped green; there was no concealing now, as he lifted his arms behind his head, yawning, the bulge of his stomach – bare freckled skin visible, even, between two straining buttons. Marsha reached for an orange.

'Coffee?' he asked Harriet. 'We could have it inside.'

'Yes, that would be nice.'

One of the kittens was mewing; Marsha turned, and picked it up. 'I want to stay out here.'

'Okay.'

Harriet finished a peach. Christopher picked up his cigarettes and lighter.

'Right,' he said, rising. 'Let's go.'

She followed him into the house.

The dining room which Harriet had glimpsed from the hall faced on to the street. Herr Scheiber had closed the shutters, or almost closed them, and shafts of afternoon sunlight slanted into the room, spinning with dust. There were only five or six tables, and only two other guests, a couple of businessmen, cradling brandies. The bird in the glass case, some kind of hawk, glared from a mossy branch as they went past the sideboard. Bottles and decanters clinked at their footsteps.

'That bird doesn't like me,' said Christopher, leading the way. 'Can't think why.'

They sat at a table between the windows. Coffee was brought in by a girl they had seen in the kitchen, and served on a little red tray.

'Scheiber's granddaughter,' said Christopher, when he had thanked her; she went over to the two men in the corner, who were asking for the bill. He sat back, and lit another cigarette, watching Harriet pour. Smoke drifted in and out of the shafts of sunlight. 'Well,' he said slowly. 'Here we are again.'

'Indeed.' Harriet put down the jug and looked at him. She waved away smoke. 'How many do you have a day?'

'Too many. I've tried to give up and I can't. One of the few pleasures left to me.'

'Dear, dear.' She sipped her coffee. 'You realise you're running a terrible risk.'

'What with my weight and all.' He inhaled again, more deeply. 'Too bad. Who cares?' He raised his coffee cup. 'Cheers.'

'Cheers.'

The businessmen at the corner table were pulling out wallets, signing for credit cards, leaving a tip. Harriet was aware of these sounds, but she was also thinking of another table; in the dining room in Brussels, as the sky beyond the window grew dark; of Christopher leaning across to light a cigarette in one of the candles reflected in the polished surface, narrowing his eyes in the light. *They're sexy as hell, and they kill you,'* he'd said to Susanna. Did he really not care?

The two men got up to go; Scheiber's granddaughter saw them to the door with a smile. Out in the street, footsteps went past the shuttered windows, and voices faded. The girl came back and cleared their glasses and coffee cups; then she was gone.

Harriet looked at Christopher, smoking, watching her. She became acutely aware of the quietness and emptiness of the room, the whiteness of the linen, the stillness broken by the spinning dust in the beams of light. She, who was always busy, always moving quickly on to what came next, on impulse wanted to stretch out her arms, to open herself – to the place, the space, the atmosphere it contained, and she felt as if all this were all of a sudden narrowing: forced, like the light at the gap in the shutters, into something with a timeless intensity: a single, unforgettable moment, on which you might look back for the rest of your life, thinking: *then*. That's when it was.

'Harriet?'

'Yes.'

'What are you thinking?'

'I suppose,' she said carefully, 'I'm thinking about you.'

'Yes?'

They looked at each other; Harriet looked away. The stillness of the room possessed her; she looked back; she said, as though something were making her say it, 'Tell me about your wife.'

'My ex-wife.'

'Yes.'

He stubbed out his cigarette in a thin, beaten metal ashtray, the kind of thing you never saw in England now – something else which seemed uniquely to belong to this room, this moment.

'My wife was – my wife is – ' He shut his eyes for a moment, then opened them, looking beyond her. 'Susanna knows about my wife, but it's a long story.'

She felt her stomach contract.

Footsteps crossed the hall, came in through the open doorway. The bottles on the sideboard clinked.

'You're being an awfully long time,' said Marsha. 'Can we go swimming now?'

The swimming pool was set within a modern housing complex in Ernst Thälmann Park, on the other side of Dimitroff Strasse, a busy thoroughfare to the north of the hotel. They crossed at the lights. Petrol fumes shimmered in the heat and Christopher wiped his brow.

'I'll be glad to get in the water, won't you, Marsha?'

'Yes.' She had not wanted to get in the water with Christopher, that had been abundantly clear to Harriet as the three of them sat in the shuttered dining room making plans. Marsha's legs swung beneath the table; she kicked Harriet, sharply, when Christopher had suggested accompanying them to show them the way. Harriet frowned at her, with almost equal sharpness, feeling what she did not often feel with Marsha: a real resentment. The moment of stillness had been taken away, the moment of revelation postponed. Was she never to have adult company without interruption? Marsha looked hurt; Harriet felt guilty.

Now, Marsha said to her: 'It won't be like this in Prague, will it?'

'What do you mean?' And please don't say, under your breath, '*He* won't be with us, will he?' willed Harriet, following Christopher's stride along the pavement.

'So hot all the time.'

'Oh. No, I shouldn't think so.'

'And *he* won't be with us all the time, will he?'

Harriet almost smacked her. Unheard of. 'Ssh!'

'He can't hear us.'

Christopher turned and slowed for them to catch up. 'Almost there.'

The entrance to the little park was dominated by a gigantic piece of sculpture: a head and clenched fist, sprayed violently with graffiti.

'That's not Marx,' said Marsha.

'No. But Thälmann was an important communist figure in the thirties. The Nazis murdered him, and this thing was put up in his memory after the war.' He nodded towards the graffiti. 'He seems to have fallen out of favour again.'

Skateboarders swooped in the sun up and down the concrete slopes beyond the statue; well-kept high-rise blocks rose from well-kept greenery.

'This was a sort of GDR showpiece,' said Christopher. 'Something smart and modern amidst the tenements: something to aspire to. Not that many tenement-dwellers were rehoused here – I think you had to be one of the card-carrying elite to get one of these apartments. It's all a bit luxurious in its way – ' He was guiding them through the skateboarders, at whom Marsha glanced with longing, and up shallow steps to a precinct of shops and restaurants. 'Hence, everything on tap – even nurseries, I think, no doubt with pictures of Ulbricht and Honecker on the walls. Hence the swimming pool. Mind you, it's pretty basic – don't expect a wave machine or anything, Marsha.'

'I don't like wave machines anyway.'

The entrance to the pool was on the far side of the precinct. Inside, they found green and white tiles, a bored-looking girl behind glass. Shrieks and splashes sounded from beyond swing doors.

Christopher paid for them.

'I thought you were broke,' said Harriet.

'Not that broke.'

They made their way to separate changing rooms. The women's was high and echoing, with scuffed green doors to the cubicles and an old-fashioned, bathhouse feel to them.

'Marsha,' said Harriet, as they went in.

'What?' she asked guardedly.

'Can you just try? He's giving us a lovely day. Think of the lunch. Think of the kittens.'

'He talked about *drowning*.'

'Oh, come on – he wasn't serious, it's just his manner.'

Marsha went into an empty cubicle and locked the door. 'How come,' she asked through the plywood division, 'how come you like him so much all of a sudden?'

'I didn't say I did like him so much.' Harriet locked her own door, and hung her own bag on the hook.

'You don't need to *say*,' called Marsha.

Harriet did not answer.

When they had changed, and put their clothes into a battered locker, they went through a footbath and out to the pool, which was crowded. Municipal green and white tiles lined the walls, and the pool itself, so that the atmosphere was less of summer-blue skies, as they were used to in London, and more of a steamy pond. Children bobbed about in the shallow end; three or four teenage boys raced along the side, whistled at sharply by a lifeguard with an earring. They leapt into the water, laughing. Adults swam up and down marked lanes. Harriet looked for Christopher.

'There he is.' She saw a large figure in pale blue boxer trunks at the far end, sitting on the edge with his legs in the water, a towel slung over his shoulder. He looked overweight and out of place, and as she watched him survey the swimmers, she wondered that he had chosen to bring them here, and was touched by his consideration for a child in a hot city. He turned, looking around; he saw her watching him and raised his hand, getting awkwardly to his feet. His stomach bulged over his waistband, his shoulders were fleshy and full. His legs were long and straight and he towered over everyone, but it was clear, as he came up the side towards them, that he didn't quite know where to look.

'I'm going in.' Marsha dropped gracefully into the shallow end in a gap between toddlers, and struck out. A strong swimmer, taken to their local pool by Harriet since babyhood, she was soon halfway down, avoiding the noisy group of boys.

Christopher and Harriet moved towards each other: she, more than anything, to save him from having to continue his ill-at-ease approach. He smiled down at her, approving her plain black swimsuit.

'You look good.'

'Thank you.'

'Well.' He gave a short, embarrassed laugh. 'Shall we swim?'

He dropped his towel on the ledge running alongside the pool, and they walked back down to the deep end. Children jumped in wildly; Marsha had turned, and was coming back again, sleek and straight.

'She's good.'

'Not bad. Better than I was at her age. I still have to go in down the steps.'

'Do you really?'

They had reached the end; she crouched by the top of the metal rung, and watched him walk round, and stand for a moment on the edge, waiting for a space amongst the swimmers in the lane beneath him. He ran a hand through his hair, raised heavy arms, and lifted his enormous body weight on to the balls of his feet. He plunged, and then she could see why he'd brought them. He was extraordinary: powerful and smooth, moving through the water like an animal, taking possession of it in a steady, rhythmic crawl, reaching the far end and turning without a pause. He was coming back down towards her; he hauled himself up on the side again, gasping.

Harriet gave him a clap. 'You're a pro.'

'Not enough puff.'

'Too much puffing.'

'True.' He wiped the water from his eyes and smiled, coming to join her.

'Aren't you going in?'

She swished her feet. 'In a minute. Here's Marsha.' She watched her daughter's approach. 'Did you see Christopher swim?'

'Yes.' Marsha held on to the edge of the railing. 'Aren't you coming in?'

'I am, I am.' Harriet slipped down the steps and struck out. And Marsha swam alongside, as he did in London, as she had done since she was small. Harriet usually enjoyed this companionship, and the feeling of achievement: she had given a skill to her child, and now they could share it. But in London there were often other children, or Harriet's own friends; she and Marsha could come and go from each other. Here, now, it felt as though Marsha were clinging, deliberately drawing her into an exclusive twosome. And again, with a pang of guilt – they were in a strange place, in a foreign city; they knew no one except for Christopher, of course Marsha clung – she thought: can't I have time to myself?

Up at the shallow end a few little girls were playing with an inflatable ball. They were younger than Marsha, seven or eight, but they looked happy and carefree, and as the ball made an arc through the air and landed in the lane beside her, Harriet, picking it up, said: 'Why don't you join them?'

'They don't speak English.'

'So? You don't have to speak German to play catch.' Harriet lifted the ball above her head and threw it across the markers to the furthest child, who leapt up, and threw it back, laughing. Harriet passed it to Marsha. 'Go on.'

'You just want to get rid of me.'

'Don't be so silly. I want you to have fun with other children.'

'I don't *know* them.'

'You're usually so sociable.'

The circle of little girls was waiting, listening to this exchange between foreigners. One of them bobbed up and down, waving.

'Her wesen! Her wesen!'

'That means throw it over here. Go on – throw it. Go and play.'

'Oh, all right.' Marsha threw, and ducked under the markers. She came up next to the circle of children, and stood there, waiting her turn. Harriet, with a mixture of guilt and relief, watched for a moment, then swam away.

Christopher was standing at the edge of the deep end, watching her approach. Harriet swam slowly, not acknowledging this, trying to concentrate on her steady breast stroke, on avoiding the other swimmers. Were she and Christopher going to swim together? How would that feel? Shrieks and shouting echoed all around her: in this public, crowded place, those charged, still moments in the empty dining room felt distant and dreamlike. She longed to recapture them.

Was that true?

It was true.

She wanted – oh, how she wanted – to be seated opposite this man again, to feel his gaze upon her, to return it, to sense between them – what? What was between them now?

Susanna knows about my wife, but it's a long story –

What did that mean?

Someone coming the other way bumped into her; Harriet moved aside, and looked up. Christopher Pritchard, tall and heavy and almost naked, was still on the edge of the deep end, waiting.

You could only swim so slowly. Harriet, more than halfway down the pool, swam slowly on, thinking, as she had not thought for a long time, of other naked bodies she had known. Not many. Not Karel's, so long and lean and beautiful, so much desired. There had been Martin's, well-made and compact and – yes, it was true – often turned away from her. One or two others before him, one or two others since. None of them, at this moment, seemed to have mattered much.

The body Harriet knew best was Marsha's – slender and straight and boylike. As for her own . . .

She had come to the end of the pool. Above her, Christopher was lowering himself, slipping into the water beside her. 'Marsha seems happy.'

'Does she?' Harriet turned, holding on to the edge with one hand. Down in the shallows the circle of children had widened, and Marsha, the tallest, was in the middle, throwing the bright striped ball and laughing. Guilt evaporated, and with it came a sense of freedom. She was, after all, doing what a child should be doing.

Christopher said: 'Will you have supper with me tonight?'

'That would be nice. But Marsha – '

'We don't have to eat late. Scheiber's got a sitting room – she could stay in there with the cats.' He looked at her questioningly. 'Does that sound all right?'

'It does.' Harriet wiped her face. 'Thank you.'

'Good. Well – shall we swim?'

'I'd never keep up with you.'

'Try.'

She followed him through the water.

Herr Scheiber's sitting room, up on the first floor, was more of a snug: the kind of room which in Harriet's experience as a waitress in long-ago student days was only to be found in small hotels and restaurants, where almost all family life was lived in public and the one room marked Private was consequently precious, and crammed with belongings which in an ordinary house might be spread all over the place.

Marsha was curled up with the kittens on a low sofa behind the door, watching television. A window on the far wall overlooked the little garden where they'd had lunch; the hot summer sky was cooling and darkening, now, smoky fingers of cloud stretching towards each other above the hill of Prenzlauer Berg. Harriet, watching their gentle drift, saw lights come on in the streets below and in the tenement buildings. She imagined families returning from work, preparing a meal, watching whatever Marsha was watching now, and she imagined herself, watching Christopher Pritchard across the white linen tablecloth in the hotel dining room.

Light spilled out from the kitchen window below on to the square of garden; through the open back door she could hear dishes and saucepans clattering, and then Frau Scheiber, to whom they had been introduced on their return from swimming and tea in the park, came out of the door with a crate of empty wine bottles, dumping them down on the flags. Harriet turned from the window.

'Shall I draw the curtains?'

Marsha shrugged. 'If you want.'

Against the wall opposite the window stood an upright piano, with heaps of yellowing music piled on top and a mildewed mirror on the wall above. Next to the television an embroidered screen stood before the fireplace. There were bookshelves, a chair piled high with clean aprons, stacks of magazines on the floor. The walls were hung with family photographs, going back to distant pre-war days. The room could not have been cosier; Marsha, even with kittens, could not have been grumpier. Harriet left the curtains as they were.

'Right,' she said briskly. 'I'll see you in a bit.'

Marsha gazed fixedly at the screen. 'I don't understand a *word* of this.'

'Shall I switch it off?'

'No. It's better than nothing.'

'Have you had enough to eat?'

'Yes.' She had been given a cutlet and fried potatoes and salad down in the kitchen by Scheiber's granddaughter, whose name, they discovered, was Liesel. This had been followed by a pancake with a hot vanilla sauce, the presentation of the kittens, and the freedom of the snug. Harriet, faced with such mulishness after such treats, did not feel inclined to pander to moods any longer. She gave Marsha a peck on the cheek, which was not returned, and went to the door.

'I'm downstairs if you need anything. We'll leave about half-past nine and take the U-Bahn home.' She had said it all before.

'It isn't *home*,' said Marsha, addressing the screen.

Harriet gave up and left her. It was true.

She went to the bathroom along the landing, and washed her face and brushed her hair, which was rather flat after the swimming. She put on some lipstick, and looked in the mirror once more before leaving. The woman who returned her gaze seemed apprehensive. 'Come on,' said Harriet aloud. 'Let's see what's what.'

She went down the steep stairs into the hall and into the dining room. Christopher Pritchard was sitting at the same table they had occupied at lunchtime, smoking and looking at the wine list. Now there were no shafts of sunlight, but candles. There were other guests, at other tables, but Harriet did not take them in as she crossed the room towards him, and he rose, and kissed her on both cheeks. They sat down.

'Well,' said Christopher, picking up the menu.

'Here we are again,' said Harriet.

Liesel came to take their order. She brought them a bottle of wine and a basket of bread, and Harriet broke a roll into little pieces, absently. Wax trickled down the side of the candle, whiter than white;

smoke from his cigarette drifted in and out of the flame. The voices of other guests murmured through the room.

They looked at each other in silence.

'Tell me about your wife,' said Harriet. 'Tell me about Susanna.'

'They are one and the same,' said Christopher. He put down the glass and his hand was trembling. He drew in smoke and blew it away from her. 'So. Now you know.'

The room seemed to rock, and then it was steady again. Harriet, sitting absolutely still, knew that she had gone white; she could feel the blood drain from her face – as though, in a great gush, it were flooding out of her body entirely, leaving her lifeless, a white shocked thing of no use to anyone.

Christopher said: 'Harriet – ' He was leaning forward, his face full of concern. He was speaking to her from a long way away, from down in a tunnel, dark and endless. 'Here.' He put her full wine glass into her hand. 'Or perhaps you should have a brandy. Would you like a brandy? Harriet?'

'I – ' she raised the wine glass and spilled it, and wine spread everywhere, like blood.

She watched it seep into the white linen cloth. From a long way away came the murmur of voices: she saw herself standing, a long time ago, at the half-shut door of her parents' dining room, hearing the murmur of a voice inside, a river of words which she could not catch. Legs in long grey socks swung back and forth beneath the polished table, fingers drummed. A child so lonely, so locked away. Her eyes filled with tears.

'Harriet – please – I'm so sorry – '

'It's all right, I'm all right.' The tears were hot and comforting, a release, but she could not cry here, in front of everyone.

Susanna cried in front of everyone. She cried in galleries and gardens and in her apartment at night, and could not stop.

'*I've been like this all my life –*'

Christopher was passing a handkerchief. Harriet swallowed and wiped her eyes. She drank what was left in the wine glass – quickly, all in a rush. There.

'Are you sure you're all right?'

'A bit better.'

She sprinkled salt from an old-fashioned salt cellar on to the wine stains and covered it all with a white linen napkin, remembering, in the kind of association you might make in a dream, Lot's wife, who had dared to look back on Sodom, and was turned into a pillar of salt. How extraordinary, how absurd: why salt? But still – there was a lesson: never look back.

That couldn't be right: the past was everything.

'What you were yesterday is still with you today.' Truffaut had said that, in some long-ago film seen on some long-ago winter's evening down on the South Bank, down at the NFT. Hugh had never gone to the NFT, he'd told her. He spent all his time making money.

Christopher Pritchard had no money. Susanna, a banker's daughter, had lots.

Lot's wife.

No, Hugh's wife.

No, Christopher's.

Liesel was beside them again, smiling. Harriet, with apologies, indicated the napkin, the wine stains, the salt. It was not a problem. A clean white cloth was brought, the table relaid; hot, heavenly-smelling dishes were set before them: schnitzels in paprika sauce, red cabbage, potatoes fried in garlic butter. How could you eat, now?

'Please,' said Christopher. 'Just a bit. It'll do you good.'

She ate, just a bit, and it did her good.

'So,' she said, wiping her mouth, 'tell me. Please.'

'I've shocked you – I didn't mean to – '

'Perhaps I over-reacted. I don't know. It's just that Hugh – '

'Hugh is a very nice man, I know.'

'He's my brother,' said Harriet, and could not eat any more. How was it possible to convey that bond, which went back further than any other, which lasted, unlike marriages now, until death? 'Do you have a brother or sister?' she asked.

'No. I'm an only child.'

'Like Marsha.'

'Yes. Like Susanna.'

Harriet drew a breath. 'Go on.'

'It's a long time ago,' he said slowly.

'A lot of things are, when you get to our age.'

'Like the start of your sentimental journey.'

'Yes. Go on.'

Christopher put down his knife and fork. He lit, with a tremor, a cigarette. 'We met when Susanna was very young – in 1983. January. I was working in London, as a broker – I told you, didn't I? The firm had connections with her father, very useful ones, and we met at a New Year party. Susanna was twenty-four, but looked younger. She was – ' He spread his hands – 'completely beautiful.'

'I can imagine.'

'And close to the edge.' He paused. 'I don't know how well you know her – '

'Neither do I.' It was Harriet's turn to pause. 'Anyway, you tell me. I'm not in the business of disclosing confidences.'

'Discretion itself. Like your brother.'

She did not answer.

'Well.' He was smoking, smoking. 'She has a very dark side, which in some ways I shared. Dark and destructive and fatal in marriage. I was almost eight years older, but not exactly on course myself.' He gave an ironic smile. 'Now, of course, I'm completely balanced.'

Like Susanna, thought Harriet, and then, with a feeling of dread: and Hugh? What is to become of Hugh in all this?

'So.' Another pause. 'This isn't an unusual story, you know, Harriet. Lots of young marriages burn out fast.'

For the hundredth time, Harriet recalled the Cockatrice, the complicity, the look. Burning, she realised now. It was burning.

'Go on.'

'We fell upon each other. That's what it was. Not falling in love – devouring.' He was no longer looking at her. 'We were married in April, we bought a little house in Chelsea. Stretching it a bit. I was making money, but I was losing it, too, investing rather unwisely. That's another story. And in this little house we proceeded to tear each other apart. She wanted a baby, because she didn't know what else to want, she didn't know what to do with her life. I was drinking. I was worried about money, I couldn't even think about children. I refused, or at least I wanted to put it off, and she began to hate me. Except that Susanna doesn't really allow herself to hate other people, she turns it all in on herself, and becomes – ' He broke off. 'When she was in her teens she went through some kind of religious thing. She called it a conversion – I thought of it more as an obsession, the way she described it. Controlled by God: every thought, every wish . . .'

'When I was younger, I wanted to be a nun . . . Would you like to visit a convent? The Béguines live as a sisterhood but without vows. They have power to return to the world . . .'

They had been sitting in the Little Church of the Carmelites, where Susanna came to listen to Bach at lunchtime. She leaned back, closing her eyes, excluding everyone.

They were walking through the quiet rooms of the convent at Anderlecht.

'Did you really want to be a nun?' asked Marsha.

'You want all sorts of things when you're young – '

And when you are older, too, thought Harriet –

'Some of all this came back,' Christopher was saying. 'She was praying for a child, like a woman in the Middle Ages, praying I'd change my mind.' He stubbed out his cigarette, rubbed his face. 'She was in such a state that I couldn't bear to come home at night.'

Liesel was beside them, smiling again. They had enjoyed their meal? They would like dessert?

'Dessert,' he said. 'How does that sound?'

It sounded like something from another planet. Harriet shook her head. 'Just coffee, please.'

'And brandy. I think we need one. I do, anyway – I haven't talked like this for years.'

Coffee came on the little red tray. The brandy came from the sideboard, near the hawk. The bottles and decanters clinked, the conversation of other guests rose and fell, the candle flame was getting low. Wax dripped, solidified. The room felt smoky and intimate and warm, but there was, for Harriet now, none of the feeling that had been here this afternoon: of a moment concentrated, held, breathless, waiting for something to happen. Everything, it seemed, had happened already to Christopher, in long-ago unhappiness. And here he was: overweight, drinking and smoking, someone who seemed, on first impression, to be just a loud-mouthed boor.

And now?

'The thing is,' he said, swirling the brandy over the flame, 'that I make it sound as if it was all Susanna. It wasn't, of course.'

'You said you had a dark side, too – '

'I did. I suppose I still do.' He raised his glass. 'Anyway, I got in a bit of a mess on the market. A hell of a mess, actually.' He stopped. 'I don't know if I should be telling you all this, I don't really know why I am, except – ' He lit a cigarette. Another cigarette. He saw her expression. 'Tut tut tut. It's all a far cry from the history department, isn't it? Or perhaps there are swindlers in education, too. I expect there are –

I shouldn't think many places in the Eighties were untouched by corruption.'

'Probably not,' said Harriet, 'but please don't patronise me. I know very well what the Eighties were like, I spent quite a lot of time fighting what Thatcherism was doing to schools. I told you in Brussels – I've been a socialist all my life.'

'*More fool you*,' Christopher had said, and Marsha had been furious. '*Don't speak to my mother like that!*'

'I'm sorry,' he said now, and sounded as if he meant it. 'You must forgive me – my manner. At least, you don't have to, but I'd be grateful.' A rueful smile, full of charm. 'I am a bit of a wreck, you know.'

Harriet looked at him, trying to work him out, feeling out of her depth, uneasy.

Getting my fingers burned – What had he done?

'What are you thinking?'

'I don't know what to think. Go on, tell me what happened.'

He rubbed his face again. 'The atmosphere in the firm was vicious. Long knives everywhere. Someone who didn't like me suggested I put money in crude oil. I thought I'd recover my losses and pay off my debts. So I did, like a bloody fool, the one thing you should never ever do, which was play with the firm's money. I played with it quite a bit. Crude oil plummeted, and I got caught.' He was watching her, waiting for her to react.

'Oh,' she said, and didn't know what else to say.

'It *is* a long way from the history department, isn't it? Well. There we are. I should have gone to prison, I very nearly did go to prison. But Susanna's father got me off – another little piece of corruption, I suppose – and by the skin of my teeth I was fined. And booted out, of course. We sold the house, but I'm still paying the fine off. And that was the end of the marriage, no question. Susanna's father saw to that – but it felt as if we'd run our course by then anyway. Too many tears, too much shouting, too much pain. Better to kiss and part. Which we did. She went back to her family, they moved to Zurich, and then Brussels, though I didn't know that. We broke off all contact. And in the meantime, naturally, no one would employ me. No one would touch me with a barge pole, actually – ' He gave a little laugh. 'This is the point where people throw themselves off bridges, or end up sleeping under bridges, isn't it?'

Harriet was silent, listening. She didn't know what to say.

'I don't know – I suppose so – I'm sorry, it must have been terrible – '

It was also – it was true, he was right – unthinkable, beyond her experience. All those years in meetings, on marches, had not prepared her to sit face to face with one of Thatcherism's casualties: a bent ex-public schoolboy who'd fallen horribly foul of get-rich-quick.

'It was terrible,' he was saying, 'but I have lived to tell the tale. A round of applause, please.' Liesel was at the next table, taking an order. He gestured to her, when she looked round. 'I'm going to have another brandy. Will you join me? No? It isn't good for a man to drink alone, you know, but I'm used to it. Bring on the violins.'

Liesel brought brandy from the sideboard. Around them, early dinner guests were leaving, later ones arriving. Harriet looked at her watch, feeling dazed.

'It's almost nine – I must do something about Marsha, soon.'

'I've unnerved you, haven't I?'

'Yes,' she said, looking down at the tablecloth, turning a spoon over, trying to collect her thoughts. 'I think you probably have. And I still don't understand – ' She looked up at him. 'Brussels. You're working in Brussels. You came to dinner that night, you'd looked Hugh up – that's what he said. Someone from his old school had telephoned out of the blue – '

'*Pritchard was a bit of a bully . . . I kept out of his way . . .*'

That was on the night of their arrival: Marsha relaxing, beginning to enjoy herself; Harriet, too. Susanna quiet, withdrawn. Had that phone call really been out of the blue?

She and Hugh were walking along the canal at Charleroi. Leaves blew ahead of them, riverboats came and went.

'*Did he ever do anything to hurt you?*'

'*No, never, he just had a reputation – *'

They were all having lunch at the Cockatrice. Across the table, that look: just for a moment, but she had seen it –

She said, hearing herself sound cold and direct: 'If you do anything to harm Hugh, I'll – '

She would what? What would she do? Rise from the table and leave the hotel with Marsha and never set eyes on this man again.

But then – if she never saw him again –

She felt as if she were being drawn in towards darkness: towards someone she did not know, and did not understand.

Was it him, or was it herself? She covered her face.

'Harriet.' She felt his hand on hers: a large hand, with a warm touch, and a tremor. 'Harriet?'

She uncovered her eyes, but she could not look at him. 'What?'

He said gently: 'I don't want to harm Hugh. Or anyone. Please believe me. I said I didn't know why I was telling you these things. That isn't quite true – I think I do know. I want to get them out of the way. I want you to know the worst. Then – '

'Then what?'

'And then we'll see,' he said slowly. 'Shall I explain?'

She nodded, unable to speak.

He was drinking again, cradling the glass. 'There are people who are good for each other, and there are people who make each other unhappy. Susanna and I – I've told you. When she went – when her father took her away – I was in pieces. Not just because of her, because of the trial, the aftermath. Close to skid row, I was, really. Anyway. I did, in the end, get back on my feet. I did things like sell on commission – that's a whole world in itself, bloody awful, but I did it.

'Then I had a break. I had a poor old aunt in a home in Hastings, whom I never went to see. She died, and left me a bit, just enough to keep paying the fine off and start up on my own. But I wanted to get out of London, start again, travel. When everything changed in '89 it seemed like the perfect opportunity – go east, young man, go where your heart is. My heart wasn't anywhere, of course, it didn't matter where I went. I came here, to Berlin, I nosed about, talked to people, went to Warsaw, went to Prague ... Things began to take shape – I saw I could act as east–west middleman, and Brussels seemed as good a place as any to have a base. It's solid and respectable and full of useful contacts, so that's where I moved to.'

'You didn't know Susanna was there?'

'No. I told you, we'd lost all contact.'

'You said you'd been living there for a year or so.'

'Yes. And one day I bumped into her. I was walking one way, and she was walking another – it was as simple as that. A lunch-hour encounter on the Grand Place, outside the Hotel de Ville. Neither of us could believe our eyes. We went for a drink, we talked – she told me she had married again, and that she was happy. I was pleased for her, but I didn't quite believe it, and I was right.' He had put down his glass. 'Wasn't I?'

Susanna was weeping, inside the Hotel de Ville. Before her was a tapestry: two lovers, a delicate glance of desire. 'I have watched you, and watched you: at last you are mine – '

Harriet closed her eyes, remembering. 'Go on. Did she tell you who she had married?'

'Yes – she told me his name and I recognised it, and at first I couldn't think from where and then I remembered. And then, I'm afraid, I couldn't resist looking him up, and phoning. I thought he'd be a good contact anyway, and I was curious.'

'But you didn't tell him who you were – I mean that you and Susanna – '

'No. She had asked me not to – she didn't know I would get in touch, but she said, if I ever bumped into him, that she didn't want me to tell him.'

'But why? Why?'

Christopher was silent for a few moments, thinking. 'The truth is I don't really know. Susanna's a great one for denial – to herself and to other people. And a great one for wanting to make everything right – to start again, and have everything perfect. She did that all through our marriage – such as it was, short as it was. A terrible row, and then: please, let's pretend that didn't happen, let's have a baby, let's pretend that you're not drinking, and I'm not depressed – '

Harriet said: 'Don't most of us want to put bad things behind us, and start again?'

'Yes, but with her it's a refusal to look at things at all. Believe me, I know her.' He stopped again. 'Even so, I don't fully understand why she didn't want Hugh to know about me. She'd told him she was married before, of course, she had to. But she'd never told him who I was – perhaps because of all that misery, and the scandal. And perhaps, to be honest – ' again, that gesture, rubbing his face, over and over, as if trying to wipe things away – 'Christ, how hard it is to be honest. Perhaps because, when we saw each other again, we both knew there was still something between us.'

Yes. Of course. Because, if Hugh didn't know, she and Christopher could meet without question, exchange looks without being noticed.

Harriet said shakily: 'I know. I knew. I knew the first moment I saw you together that evening, the way you looked at each other. And then at that lunch.' She stopped, reliving it all. 'I feel ill. Why did you ask us all to lunch? How can you say you don't want to harm anyone?'

Her voice was rising: the couple at the next table were turning discreetly to look. Marsha's right, she thought miserably: she's sensed everything wrong about this man, she knows he's not to be trusted –

'Harriet – please.' His hand came towards her across the table; she withdrew her own, and feelings of loss and betrayal swept over her. He said carefully, 'Can I ask you something? What is the worst thing that's ever happened to you?'

She looked at him. 'I'm tempted to tell you to mind your own business.'

He was visibly taken aback. Then: 'I'm sorry. You're right. Just because I'm talking as if I were in the confessional – '

Lucy Snowe, broken and desperate, had gone to the confessional in Villette. For that read Charlotte Brontë, in Brussels, suffering the anguish of unrequited love. For that read who? Who was broken and desperate?

Susanna.

Christopher.

Susanna: pacing, weeping, craving a child, a purpose.

Christopher: divorced, disgraced, close to skid row.

She said distantly: 'I suppose it was when my husband left me. Marsha was only a baby. And before that – ' No, she was not going to talk about Karel, who just at this moment could not have felt further from her thoughts, her life. 'Never mind about before that. Let's say when my husband left us. Why?'

'Just – you don't have to tell me anything about it, of course. But you see, when Susanna and I broke up, and I was kicked out of the firm, and all that – I suppose I did hit rock bottom. The worst. And when that happens, you go under, or else you come through. Isn't that right? Isn't that how you felt when your husband left? And I've tried to come through. There's still a side of me which is – well, I suppose you could call it dangerous. The impulse to ring up Hugh, and invite myself to dinner – inviting you all out to lunch – I can remember how I felt; on the edge, tensed up, waiting to go, wanting to stir everything up with a stick and see what happened. I don't think I really knew what I was doing, except getting high on a risk. That's what it was like as a broker, it's in my blood, I almost can't help it. I'm still involved in one or two things I'm not very proud of – in work, I mean. But not with people. That I can do something about.'

He pulled out a cigarette. 'I mean it,' he said, lighting up. 'That's

173

what I mean when I said I don't want to harm anyone – not Hugh, not Susanna, not myself. I've had enough. You may not believe me, but it's true. Never again.' He smiled at her, a smile full of warmth and liking. 'And now I have told you the worst, and now you know.'

There was, after that, a silence.

The voices of the other diners rose and fell, smoke drifted through the candlelight, as it had drifted through the shafts of light that afternoon. Harriet had her face in her hands, thinking, thinking. And something of the moments in the afternoon were returning, now – perhaps, after all, recapturable. She looked at Christopher, and he looked at her, and she thought: I am on the brink. We are on the brink. How completely unexpected, and how disturbing.

So. She drew a long, long breath.

'I've exhausted you.'

'Yes.' She looked at her watch. 'And I must go home. Poor Marsha.' She pushed back her chair. 'Thank you for – well, for talking to me.' A sudden thought. 'Christopher?' It was the first time she had used his name. It really was. And how did that feel? It felt right. How very unexpected.

'What?'

'You being on the train – you hadn't planned that, had you? You weren't following, or anything – '

He smiled again. 'I wasn't following or anything. As I said at the time, it was an extraordinary coincidence.' He drew in smoke, and blew it away again. 'Or fate. However you want to think of it.'

'Mmm. I don't know how I want to think of it. Or anything. I've got a lot to digest.' She stood up; he rose, too. The couple at the next table were watching, she could feel it, as he leaned towards her, and kissed her on the cheek.

'Thank you for listening.'

'Thank you for telling me. I must go – '

He walked beside her to the door. 'I'll see you to your hotel.'

'You don't have to do that.'

But the thought of going out now, with a tired, cross Marsha, getting on to the U-Bahn across the city, back to their bleak hotel room –

They walked across the lamplit hall, and up the steep stairs to Herr

Scheiber's sitting room. Marsha, on the sofa, was fast asleep, and someone had covered her up with a rug, turned off the television, and taken the kittens away. How very kind. How comforting.

'What a nice-looking child she is,' said Christopher.

'Thank you.' Harriet crossed quietly over, not knowing what to do. Marsha was sleeping peacefully, deeply: terribly tired. She'd been travelling from Brussels, then all across Berlin; she was about to do it all over again, to Prague.

Remember Prague?

Harriet touched her daughter's cheek, and listened to the light high breath. How could she wake her now?

'Leave her,' said Christopher. 'Scheiber won't mind for a night.'

'Are you sure?'

'Yes.'

'But – '

'But where will you sleep?' he asked, smiling down at her. 'Now there's a question.'

She stood up slowly; she could not look at him. He reached out towards her and touched her cheek, a little as she had touched Marsha's – just a fingertip, just a brush. She felt as though she had brushed an electric fence.

'I'll find you a room,' he said gently. 'Yes?'

She came back from another country. 'Yes.' And then: 'It seems dreadfully extravagant, two hotels, our rooms already paid for – '

'Well. Perhaps it should be one hotel. Much more economical. Why don't we talk about it in the morning?'

And then he was gone, and she sank to the sofa at Marsha's feet, and did not know what to think.

4

Harriet woke in a high iron bed in a small white room at the top of the hotel. Last night, conducted up precipitous uncarpeted stairs by Frau Scheiber, she had barely taken in where she was, turning out the lamp as soon as she climbed into bed and reliving, in a daze, the evening's conversation. Now, lying against snowy square pillows, beneath a heavy quilt, she looked sleepily at bare walls, stained floorboards, tall shutters through which she could hear, from down in the garden, the hotel day beginning. The back door was opened, and bottles put out; water ran into a drain; there was a saucer put down on stone – someone was feeding the cat. She could smell coffee. She looked at the clock on the chest of drawers: twenty to eight. She must do something.

Footsteps up the uncarpeted stairs, a tap at the door.

'Frau Pickering?'

'Mum?'

'Marsha?' Harriet sat up, calling out 'Come in, please,' and Liesel and Marsha came in together, Marsha unbrushed and rumpled but clearly content, and Liesel with a large cup of coffee.

'Good morning.' She set it down on the bedside table and returned to the door.

'Hang on a minute,' said Harriet, and then, in German, 'Wait, please – '

Harriet indicated the coffee; the child, who had been cared for. 'Thank you.'

Liesel smiled. It had been a pleasure. Breakfast was served until nine. Harriet had slept well?

'Very well, thank you.' She looked at Marsha, who had gone across to the window and was opening the shutters. 'What about you, on the sofa? Did you know where you were when you woke up?'

'Of course I knew where I was.' She lifted the flat iron bar. 'I've been feeding the cat.'

'It was you.'

'It was me.' Marsha unfolded the shutters and the room was filled with pale morning light. 'I wish we had shutters at home.'

Liesel was leaving. If there was anything else they wanted, please ask. The door closed behind her; they heard her light step on the stairs.

'Well,' said Harriet. She reached for her coffee and leaned back against the pillows. Bliss. She patted the quilt. 'Come here.'

Marsha came. They kissed; she perched, and looked round the room.

'It's lovely, this place.'

'Isn't it?'

'I like it better than Brussels.'

Now there was a thing. Harriet sipped. 'Why?'

'Just – this room.' She indicated the bare stained boards, the rug, the wicker chair in the corner, where Harriet had folded her clothes. 'Our room in Brussels was so posh and grand – I mean, I did like it, but this is nice and simple.'

'Isn't it?'

'Like the convent,' Marsha said suddenly. She got off the bed and walked round it. 'It's like a nun's room, sort of.'

'Yes. Yes, I suppose it is.'

'When I was younger, I wanted to be a nun –'

'She called it a conversion – I thought of it more as an obsession . . . . She was like a woman in the Middle Ages, praying for a child –'

Harriet closed her eyes. Christopher's face across the candlelit table swam into focus again, as it had followed her into sleep last night: heavy, intent, unlike any face she had ever been used to looking at, or wanting to look at.

'Mum? What are we going to do today?'

She opened her eyes. Marsha was beside her again.

'Have breakfast.'

'Then what?'

'And then we'll see.'

'I don't know why I'm telling you all these things – well, perhaps I do – I want you to know the worst –'

'And then?'

'And then we'll see . . . '

Marsha was frowning. 'You're still half asleep. And what on earth are you wearing?'

'I don't know, what am I wearing?' She looked down at flowery nylon. 'Oh, yes. Frau Scheiber lent it to me. It was very kind of her.'

'But how come we stayed the night? You said we'd be going back on the U-Bahn.'

'I know, but you fell asleep.'

'Only because you were downstairs for such a long time. What on earth were you talking about?'

'Oh.' Harriet finished her coffee. 'I can't remember now.'

'Yes you can.'

'That's enough.' She pushed back the heavy quilt and got up. There was no basin in here. 'I'm going down to the bathroom.'

'That nightdress is awful.'

'Marsha.' With the memory of last night's ill-humour from Marsha returning, Harriet turned to look at her. Nylon static clung to her legs. 'We are in east Berlin. A lot of things here are still awful, you little snob. Just because we're staying in a nice hotel. What happened to the girl who worried about people sleeping rough? People are putting up with a lot worse things than nylon nightdresses here, I can tell you.'

Marsha's mouth was hanging open. 'Mum! I only said – '

'Well, stop saying. Just for once, stop.'

'What on earth's got into you?'

Marsha had gone pale; Harriet was flooded with remorse. What had got into her? She was barely awake, they hadn't even had breakfast. Perhaps that was it. Of course it wasn't. She held out her arms.

'I'm sorry,' she said, as Marsha came into them. 'That was unforgivable. You've been absolutely wonderful, I don't know what all that was about – ' She kissed the unbrushed hair. 'I'm really sorry.'

'So long as it wasn't me.'

Marsha drew away; Harriet felt some of their usual spirit returning. 'Of course it wasn't you. Last night, after all, you were an angel.'

Marsha frowned again. 'Are you getting at me because of that?'

'I shouldn't be getting at you for anything. Come on, let me go to the bathroom – or do you want to come too? Let's have a bath to make up for no clean clothes. And then we'll have breakfast.'

'Okay.' They went down the precipitous stairs one by one. 'Mum?' asked Marsha, in the airy bathroom, as Harriet ran a bath from ancient taps.

'Yes?' Pipes banged, water spurted wildly, there were clouds of steam.

'We don't have to have breakfast with Christopher, do we?'

A civilised hush hung over the dining room. The shutters were open but the morning was hazy still, and the light still pale. The smell of hot coffee and warm bread filled the room; there was the rustle of newspapers, quiet conversation. Christopher had not come down yet.

'Thank God for that,' said Marsha.

Harriet said nothing. There had been enough misplaced reproaches already this morning; she would save up one suited to this particular attitude for a moment when it might become really necessary.

What sort of moment might that be?

'Let's sit over here.' Marsha was leading the way to a corner table, laid for two. 'I'm starving. What can we have?'

Harriet's mouth was dry, She could not, at this moment, waiting for Christopher's arrival, imagine eating anything much. She hadn't eaten anything much last night, either.

'You can have what you like,' she said, sitting down.

'I love the smell of the bread.' Marsha was looking round the room. 'Who do you think killed that bird?'

'An ancient Scheiber.' Harriet shook out her napkin. 'Here comes Liesel.'

Dear Liesel. She began to feel like a friend. They ordered coffee, hot chocolate, a platter of *Wurst* and *Käse* for Marsha, and lots of bread.

'What about you, Mum?'

'I'll wait.'

A sigh.

Harriet said cautiously, 'I'd like to go a bit further east today, if we can. I haven't arranged it properly with Christopher yet, but – '

Silence.

'What would you like to do?'

A shrug.

Coffee and hot chocolate arrived, and a basket of bread. Marsha fell upon it.

'If you really like it here, we might be able to move from Schöneberg, fetch our stuff . . .'

A long look. Bread dunked in hot chocolate.

Harriet poured coffee.

'Good morning.'

He was in the doorway, he had crossed the room, he was beside them.

'Have you slept well?' He was looking, himself, as though he had been through a difficult night, and had made efforts to disguise the fact. He had washed his hair and shaved and was wearing a different shirt, but he still looked tired and wrung out.

'Very well, thank you,' said Harriet. 'What about you?'

'Not bad. May I join you?' He took a chair from the next table and sat down, his back to the room. Marsha looked past him, as Liesel approached with her platter. He ordered more coffee, and hot rolls. Liesel brought him a cup while he waited. Harriet filled it from her pot, and reached for the milk jug.

'No, no thanks. Black is what I need this morning. So. How are you this morning, Marsha? Pass a quiet night on the sofa?'

'Yes, thanks.'

'And how are the kitty-cats?'

'Fine.' She was cutting a piece of Emmental into tiny cubes. He watched her. 'Is that for them?'

She gave a sigh. 'No.'

'Marsha fed the mother cat this morning,' Harriet said helpfully.

'Did she? How charming.' He raised his cup and blew gently on the hot coffee; he drank. 'Ah. That's better. The day begins to have possibilities.' He looked at her, and smiled. 'And what about you? How is the mother cat this morning?'

Harriet returned the smile, sipped her own coffee and felt warmth spread through her. 'Okay.'

'Good.'

'Here are your hot rolls,' said Marsha briskly.

'So they are.'

The hot rolls arrived in a basket and with them unsalted butter in a cut-glass dish and two kinds of jam, in china pots. At the Hotel Kloster these things came in little plastic tubs with peel-off foil on top.

They ate, and poured more coffee. Other guests came and went.

'Did you know,' asked Christopher, passing Harriet the basket, 'that the first people to cross the wall did so from Prenzlauer Berg? A young couple – they went through the border crossing on Bornholmer Strasse, a mile or so north of here.'

'I must go and see.'

He shook his head, reaching for the jam. 'You won't see a thing. In most parts of the city it's as though the wall has never existed – there are a few chunks in Potsdamer Platz, and as I told you, you can buy dubious chips of it from stalls round what was Checkpoint Charlie, down the road, but other than that – poof. She vanishes.'

Harriet took another hot roll, and broke it. 'Well. If we can't see anything of the wall, might we see something of the place you were talking about yesterday? Where the Scheiber factory is?'

'Marzahn? I'm not sure about that, actually – '

'Oh, please. I really shan't feel we've been to Berlin unless we go east, and see some of the changes. And it does sound interesting, from what you were saying – the factory, I mean, and the changeover to a market economy. Unless – ' she looked at him, wondering about his reluctance. 'Perhaps you're too busy?'

'No, no, I have to go there anyway. I can make a phone call, tell them I'm bringing visitors, if that's what you'd really like.'

'I'm interested, that's all.' And also it would provide an emotional breathing space, a distraction – to be thinking, once again, about issues in the public arena, as she was used to doing in London. 'If you're sure that's okay – '

'Yes. Just – ' he hesitated. 'Forgive me – you won't make too many enquiries, will you? Dieter's still feeling his way, and it isn't always easy, with his workforce and so on. And east Berliners still keep their guard up – they're not used to being questioned. Or perhaps I should say they don't like it – '

She took the point. 'I'll do my best.'

'And what about Marsha?' He turned to her; she was smothering her third hot roll in butter. 'How would you like to visit a factory in one of the grottiest parts of Berlin? Just for the experience.'

'It's up to Mum.' She went on spreading, concentrating on every crumbling corner.

Harriet hesitated, torn once again between her own desires and Marsha's. Even before they'd come to the Hotel Scheiber the dilemma had been with her – wanting to see the whole city, wearing both of them out. And now there was another factor: she wanted Christopher's company. Marsha didn't.

'We could go back to Schöneberg, Marsha,' she said. 'Would you prefer that?'

She studied the tablecloth. 'I'd like to stay here, really. With the kittens.'

'Yes, but – '

Christopher finished his coffee. 'I think I'll leave you to it. I'll have a smoke and a look at the papers.'

When he had gone, Harriet and Marsha had a discussion, which became an argument. Harriet won. She reached across the table for Marsha's hand, which was withheld.

'I just want to feel I've seen both sides of Berlin, and understood things a bit more, and I really don't think I can leave you here for hours on end. But then we'll come back here, and do whatever you want tomorrow, your birthday, of course, and then – ' She stopped. 'God. And then we're leaving for Prague.'

'Yes,' said Marsha, pointedly. 'To look for Karel.' She rose from the table. 'I'm going to look for the kittens.'

There was no direct U-Bahn connection betwen Prenzlauer Berg and Marzahn, so they took a tram, leaving the tenement-lined back streets and humming along the lines going east, on wider main roads. Much of the traffic was heading in the opposite direction, carrying workers to the western side of the city; many of the roads were in visibly bad shape, pitted with holes or badly surfaced: every couple of miles they passed boarded-up sections enclosing pounding drills and smoking barrels of tar. Tower blocks stretched into the distance, beneath a brightening sky.

When they got on, the tram had been crowded. Harriet and Marsha had found a couple of seats at the back, leaving Christopher to strap-hang, like a great tree, amongst the press of local commuters down near the driver. Gradually the commuters thinned out, and now, as they stopped at traffic lights, he came up towards them.

'Another twenty minutes or so. Mind if I smoke?'

It felt like years since London Transport had banned smoking: already, Marsha had voiced objections as people around them lit up.

'Actually,' said Harriet, 'do you mind if you don't? It does feel a bit airless in here.'

'Sorry. Of course.' Christopher put his cigarettes back in his pocket, but Marsha was already rising.

'Go on, if you want, you can have my seat. I'd like to go to the front, anyway.' She turned to Harriet. 'Is that okay? It looks cleaner down there.'

'All right.' They watched her move along the slatted floor, holding on to the back of an empty seat as the tram swayed, then stretching up to get hold of a strap. She could just about reach, and seen from the back she could, because of her height, just about be an early teenager, travelling alone. This was, Harriet realised, the effect she was aiming for, and the state she probably desired. In another few years it would not be possible to win arguments so often, to take her hither and thither across Europe without consultation. In another few years . . .

Christopher, beside her, said, 'She wants to do her own thing.'

She turned to him. 'That's just what I was thinking.'

'Well. There we are.' He looked at her directly. 'And what else have you been thinking, after last night? I hope all that talk didn't shake you up too much.'

'No, no, I – ' She what? She was sitting next to him, which felt quite different from being across the table. It was always awkward to talk to people next to you, rather than opposite, unless you knew them so well that it didn't matter where you sat, or looked, you could just chatter away, as she and Marsha did. She did not know Christopher so well, she was very aware of him being so close, and she did not, above all, want to reopen last night's conversation. Later, perhaps. Not on a tram to an eastern suburb of Berlin first thing in the morning, with Marsha only yards away from them. She shifted along the seat towards the window. They were passing a parade of narrow-fronted shops, which looked as though they had been there since the Fifties, and then a very Nineties supermarket, brightly lit, plastered with notices of special offers.

'A lot of big chain stores have opened up in the East in the last couple of years,' said Christopher, following her gaze. 'Seizing the moment. I think some have lived to regret it – after the first rush for western goodies a lot of people lost their jobs and had to tighten their belts again.'

The tram stopped at a junction, and its doors opened; a couple in their early fifties climbed on, he in an ill-fitting suit and open-necked shirt, she carrying an ancient shopping bag.

'It's been a complete social upheaval, hasn't it?' said Harriet, half-watching them, glad of the opportunity for impersonal conversation.

'Of course. And especially for people like them.' He nodded towards the couple, settling into a seat. 'They're of an age which is caught in the middle – they've never known anything except communism, they've no pre-war memories of a united Germany to make them feel hopeful about reunification now, but they're too old to benefit from capitalism. They're not going to become the new rich in the West. If they've lost factory jobs they probably won't work again. And unemployment is something they've never known. Unlike the young – there's a whole lot of the new generation who've never known anything else.'

'I know.'

He smiled at her. 'Of course you know. You've read it all up, haven't you?'

'That's what Susanna said – ' She broke off. 'Let's not talk about Susanna or anything now. Anyway, it's not a question of "reading it all up", that sounds – '

'I know. It sounds like a tourist. Whereas you, of course, are a traveller, quite different, taking a lively interest in contemporary affairs.'

'Oh, shut up.'

He raised an eyebrow to comic effect.

She laughed. 'Go on.'

'Go on what?'

'Go on telling me what I already know.'

'On the contrary, I feel I should sit back and let you educate me.'

'Don't be silly.'

The tram had stopped again, and Marsha was at the door, looking out. They were near a little park, an oasis in what was now a succession of sprawling high-rise estates. Marsha stepped back as the doors closed again, and a young mother carried a heavy toddler up the aisle. The child was wearing a bright blue and green tracksuit, which looked like something out of Marks & Spencer – certainly smart and new. Harriet remarked on it.

'Well, yes. People do spend money like water on western stuff when they've got it, especially for kids. Shiny new bikes, and all that. Colour. Of course there are changes and some people are making good – making better, anyway.' He shifted in the seat as the tram gathered speed. 'I can remember when I first came here, in '88, how grey everything looked. It really did. You came through Checkpoint Charlie and stepped back thirty years: virtually no traffic except for ancient trams, half-empty shops, half-finished housing, shell damage, cobbled streets. And at night you went about in the half-dark.'

Christopher nodded towards the press of traffic alongside, the secondhand Golfs and Audis amongst ancient Skodas and Trabants. 'All that's changing in some places, but it's not going to keep pace with what people want, and in some ways things are worse, as I said. There's a lot of disappointment, a lot of anger – since unification the East Germans feel like the underclass. There are dole offices on the estates now – that's new. And not only is there massive unemployment, but when they go for jobs in the west they're treated like idiots, stuck in a Fifties time-warp, who've never seen a computer.'

'And that's why they're looking for scapegoats,' said Harriet, thinking of events in Rostock and Mölln, last summer, all over the papers at home. 'Guest workers. Asylum-seekers.'

'Exactly.' He banged his fist on the seat rail, making her jump. '"Deutschland den Deutschen! Germany for the Germans! Foreigners out!"'

She shook her head. 'The Jews have gone, and now – the asylum-seekers are the new Jews in a way, aren't they? For the young neo-Nazis. It's very disturbing.'

'It is, but all the right conditions are there for it. The wrong conditions, I should say. And of course the asylum laws are crazy. Far too lax.'

She was startled. 'Come off it.'

'They are. You must realise that. Asylum for all – it was built into the constitution after the war as an act of guilt and atonement.'

'Of course. So it should have been.'

'But no one could have predicted then what would happen now. Do you know how many people applied for asylum here last year? Almost five hundred thousand. This year it'll probably be higher. There's a barracks-like place on an estate not far from Scheiber's new premises, apparently. Housing God knows how many Romanians. There are places like it in depressed towns all over East Germany, as you know. What's supposed to happen to all these people?'

'I don't know,' said Harriet, suddenly on her mettle, 'but I do know they're not supposed to be burned alive in overcrowded hostels.'

Christopher frowned. 'Don't get on your high horse. Did I say they should be?'

'No, but – '

'But what? You sound like the person I met in Brussels.'

'I am the person you met in Brussels.'

'Yes, but – ' His hand on the rail was trembling; he reached into his pocket. 'I need a cigarette, sorry.'

Harriet found she was shaking too. She bit her lip. What had happened?

'No,' she said quickly. 'I'm sorry. I've already snapped Marsha's head off this morning, I don't quite know what's got into me.'

He was inhaling deeply. 'Let's forget it.'

'I think I'm actually very tired,' she said, suddenly aware that it was true.

'And emotional.' He was looking at her, now, with renewed concern. 'It's my fault. I did upset you last night.'

She looked out of the window. 'I don't know. Anyway, I shouldn't have jumped down your throat.'

'Not a problem. Let's talk about something else. We're almost there.'

But Harriet did not know what else to talk about, and a silence fell. Christopher went on smoking; she gazed out of the window at tower blocks stained with meandering brown rivers of damp, feeling ill at ease and confused.

It was true that she had over-reacted, going on the attack before he had made his position clear. And yet. A gut reaction was a gut reaction, and it told you who you were. And she was a political animal, who had always, despite the circumstances of Karel's return to Prague, been drawn to the left. Christopher, it seemed, stood on the right. How far to the right? How much did it matter? What was the point at which you might say: it matters a lot, and more than anything else?

An abandoned car with an open bonnet, the engine gutted and the seats ripped out, stood at the side of the road on sunken tyres. Beyond, a scuffed stretch of green and a concrete path led to a windswept concrete precinct, shadowed by monstrous tower blocks. They were in the heart of Marzahn, where for mile upon mile this grid was repeated: precinct, high-rise, dark connecting alleyways, parade of shops. Here and there young trees swayed in the wind, here and there were windowboxes; in some blocks bright murals had been painted round identical doorways, perhaps to help people locate their own apartment. But these signs of individuality were few. They were walking through a vast, featureless estate, stretching for miles towards the eastern edge of Berlin, a place built in the mid-seventies to house hundreds and thousands of workers brought up in decayed tenements who wanted hot water, a convenient, modern apartment. Already, it looked outdated – more than outdated: desolate. Who, with a choice, would choose to live here?

Litter blew in and out of the muggers' paradise of alleyways, in the path of young mothers wheeling pushchairs across bleak concrete spaces to the shops. There were broken windows on the lower floors; graffiti was scrawled everywhere. Harriet, holding Marsha's hand, felt that they were being stared at: by women carrying heavy shopping in plastic bags but more by the young men with close-cropped hair hanging around computer games arcades or walking four or five abreast across the precincts, in jeans and heavy boots. She could feel them looking her up and down, and looking at Christopher, in his creased linen jacket, carrying a good leather briefcase.

She remembered the first afternoon in the city, eyed by punks lolling on the steps of the Kaiser-Wilhelm-Gedächtniskirche on the Ku'damm. She had wondered then if they came from the eastern districts and whether she would feel like a voyeur coming out here, and she realised now that she did, that she felt tense and uneasy, menaced by these young men with the cold stares. It seemed now unthinkable that she might ever have brought Marsha here alone, but she also felt that Christopher, though affording protection, drew attention and hostility.

They walked on. He was talking neutrally, over Marsha's head, about the activities of the *Stasi*, whose old headquarters were in the adjoining district of Lichtenberg, and who, it used to be rumoured, had penetrated the Marzahn estates so effectively that almost every other apartment had housed a paid informer. When the citizens' files were discovered and opened, after the wall came down, there were people who learned that their own mothers had been reporting on them.

This talk only served to increase Harriet's feelings of alienation. She was also aware that the easy banter which had been developing between her and Christopher had evaporated in the wake of their exchange on the tram, and that Marsha, beside her, had barely spoken six words together since they got off. She began to feel as if this might go on for ever: the two of them listening, as if to a stranger, looking about them, out of place and uncertain of their destination, and she said abruptly, hearing herself sound like Marsha:

'When are we going to get there?'

He gave a little laugh. 'Had enough?'

'Well – ' She looked down at Marsha, between them.

'I thought you wanted to see all this.' He gestured at the towering blocks of flats, the mean-looking shops below. 'If you find it unpleasant, think what it must feel like to live here.'

She was made uneasier by his tone; she bit back a sharp retort.

'This is communism,' he said. 'Socialism. Isn't socialism what you believe in?'

'Christopher – '

'What?'

She shook her head, not knowing what to do. She confronted him, and they had a full-scale argument, impossible with Marsha here, or she shut up. She shut up. They walked on.

'We get another tram in a minute,' he said. 'Out to the factory, but it's not far.'

'Okay.' She looked down at Marsha. 'All right?'

'Yes, thanks,' said Marsha, looking straight ahead.

The railway line ran through Marzahn, and from the tram they could see goods trains being shunted into sidings, and workers in overalls and luminous jackets moving along the track. Gigantic cranes swung above building sites, clearings in the midst of a tenemented district which would soon be gone.

'This is where Dieter's old factory was.' Christopher indicated a maze of half-demolished cobbled streets off to their right, and Harriet looked out at soot-grimed warehouses. Windows were barred; signboards swung in the wind. The double doors of one building stood open; boxes at the entrance were being loaded into a waiting lorry squeezed into the narrow street.

'So people are still working there.'

'Oh, yes. In pretty grim conditions – it's sweatshop land, really.' The tram moved on. 'Dieter's new premises are on a development a couple of miles away. They moved there only at the beginning of the year: it's still something of a wasteland, but he's not complaining.' He had been talking neutrally, generally, since they left the estate; now he turned to her and said, 'What about you? Are you complaining?'

She looked towards Marsha, across the aisle, her face turned to the window, and said carefully, 'I don't really understand what happened, earlier on. I didn't mean to make a fuss, but you didn't need to – '

'I know. Apologies. I get irked by your holier-than-thou-ness.' He smiled at her. 'Have you always occupied the moral high ground?'

'Always.' She returned the smile with caution. 'You must forgive me – '

'I think it's those on the moral high ground who have the power to forgive.'

The banter was returning; she gave an inward sigh of relief.

'Let's call it quits.'

'Let's. And later we must talk.'

'Yes.' She looked away. Later, she must think. Across the aisle, Marsha's face was pressed to the glass. If she were travelling with two parents, she might be used to differences of opinion expressed between them; she might be used to a quarrel, and a reconciliation. In such circumstances, this, now, would be the moment for Harriet to reach over and reassure: it's blown over, you can come out now. They could all have an ice, or something, and forget about it. As it was –

'Marsha?'

'What?'

'We're nearly there.'

'Who cares?' It was spoken to the glass.

On the outskirts of the district, a piece of derelict land was crossed by a newly made road. Bulldozers were working on one side; on the other, a high wire fence surrounded a car park and low modern buildings beyond a barrier. A prefab cubicle stood at the gate and Christopher showed his card to the attendant, a thin young man in a peaked cap, who waved them through. They looked like a family, Harriet thought fleetingly, as they followed Christopher along the pedestrian path by the barrier. Businessman, wife and child. He raised his arm as they walked across the windy car park, indicating the outskirts of a small town a mile or so beyond the perimeter.

'That's the place I was talking about, earlier on. Where the refugee hostel is.'

'Have you ever been there?'

'No, of course not. I've never had reason to.' He ushered them suddenly out of the way of an enormous lorry, moving towards the gate. There was lettering on the side: INDUSTRIELLE MATERIALIEN FÜR WEITERE WERARBEITUNG – RÜCKSTAND WIEDERVERWERTEN – NICHT SPEZIFIKATIONGERECHTES MATERIAL. The driver nodded towards Christopher, who briefly raised his hand, drawing them aside. 'Somebody told me one of the hostel occupants scrawled up *Azilant gut* on the hostel door,' he went on, leading them across the car park as the lorry left the compound. 'I shouldn't think many of the neighbours agree.'

'What are you talking about?' asked Marsha.

'Tell you later,' said Harriet, feeling that to give one of her state-of-the-world lectures to Marsha now would bore her and risk reopening the earlier argument with Christopher. 'Are you okay?' she asked, trying to take her hand. 'It's nice to hear you speak.'

'Don't be silly.' Marsha kept her hand to herself.

They accompanied Christopher across the compound. Harriet was aware of the change in the air – a faint smell of something industrial she couldn't identify, which wasn't very pleasant. Then they were at the entrance of one of the first buildings, where a sign for Wilkendorf und Scheiber, and the logo, was nailed to the door.

Harriet said to Marsha as they went in: 'You're being wonderful. I'll make it up to you.'

'How?'

'Your birthday. You name it, it's yours.'

'A kitten? The little tabby?'

'We can't take a kitten to Prague . . .'

Marsha moved away.

Christopher was talking to the receptionist. They were in an open area floored in pale vinyl, with a few low chairs upholstered in a beige moquette. Plastic flowers stood on a plastic table; there was a drinks machine.

Christopher returned as Harriet looked about her. 'Okay, Dieter's expecting us. Follow me.'

He led them off to the right. Marsha looked longingly at the drinks machine.

'On the way back,' said Harriet.

On one side of a corridor windows overlooked the car park; on the other was a long line of partitioned offices, featureless boxes adorned here and there by plants and postcards. The occupants sat at bright green computer screens surrounded by sheaves of print-out. Phones rang, keyboards tapped, a man in a cheap suit came out of a doorway carrying files and hurried past them, with a nod.

'Dieter's in here,' said Christopher, and knocked on the glass of the next office. A dark-haired man in shirt sleeves swung round from his desk with the phone in his hand, and made a gesture: one minute. Then he saw Harriet and Marsha and made another: half a minute. Harriet smiled. He beckoned them in.

'The last office we visited was Hugh's,' she said to Marsha, as they went through the door.

'I know.' Marsha looked round the prefabricated piece of twelve-by-twelve in which she now found herself.

Dieter Scheiber finished his call and rose to greet them. He was a short, well-made man – dwarfed, like most people, by Christopher, with whom he was clearly on good terms. They were introduced; he greeted them in English.

'Welcome. My apologies for detaining you. You would like some coffee – ' he turned to Marsha ' – some Coke, maybe?'

'Please.'

'This way, please.' He led them back to the reception area, making polite enquiries. They were enjoying Berlin? The hotel? His uncle was looking after them, he hoped. Good, good. And now –

'Our dazzling choice.' He made a sweeping gesture at the vending machine. 'And then I will show you the shop floor, if you are interested. I have the right expression?'

'It'll do.' Christopher was feeling in his pocket for change. 'And my friend is interested. I have been telling her of your new set-up.'

They took their drinks to the low beige chairs.

'I understand you have had quite a few changes,' said Harriet.

'In Berlin?' He laughed.

'In Berlin, but also for you, yourself. You were working in a nationalised factory. Now – '

'Now – ' He spread his hands. 'Now we are capitalist at last.' Another laugh. 'The world waits for Wilkendorf & Scheiber. But seriously. We are doing okay. My friend here is helping us a little.'

'You don't need to bore her with details,' said Christopher. He had not sat down, but was smoking and drinking his coffee, looking out of the window. He frowned. 'Is something happening out there?'

'There is always something happening here.' Dieter turned and looked over his shoulder. They exchanged a glance. 'It is deliveries only.'

'No – I don't mean the lorry. Outside the fence. You seem to have visitors, Dieter. I think you'd better – '

Now Dieter was frowning. He got to his feet and looked out. 'A little problem, only. Excuse me.' He nodded to Harriet and went quickly over to the reception desk, speaking quietly in German.

'What's happening?' Marsha asked.

'I'm not sure.' Harriet stood next to Christopher at the window. Outside the compound, beyond the perimeter of the high wire fence, a group of demonstrators was marching towards the gates, shouting. They carried a banner, and placards; she could see the company logo, W & S, violently crossed through in red. There were slogans, but these she could not understand. There was a skull and crossbones –

'Christopher?'

'It's okay – just a little local demo.' But he was still frowning.

Behind her, the receptionist was speaking on the phone. Then the barrier at the entrance was raised, and a lorry pulled out, rather fast. The gates swung to behind it, and the barrier swiftly descended.

'Excuse me for that.' Dieter had rejoined them. 'Shall we begin our little tour?' He gestured towards the entrance.

Harriet looked at Christopher, stubbing his cigarette out in a tubular ashtray. 'What was all that about?'

He ushered her forward. 'Tell you later. I'm going to go and talk to a few people now, okay?'

Dieter was holding the door at the entrance: they went out and he led them across the compound, away from the gates. A smell hung in the air as they approached the factory itself, and Marsha covered her mouth.

'My apologies,' said Dieter. 'Some of these industrial processes do cause unpleasantness in the atmosphere, but – ' he shrugged – 'Soon we shall be improving this side of things.'

They followed him in through heavy swing doors: at once, the smell became worse, and the noise was deafening. A foreman gave them earmuffs, and led them through more swing doors. Even to Harriet's untutored eye it was clear, as she put on her earmuffs and looked around, that what was here was a mixture of ancient and modern: enormous hunks of ironmongery, thick with decades of black grease, stood alongside sleek, scaled-down Nineties machines equipped with sophisticated calibrators. They followed Dieter round, greeted with nods by the operators. Vats and powders and chemicals were everywhere.

'You see we are still in the transition,' Dieter shouted. 'We have much outdated equipment still.'

Harriet nodded. 'I don't know much about these things, but – '

'But you can see, yes? Some of this machinery we have since the 1960s. In time we shall be completely modernised. Well – ' They were nearing the door again; he looked towards Marsha, who was watching thick liquids swirling in enormous vessels. She looked pale and bemused. 'You have seen enough, now?'

'Yes, yes, thank you for showing us. I'll fetch my daughter.'

She made her way over and touched Marsha on the shoulder. She jumped.

'Ready to go?' mouthed Harriet. 'Are you okay?'

Marsha nodded dazedly.

'So,' Dieter said to her, as they came out into the fresh air once more. 'You have enjoyed our factory, Marsha?'

'I feel a bit sick.'

'I am sorry. That unpleasant smell?' He reached into his pocket. 'Your mother allows you a peppermint?'

'Her mother allows her anything today,' said Harriet. 'She's been wonderful, a true travelling companion. In a couple of days we're going to Prague, did Christopher tell you?'

'To Prague?' They had reached the main office building: he held the door. 'So he can show you around there, also. Or perhaps you know it well?'

'No, it's our first visit.'

'They're going on a mystery tour.' Christopher was waiting for them, looking out of the window again. 'Your friends seem to have gone for lunch,' he added.

Dieter followed his gaze. 'Very good. So – ' he looked at them questioningly. 'I have one or two phone calls, and then perhaps you will like some lunch in our canteen? You will wait here, or you will go direct – ' He indicated another passage, behind the reception desk.

'I want to go to the loo,' Marsha told Harriet.

Dieter pointed them in the right direction, down the passage away from the canteen.

Inside, Harriet said, 'You're not going to be sick, are you?'

'I don't think so.' Marsha went into a cubicle. She wasn't sick, but she still looked pale when she came out.

'Better now? Want to sit down?'

'It's all right.' She dried her hands and moved out of the way as a young woman in overalls, from the machine room, pushed the door open. 'Let's go.' She went out; Harriet followed, feeling that Marsha was lost to her, and feeling, once again, the mixture of guilt and irritation which had begun to be a feature of the last few days. Out in the passage, she said, 'I know this isn't exactly fun, but could you – '

Marsha ignored her, striding ahead.

Out in the reception area Christopher was smoking, his back to the desk. Harriet walked up beside him, and looked out of the window. The barrier was still down, and the gates were closed, but the group of demonstrators had gone.

'What was all that about?' she asked him again.

'Dieter's had to lay off quite a few people in recent weeks,' he said. 'And not just him – quite a few factories on this estate are finding things difficult. It's what we were talking about – out in the open market, things get tough. A lot of local people had high hopes when industry moved out here; they get a bit heated when jobs have to go, or they're put on *Kurzarbeit* – short-time work.'

'And that's who those people were? But Dieter's supposed to be doing well.'

'We're in a recession, remember? Nothing's guaranteed. And Dieter has to be careful – his other half wants to see his money well invested.'

'Wilkendorf.'

'Wilkendorf, indeed. Anyway, the moment seems to have passed. Where's Marsha?'

'Right here.' Harriet turned to where Marsha was seated on one of the low beige chairs, swinging a foot. 'I think she's had enough.'

'Sure. We'll go back after lunch, yes? And continue our conversation?' He looked down at her. 'You realise, after all my talk last night, that I still know almost nothing about you at all?'

'Yes. Well . . . ' She looked round, as Dieter rejoined them.

'So. My apologies again. Let me show you our canteen.'

They lunched on meatballs, fried potatoes and salad in a new canteen – all white tiles and shining saucepans. Harriet, looking around her, observed among the men and women in middle age faces which she felt instinctively that you might see on any street in Eastern Europe: the faces of people who had queued for too long, done without for too long, smoked too many cheap cigarettes and had about them in consequence an air of grey fatigue which in these optimistic new surroundings made them look washed up from another era.

Marsha had a plain bowl of chips and a bottle of mineral water. She ate in silence as the grown-ups talked. Harriet, without thinking, asked Dieter about local unemployment, and feelings about the industrial estate. He gave a little frown, looking at Christopher.

'These things are inevitable,' he said, taking salad, 'I am afraid that sometimes there is no choice.'

'It's none of my business, of course – I'm just curious.'

'Naturally. You are visiting the Third World.' He raised his spoon, and she blushed. He smiled: he was joking, she must not take him personally, please. 'I explain to you before, we are in transition. It is not so long since I was carrying the party card, you know. Some of the people I had working for me now are my friends from a long time.' He paused. 'Except, of course, that in East Germany we were cautious friends, you understand. There were informers in every workplace.' He shrugged, finishing a mouthful. 'Perhaps still. It is a risk I take, like others. I do not like to see people without jobs, but in the end I must look to make a profit, to succeed. It is the same for the other factories here. That way there will be a future. So.' He turned to Marsha. 'They are good, your chips?'

'Yes, thanks.'

'Your family have been very kind to us,' said Harriet. 'Particularly to Marsha. Haven't they, Marsha? Tell Dieter about the kittens.'

'You tell him.'

'Marsha – '

Dieter ignored this exchange, but he picked up on the change of subject and began to talk at some length about his uncle and aunt and their new way of life, now that the hotel was theirs. He did not ask about Harriet's life, or her work, or about Marsha's school, and she commented on this to Christopher when he went to fetch coffee.

'It's as though he has no curiosity about us at all.'

Christopher shook his head. 'It isn't that.' She could see him think about lighting up, but they were, out of deference to Marsha, in the non-smoking part of the canteen, and he took his hand out of his pocket. 'You must understand that for decades people looked for the meaning behind every question. It's true what I was saying earlier on – and he's just mentioned it, hasn't he? Even your own mother could be informing on you – people learned to be very suspicious of questions, and it wasn't good form to ask too much. You can forget all the London chat: and what do you do, and where do you live, and oh, really, and how long have you lived there? If people want to tell you things, they'll tell you. They assume you'll do the same.' He watched Dieter coming back towards them, carrying a tray. 'And also, of course, he's enjoying the opportunity of telling you about his family's success.'

'I'm sorry if I was tactless – about laying people off, and so on.'

He looked at her steadily. 'I thought it was one of your milder moments, actually.' He pulled a chair out of the way as Dieter put down the tray of coffee.

Afterwards, they were given a tour of the rest of the estate. They visited a workshop making electrical goods, a printer's, a plastics factory where the smell was worse than amongst the dyes and paints. By the time they came out into the car park the afternoon was almost gone. Harriet noticed a building on the far side of the compound, bolted and barred.

'What's in there?'

Christopher glanced towards it. 'No idea. Storage, I should think.' He took her arm. 'Time we were off.'

Dieter offered them a lift.

'Are you sure?'

'Of course.' He looked at his watch. 'I am not able to take you to Prenzlauer Berg, unfortunately, but back into Marzahn is no problem. This way, please.' He led them over to a Volvo parked near the factory entrance. 'Please.'

The barrier was raised at their approach; they swung out into the road and turned left. Within two hundred yards their way was blocked by a bulldozer and an articulated lorry, at right angles: one unmanned, the other tipped up and pouring sand out in a heap at the roadside.

'Fantastic.' Dieter leaned on the horn.

'In England you'd think nothing of it,' said Christopher. 'This kind of thing goes on all the time.'

Harriet and Marsha sat waiting in the back.

Dieter looked at his watch again. 'We make a detour, I think.' He reversed a little, and turned in the road; a line of vehicles behind them were doing the same.

'Tch, tch.'

They left the industrial estate behind, and travelled then through wasteland in either side of the road. To their left, the building works gave out, and the land was abandoned to weeds and a rubbish dump. To their right, after half a mile or so, Harriet looked out on the now familiar drab surroundings of another housing estate.

'Quite a number of our workers live here,' said Dieter, overtaking a bus.

Gathering clouds hung low over apartment blocks whose cramped balconies were draped with washing; below, children biked up and down along cracked paths. It was not quite as densely built-up as the gigantic sprawl of Marzahn, and the blocks, on the whole, looked older, bordering a characterless main street. They drove past a line of shops, a post office, one or two bars, a crowded pinball arcade.

'Christopher?' Harriet leaned forward. 'Where do you think this hostel might be?'

He looked at her in the mirror. 'Is it really on your sightseeing agenda?'

She bit her lip. 'I just – '

'I know, I know.' He turned to ask Dieter.

'The refugee hostel? That is another of our problems.' He slowed down as they came to the end of the main street, and nodded towards low, barracks-like buildings set in the middle of a piece of open land. 'There.' He stopped the car for a moment. A wire fence surrounded the buildings, much like the one at the factory, and on the other side they could see women in kerchiefs hanging out washing and children kicking a ball about. The doors were open, revealing dark interiors: men sat smoking in silence on the steps, or walked up and down beside the wire.

'It's like a prison camp,' said Harriet. She knew she was staring, but could not help it. The sun was low now, and longer shadows stretched across the ground: the figures behind the wire fence – pacing, smoking, waiting – had in this thickening afternoon light a timeless quality: everyone who had ever waited, far from home, with dwindling hope. A few other women in headscarves were walking up towards the gate in the middle of the fence, returning from the shops. Every now and then they looked round, as if they were checking something.

'It is something like a prison camp,' said Dieter, 'but what are we to do? And the truth is, they are safer behind that fence.'

'How long have they been there?'

He shrugged. 'A year? Two years?'

Harriet said: 'Would you mind very much – do we have just a few minutes – I'd like to get out.'

'And do what?' asked Christopher.

'Just – I don't know. Be here.'

'I really don't think that's a very bright idea. Dieter?'

'I have a few minutes,' said Dieter. 'But it is wise if we all go.'

'That does feel like sightseeing. I'm sure I'll – ' She looked at Marsha. 'Or do you want to come with me? Stretch our legs before we go home?'

'It isn't *home*,' said Marsha. 'Why do you keep calling everywhere home?'

'Oh, Marsha – '

'What?'

Harriet got out of the car. Dieter and Christopher followed.

'You will accompany us?' Dieter opened the door on Marsha's side. She came out slowly; he locked all the doors. They walked past the last two blocks of flats, and over the rough dry ground.

Much later, when she relived, over and over again, what happened next, Harriet realised that it was then, almost as soon as they left the car, that she had the uncomfortable feeling of being watched, or followed. Marsha was lagging behind. Harriet turned, to chivvy her along; she held out a hand, which was ignored; she became aware of a group of youths, standing quite still on the path between the blocks of flats. They wore jeans and black T-shirts: she noticed some kind of white decoration; she felt, as she had felt in Marzahn, a prickle of unease at being stared at, but she was concentrating on Marsha.

'Come on, please. We won't be long.'

Her English voice carried over the open ground.

One of the youths said something; another drew on a cigarette and threw it to the ground.

Harriet gave up. Christopher and Dieter were a few yards ahead by now: they stopped to let them catch up, and turned round.

Was it then that Dieter was recognised, or had they seen his car?

Harriet hurried to join them. She turned again to wait for Marsha; the youths had gone. Long shadows followed them over the grass as they continued walking towards the hostel ahead, its outline growing darker as the sun sank low. Beyond were a few trees. The women with their shopping were going through the iron-framed gate in the wire. There were greetings; the gate clanged shut again; then it was quiet.

'Scheiber!'

Footsteps behind them; the rattle of a chain.

Later, much later, Christopher translated the brutality which followed.

'Scheiber! What are you doing here?'

Dieter swung round; for a moment, Harriet was frozen. And then they were surrounded. A gang – how many, how many? Six, eight, more? – with a dog on a chain, straining and panting.

'Marsha – '

She was beyond them, rooted to the spot, white-faced.

'Marsha! Christopher, please – '

He was beside her; he made a move forwards. At once the dog on his chain leapt forward, snarling, and he recoiled. Harriet felt fear dissolve her as one of the youths thrust a fist beneath Dieter's chin.

'You put my father out of a job and you walk up here like it's nothing? You are taking your friends to see this rubbish that we live with?' He jerked his head towards the hostel, and Harriet, in her terror, took in the white decoration on his T-shirt: the German eagle, scrawled with a swastika. 'These people that are living off us? Receiving the same as my father?'

Dieter was pale. He stepped back, away from the fist, and was grabbed by the collar. From behind the fence of the hostel came the sound of voices, doors closing, a bolt slammed shut. The youth spat on the ground.

'They are scum, they are shit, they are cowards.'

Dieter said, his voice shaking: 'My friends are nothing to do with this – there is a child here – will you please – '

'Please *what*? You would like to walk freely here? You would like to drive up in your Volvo and show them the sights and drive away again? You would like to be able to lock your factory gates when we come to visit?'

Other youths running towards the scene from the flats were shouting.

'Mum!'

'Marsha – ' said Harriet, shaking. 'Please – my daughter – I must – '

The youth swung towards her. 'You are from England?'

'Yes.'

'You are visiting this rich shit Scheiber? You are a piece of rich bitch shit yourself, I think.'

Christopher moved towards him. 'That's enough. Let us go.'

The youth spat again, and it landed at Christopher's feet. 'You would like to fight your way out?'

The youths running up over the grass drew near; one of them knocked into Marsha and sent her flying. She fell to the ground and scrambled up again.

'*Mum!*'

Panic and fury swept over Harriet: she heard herself screaming: '*Let me through!*' and lunged towards a gap in the circle. It closed. She thought in despair: we shall die here, and no one will know. As if she were drowning, she saw in a swirling film before her Karel in a sunlit basement; Marsha, a baby, held in her arms; saw Martin walking away, and Hugh beside her, and Hugh and Susanna, Christopher –

Then everything happened at once. A punch, a groan. Fists flew, the circle broke apart, the dog on its chain was barking hysterically.

'Run! Run!'

She ran, but Christopher was ahead of her, panting, stumbling over the ground towards Marsha. Sirens sounded, lights flashed, cars roared over the grass. Christopher grabbed Marsha and flung her over his shoulder.

'Run!'

The cars screeched to a halt, doors were flung open, armed *Polizei* were everywhere. Christopher was racing after Dieter, towards his car. Harriet heard the horrible sound of metal dragged across metal, and breaking glass. She saw people running away from Dieter's car, yelling, and she heard Marsha, sobbing wildly:

'Let go of me! Let go of me! You're not my father! Let me *go!*'

5

Marsha lay in the high iron bed, and Harriet sat beside her. It was late, it was dark, and the shutters were closed; a lamp on the bedside table made the room shadowy and soft. Marsha glared at Harriet from the pillows.

'You drag me around as if I was a *suitcase*. It doesn't matter what I say, I have to come, I have to do what you want, I have to listen. You keep on saying it's just for now, it's just for today, and I just want to see this, and I must just show you that, this is a statue of Marx, and this is a statue of someone else, and do you know what happened in 18 this and 19 that, and now I'm not going to talk to you at all because I'm talking to *him*, and we can't take a kitten to *Prague*, oh no! And then you drag us all into that horrible place and we were nearly *killed* – ' She began to cry again.

Harriet held her hand and listened. She stroked her face, and wiped her eyes, and said she was sorry, over and over again. After a while, Marsha slowed down, and stopped crying.

Harriet said: 'Darling Marsha, how can I make it better?'

Marsha yawned.

'Would you like a hot drink?'

'Don't go.'

'Okay.' Harriet leaned back in the wicker chair, and closed her eyes. Bright lights flashed before her, the voices of the *Polizei* were curt and demanding, Dieter was shaking, looking at his car. The tyres were slashed, and the windscreen shattered; long, ugly scars ran over the paintwork. Marsha, incoherent, was in her arms, Christopher had lit a cigarette and was trying to calm things down.

'An unprovoked attack – we were just visiting – no, no purpose . . .'

A police car took them back to Prenzlauer Berg; Dieter stayed to supervise the removal of his car.

'I am so sorry,' said Harriet. 'What can I do?'

He shook his head, his face blue-white in the revolving light of the van beside them. 'It is insured, it is not a problem.'

Of course it was a problem, but she could only say again: 'I'm sorry,' as the *Polizei* radioed for a breakdown lorry. They left him standing at the roadside.

Harriet, leaning back in the wicker chair, hearing Marsha's breathing grow steady and slow, saw all this over and over again. She saw the circle of youths with their swastika T-shirts close round them, heard the slavering dog, the angry voices, and Marsha's voice, from outside the circle –

'*Mum! Mum!*'

'Harriet?'

Someone was knocking at the door: she jumped, and her eyes flew open.

'Harriet?'

'Ssssh!'

She looked at Marsha. Marsha was sleeping. Thank God. She crossed the room slowly, her limbs like lead. I am in a state of shock, she thought distantly. That is what happens to people on occasions like this.

I have never known an occasion like this.

She opened the door.

'How are you?' Christopher asked.

'Sssh!'

'Sorry.' He had a bruise on his right cheek; he was enormous, he was occupying every inch of the square of landing at the top of the stairs. 'How is she?' He was whispering now. She nodded towards the bed; he looked over her shoulder. 'Good. And you?'

'Okay.'

They went on standing there on the threshold, he looking down at her, she looking up.

She said, as she had said in the speeding *Polizei* car: 'I was a fool.'

'Stop saying that. None of us were very bright.'

Behind them, Marsha stirred. Harriet jumped. 'A brandy?' he asked her. 'Would that help?'

She shook her head. 'I don't want to leave her.'

'I'll bring you one up. Yes?'

'No. I'm a bit – I think I'll just unwind, thanks. Please tell the Scheibers again – I'm so sorry.'

'You've told them – come on, now. It's all right.'

She looked at his bruised face. 'What about you? Are you all right?'

'Terrific.' He touched his cheek. 'Could've been worse.'

'Don't. Would you do one thing for me – would you phone our hotel? Otherwise they'll think we've done a bunk.'

'You have done a bunk.' He put a hand on her shoulder. 'I'll phone them now. Sleep well.' He bent down and kissed her on the cheek – just a touch, so light from someone so heavy – and turned to go.

She said, filled with emotion, 'Thank you for rescuing Marsha.'

'I'm afraid she didn't enjoy it much.'

'She was very frightened.'

'Mmm. Goodnight.'

'Goodnight.' Harriet closed the door behind him. She stood in the middle of the room with her hands pressed to her face. She stayed like this for quite a long time, trying to collect herself, breathing deeply, listening to the quiet tick of the clock on the chest of drawers. She remembered standing in the middle of the bedroom in Brussels, the afternoon of their arrival, feeling uncertain and new; remembered Marsha tired after a long journey, dropping things on Susanna's perfect drawing-room carpet. She had settled in so quickly, after a shaky start, but then she was with her family, loved and cared for and made to feel special. Which she was. And now –

Harriet took her hands from her face and walked slowly up and down the bare floorboards. Thinking, pacing – like the man in the refugee hostel behind the wire. The wall had come down, but they were shut out of everything –

'*They are shit, they are cowards – You are a piece of rich bitch shit yourself, I think . . .*'

'*Run! Run!*'

'*Let go of me! Let go of me! You're not my father!*'

She went over to the bed and looked at her daughter, listening to her breathing as she had listened on their last night in Brussels, thinking of Christopher Pritchard, flying to Prague, wondering about him and Susanna.

Well. Now she knew. All that unhappiness, all those years ago.

And now?

'*Never again.*'

His face in the candlelight yesterday evening swam before her, she saw him a few minutes ago, standing in the doorway, taking up every inch of space, looking down at her, kissing her cheek – just a brush, just a touch.

She sank down into the wicker chair and stretched her legs out before her. She thought: this man is a potential danger to my brother, whom I love. I think that's true. He is potentially dangerous, still, to Susanna, whom I care for. No matter what he has said, I think that is also true. He has ideas I do not agree with, a past which I do not begin to come to grips with. More than all this, he threatens and disturbs my daughter, who has been my life, who is my first responsibility in everything.

And yet. She craves her father. That is clear to me now. I am not enough.

The wicker chair creaked as she leaned forward and turned off the bedside lamp. A thin pencil of light from the buildings beyond the hotel garden came through the shutters – as afternoon sunlight had shone, spinning with dust, through the half-closed shutters in the hotel dining room. Was it really only yesterday? She had sat opposite Christopher then, wanting to stretch out her arms and embrace the moment –

She thought: I am not enough for Marsha, but I must be enough. This man is an unknown quantity, still, and she dislikes him deeply: she has made that clear. I have been unforgivably selfish these last few days. She has made that clear, too.

So. That must be enough for me.

The clock ticked, the pencil of light fell upon the high iron bedstead. Harriet, in turmoil, fastened upon these two constants as if in meditation, and fell asleep.

'Mum?'

'Hello.' Harriet looked down at Marsha, snuggled up in bed beside her. 'Happy birthday. How did I get here?'

'You've still got your clothes on.'

'So I have. No wonder we're snug.'

'A bit hot.' Marsha pushed back the heavy quilt. 'I can't believe it's really my birthday.'

'It really is.' She put both arms round her. 'Dear Marsha. I can hardly believe it myself: ten whole years of having you.'

Marsha didn't say anything, and for a while they just lay there, recovering. Harriet looked at the clock. It was after eight. She could not remember – oh, yes, she could, just – waking in the small hours, stiff in the wicker chair, and climbing into bed. Her mouth felt dreadful.

'I haven't cleaned my teeth.'

'A terrible punishment will befall you,' said Marsha, sounding happier than she had done for days.

'You didn't brush yours, either. Well. Ready for some breakfast? What would you like to do today?'

'Nothing. I don't want to go anywhere or do anything. I just want to stay here and play with the kittens.'

'Okay, that sounds fine. You realise we have to go back to Schöneberg.'

'But not yet.'

'No. Not yet.' Harriet pushed the quilt right back and climbed out of bed.

'Mum? As it's my birthday – could we phone Hugh and Susanna?'

'Yes. Yes, of course.' She went to the window.

Dear God – how would it feel, now, talking to them?

She opened the shutters and looked down on the now familiar flagstoned garden: Frau Scheiber was out there, watering the plants before the heat of the day began. How could she face the Scheibers? She thought of Dieter, grabbed by the collar, yelled at, as the circle closed round them; she thought of his face blue-white in the flashing light of the *Polizei* van, as they left him standing by the roadside –

'Mum?' Marsha was sitting up in bed, her arms round her knees.

'Yes?'

'I can't stop thinking about it.'

'No,' said Harriet. 'Neither can I.'

They had a bath, and dressed in the same clothes for the third day running, and then they went slowly downstairs to breakfast. A civilised hush hung over the empty hall, and the dining room, as it had yesterday morning, but today the quietness felt to Harriet full of unspoken reproaches.

There were two or three guests down already, but Christopher was not among them. Liesel was not there, either.

'Perhaps it's her day off.'

They sat at their table and waited, and Harriet felt anxiety rise within her. The Scheibers had been kindness itself, and her foolishness had put everyone, including their nephew, in danger. How would they look on her?

She need not have worried. Frau Scheiber arrived after a few moments, with a pot of coffee. She had left them to sleep; she was leaving Herr Pritchard, also. How were they both this morning? The little one was feeling better now? It had been a terrible experience, but they were not to let it spoil their stay. Dieter? He had telephoned this morning: he was recovering, the car was in the repair garage, he sent his best wishes.

Harriet was touched – overwhelmed, even.

'You are much too kind.'

Frau Scheiber shook her head. Nonsense. What would they like for breakfast? The little one was probably hungry. Like the cat – she would like to come and feed her?

'Will you tell her it's my birthday?' Marsha asked Harriet.

Harriet conveyed the news. Frau Scheiber kissed them both. But this was special – they should have told her before! Harriet translated. Marsha slid off her chair at once.

'Where's Liesel?'

Liesel? She had gone shopping, she would be back at midday. Harriet would like coffee? Hot rolls? Very good. Marsha could help to bring them.

They left, and Harriet sat in the quiet room, listening to the pages of newspapers turned at other tables, the chink of cup on saucer, footsteps across the hall.

He was there in the doorway, he was looking round, he had crossed the room and was beside her.

'Good morning. No Marsha?'

Harriet explained, pouring coffee. He sat down, and reached for a cup from another table. The bruise had spread exotically. He said it was tender, but that he would live. And so. He drank his coffee. What did the day hold now?

'We must go back to Schöneberg,' said Harriet. 'Marsha wants to rest, and I've said we can do what she wants on her birthday, but then we must go. Did you manage to phone the hotel?'

'I did. Not a problem. I said you would ring them this morning.'

'Thank you.' She drank her coffee; very hot, very strong.

He said: 'I have meetings today, and I think I'd better go and see Dieter, but perhaps this evening – '

'This evening I must stay with Marsha.'

'Yes, yes, of course you must. And I must buy her a present.'

'Please, there's no need.'

There was a silence.

Christopher said: 'Well. Tomorrow I leave for Dresden.'

'Yes. And tomorrow we're leaving for Prague.'

'Yes. Well – I'll be there on Sunday. I'll look you up.' He pulled out his cigarettes, and tapped the packet. 'I still don't really know why you're going. We haven't had a chance to – '

She said slowly, deliberately, addressing a point in the middle distance: 'We are going to Prague to find someone I knew when I was young, and cared for very much, and have never forgotten. I very much want to see him again.'

How quiet the room was, how subdued the conversation of the other guests, how concentrated and how still and sad this moment.

'Ah.' He cleared his throat. 'So . . . yes. I see. Perhaps I should not intrude on this reunion.'

She said to the middle distance, 'You have been very kind to us. It's been lovely staying here, I am very sorry about yesterday. But now I think – '

'Okay, okay.' He had finished his coffee, and lit a cigarette, without asking. 'Not to worry.' Clouds of smoke rose into the air. 'I understand. Well. Good luck.'

'Mum?' Marsha was back again, bearing a basket of hot rolls in a snowy napkin.

'Hello, there,' said Christopher, rising. 'How's things?'

He sounded as he had sounded when they met: clumsy, full of jolly, inappropriate phrases. 'Happy birthday,' he added.

'Thank you.' Marsha put the basket on the table. She waved away smoke, and sat down.

Christopher remained standing.

'Are you not joining us for breakfast?' Harriet asked.

'I have to make a couple of phone calls. You go ahead. I expect I'll see you before you leave.'

He turned, and crossed the room, nodding to one of the other guests, passing the hawk in its glass case, passing Frau Scheiber, bringing butter and pots of jam.

Harriet watched them exchange German pleasantries, then he was gone. She thanked Frau Scheiber, she listened to Marsha talking about the kittens, she watched a thread of steam rise into the air from within the snowy napkin, and evaporate to nothing.

Marsha said: 'Today it's going to be just us?'

'Yes,' said Harriet.

'And in Prague?'

'Just us.'

They said their goodbyes in the hall. The front door was open to let in the morning sun, and it fell upon the rugs, the polished desk, and lamp and brass pinger, with its single, pleasing note. Marsha sounded it, just for fun.

'Right, then,' said Christopher, looking at his watch. His briefcase was in the other hand, and he was in a hurry.

'Marsha,' said Harriet.

Marsha came away from the desk. 'Thank you for having us.'

'My pleasure. Happy birthday once again.'

'Thank you. We're going to phone Hugh and Susanna.'

'Oh. Good. Well – give them my love.'

Herr Scheiber came out to the hall in his apron, answering the ping. Harriet explained. He wagged a finger at Marsha. She followed him back to the kitchen.

Outside, the traffic was building up. Christopher looked down at Harriet.

'Have a good trip.'

'Thanks. And you.'

He put down his briefcase, he felt in his inner pocket, he pulled out his pen, a card. She watched him go over to the desk and lean on it, writing quickly. His jacket was still crumpled and creased, he looked older, and tireder, and the bruise was very dark. As she had felt in the dining room at lunchtime two days ago – beams of sunlight, dancing dust, smoke rising softly into the air – she thought now: this is a moment I shall remember, a moment I shall look back upon, thinking: Then. *That's* when it was –

He put the cap back on his pen, he came over.

'Here. The main post office in Prague. Not far from Wenceslas Square. I'm sure you won't want to meet, but if you do need anything, you can leave a message – '

'Thank you.'

He picked up his briefcase, he went to the door.

'Goodbye, then.'

He hurried out into the street.

Birthday celebrations followed. They sat in the garden and played with the kittens, and Frau Scheiber, at mid-morning, brought Marsha a strawberry ice in a cone, and a birthday card with a picture of a girl in a check skirt on a bicycle in front of a stream, saying 'Hi!' in German. There was a large 10 embossed in gold, and long German verses, with lots of exclamation marks, in flowing italic script inside. Marsha was very pleased.

'Thank you. Danke schön.'

Then Harriet and Marsha went into the hall and sat at the polished desk, and telephoned Brussels.

'Hugh first.'

Harriet's heart was pounding, but Hugh was out, today, at a meeting in Antwerp. Marsha's face fell. They tried the apartment. Please, willed Harriet, please don't answer. Susanna did not answer. Her cool light voice came over the answering machine, in English and French.

'Hello,' said Marsha. 'It's my birthday. I miss you. We'll phone you from Prague – ' she looked questioningly at Harriet, who nodded. Anything, anything. 'Goodbye. Thank you for having us. We met – '

'Okay,' said Harriet, taking the receiver. 'There's no need to waste money.'

Marsha looked at her. 'It's my *birthday*.'

'I know. I'm sorry. There's a present from them in my suitcase.'

'*Is* there?'

Liesel came in through the open front door with her shopping.

'Tell her,' said Marsha.

Harriet told her.

Marsha's birthday? She was ten? But wait a minute –

She went out, and they went back to the garden. Liesel returned, with a present, wrapped in flowery paper and tied in green ribbon. Marsha unwrapped a T-shirt, printed all over with postcard views of the city.

'It's lovely.' She held it up against her. 'Will you come and visit us in London?' she asked Liesel. 'You could be one of our lodgers.'

Now there was a thought.

Harriet went to pay their bill, and Herr Scheiber told her that Herr Pritchard had already settled their account.

'But – ' She could not speak. She sat in the empty, sunlit dining room and wrote a letter, and tore it up. She wrote one to Dieter, instead, full of apologies.

They had lunch in the garden, and then they said goodbye to the cat and the kittens, who could not, please be reasonable, come with them to Prague, and goodbye to the Scheibers, and Harriet gave them the letter for Dieter.

And then they walked out of the hotel in the heat of the afternoon, and through the narrow streets of Prenzlauer Berg.

'And now I must buy you a present,' said Harriet.

'But where? But what?'

'I really don't know. I really don't know how I can have been so hopeless. What a mother. I somehow thought, that when we got to Berlin – '

'Things are almost always different from how you imagine, aren't they?'

It was true, it was true.

They walked along the cobbles hand in hand; they came, in a while, to Kollwitz Platz. It was very hot now; they sat on a bench beneath trees, and talked, watching the afternoon café life go on.

Marsha said: 'Tell me again about when I was born.'

Harriet said: 'It was hot, like today, and I'd woken at four in the morning. I walked round the house – '

'Without waking Daddy – '

'Without waking Daddy – ' Harriet stopped. Dear God. She put out her hands in front of her: left, right. On the left was the house in darkness, the dawn beginning to break, the birds to wake. She stopped on the landing, feeling another contraction – so that's what they were like: breathe, breathe – straightening up again, hearing Martin turn over in bed and sigh. She went downstairs and out to the garden, walking up and down as the sky began to lighten, waiting for her life to change. There was that. There was then. And on her right hand was now: a hot afternoon in Berlin, with a ten-year-old daughter beside her, ten whole years of just the two of them in between. And in the last few days –

Well. It was still just the two of them. That's how it was.

'Go on,' said Marsha. 'Why have you stopped?'

'I'm thinking.'

'Go on.'

'Sorry. So. At about six o'clock I made tea, and took some up to Daddy, and woke him, and told him you were on the way – '

'And he was very pleased.'

'He was. He drove us to the hospital, and he stayed with me all the time, and he saw you being born – '

'At quarter-past four in the afternoon.'

'Exactly. The most beautiful baby in the entire world.'

Marsha leaned over and looked at Harriet's watch. 'That's in two hours' time.'

So it was.

'I know what I want for my birthday. A watch.'

Of course. Just the right age. They went off to look for one. It was too hot to think about taking the U-Bahn: they walked through to Prenzlauer Allee, and down towards Alexanderplatz. Prenzlauer Allee was tree-lined and full of shops, less daunting than the Ku'damm. They found a jeweller's, they found a watch. It was small, with a gold face and a white strap, and it suited Marsha perfectly. She wore it out of the shop and couldn't stop looking at it.

'Now it's an hour and a quarter till I was born.'

'So it is.'

They came into Alexanderplatz, with its crowds and its stalls in the shadow of the television tower.

'I know what I'd like to do,' said Marsha.

'What?'

'Go up that thing. Go to the top.'

Harriet gazed upwards. Two hundred metres of concrete column rose towards the summer sky. A globe turned slowly, transmitters clung to it, an aerial pierced the blue. 'Are you sure?'

'Yes. Don't you think it would be fun?'

They took the lift up, up. There were other tourists: Marsha told two Australians she was ten, and showed them her watch. They said that was brilliant, they thought it was neat. At the top was a viewing platform. They all got out. There was quite a wind up here.

Harriet and Marsha stood side by side and looked far out over the city. They looked towards the East, its tower blocks and tenements stretching far into the distance. Somewehere over there was Marzahn, and Dieter's factory. Tomorrow they would be travelling much further east, to a new city. They went round the viewing platform and looked west, along the straight, beautiful boulevard of the Unter den Linden, with the ordered, pleasing lines of old Berlin on either side.

Marsha looked at her watch. 'And now I was born,' she said.

'So you were.' Harriet kissed her. 'Happy birthday. You do know I love you, don't you?'

'Yes.' Marsha leaned against her, the wind blew her hair across her face. She said: 'I just wish – you know.'

'About Daddy?'

'Yes.'

'I'm sorry,' said Harriet. 'It's just how it is.'

'I know.'

Summer clouds drifted over the sun.

'Anyway,' said Marsha. 'Tomorrow we're going to Prague.'

'Yes. Are you excited?'

'Yes. How long do you think it'll take us to find Karel?'

'I don't know. We might not find him.'

'I bet we do.'

'Dear Marsha.'

'And if we do – '

'Then we'll see,' said Harriet.

'That's what grown-ups always say.'

The wind blew, the clouds moved on, the sun shone over Berlin. Harriet could just see the Brandenburg Gate, where Rosa Luxemburg had made speeches, where there had been a wall. She thought: as the West to the East, all those Cold War years, so Karel to me, perhaps, all this time. Beyond the wall there is something to dream of, offering hope.

PRAGUE

Leaves falling, supplication

I

A bell was ringing, a single mellow note sounding across the terracotta rooftops of the Little Quarter, bathed in evening sunlight. Marsha was leaning out of their gabled window. Harriet put her box of letters on top of the edge of the chest of drawers. Sun caught the edge of the wood.

'Come and look,' said Marsha, at the window.

Harriet joined her. The buildings were crammed together; tiny dark courtyards huddled beneath; electricity cables were strung from housetop to housetop. They looked down on pitched pantiled roofs, the fantails of gables, on skylights, tall chimneys, clay gutters, peeling stucco. The sun was low, the bell rang steadily, a haze hung over the city.

'It's lovely,' said Marsha.

'Isn't it? Aren't we lucky to have a room here?'

Their train from Berlin had pulled in after five hours to the station in Holesovice, an industrial suburb in the questioning curve of the river Vltava; they had taken a taxi, a first-day luxury, following the road winding along the embankment, gazing out over the broad river, the bridges, the domes and spires of the Old Town churches across the water. The hotels there were for rich Americans; those on the city's perimeter were modern and ugly, a ring of cheap skyscrapers beneath the forested hills beyond. Their taxi had brought them to the pension room Harriet had booked through Cedok in London last spring: impossible, had she not done so, to have found space here, in the shadow of the castle, in a quarter where everyone wanted to stay. She gave a passing thought to their arrival in Berlin, and the disappointment of the Hotel Kloster, and patted herself on the back: this time she'd got it right.

'Where does Karel live?'

'If he's still at his old address, it's across the river.' Harriet leaned on the narrow windowsill. The unpainted wood was rotting: you could pick little bits of it away. 'We'll go and knock on his door tomorrow.'

'I can't wait to meet him.' Marsha had discovered the rotting wood also, and was flicking small, picked-out pieces down into the gutter. Harriet stopped her.

'And please don't be too disappointed if we can't find him.'

Marsha stopped picking, and looked at her. 'Won't you be disappointed?'

'Yes, of course.'

'Well, then.' She yawned.

'Shall we have a rest?' Harriet felt suddenly that she could do no more. 'And then we'll go and look at the river and have something to eat.'

'Okay.'

They lay on high iron beds with creaking springs. The ceiling sloped steeply, and the room, even with the window open, was close and warm. They talked sleepily, with long pauses.

'Everywhere we stay is nicer than the last place.' Marsha was yawning again. 'Except for the Hotel Kloster. But the Hotel Scheiber was better than Brussels, and this is the best of all.'

'Why?'

'I like being up in an attic. I like the rooftops.' The bedsprings creaked as she changed position. 'I'm thirsty, though.'

'We have to be a bit careful here,' said Harriet. 'Everyone drinks mineral water.'

'Why?'

'There's a lot of pollution. In the air, in the water.'

'That's why Hugh's giving money for that thing. That pollution thing, that sulphur thing.'

'Yes. How clever of you to remember. In the Krušne Hory mountains. We might go and look at it.'

'Why did I speak?'

'I'll try not to drag you about too much.'

'Good.'

'But I do want us to see – '

'Everything. I know.'

After that, there was silence. Harriet lay watching Marsha fall asleep. She watched a fly sail into the room and sail out again. She looked at the sloping whitewashed ceiling, at their open cases on the dusty bare floor, the crucifix above the chest or drawers, the box of letters. They were here, she had done it. She closed her eyes, summoning images of the city – from her reading, from photographs, from her lined black notebook, tipped in Chinese red.

Prague was chalk and pastel colours, gleams of gold, rippling terra-cotta. It was washed-out blue and faded rose; copper-green domes and dark slate towers. It was the façades of medieval houses painted in shades of parchment and linen, coffee and cream and ochre. It was five medieval towns, one a ghetto, on the east and west banks of the river; the centre of a holy empire under a visionary king who gave his name to the Charles Bridge. It had not become one city until the end of the eighteenth century.

Prague was a castle and cathedral on a forested hill; it was Roman-esque and Gothic, Renaissance and baroque, onion domes and soaring spires, intricate turrets and gabled roofs; art nouveau avenues modelled on Parisian boulevards, cobbled alleys and quiet squares. It was bells, ringing across the city, it was string quartets in churches, it was Mozart, Mozart, Mozart. He had visited Prague four times in the last four years of his life, overjoyed by his reception. *Figaro* had flopped in Vienna, but the Czechs loved it, whistling arias in the streets.

Fairytale, musical, picture-book Prague.

The capital city of Bohemia, one of the most polluted quarters of Europe. Behind the parchment and ochre façades was rot and decay, and the water was unfit for drinking. Along the border with East Germany clouds of sulphur rose into the sky from factory chimneys, and the trees were stripped bare by acid rain.

'The countryside in northern Bohemia is choking to death ... the children have to stay indoors in winter ... we're financing a loan for a plant in the Krušne Hory mountains ...'

Harriet heard Marsha's breathing, steady and light. She turned over, thinking of their twin-bedded room in Brussels, the acres of pale carpet, the padded headboards and gilt mirrors, the sound, late at night, of Susanna, weeping. She thought of the conversation with Hugh, his laid-back enthusiasm for this project, his casual mention of a casual encounter with an old school contemporary, coming to dinner. She saw the hotel in Berlin, and Christopher hurrying out into the street, with a curt goodbye, and she felt a wave of sadness and confusion, blotting it out at once by returning to Prague, its history and her expectations.

The past has become more to me than my own life –

Well. Perhaps there were very good reasons for that.

Prague was a Protestant martyr, burned at the stake. Jan Hus, the university rector, preaching against a corrupt papacy. In 1415 his death ignited two hundred years of war.

Prague, centuries later, was tormented, emaciated Kafka, who once described himself as a memory come alive. He was born and died in the Old Town – 'the most beautiful setting that has ever been seen on this earth' – but for a while, in the winter of 1916, he rented a house in Golden Lane, here in the Little Quarter, writing all night and walking back across the Charles Bridge to go home and sleep.

Prague was Alexander Dubcek, whose sweet, charismatic smile showed liberalism to the world for a few brief months in 1968, when Harriet and Karel had met. By the last week of August he was lying drugged and incoherent in a back room in the Kremlin.

Prague was a bitter January day in 1969, a human torch in Wenceslas Square, where a young philosophy student stood next to a fountain and poured a can of petrol over himself. When he died, three days later, Dubcek – back from Moscow, humiliated, clinging to the last shreds of authority – ordered black flags to be hung throughout the city.

Prague was Charter 77. It was Vaclav Havel, one of its signatories, in and out of prison. It was thousands of East Germans in the autumn of 1989, besieging the German Embassy here in the Little Quarter, camping out in the gardens, demanding the right to travel freely. It was the heady days after the fall of the Berlin Wall a few weeks later, a student demonstration brutally suppressed, a Velvet Revolution.

In the cold days of that November, Dubcek returned from banishment. He smiled from the balcony of the national Museum overlooking Wenceslas Square, on the thousands ringing handbells in the snow, and Harriet, in London, watched it all on television and reread her bundle of letters by the fire.

Prague was a playwright president installed in grand offices in the Castle. For 900 korunas you could now have bed and breakfast in Havel's old prison cell. Prague was liberated, Prague was westernised, the ring of cheap hotels was built round the perimeter, and everyone's aunt let rooms.

And here they were, in one of them. All this way, after all this time.

Prague was Karel, returning, leaving Harriet to walk with awful slowness home from school, all through the autumn of 1968, changing her briefcase from hand to hand, watching damp leaves pile up in the garden square and smoke rise thinly towards the trees. Her footsteps dragged as she came to the house ...

– *dreading the rack of expectation, and the sick collapse of disappointment*

. . . I suppose animals kept in cages, and so scantily fed as to be always on the verge of famine, await their food as I awaited a letter . . .

She climbed the steps, she rang the bell, she gave the merest glance towards the hall table as her mother let her in.

'Had a good day?'

'Fine, thanks.'

'Much homework?'

'Quite a bit.'

It wasn't there, it wasn't there. He had forgotten her. Well. She had tea, she went upstairs to her room, she worked. On a wet night in April, the following year, she sat in the striped armchair by her bedroom window reading black pen on thin paper.

London seems a very long way from me now. Since my return life has been – I hope to study law again one day, but at present I am working as a porter – I think of you . . .

The fly who had sailed out through the open window had returned, and was buzzing. Harriet sleepily opened her eyes. The beam of light which had touched the edge of the box of letters had moved, holding the whole box now. Seeing this, hearing the summer sound of the fly, and the bell beyond the rooftops, she was put in mind all at once of another film seen on a long-ago evening in London, down at the NFT: an Italian film, following the life of a village through the seasons. An old man in a clean white shirt put his dead wife's wedding ring into a box on a chest of drawers, and put his own beside it, preparing for death. He left the house and walked along a flowery path in high summer. The rings lay next to each other, gleaming in the sun at the bedroom window. A whole life together.

The room was warm, the bell rang steadily, the fly had gone. Harriet closed her eyes and slept.

The air was balmy and still when they left the pension. They bought two bottles of mineral water from a dark little shop on the corner, and wandered through the streets in the general direction of Malostranské Square. The Little Quarter was full of charm: hilly cobbled streets, with here an arch, there a sudden, surprising descent of steps, an elaborate gateway or shady courtyard. The streets were narrow, but the houses fine – pleasing, regular, eighteenth-century facades bathed in the deepening evening light. Every now and then they came to a little square, or broader thoroughfare, from where they were able to look up the hill towards the castle, and the soaring Gothic pinnacles of St Vitus Cathedral. Strains of Mozart floated now and then from open café doorways. *Don Giovanni* was completed and premièred here, and here, while Mozart lay in a pauper's grave in Vienna, four thousand people stood in the aisles of the great baroque St Nicholas Church, listening to his *Requiem Mass*.

St Nicholas towered over and divided Malostranské Square: Harriet and Marsha, drinking their mineral water, taking their time, could see ahead of them its mighty copper dome and tower, overshadowing a cobbled hill lined with tramways. Awnings still shaded the café tables spilling on to the pavements, shops were still open, the last of the day's tourists were coming down the hill from the castle, stopping for a drink or making their way through the square towards Mostecka, the long sloping street which led to the Charles Bridge. Marsha and Harriet followed them, seeing the gleam of the sunset on water, passing through an arch between two massive Gothic gateways.

Black-headed gulls wheeled above the cobbled bridge, and over the broad Vltava. Barges rocked on their moorings, swans drifted beneath the buttressed arches, and a procession of stone saints all along the parapets stood in silhouete against the sinking sun. On the far side were the clustered buildings, the towers and spires and domes of the Old Town. For four hundred years this medieval bridge had been the only link between the two settlements. It had been a trade route, a battle ground in the Thirty Years War, a place of execution for Protestant martyrs. Now, as the sun fell on the water, a path of gold, it was crowded with students, with tourists, with hawkers and buskers.

A young man with a violin was playing *Eine kleine Nachtmusik*, very fast and not very well, but the effect even so was tuneful and light. People were wandering amongst stalls of painted eggs, postcards, secondhand books, a hot-dog stand. Everyone, it seemed, had a bottle of mineral water, and no one was in a hurry. The gulls wheeled, the sun sank lower, the violinist changed his tune to a slow and gentle air which floated out over the water.

'I feel happy,' said Marsha.

'Yes,' said Harriet, 'so do I.'

They found a space betwen two statues on the parapet, next to one of the tall, copper-topped street lamps; they leaned on the stone, looking out over the river, spanned by bridge after bridge. To the south the right bank was lined with the buildings of the Old Town, the New

Town, the suburb of Vysehrad; to the north it made a great, questioning meander, in whose curve lay Josefov, the old Jewish quarter, a once-walled ghetto whose slums had been razed to the ground at the end of the nineteenth century. A synagogue remained; so did the old cemetery, an overcrowded plot of broken headstones which Harriet intended to visit, Marsha permitting. She also intended to visit Kafka's grave, in the New Jewish Cemetery in Žižkov, near to where Karel's family had their apartment. Palach, also, was buried near there. Tomorrow, she thought, watching the lazy progress of swans, tomorrow I shall be walking along the street from where Karel used to write to me. I shall find his apartment building, I shall ring the bell . . .

Someone had lit a cigarette, and the smoke drifted past her. She turned, and saw a little stall selling packets of Marlboro – 'Cheap Americans' – and for a moment her heart turned over.

Karel, lighting up in a long-ago summer, held the precious western cigarette between long thin fingers, inhaling, looking at her across a cheap brown table. He held her in his arms as they lay on an Indian cotton bedspread.

'There must be many beautiful girls in Czechoslovakia.'

'That is true. But none of them called Harriet.'

She felt herself on the threshold of a journey, which began with the expression in his eyes and ended – where would it end?

There it was: the reason for her journey now, the moment which had brought her and Marsha halfway across Europe, to lean on the parapet of the Charles Bridge on a heavenly summer evening, filled with expectation.

And then there was someone else who smoked – far too heavily, embracing its danger – and Harriet, looking out over the water, recalled moments in the dining room of the Hotel Scheiber, the smoke wreathing in and out of a shaft of sunlight, a candle flame, a heavy, serious face across the table.

'I suppose I did hit rock bottom . . . There's still a side of me which is – well, I suppose you could call it dangerous . . . Getting high on a risk – it's in my blood . . . But never again.' He smiled at her, a smile full of warmth and liking. *'And now I have told you the worst, and now you know.'*

Smoke drifted through the candlelight. She thought: I am on the brink. We are on the brink –

Žižkov was set on a hill, a mixed district of nineteenth-century working-class tenement housing and postwar rebuilding, where new streets of skyscrapers and lingering cobbled alleys climbed to a strip of green. To the north, the strip overlooked the district of Karlin and the bend in the river; to the south was a windswept expanse of cemeteries. On this hill the Hussites had won their first battle; from this hill you could see much of the city spread out before you. Or you could do that by taking the lift to the top of a smooth grey television tower, in the south-west corner of the district, as Marsha and Harriet had done in Berlin, feeling the summer wind on their faces as they slowly revolved above Alexanderplatz.

They did not do that here. They came out of the metro station next along the line from the tower – Flora, on the corner of the cemetery – and began to climb the hill, walking up Jirinska, broad and straight and tree-lined. The cemetery was endless: row upon row of graves and tombstones crisscrossed by cobbled paths: how to begin to find Kafka's? Well, that was for later. Harriet looked at her Cedok map, searching for Baranova Street. It wasn't hard to find on the grid: they turned left, walking a couple of blocks, turning into a featureless thoroughfare where a local tram was humming to a halt. She checked the map once more. The centre was richly decorated with little symbols for churches and restaurants and museums, but here, apart from the cemeteries, was mostly as ordinary as the district itself – much as the winding streets of the Little Quarter had early this morning already been crowded with tourists, while here they were mostly among families doing the weekend shopping. She stepped aside for a young mother with a pushchair, and said to Marsha, 'Karel's street is just off the next block. We turn right.'

'He'd better be there, he'd better be there, if he isn't there I'll die.' Marsha skipped along the pavement.

'It's Saturday morning,' said Harriet calmly. 'It's a good time to find people in.' And a bad time to disturb them, after a hard week. She followed Marsha round the corner, keeping a measured pace, feeling her heart racing.

'What number, what number, what number did you say?'

'Slow down, calm down, you're making me terribly nervous.'

'You're terribly nervous already.'

'Nonsense.' Harriet looked about her. This street was narrower than Baranova, impassable for a tram or indeed anything but a small car or motorbike. It was quiet, with few people about, the morning sun slanting thinly from the far end on to windows where the curtains were still drawn, and narrow brick balconies where one or two women were taking down washing, or watering plants. A child ran out of a doorway and ran back in again; a man came out of a shop, opening his paper as he walked along the street, stopping to light a cigarette. Everyone smoked in Prague. Harriet glanced at his paper as he lit up and walked on. *Céský Expres*, a cheerful-looking tabloid. Žižkov had been a communist heartland even before the war: until a few years ago everyone would have been reading *Rude Prâvo*, the Party paper. Now, the fashionable broadsheet was *Lidove Noviny*, a samizdat publication all through the 1970s and 1980s, when many of its contributors, like Havel, had been signatories to Charter 77. These days it was revamped, readily available – she'd seen it at the metro kiosk this morning, amongst English-language papers like the *Prague Post,* and the dozens of western magazines.

What did Karel read? What had he been doing, all these years? He had grown up in this quiet, ordinary back street, a child of the working class for whose Party-member parents communism had turned sour, who had through his studies climbed into the intelligentsia, and made the classic trip to the West. And there he had met a nice young English girl . . .

A dog ran out of an alleyway; someone went past on a bike. Marsha reached for the map in Harriet's hand and turned it so she could read the address written upon the corner.

'Six/eight. What does that mean?'

'House number six, apartment number eight.' Harriet felt sick. They were intruders, they were unwanted. If they had been wanted, he would have answered her letter. To turn up on the doorstep uninvited and unannounced –

'Mum,' said Marsha, giving the map back, 'we're visiting, that's all. Don't look so dreadful and doomy.'

'Sorry. Do I?'

'Yes. If it's a problem we have a cup of coffee and go away again, okay?' She took her hand in motherly fashion, and led her along the street.

Harriet smiled at her weakly. 'How right you are. How wonderful you are. Of course. That's just what we'll do.'

'And here we are,' said Marsha.

They stood before the door.

It was dark blue, and needed repainting. Set into the wall alongside were the bells to ten apartments. Marsha looked questioningly at Harriet, reached up and pressed number eight. There was a buzz, a silence, a receiver lifted. A woman's voice.

'Yes?' She sounded as though she were under water. 'Hello?'

Harriet summoned guidebook phrases. 'Good morning. Excuse me. I am from England.'

'From England?'

'Yes. From England. I am looking for Karel Miluvić.'

'Karel is not here. He is – '

Harriet could not understand where he was.

'I'm sorry?'

'He is – '

Incomprehensible, beyond the guidebook. She said slowly: 'I am sorry. I do not understand.'

There was a sigh, another unintelligible murmur. Then the buzzer sounded, and the door gave a click, and opened. Marsha and Harriet looked at one another, and went inside.

They found themselves in a chilly hall, beneath a winding stairwell. Doors to two apartments were to the right and left; light fell from a landing window. Far above a door was opened, and the woman's voice came down towards them.

'Come up, please.'

They climbed the stone stairs, their footsteps loud and echoing. The metal handrail was painted green; the air felt cold and damp, acrid with stale cigarette smoke. They came to the second floor, the third. On the fourth landing the door to a dark interior was held open.

The woman at the doorway was in her late sixties. She was thickset; she wore a wraparound print pinafore over a brown polo-neck jumper and drooping skirt; her grey hair was plaited round her head. She looked at Harriet and Marsha with sharp dark eyes.

'Yes?'

'From London,' Harriet said again, panting after the climb. 'Karel's friend. I am Harriet.' She gestured towards herself, and then to Marsha. 'My – ' but she could not remember 'daughter', nor 'child'. 'Marsha,' she said, recovering her breath.

Footsteps sounded in the dark interior. The woman regarded Marsha and said something. From behind her came a child's voice in answer, and then a girl with long dark plaits and a bright, lively face appeared at the doorway. She looked at them, and they looked at her, and Harriet felt a quarter of a century tilt backwards and swing, like a great slice out of a clock, spinning her back to a summer's day and a basement room, and a lean, dark, lovely face gazing at her, as his daughter – so like, so unmistakably, perfectly like – was gazing at them now.

'Gabrielle,' said the woman, and then, pointing at herself, 'Hannah.'

Gabrielle smiled at Marsha.

'I learn little English.' She looked enquiringly up at her grand-mother, who nodded. 'Please to come in.'

They sat at the table in a cramped tiled kitchen, and Karel's mother put coffee in a saucepan on the stove, moving slowly to a rack of shelves on the wall for cups. The kitchen was at the end of the passage and was unexpectedly sunny and light, with a large window taking up most of the end wall, overlooking the trees on Jičinská Street, bordering the cemetery. Harriet, looking out, saw passing traffic, distant rows of graves. She looked back again, smelling strong, reheated coffee.

It was set before them, with a plate of fat iced biscuits. Hannah sat down heavily, saying something. Harriet caught Karel's name again.

'My father is working,' Gabrielle translated. 'His bureau is in Nove Mesto – New Town.'

'Oh. Thank you.' Harriet smiled at her. She was sitting next to Marsha, politely passing biscuits. Marsha regarded them with interest, taking a pink one. She looked at Gabrielle.

'How old are you?'

'How old? Eleven years. You?'

'Ten. I was ten in Berlin.'

'Berlin?' Hannah frowned. 'London?'

'Yes, but – ' Harriet stopped. How to convey it all? To say that she had been making a kind of pilgrimage across Europe in search of Gabrielle's father? It wasn't possible. 'We are on our holidays,' she said simply. 'Travelling. We just wanted to see if perhaps Karel – '

Gabrielle translated. Hannah looked carefully at Harriet.

'How – how you know him?'

'A long time ago,' Harriet said slowly, drinking her coffee. It was bitter, and very hot. 'A long story. I wrote to him to tell him we were coming, but perhaps he did not get my letter.'

Hannah turned to Gabrielle, who was clearly enjoying her role. She translated, then said to Harriet: 'I speak little English, my grandmother tiny, tiny.' She held up finger and thumb.

'And my Czech even smaller,' said Harriet, putting her own finger and thumb even more closely together. They all smiled: agreeably, feeling their way with strangers.

'My father's English is good.' Gabrielle spread her hands wide. 'But I do not think a letter came.' She shrugged. 'You would like to telephone the bureau?'

'I – ' Harriet took a moment to think about this, and Marsha seized it.

'Where is your mother?' she asked Gabrielle.

'My mother? She is at the bureau also. They are working together, they are both – ' She frowned, her English failing her. 'Wait, please.' She pushed back her chair and went out to the long corridor.

Harriet and Marsha looked at one another, and although Harriet was concentrating hard on keeping her own face neutral she remembered for a long time the expression on Marsha's: an unguarded moment in which sadness and disappointment were clearly visible, quickly wiped away. Had she really hoped for so much?

Gabrielle was back again, carrying things.

'Law–yers,' she said, thumbing the pages of a dictionary, stumbling over the pronunciation. 'They are both.'

'Lawyers,' said Marsha, having a look.

'Yes.' From underneath the dictionary, carefully held, Gabrielle withdrew a photograph – small, in a brown frame. She set it up on the table. 'My – '

'Parents,' said Marsha flatly.

'Yes. Before I am born.'

Harriet and Marsha, on opposite sides of the table, leaned across. They looked at the photograph and the young couple there looked back at them, smiling radiantly. He, in a jacket and tie, was tall and dark and lean, his hair rather long, as if in the Sixties; she, leaning against his shoulder, had shining fair hair in a bob. She wore a cheap-looking

226

white suit, and lipstick; she carried a bunch of flowers. They were outside a modern building which must be a register office.

'Their wedding day,' Harriet said slowly, looking at this different version of Karel, with his would-be western hair, a decade after everyone in the West had been to the barber. 'Very nice. When?'

Gabrielle tried and failed, she found a pen on the cabinet and wrote it down inside her dictionary, in neat continental writing.

'1980,' read Harriet, and smiled at her. 'It's a very nice photograph,' she said again.

'Thank you.' Gabrielle picked it up. 'They are divorce now,' she said calmly. 'They divorce when I am six.'

'Oh. Oh, I see.'

There was a silence. Well. Well, then. The morning lay ahead.

Across the table Marsha said: 'My parents are divorced, too.'

'Yes? They are friendly?'

'No. I never see my father.'

'Marsha – '

'Mine are friendly,' said Gabrielle. She translated all this for her grandmother, whose expression was unreadable. She turned back to Marsha. 'You come to see my room?'

'Yes.' She looked at Harriet. 'Yes?'

'Of course. And then perhaps – '

Marsha glanced at her watch as she got down. Gabrielle asked if she was in a hurry.

'No. I just like looking at it. It's my birthday present, we bought it in Berlin.'

Gabrielle admired it. They went companionably out of the kitchen. Well. How nice.

Harriet finished her coffee. Hannah offered more, with a gesture. She offered biscuits. Harriet shook her head.

'No, thank you. You are very kind.'

They looked at one another.

Hannah was like Karel, just as Gabrielle was like him, mostly in the eyes: dark, intent, expressive. The build was very different: height and leanness must come from his father. Harriet didn't like to ask about his father.

Giggles came from along the corridor.

'Nice girl,' Hannah said with difficulty.

'*Dekuje*. Thank you. Gabrielle also. Very nice.'

Another silence. Now what?

'Karel . . . ' A struggle. 'Bureau. You . . . ' Hannah made telephone gestures, looking at Harriet enquiringly.

A rush of adrenalin. Well – yes. Why not? 'Please,' she said. 'If you give me the number – '

Hannah rose; Harriet followed her out of the kitchen. They went down the dark corridor. Kilims hung on the walls; there were brown-painted doors. More giggles: they looked into Gabrielle's room.

'Hello.'

'Hi.' Marsha, looking happier than Harriet had seen her all holiday, was curled up next to Gabrielle on a bed pushed up against the wall. They were sharing a comic. Posters of pop stars were on the wall, there was a crowded bookcase, with more photographs on the top, a desk at the window, a rug on the floor.

'How snug.'

'Snug?' asked Gabrielle, and her accent made the word sound so comical that they all burst out laughing.

'Snug?' mimicked Marsha.

The two girls clutched at each other.

Harriet left them to it, following Hannah to a sitting room at the far end. The room was neatly kept, furnished with a mixture of what looked like Fifties armchairs and shiny sideboard, and rugs which might have come from Habitat. Enormous house plants stood at the balcony window, an ancient black telephone stood on a spindly table, with a worn address book.

'I speak.' Hannah picked up the phone and dialled, and Harriet, now, was no longer trying to suppress a tide of nervous excitement. Hannah was answered, she asked for Karel; she explained the situation. Harriet needed no Czech to understand: visitor from London – a little girl like Gabrielle, yes – her own name, with a heavy accent, an astonished silence. Yes, yes, it was Harriet. Hannah passed the receiver with a smile.

'Hello?'

'Harriet?'

'Karel?'

'It is really you?'

'It is really me. I – ' she stopped, overwhelmed by nerves. Hannah was quietly leaving the room. 'How are you?' she asked. 'It's a very long time – '

'It is for ever.' He was laughing, he was delighted. 'What are you doing in Prague?'

I came to look for you – No.

'I'm on holiday. I'm a teacher, we have a long summer break. I brought my daughter.' She swallowed. 'You didn't get my letter?'

'Your letter? From university? I remember. You gave me – ' A hesitation. 'The brush-off? The boot? I have the right expression?'

'Oh, Karel – '

Since it is so hard for us to communicate, perhaps it is better that we do not try . . . I shall always remember you with affection . . .

How could she have done that? Hurrying across the campus, dropping it into a letterbox, forgetting all about him –

'Not that letter. I wrote to you quite recently, early in the year, when I was planning this journey – '

'I did not receive it. If I had received it I would have replied, naturally. So – ' She could sense him glance at his watch. 'I am working now, but we must meet.'

'Yes, yes, I'm sorry to disturb you. What – have you got time to tell me what you are doing now? You are a lawyer, you finished your studies. I'm so pleased.'

'Yes. I shall tell you more when we meet. The telephone is not always such a good idea – '

'Of course. Well – ' Should she go to his office, or was that an intrusion? Would his friendly ex-wife mind a visit from the past?

'Listen. If you stay there, my mother will look after you. I come home for lunch on Saturdays.'

'That would be lovely. Thank you.'

'And your daughter? She and Gabrielle are friends?'

'They seem to be.'

'What is she called?'

'Marsha.'

'Marsha. It is a diminutive?'

'No. It's just Marsha.' She hesitated. 'Her father chose it.'

'And he is with you now, your husband?'

'No, no. We separated a long time ago.'

'I see. Well – I shall finish here at just after one – I'll be home by two. Yes? That suits you? Or perhaps you have other plans for this afternoon?'

'No. No other plans. That would be fine.' She looked at her watch. Perhaps, in the intervening hours, she could visit Kafka's grave.

'You can visit Kafka's grave,' said Karel. 'Would it interest you?'

'Yes. I was just thinking that.'

'Naturally. It is like this always. No one comes to visit me, they come only for Kafka.'

She smiled. 'It's in the New Jewish Cemetery, isn't it? Will I find it all right?'

'There are signs in five languages.'

'Ah. And Palach?'

'He is in the Olsanska Cemetery nearby – you have a map for all this sightseeing? Good. There are janitors, they will show you Palach.'

'Good. Thank you. I shall visit them both.' She could hear another phone ring in his office. 'I must let you go. I'll look forward to seeing you.'

'And I you, also. Now if you will kindly pass me my mother – '

Harriet went down the long dark corridor to fetch her. The girls in the bedroom were quietly content, she could feel it. As Hannah returned to the telephone, she put her head round their door.

'Snug as a bug in a rug?'

They were helpless.

'Listen,' said Harriet, as they rolled. 'Marsha. Listen, please. I've spoken to Karel – '

'What?' She stopped laughing and shot upright. 'What happened? What did he say?'

Harriet explained things. 'And until Hannah is kind enough to give us lunch, I thought I'd go for a walk, if she doesn't mind, and visit the cemetery.'

'That sounds fun.'

'Kafka,' said Gabrielle. 'Everyone comes to see this grave.'

'Would you like to come with me?' Harriet asked. 'Marsha – would you like – '

Marsha looked at her. 'Do I have to?'

'No, but – '

'I can stay here.' She turned to Gabrielle. 'Can I?'

'You do not know this writer?' Gabrielle looked at her with mock severity.

'What did he write?'

'*The Castle* – '

'The same castle near where we are staying,' Harriet put in, hearing the telephone being put down, and Hannah returning. 'Up on the hill behind us.'

230

'*The Trial*,' continued Gabrielle. '*Metamorphosis*.'

'What?'

'You do not know this story? It is about a man who wakes in the morning and finds he is a fly.'

Marsha looked at her. They almost fell off the bed.

'Idiot,' said Harriet, with affection. Hannah was beside her. 'Gabrielle, your services, please. Will you be kind enough – listen – will you be kind enough to explain to your grandmother? And thank her very much for having us?'

Gabrielle explained. Marsha spluttered.

'You're hysterical,' said Harriet.

'And you're historical.' She wiped her eyes.

'Very funny. So. I shall leave you to it?'

'Please.'

Out in the corridor, Harriet, on impulse, took Hannah's hand. 'Thank you. You are very kind.'

'Please. Nothing. We eat – ' she pointed to her watch, indicating one o'clock.

Harriet nodded, and went to the front door. For a moment, as she closed it behind her, and began the descent of the echoing stairwell, she wondered: was it all right? Leaving Marsha with strangers, people they'd barely met? Well, yes it was. They did not feel like strangers.

'Mum?' A voice from above, a sudden dash of footsteps. She stopped abruptly, turning. Marsha came flying down towards her.

'Hey – '

'It's all right. Just – you don't mind, do you? Going off on your own?'

'Oh, Marsha – '

They stood on the stairs and hugged.

'My dear companion,' said Harriet. 'Thank you. Yes, I'll be fine. I've dragged you round quite enough for a bit, haven't I?'

'So long as you're okay.' A pause. 'She's nice, isn't she?'

'Gabrielle? She's lovely, yes. Go on, off you go and enjoy yourself. I'll see you soon.'

'And then we'll see Karel.'

'And then we'll see Karel.' She felt light with anticipation.

'Did he sound nice?'

'Very nice.'

A last hug, and Marsha raced back up the stairs.

Harriet continued her descent, passing closed doors, smelling the cold, unpleasantly acrid air. The windows on the landings were grimy, cigarette butts lay on the stairs. Everyone smoked in Prague.

'They're sexy as hell, and they kill you – what do I care?'

She pushed away the memory, going out into the street.

'What have I in common with the Jews? I have scarcely anything in common with myself.'

Dandelion seeds drifted on a summer breeze across the New Jewish Cemetery. Despite the breeze, it was warmer than when Harriet and Marsha had set out this morning, and the air smelt faintly of buttercups and hay as Harriet walked down the long path to the right of the entrance, following signs. The cemetery was large and quiet; untended and almost empty. Ivy tumbled over headstones, tall weeds grew amidst uncut grass; the walled acres stretched to right and left but there were few visitors and, indeed, few graves. Whole plots lay empty, and Harriet, walking along the path, hearing the birds in the trees, sensed, despite them, and despite her pleasure at the prospect of reunion with Karel, a deep sadness and desolation.

There were almost no Jews left in Prague. The dates on the headstones faded out after the 1930s: these empty plots, these acres of undug earth and waving grass would have received the bodies of a whole generation who had perished, instead, in the camps. Rounded up from the Jewish quarter of Josefov, and from hiding places all over the city, they had been transported: to Auschwitz, Treblinka, Ravensbruck, or much closer to home – to the 'model' camp at Terezín, some fifty miles north of Prague, whose neat streets and windowboxes had fooled even Red Cross visitors.

Harriet intended to visit Terezín, on the way to the site of Hugh's power plant. She also intended to telephone Hugh, and tell him they had found Karel. Now, she walked past gravestones with worn Hebrew obscured by trailing ivy; past the unfilled acres: a whole generation missing, rising in a dark cloud of smoke to the sky above the crematorium.

And after the war? After the war, anti-Semitism had driven the survivors away, as it had driven out survivors in Warsaw, in Budapest – the Jews of Eastern Europe had fled again: to Israel, to Australia, to England and America, to the four corners of the earth. In Prague, now, less than two thousand remained: to worship at the synagogue in Josefov; to die, one by one, and be brought here, one by one, for burial.

'What have I in common with the Jews ... ' Tormented Kafka, suffering a fury of boredom in interminable childhood hours at his father's side in the synagogue, grew up to hate both: his race, and his overbearing father, with whom he was buried.

'I have scarcely anything in common with myself – '

Harriet felt, all at once, that extraordinary evocation of a dislocated spirit possess her so powerfully that she almost spoke the words aloud. And realised, as she held them back, that they could have been uttered by Susanna. Or by Christopher.

There's a dark side to both of us –

He was somewhere in Prague, but she wasn't going to seek him out.

I'm sure you won't want to meet me, but you can leave a message –

No. Whatever they had shared belonged to Berlin, to moments in a hotel dining room, in a city left behind.

I thought: I'm the one who has been walled in. They have built a wall around me –

The secret self. The forbidden room. Images that might have come from Kafka.

Kafka had spent the last few months of his life in Berlin, coughing and growing thinner, too poor to buy a newspaper, meeting the last love of his life, a young Jewish girl called Dora. It was 1923, and people were taking their wages home in wheelbarrows. He and Dora rented a little apartment in a leafy suburb and could not pay the electricity bill. She heated ill-cooked vegetarian meals with a kerosene lamp; they read Hebrew to each other by candlelight; she worshipped and adored him. Tuberculosis ate him away; he came back to Prague a skeleton. He wrote his last story; he went, on a last, desperate journey, to a sanatorium in Vienna; he died with Dora beside him.

'Put your hand on my forehead for a moment, to give me courage – '

She followed his body back to Prague; when he was buried they had to hold her back from leaping into the grave.

Dear God, what intensity, what grief and loss. Harriet, seeing ahead of her a little group with cameras, thought: perhaps I have made a mistake. These hours should be ones of pleasurable anticipation – why am I seeking out sadness?

Well. I did not intend to seek it out. It has come upon me. My own dark side, perhaps; my shadow, or a warning.

A warning of what?

Cameras clicked in the morning sun. She joined the little group at the graveside.

*

He died unpublished; for decades, under the communist regime, his name was reviled. Then, in 1963, a Writers' Union conference made a brave attempt to rehabilitate him. Such events began to change the climate: they made possible the spring of 1968.

And in the winter of 1969 a young philosophy student set fire to himself in Wenceslas Square. He was buried near here, too, though not among the Jews. Harriet retraced her steps toward Karel's apartment, walking outside the wall of the Jewish Cemetery and then along the Vinohradská boulevard. Here was the entrance to Olsanská, one of the largest cemeteries in the city, built for the victims of the Plague and crowded, now, with every kind of monument: elaborate tombs, marble obelisks, Russian Orthodox crucifixes, row upon row of the crosses of war graves. She walked through the main gates.

The grass was cut, and the mower still moving along a distant plot. Flowers lay in cellophane on freshly dug graves, and here there were quite a number of visitors, walking along the paths beneath the trees – Saturday morning was probably a good time to come and lay flowers, light candles, say a prayer. It was a long time since Harriet had said a prayer – that was Susanna's territory, though who knew whether it brought her comfort?

She was like a woman from the Middle Ages, praying for a child . . .

It had not brought her a child.

And why, wondered Harriet, looking about her, is Susanna so much with me today?

She saw a uniformed attendant, walking amongst the graves.

'Excuse me – do you speak English?'

'Little only.' He smiled at her from beneath his cap, a sweet-looking man with a frail moustache.

She smiled back, feeling the loneliness of the neglected Jewish Cemetery evaporate a little.

'The grave of Jan Palach?'

He nodded – everyone must ask him where that was – and pointed to a path along the right, just inside the gates. She saw another little group, more cameras.

'Thank you.'

'Today is anniversary,' he said slowly.

'I'm sorry?'

'Anniversary,' he repeated, and then, as an old woman in black approached him, he turned away.

234

Harriet stood thinking. Palach had burned himself in winter, on a bitter January day. What anniversary? She looked at her watch, at the date. The dial showed 21.

August 21 . . .

A prickle of gooseflesh ran all over her. She was here twenty-five years to the day. She had not planned it – somehow, amidst all her reading and preparation, she had not even realised it would be so. Marsha's birthday had been the key date on this journey. But here it was: the anniversary not just of Czechoslovakia's invasion but of one of the most important days of her life. She had come downstairs to breakfast, still in her nightdress, still not quite awake, and seen her parents and brother listening intently to the kitchen radio. Tanks had crossed the border in darkness, they were moving through Prague –

She had known even then that Karel was lost to her.

And now he was found again. In a few minutes she would return to his street, she would ring the bell, she would climb the stone steps to his apartment –

A rush of joy replaced the gooseflesh; melancholy disappeared.

But first –

A handful of tourists stood at a martyr's grave. She went to join them.

The headstone was unmarked; there was only a photograph, wrapped in cellophane. She stood gazing at it, as she had gazed at the Athena poster pinned above her desk, in the room of her childhood, all those years ago.

'A good thing they've moved him back here, hey?' said a young American behind her.

She looked at him. 'What do you mean?'

'You know they dug him up? Back in the Seventies?'

'No, no, I didn't know that.' Something else she had missed. 'Tell me.'

'Well, I guess it was because this place was becoming a kind of shrine, you know? Candlelit vigils and all that – could be trouble. So they dug him up and moved him to some place about forty miles outside the city, where he was born. He only came back after '89.'

Harriet shook her head. A few more people came to join them.

'Been here long?' he asked her, coming up alongside as she moved away.

'This is day one.' She followed the cobbled path towards the gates.

'Terrific. You'll love it. Have you done the Old Town yet? The medieval clock – the astronomy clock? It's really something.'

'Yes, I've seen pictures.'

They had reached the gates. 'Fancy a coffee?' he asked her.

She turned to look at him properly. He was tall and well-fed and shining and he hadn't even been born when the tanks came in.

'I'm old enough to be your mother,' she said primly.

'So? We're talking coffee here, not a roll in the hay.'

She laughed. He was okay, he was nice.

'Thanks, but I have to get back. My daughter – '

'Sure. Well – ' He held out his hand.

'Don't tell me,' said Harriet, full of good humour. 'Have a nice day.'

He rolled his eyes. 'She's so *English*. Okay, so long. Have one anyway.'

'And you.' She watched him stride away, towards the endless crosses of the war graves.

And then she was outside the gates, walking beneath the trees along the boulevard. Traffic went past; it was getting busier now. But where were the demonstrations, the celebrations – did August 21 go by unnoticed now?

She turned the corner into Jičinská, and walked up the hill; she waited at the traffic lights to cross; she tried to keep steady and calm but her stomach was churning.

She came to Baranova, she made her way through the crowd of shoppers, she turned into the quiet, ordinary street where Karel had grown up, from where he had written to her.

Please understand that things are rather difficult now –

I think of you . . .

Someone was walking ahead of her, towards his apartment building. He was tall and lean and dark, and swinging a briefcase.

'Karel?' She quickened her pace, passing the shop. A child coming out of it, unwrapping a bar of chocolate.

'Karel?'

He turned, he saw her.

'Harriet?'

He was older, with grey in his hair. He hesitated, and everything seemed to stop: the summer clouds sailing over the tenement buildings, the passers-by on the narrow street, all the hopes of this journey, this moment.

Then he smiled – that beautiful, heart-stopping smile – and came towards her.

3

'Dobry den, Harriet.'

'Hello, Karel.'

He took her hand and kissed it; they stood there looking at each other. He shook his head.

'This is a very great surprise.'

'Yes,' said Harriet, and could not stop smiling.

A little boy went by with his mother. Somebody across the street was whistling, hammering a nail; a light, carefree sound which for Harriet had at that moment the quality of a lark.

'So,' said Karel. He took her arm, drawing her aside as two teenage girls went past laughing. 'Welcome to Prague. You have had a good journey?'

'Long,' said Harriet, 'especially for my daughter. We have visited Brussels, Berlin – we've been travelling for two weeks. But we are very glad to be here.'

'And I am very glad to see you.'

They were walking along to his door; he pulled out his key; he held the door open for her. They climbed the echoing stairs.

'She is like you, your daughter?' he asked.

'I think so, a little. And Gabrielle looks so like you. She has been acting as our interpreter.'

'Good girl.'

They had reached the second landing. An elderly woman came out of her apartment with a shopping bag. She and Karel greeted each other; she looked at Harriet with curiosity as they went past.

'You have lived here all your life?' asked Harriet, as they went on up.

'Always. And my mother also: she was born here. Her parents lived with us when I was young until they died; my wife lived here – until recently it has been so difficult to change jobs, or apartments or move to another city: there are many families like us. Gabrielle sleeps in my old room, which was my mother's.'

They had come to the top; Harriet was out of breath.

'It keeps you fit,' said Karel, unlocking the door.

There was a rush of footsteps: Gabrielle and Marsha were in the corridor.

He greeted Gabrielle in Czech, with a kiss, then turned to Marsha, smiling.

'So. You are Marsha? My English friend?' He held out his hand. 'How do you do?'

Marsha shook his hand, looking pleased and suddenly shy. 'How do you do.' She flashed a glance at Harriet – I like him, he's nice – and then Hannah was behind them all, with a little wooden tray of glasses.

'And now,' said Karel, 'we celebrate.'

In the gloomy sitting room, with its plants, brown postwar furniture and modern rugs, he opened a bottle of wine.

'*Na zdravi*. Cheers.'

They raised their glasses; there was a general murmur of pleasantries and enquiries. The wine was sweet, and faintly fizzy. The girls, sitting next to each other on a couch, were polite, lapsing occasionally into giggles.

'You are drunk already,' said Karel. He caught Marsha's inadvertent grimace as she sipped. 'You do not like it? I am poisoning you?'

She blushed, and tried again. 'It's okay.'

'She's not really used to wine,' said Harriet.

'No? In Czechoslovakia the children are all alcoholics, even from the cradle.' He translated to the others. 'Tell them that this is true, Gaby.'

Gabrielle looked at Harriet. 'We drink only on special times.'

'Special occasions,' Karel corrected. 'But I think we can find something else for Marsha. You like Coke? Mineral water?'

'Coke, please,' said Marsha, and as Gabrielle went to fetch it, she said 'Everyone drinks mineral water here, don't they? Because of the bad water.'

'This is true. Prague is a very polluted city – the water, the air. Like much of Eastern Europe.'

'Yes. My uncle in Brussels is trying to help.'

'He is? That is kind of him.'

Harriet explained a little, as Gabrielle returned. 'I'm hoping to visit the plant,' she said. 'There's so much I want to see.'

'But this is very interesting. I am a supporter of the Green Party, you know – the environment issues have been important here for a long time, as part of the political opposition. And the European Bank is funding some useful projects. You must tell me more about your brother.'

'He's lovely,' said Marsha, drinking her Coke.

'I am sure.' He turned to Harriet. 'I did not meet him?'

'You did – don't you remember? He had a summer holiday job, like me, but he was at home sometimes. He was at home at the time of the invasion – '

He frowned. 'I think I remember.'

Hannah rose. They followed her down the corridor.

Lunch in the cramped tiled kitchen was cold roast pork, steaming dumplings, sauerkraut. A thick plum tart stood on an enamel-topped cupboard. Karel refilled glasses, dishes were passed. Marsha tucked in with a will, leaving the sauerkraut.

'You like dumplings?' Karel asked her, seeing them disappear.

'They're yummy.'

'They are what? What is this yummy?'

The girls were off again. He shook his head in despair.

'It means they're delicious,' said Harriet, laughing too. 'It means she likes them.'

'That is good. She will see a lot of them in Prague.' He drank. 'And what else have you seen in Prague? You are fulfilling your duties as tourist?'

'There hasn't been much time yet. We're staying in Malá Strana, the Little Quarter – '

'It is charming there. And so convenient for the President.'

'Quite. Last night we went to the Charles Bridge, of course, and today I've visited the cemeteries. Somehow I hadn't realised that it was the anniversary – ' she broke off, suddenly, recalling his earlier frown at her reference to the invasion. Perhaps she should be careful, not tumble over herself with references to a past they had shared so briefly.

'You are hesitating?'

'I – I think I must have expected some sort of celebration, something to mark the end of that time.'

He refilled her glass, his mother's glass. 'Celebration? If you had been here in 1990, yes – you would have seen something then. Cars turned over, everyone out on the street . . . Now? Now we are getting on with living again. Rebuilding.' He turned to his mother, translating. She nodded. 'You see,' he said to Harriet, 'my mother has been through a great deal. She and my father hoped for so much after the war – they had been communists since the early days. They suffered in the war, and then afterwards – they suffered in ways they had not

239

expected. Now, sadly, my father is no longer with us, and my mother – she looks for the good life at last, though without him it will never be the same. Still – ' He smiled at her. 'All this is part of many conversations. I ask you about tourism.'

'I've told you, I visited Kafka's grave – ' And walked into a well of sadness, but this she could not talk about, yet, either. Not the past of twenty-five years ago, nor the more recent past of this journey.

'We haven't come all this way to see the sights,' said Marsha all of a sudden. 'We've come to see you.'

He bowed towards the end of the table. 'That is a charming thing to say.'

'It's true. We didn't know if we'd find you, but I thought we would, and as soon as I saw you I thought – '

'Marsha – ' said Harriet firmly.

'What?' She turned to Harriet, flushing. 'Can't I say what I want?'

Hannah, watching in amusement, turned to Karel for explanation. There was a small flurry of Czech, then he said kindly to Marsha, 'Sometimes parents are a great problem. Gabrielle finds it the same, isn't that so, Gaby?'

She nodded. 'Especially you, Father.'

He spread his hands. 'You see? Even with the nicest father in the world. So. Who is going to have a little more? Marsha? Your dumplings are vanished. Surely they cannot be all in that English tummy?'

She held out her plate.

The difficult moment passed: they all had second helpings. And then plum tart, groaning. And then they could not move.

'You would like coffee?' Karel asked Harriet. 'A glass of tea?'

'Coffee, please.'

'She's a coffee addict,' said Marsha.

He looked at Harriet. 'This is true?'

'I suppose it is.' She smiled at Hannah, gestured at the table's remains. 'Thank you for a wonderful meal.'

Hannah nodded; the girls asked permission to get down, and made an unseemly scramble for the door. Harriet offered to help with the washing up and was refused. Hannah made fresh coffee in a metal pot with a glass lid which reminded Harriet of something from her childhood. She made a glass of lemon tea for Karel. She put all this on a tray and gave it to them.

'Go. Talk.'

Karel took the tray from his mother and kissed her.

In the sitting room, he leaned back in an armchair, drinking, his long legs stretched out in front of the television. Harriet, in another, drank her coffee, watching him. Now. Where should they begin? Should she ask about his life? Careful, careful – she thought of Dieter Scheiber, in East Berlin: defensive, asking her little. Karel, similarly, might not wish to be questioned about his activities, personal or political. Should she talk about herself? She had, all at once, something of the same, disconcerting sensation she had experienced on the first day in Brussels: of seeing her life in London become small and distant, an unknown quantity, even to herself. And Karel, certainly, even though he was welcoming, charming, was an unknown quantity to her now. Everything in his country had changed; how much, over two and a half decades, had that changed him?

He finished his tea and leaned forward, putting the glass down on a low, spindle-legged table. He smiled at her – such a heavenly smile – and she was taken all over again to that basement bedsit: to a smile, a glass of lemon tea, a cigarette . . .

'You don't smoke,' she said suddenly.

'No, not for a long time.'

'Everyone smokes in Prague.'

'This is true.'

'And you used to smoke all the time.'

'Did I?'

'Yes, Marlboro, don't you remember – '

Long, elegant fingers unwrapped the cellophane, tapped the packet. He inhaled deeply, talking rapidly.

'In my country we are fighting for the essentials, for liberty to meet and make discussions, to move without the police spies, to publish . . . '

He was frowning again. 'I remember some things about those days, and some of them become a blur. Everything that happened then – it was made small by events afterwards.'

'Of course.' Yes, yes, of course it was.

. . . watching the faces of her parents and her brother as they listened to the news, realising, even then, that nothing could last for ever, and that falling in love, which had seemed to encompass everything, was, in the scale of world events, only a little thing really . . .

'But I remember I was smoking a little in London,' Karel said now.

'It was Marlboro, even then? You see them everywhere now, like McDonalds.'

'When did you give up?'

'When I married. My wife does not like smoking, and she is right, of course.'

'Of course,' she said again.

'Mind you, it was hell.'

She laughed. 'And your wife – ' she hesitated. 'She is working with you now? Gabrielle mentioned that you are both lawyers.'

'Yes. In the same bureau – office, I should say – but our specialisations are different. She is a property lawyer, so she is very busy these days. Restitution is our buzz word now – people are claiming their rights to property taken over by the regime – land, old family houses. Danielle is an expert in this field.'

Harriet thought of the Scheibers, and the family hotel reclaimed in Prenzlauer Berg. She wondered about Danielle.

'But there are many problems,' Karel went on. 'Such places are often too big to look after nowadays, so they are rented out, turned into hotels, and so on. All the foreigners come, and the local people cannot afford what then is in the shops. They move out. The butcher becomes a boutique. It is a kind of economic destruction of a class, a downside of the new capitalism, and people – I am not talking about people like your brother, you understand, but many people from the West are taking advantage. We have had to create a new legal system, new tax structure and so on – while we are working it all out, the big fat cat makes a big fat profit.'

'Yes,' said Harriet thoughtfully. 'He normally does.'

In the dining room in Brussels the polished table shone. Bruise-coloured clouds went past. He leaned forward, lighting a cigarette from a candle flame, his hand trembling a little.

'Buy here, sell there, or vice versa – they need practically anything I can get them, I'm delighted to say ... the whole of Western Europe has its mitts in Eastern Europe these days ... '

He looked at her. 'I am talking too much? You are interested in these things, in politics?'

'Of course I'm interested. I'm a political person.' She leaned forward, pouring coffee. 'Tell me what your own field is. Danielle is property, and you – '

'Civil rights.'

'Ah. In that case – ' she stopped again.

'Go on. In that case. Why are you so cautious, Harriet?'

'I just don't like to intrude, to keep asking questions. And if you are active in civil rights then perhaps there are things from the past years you don't want to talk about.'

'In that case,' he said gravely, 'I will not talk about them.'

He was leaning back in the chair again, long slender fingers pressed together, watching her intently. She returned his gaze, looking at the face she had for a few weeks known so intimately, craved to see so ardently after his departure. It was fuller, with more lines; there was grey not just in his hair but in his eyebrows. But it was the same face: well-made, clever, full of vitality. And now there was confidence and assurance there, too: he was impressive-looking, there was no denying it – this was someone who knew what he was doing, whom you would turn to for guidance, and could trust.

'Mum?' Marsha was in the doorway.

'Ah, my English friend.' Karel turned and smiled at her: Marsha blushed, and smiled back.

'Mum? Gabrielle says we can go to the park. Is that okay? It's only a couple of blocks.'

Gabrielle appeared behind her, looking sensible.

Harriet looked at Karel again. 'What do you think? Is it all right to go there without a grown-up?'

'Gabrielle goes there, and I used to go there myself at her age. Before that my grandfather took me – he made me a little boat, for the pond.'

'Have you still got it?' Marsha asked.

'I have. Gabrielle and I used also to sail it, didn't we, Gaby? I think it is perfectly safe there, but you never know. Would you permit me and your mother to accompany you? Harriet – would that suit you? We can continue our conversation while they play on the swings.'

'Yes, that sounds fine.'

'You could bring your boat,' said Marsha.

He looked at her in amusement. 'I could.'

They left Hannah resting; they walked the couple of blocks. The park was like any park anywhere: trees, railings, old people on benches by the flowerbeds, children on the swings. When there was nothing else to do, you went to the park: there was always that feeling, thought Harriet, as they walked through the gates. And it was the end of the

243

summer: a dryness and dustiness hung over the grass. But there was the warm light breeze, and there was the pond. Ducks swam, and preened themselves on a little island of bushes and mud. Children leaned forward with bread crusts and mothers pulled them back. It was the same everywhere, but it still had charm. And Karel had brought the boat.

It was a simple little sailing boat, its sides painted in a utilitarian blue which was chipped and faded. The deck was white, yellowing with age, like the two cotton sails, run up on fraying string.

'It's sweet,' Marsha had said, when he took it out of a cupboard in the corridor.

'You think so?' He examined the chips, the drooping sails. 'It has been through a storm, I think. But it is well made – my grandfather was so good at these things.' He held it out. 'You would like to carry it?'

Marsha shook her head: she was, after all, ten, not six.

But now, as he set the boat carefully in the water, and it rested, steady and upright, she was enchanted. Impossible not to feel a lift of the heart as he gave a push and it moved alongside them in the breeze, the sails filling a little, stirring a little, the water parting. People stood watching, small children ran after it.

'It's lovely,' said Harriet, as they walked alongside.

'Yes. It brings back happy memories – with my grandfather, and with my daughter. She is too old for it now, of course, but – '

'I don't think you're ever too old for something like this.'

'Exactly.'

A large Muscovy duck came waddling up the muddy slope at the edge.

'She's afraid,' Gaby said.

'She's almost as big as the boat,' said Karel.

The breeze fell, the little boat slowed and stopped. For a while they tried to encourage it along with a stick, but it didn't work. The boat rested on the water, rocking a little as ducks went by; then it was steady and still again.

'You would like to swing?' Gaby asked Marsha.

They ran off over the grass.

'So.' Karel reached out, and drew the boat in; he picked it up, dripping, and shook off the water. 'We were talking, I think.'

'We were.' Harriet watched him, wiping the sides of the boat with a handkerchief; she turned to watch the girls, racing towards the swings.

The last time Marsha had been in a playground was in the Berlin Zoo, the morning after their arrival.

She told Karel this, as they walked away from the pond.

'There was a boy there who looked a little like you,' she said. 'He might have been your son.'

'Yes? And instead we both have daughters. We are fortunate – they are both good children, I think.'

'Yes. And it's nice for Marsha to have someone of her own age, after travelling just with me for two weeks.'

'Brussels, Berlin – it is a long journey. You could have flown here.'

'We could, but – '

But I wanted to follow your route, to think of you, travelling by train, crossing the Berlin Wall, coming back to an occupied city –

She could not possibly say all this. Caution had long been part of her nature – had been there, probably, ever since Martin left: she had not quite expected to feel it now, but feel it she did. She and Karel had only just met again: it was early days, and who knew what course the rest of this week might follow?

'But I wanted to see my brother,' she said. 'And get to know my sister-in-law a little. I must phone them this evening, we haven't spoken since we left, though I tried in Berlin. I had to visit Berlin, now the wall is down. As for Prague – it's a dream city. Everyone wants to come here now.'

She could hear herself talk fast; she felt like a skater, skimming over the ice, over everything of importance.

They had come to the playground: Marsha and Gaby were standing up on their swings, going high. Marsha took off a hand and waved, Gabrielle's plaits swung out behind her. Harriet waved back; they stood for a few moments, watching. The girls began to play a game, trying to catch each other's hands as they swooped past.

'They get on well,' said Karel, putting the boat down on a bench.

'Yes, I'm so pleased. I think it's hard for Marsha sometimes, being an only child.'

He shrugged. 'It does not seem to trouble Gaby, she is mostly content. I also was an only child – I was happy, I think. And in any case – Prague is full of only children. Like East Berlin, I believe; like much of Eastern Europe. When times are difficult, the birth rate falls. It was difficult until recently to think of having more than one child.' He looked at her. 'But you would have liked another?'

'I think so. But my husband left when Marsha was still a baby – '

'It must have been hard for you.'

'We've survived.' She stepped out of the way of a toddler with a pushcart. 'Anyway,' she said carefully, 'you are also divorced.'

'Again, it is rather common: families live on top of one another, times are difficult, there are problems. Domestic life makes Danielle restless – she likes to work, to be free. She is happier now, I think, living in her own place, and my mother likes to take care of Gabrielle. And Danielle and I are friends.'

'Yes. Gabrielle said that.'

And what about him? Was he happy? Had this splitting of a family asunder left no mark?

He called to Gaby, pointing to the boat: she should keep an eye.

They walked round the playground, they walked along the path. Late-blooming roses stood in the flowerbeds, petals lay on the earth.

'We still haven't talked about your work,' she said.

'We have not talked about your work. You say you are teaching now?'

'Yes. I teach in a comprehensive – a secondary school – in west London. I run the history department.'

'That must be very interesting.'

'It's hard work.'

'Of course. But important, yes? What is more important than history?'

Someone was scattering bread on the path: a flutter of pigeons alighted. Harriet and Karel stepped round them, and walked on round the park, beneath the trees.

'I do want to know about you,' she said. 'What you've been doing, what happened to you, when you came back. But only if you want – '

'I want.' He smiled at her. 'Everyone is talking, now. East to West, West to East.'

We are one people.

So are we –

He said: 'When we met I was in the second year at the university, I think. After the invasion it was difficult at first to resume my studies: the department was undergoing a certain amount of restructuring, as they called it. There were revisions to the syllabus. You can imagine.'

'I can.'

'*I hope to study law again one day, but at present I am working as a porter . . .*'

'But then the department reopened, and we began again. I used to have interesting conversations with my father in those days. He was a communist since before the war: he believed very strongly, but for him it was associated with a humanitarian perspective, you know. It was after '53, after Stalin's death, when the party members of his generation saw the light. And then there was Hungary, in '56, the uprising – the shock of that. Totalitarianism. Ruthless. We could not believe that what happened to Hungary would happen to us, but of course in the end it came. My father's spirit was broken the day the tanks came in. I think it helped his death, truly. But for me, for my generation: we had to fight, to resist.'

Harriet listened. She and Karel had come full circle: she glanced towards the swings. The girls were off them now, spinning on a roundabout. Sunlight flickered on the path as they walked on.

'So,' Karel was saying. 'After I qualified I had a low-grade job in a lawyer's office, but I did what I could for the resistance. Danielle also – we were members of the same group. I wrote a little, I smuggled a few books – nothing dramatic, you understand, but it was extremely dangerous to do anything dramatic. I was a signatory of the Charter in '77. I was arrested, I was interrogated, I was watched, but perhaps not important enough to send to prison.'

'You were brave,' said Harriet. 'You were very brave.'

He spread his arms. 'All this is what many people could tell you, Harriet, it is not so special. And for everyone like me there were thousands more resisting in their minds, you know – an internal exile.'

They have built a wall around me –

'And now?' she asked.

His hands were in his pockets, he was walking fast. 'You told me a little about your brother – you see, I am interested because I had a little to do with these issues in those days. In 1983 I have a friend in the Ecology Section who is helping to prepare a secret report. There is much anxiety about pollution – everyone knows the water is becoming unsafe, that the air in Bohemia is disgusting. This report makes a list of such things – it makes very unpleasant reading when it is published by the Academy of Sciences and it is at once suppressed. But one or two people in Charter 77 leak it to the West – it is these kind of things that build up towards a climate for the Revolution, you know. This issue is so important for us, it is a symbol of the repression, this pollution even of the air we breathe. It is a human rights issue. And you criticise – you are a dissident. So. After the Revolution I maintain this interest – I am working now in civil rights, but I have my old Green friends, and I keep watch.'

'Do you know this plant Hugh is investing in? Could you take me there?'

'I know of it. I should be happy to take you. How long are you staying?'

'A week.'

They had walked round the park three times at least, he talking, she listening, both looking straight ahead. The girls were off the roundabout now, and were coming towards them over the grass.

He said, watching the girls. 'Is it true what Marsha said? Did you really come all this way to see me?'

She studied the ground. 'Well – yes.'

'I am very touched,' he said, and then they looked at each other, and then the ice was broken.

It had grown very hot, and Marsha, Harriet could see, was beginning to tire. They sat on a bench in the shade and rested, watching small children trundle past on bicycles, and people playing catch on the grass. The centre of Prague might be full of tourists and McDonalds, but here, thought Harriet, they could surely be back in the 1950s, when Karel had come with his grandfather to sail a little blue boat on the pond, and the world woke up to Stalin.

Marsha yawned. Karel yawned.

'Excuse me – it has been a busy week.'

'You haven't had your Saturday rest,' said Gabrielle.

'I'm sorry, Karel,' said Harriet. 'We've disturbed your routine . . .'

'You have, it is thoughtless of you. I should say to you: you travel eight hundred miles to visit, I'm sorry, I'm having a rest.'

They all laughed, getting up to go, walking back through the hot narrow streets, climbing the now welcome cool stairs to the apartment. Hannah was out, visiting a friend. She had left a note on the kitchen table, and a cake. No one could eat a crumb.

Karel put the little boat back in the cupboard. He opened the windows and gave the girls glasses of Coke, which they took back to the sitting room, to watch Czech television. He and Harriet sat at the kitchen table, drinking their lemon tea.

'This is so nice,' said Harriet. 'Thank you for looking after us so well.'

'It is a great pleasure.'

Voices and the sounds of occasional traffic drifted up from the street; looking out of the open window Harriet's eyes rested once more on the trees of the Olsanská Cemetery. She thought of the morning, and of visiting Kafka's grave in the New Jewish Cemetery beyond: of its emptiness and melancholy, and the sadness she had felt there, thinking of Christopher and Susanna.

'I have scarcely anything in common with myself – '

Karel was not like that. He knew who he was: she could feel it.

She said, sensing now that she did not have to keep to impersonal conversation: 'This morning, out there in the cemetery – the Jewish Cemetery – I had a great feeling of sadness.'

'I am sorry to hear that.'

'Not for me, or at least I don't think so. For people I've got to know recently – quite a lot of things have happened on this journey. I wasn't expecting them.'

'No. That is the nature of journeys. Perhaps you will tell me?'

'Yes. But perhaps not yet.'

The curtain stirred at the open window, voices came up from the street again, and then it was quiet. They sat looking at each other.

She said: 'I kept all your letters.'

'Yes,' said Karel. 'I did the same.'

The sun sank lower, the air became tranquil and still. The city was bathed once again in the rich golden light which Harriet and Marsha had first experienced yesterday, leaning out of their pension window, looking over the tiled rooftops of the Little Quarter.

Now, they were sitting at a café table near the Jan Hus monument in the Old Town Square, on their way home. Karel and Gaby had seen them to the tram stop in Žižkov; they were meeting them here for lunch tomorrow, but getting off the second tram, in Celetna, Harriet had not been able to resist walking through, and getting a first glimpse.

'We're in time to hear the Astronomical Clock strike six,' she told Marsha.

'Big deal.' But Marsha, though tired, was in a good mood as they made their way through the throngs of tourists, past medieval houses with freshly painted façades in shades of ochre, pink and green, and came out into the square. They found, after searching, an empty table; they found, in a while, a waiter; they sat drinking lemonade and looking about them.

'This place reminds me of somewhere,' said Marsha, surveying the cobbles, the pastel-coloured houses, mellow in the evening sun. She frowned. 'I know – it's that place in Brussels, where we went the first morning.'

'The Grand Place,' said Harriet. 'Yes, you're right. I thought we might phone Susanna and Hugh this evening – would you like that? To tell them we've got here?'

'And that we've found Karel. And Gaby. And that they're really nice.'

'Is Karel how you'd imagined?'

'Even better. He's *lovely*. Why did you stop me, at lunch, saying what I thought?'

'I suppose I was still rather nervous. I wasn't quite sure what you were going to say.'

'Only that I thought he was lovely. Can't I say things like that?'

'Sometimes you can, and sometimes you can't.' Harriet finished her drink. 'And I don't just mean because of me, either. I mean for yourself, when you grow up. Declaring yourself can be – ' She broke off. 'Why am I lecturing you? What's the time?'

Marsha looked at her watch. 'It's half-past five, and I don't know what you're talking about.' She sipped her lemonade. 'Half the time I don't know what Gaby and Karel are talking about, either. How come Gaby speaks such good English? Why can't I learn Czech?'

'Why can't you? Behold the phrase book.' Harriet pulled it out from her shoulder bag. 'Look: greetings, food, where is the railway station, days of the week . . .' She passed it over. 'What's dumplings in Czech?'

It was unpronounceable. Marsha tried greetings, practising Dobry den, good day.

'That's easy.'

'That's what Karel said this morning, when we met.'

'Is it? Didn't he say Darling-Harriet-I-thought-I'd-never-see-you-again-come-into-my-arms?'

'No, he didn't. Don't be so silly.'

They sat contentedly for a few minutes, looking things up and trying to pronounce them. Some of the words were given in Slovak, too, which didn't help.

'The months of the year aren't too bad,' said Harriet, when they'd given up on Thursday, which had five consonants before a vowel. 'They're rather poetic, and apt. Look – January is leden – ice, February is unor – hibernation . . . June is red, and July is redder.'

'What's August, where we are now?'

'Sickle. For the harvest. And so it goes on. The year ends with leaves falling, and supplication.'

'What's supplication?'

'Begging for something. It's almost religious, like a prayer. That is rather beautiful, I must say.' She put the book down. 'There's a calendar showing the months on the Astronomical Clock. Come on, it must be almost six.'

'Ten to.' Marsha looked at her watch with affection. 'Thank you for this, I do love it. Mind you,' she added with insight, 'I'd love anything today.'

They walked hand in hand across the square, to where a group of tourists was gathering on the mosaic of blue and grey cobbles beneath the Town Hall Tower, gazing upwards. Two great dials were set one above the other in the façade, watched over by painted stone figures.

'Why is there a skeleton?'

'That's Death, waiting.'

Above stood an angel, between two shuttered windows.

'When the clock strikes,' said Harriet, who had slipped into the guidebook on the tram, 'you'll see the windows open and the Twelve Apostles go past the angel.'

'See who?'

Harriet sighed and explained. 'In medieval times,' she went on, 'They believed that the clock didn't just record the passing hours, it actually created them.'

'Like God.'

'Like God. Look. The inner circle of the dial below has the signs of the zodiac, can you see?'

Marsha craned her neck. 'Not really. Which one's Virgo? That's me, isn't it?'

'Yes. We'll have to buy a postcard, so we can see properly.'

'What sign is Karel?'

'I don't know.'

'What do you think?'

'Libra,' said Harriet, without a moment's hesitation. 'I don't believe a word of it, but Libra. Balance.'

She moved out of the way of a large German knapsack. For a moment she remembered the young American, at Jan Palach's grave, then she forgot him again.

'Anyway, there's the rural calendar – all the months.' She peered at painted figures on gold, looking for ice, and falling leaves.

'What's the dial on top, all those wheels and things?'

'That's the actual clock. It's much older than the zodiac dial; it shows the time, the movement of the sun and moon round the earth – that's what they thought, whereas in fact, as you know well – '

'The earth goes round the sun.'

'Exactly. There's the phases of the moon, the rising and setting of the stars, and I don't know what else. Look – quick – the hand's just coming up to the six. Watch those two little windows, quick – ' She picked Marsha up, something she could hardly do any more. 'Can you see? Now listen.'

The crowd was waiting, talking, pointing things out in accents mostly German and American. And then it came, the first rich chime sounding out over the square, and everyone went quiet.

One – two –

The doors on either side of the angel opened, the twelve Apostles went past him, one by one.

Three – four –

A hush had fallen.

Five – six –

The sun was sinking, the last note sounded, and faded, and died. The doors on either side of the angel closed, and then, into the quietness, came the sound of a bell, as Death, far above them, rang out his warning.

Harriet felt a long, deep shiver run through her.

'It must be so strange,' said Marsha, as the crowd thinned, and they walked away. 'To live all your life believing the wrong thing.'

Harriet looked at her. 'What do you mean?'

'I don't know exactly, but I was thinking about what you said about medieval people – believing the clocks made the hours, and the sun went round the earth. I mean – imagine believing things like that, and dying, and never knowing the truth. Or coming back again, centuries later, and finding you'd been *wrong*. I mean, like in Victorian times, believing your child had died because God willed it, and all the time it was just because there weren't any antibiotics.'

Harriet listened, trying to shake off a sense of unease. 'Every age has its own beliefs. Those are very grown-up thoughts, you know, Marsha. You do think about things, don't you?'

'I do. I am quite grown-up. Ten's *old*.'

Harriet put her arm round her. 'What do you want for supper, ancient one?'

'Lots.'

'After all those dumplings?'

'I'm *starving*.'

The familiar cry. They wandered into the path of the setting sun, feeling its warmth on their faces. 'We could eat by the river,' suggested Harriet.

'Yes. I wish Karel and Gaby could have come with us.'

'We did rather land on them – we can't expect Karel to drop his arrangements for the evening.'

'Why can't we go out with him, too?'

'Sssh, that's enough. Now, shall we telephone Hugh and Susanna?'

'Oh, yes. I'm dying to talk to them.'

A yellow phone stood in a booth on the corner, but that took only single koruna, for local calls. Discovering this, Harriet realised she didn't know Karel's phone number. She must ask him tomorrow.

Finding a phone box for an international call proved difficult. She looked in her guidebook.

There was the main, twenty-four-hour post office on Jindřišská, off Wenceslas Square – that was the poste restante address Christopher had given her. No. She didn't want to think about him now. There were a couple of modern, stress-free digital phones on Wenceslas Square itself, but visiting the square was a pilgrimage to make in its own right, with Karel tomorrow; she didn't want to walk down there this evening. The thing to do, it seemed, was to find a grey phone and, unless you had a mountain of five-koruna coins, reverse the charges.

They found a grey phone outside a nearby restaurant. Harriet made her request in stumbling phrase-book Czech. The operator replied in perfect English.

'One moment, please.'

Harriet waited. She smiled at Marsha, but was suddenly filled with nervous apprehension. Could she do it? Could she skim smoothly over Berlin, and everything she had learned there? Who might be more difficult to talk to – Hugh or Susanna?

There was a series of clicks, and then she could hear the phone begin to ring. That lovely, sad apartment. She pictured the early evening light at the balcony windows, the quietness of the drawing room, Susanna sitting on a corner of the sofa beneath her portrait, waiting for Hugh's return: turning the pages of a book, trying to concentrate, putting it aside. She rose, and began to pace: up and down, up and down, thinking not of Hugh, but –

The phone rang and rang.

Harriet turned to distract herself, looking across the square again, to the golden path of the sun on the cobbles, trying to keep calm. Pigeons were fluttering, someone who looked a bit like Karel was lighting a cigarette, putting the lighter back in his pocket. Everyone smoked in Prague.

'They must be out,' said Marsha. 'Let's try again after supper. I'm *starving*.'

'Sssh. Wait.' Something wasn't right. If they were out, the answerphone would be on. Marsha moved restlessly away from the booth and went to watch the pigeons.

Harriet waited, her stomach in knots. There was a click, an answer. Hugh, curt, out of breath. The English-speaking operator made her request. Yes, yes of course. Then –

'Harriet.'

'Hugh? Is everything all right?'

'No, not really – let me sit down. I've only just walked in – I forgot to do the answerphone. You're in Prague – ' He drew breath. 'Is Marsha with you?'

'Sort of. She's wandered off – I mean, I can see her, we're in the Old Town Square, but – Hugh, what is it? Can you tell me? Shall I ring back?'

'No. No, I'll tell you, it's such a relief to talk to you.' Another breath. 'Susanna's taken a massive overdose.'

Harriet leaned against the plastic dome of the phone booth, and everything around her – the golden light, the fluttering pigeons, the tourists at the tables in the square – all fell away into darkness.

'No. No – '

She closed her eyes, and in the darkness listened: to yesterday's discovery, and the note:

> *All my life I've been looking for*
> *God, and this is the only way I can*
> *find Him.*

4

The window of the pension bedroom was open to the night. Harriet lay turned towards it, looking at an infinity of stars.

Behind her, Marsha was sleeping deeply. She had been given an edited version of the phone call: a smooth, emergency version from adult to child. Susanna was in a clinic, recovering from a nasty stomach bug; Hugh had just returned from visiting and was tired. He sent his love.

'Poor Susanna.'

'Yes. Not very nice. But she'll be home soon.' Harriet walked on trembling legs across the cobbles. 'Now, where shall we eat? Down by the river?'

They wandered through the narrow streets of the Old Town, heading towards the Charles Bridge. The evening was warm, the streets crowded, the air full of music – Mozart in cafés, rock pounding from beer cellars beneath medieval arches. German and American accents were everywhere. Amongst the press of people, Harriet began to feel faint.

'You okay?'

'Just a bit – I think I need to sit down.'

They bought mineral water; she drained the bottle. They glimpsed a little square through an arch, a church on the other side.

'There?' Marsha suggested.

Inside, in the coolness, a string quartet was playing.

'A concert. Like in Brussels, the one we went to with Susanna, remember?'

'Yes,' said Harriet.

They found chairs at the back, behind the crowded pews, and sat listening. Dvořák, mournful and tender, went straight to the gut. There wasn't another sound, only the strains of violin and cello, rising, rising –

All my life I've been looking for God –

After a while the performance ended; after a while they left the emptying church and found a waterfront café. They ate looking out at the path of the setting sun on the river, the black-headed gulls wheeling above the silhouettes of saints all along the Charles Bridge, the slow drift of swans through the arches.

'Just think,' said Marsha. 'This time yesterday we were on the other side of the river, wondering if we'd find Karel. I'd never even met him.'

'Just think of that.'

'And now – '

And now a shadow had fallen, and night approached.

The canopy of stars above the rooftops brought some comfort. Susanna had not died. She had been brought back from a dark frontier, retching and heaving, to a white bed, an open window, daylight. Hugh, who had found her, had been beside her. Her parents were flying from England.

Was that what she had wanted? People knowing, despair made public, everyone crowding round? If it wasn't, Harriet could not envisage her being able to say so.

Susanna doesn't allow herself to hate anyone – she turns it all in on herself –

That was Christopher, in the candlelit dining room in Berlin. He knew her. Perhaps he knew her better than anyone. Was her howl of anguish for him, to come back and reclaim her?

I have watched you and watched you: at last you are mine –

Harriet slowly got out of bed and went to the window. The streets of the Little Quarter below the Cathedral were starlit and gaslit: looking down over the descent of tiled rooftops she could glimpse, through a gap between houses, softly illuminated cobbles, and somebody walking down the hill. It was very late.

In the winter of 1916, Kafka used to write all night not far from here, in the little house in Golden Lane his sister had rented. As dawn broke, he walked through the deserted streets and through the massive gateway to the Charles Bridge, drawing his coat about him as the chill rose from the river. His footsteps sounded on the cobbles; there was hardly a soul about.

I am a memory come alive –

In each of the three cities Harriet had visited on this journey, a spirit from the past had in some measure taken possession of her. Here it was Kafka, travelling deeper and deeper into himself. In Berlin, Rosa Luxemburg: passionate, political, meeting a terrible end. In Brussels, where Susanna lived, a fictional creation, a mirror of Charlotte Brontë's own torment: Lucy Snowe, pacing the walled-in garden and schoolhouse on the Rue Fossette.

I'm the one who has –

Craving a letter, enduring loneliness, creeping through the rain to the sanctuary of a church. A woman on the brink of breakdown, showing such a cool face to the world, but filled with emotion, with longing –

The interview would be short, of course: he would say to me just what he had said to each of the assembled pupils; he would take and hold my hand two minutes; he would touch my cheek with his lips for the first, last, only time – and then – no more. Then, indeed, the final parting, then the wide separation . . . Pierced deeper than I could endure, made now to feel what defied suppression, I cried –

'My heart will break!'

Was it Christopher, who understood Susanna, who should be with her now? Was death, without him, preferable?

I have built a wall around myself –

That was not a line from a novel, but that was Susanna.

The summer night was growing cooler. Harriet leaned on the windowsill, thinking of Susanna; of Lucy Snowe in a walled-in garden; Rosa Luxemburg, face down in the waters of the Tiergarten; Kafka, walking alone. There was, she must acknowledge it, something in her own spirit which identified with all this intensity and sadness, something which in a life filled with work, and duty, and activity, she had not begun to know until this journey.

Should she seek to understand it? Or push it most resolutely away?

Looking out over the starlit rooftops she began to shiver. There were aspects of Susanna she understood, and others she could not begin to. It was probably foolish and misguided to imagine that Christopher, with his own dark and destructive side, was the person to help her now.

And yet. It felt terrible to think that he did not know what had happened to her, how close she had come to death. Should I tell him? Harriet wondered. Should I let him know?

I'm sure you won't want to meet, but if you do, you can leave a message –

He was standing in the hall of the Hotel Scheiber, heavy and tired, taking out his fountain pen, writing an address.

Wenceslas Square, like many of the so-called squares in the city, was in fact a boulevard, half a mile long, broad, tree-lined and gently sloping. Once, when the New Town was founded, it had been a horse market. Now it was crossed by trams and full of activity. Neon signs flashed above restaurants, department stores, hotels and cinemas. The National Museum, with the statue of Wenceslas on horseback before it, stood at the southern end.

Harriet, in Berlin, had felt awed by her first sight of the Brandenberg Gate, recalling scenes watched on television on a grey afternoon in London: euphoric students scaling the wall behind it. Here, similarly, she felt herself making a pilgrimage: in this arena the greatest scenes in modern Czech history had taken place: the outdoor Mass which began the 1848 revolution, when Marx had returned to Berlin from Brussels; the independence demonstrations of 1918; the crowds of 1938, when the Nazis invaded.

Here, in the summer of 1968, the Soviet tanks had come to a halt. Crowds had surrounded them, sobbing and shouting; a little boy had been shot for sticking a Czech flag down the barrel of a gun. Here, in bitter weather the following winter, Jan Palach had set himself alight. In the November *masakr* of 1989, riot police had violently broken up a student demonstration, and found the world against them; days later, Dubcek and Havel stood on the balcony of the National Museum, looking down on the hundreds of thousands crammed below, ringing their handbells in the falling snow. Harriet, watching by the fire in London, had got up and gone to her desk, looking for the little packet of letters Karel had written to her, taking them out of their box. Her journey had in some ways begun that night.

And now she had found him, and later this morning would meet him, as they'd arranged, for lunch. For such a long time she had imagined seeing Wenceslas Square for the first time with him beside her, discovering what part he had played in events since his return. And perhaps, later in the day, she could come back with him. But now, walking from the metro by the Museum, the main railway station behind them, she turned to look up at the balcony and knew that this morning she must be by herself. Well – she was never by herself; Marsha, of course, was beside her, hoping, when they got to the post office, to talk to Hugh.

'We'll see,' said Harriet. 'He might have left for the clinic.' And she pointed out the balcony, and the statue of Wenceslas, taking refuge from her thoughts, disturbed and distressed, in the pleasing, familiar recounting of facts.

The fact that Karel had been amongst the crowd filling the square in the falling snow of the Velvet Revolution was the only thing that really took hold of Marsha's imagination.

'I can't *wait* to see him again. And Gaby.' She swung along in the morning sunshine. Church bells were ringing everywhere, for Mass. 'It's brilliant here.'

'Good.'

'Don't you think it's brilliant? Aren't you excited?'

'Yes, of course.'

'You don't sound it.'

'I expect I'm just a bit tired.'

And confused, she thought. Horribly confused. She put out a restraining hand as they came to a crossroads, where a tram was running.

'Look!' said Marsha. 'It's made into a cigarette packet!'

So it was: a packet tipped on its side, with slogans in English and Czech. 'A cigarette for when you are feeling good! A cigarette for when you are under stress!'

'No health warning,' said Marsha, who had been given many health warnings at school. 'Isn't that dreadful?'

'Yes. I think this is our street. The post office is along here somewhere.'

They turned right into Jindřišská, and Harriet, as they made their way amongst the tourists, saw again that heavy, serious face, smoking, smoking, the tremor in his hand as he lit up.

The post office at number 14, open twenty-four hours, was at first sight daunting: inside, beyond the fax and telegram room, was a row of some fifty windows. Even mid-morning on a Sunday, there were queues at most of them.

'There are the phones,' said Marsha, pointing.

'Okay. But I also want to . . . ' Harriet scanned the line of windows, looking for Poste Restante.

'Want to what?'

'See if there's a message for us. Leave one, maybe.'

'What?' Marsha frowned. 'I thought we were just coming here to phone. Who's going to be leaving messages?'

'Oh Marsha . . . ' Harriet found the window: number 28. She moved towards it, and stood at the back of the queue. 'It's possible that Christopher Pritchard has left a message,' she said carefully. It felt extraordinarily difficult to say his name. 'And even if he hasn't, I want to leave one for him . . .'

Marsha stood and looked at her. 'Why?'

'Just to let him know about Susanna – '

'Why?'

'Marsha – '

'Why on earth should you have to let *him* know? He won't be able to do anything, will he? And she can't stand him.'

'I'm not sure that's true.'

'Yes it is, I know it is. And if you start leaving messages he'll come back and bother us, and want to show us things. You said we'd be on our *own* in Prague.'

'Marsha,' said Harriet, feeling an unexpected but all-consuming tide of grief and frustration and anger begin to rise and course through her, 'please will you stop? Now?'

'But you *said* – '

'Shut up,' said Harriet. 'Shut up, right now, and mind your own business.'

Marsha looked at her in astonishment, and then her eyes filled with tears, and she turned away.

Harriet shook. She stood there breathing and breathing, fighting to control herself.

'I'm sorry,' she said. 'I'm very sorry, Marsha, you didn't deserve that.'

A woman in the next queue was regarding them with interest. She looked at Harriet and shook her head: in sympathy or reproach? Harriet ignored her. She reached for Marsha's hand.

'Please – '

'Every time that man comes near us,' said Marsha bitterly, 'even if you just mention his name, something goes wrong or we have a quarrel.'

It was true.

'I'm sorry,' Harriet said again. The queue was moving forward; Germans and Americans and English and Japanese were collecting their mail. 'Please will you forgive me? Sometimes I just need to be able to do things in my own way – '

'I have never known you to do anything not in your own way. We had all this in Berlin – '

It was true, it was true.

'I think we need a break from each other.'

'I think we do.'

A long silence.

'Kiss and make up and start again?'

Marsha sighed. They kissed. The queue moved forward.

There was no message from Christopher. Of course not, why should there be? They had to go to another window to buy a postcard and envelope, Harriet in her anxious state this morning having forgotten to bring them with her. She stood to one side at the counter and wrote her message, conscious of Marsha hovering.

> Susanna is ill: I'll explain more.
> I should like to meet, if you would.
> I hope all is well with you. Please
> will you ring me?

She scribbled their pension address and phone number. It felt quite extraordinarily difficult to write his name on the envelope. They returned to window 28 and left the letter for him. And then they went to phone Hugh.

He must have already left for the clinic, but he'd remembered, today, to leave on the answerphone.

'Hello,' said Marsha. 'I'm sorry about Susanna, hope she's better soon. We've met Karel, he's really nice. See you soon.'

'Hello,' said Harriet. 'I'll try again. I'm thinking of you. I'll come straight back if it'll help you – ' She gave him, too, the pension number.

And then they went out into the sun again, and walked back to Wenceslas Square and up towards the narrow streets leading to the Old Town Square, where Karel would be waiting.

He was sitting with Gabrielle, reading the papers at a café table on the other side of the Hus Monument, and at first, because he was wearing glasses, they did not recognise him. Then he lifted the paper and folded back its pages with long slender fingers, and the movement, graceful and deft, identified him to Harriet at once. She pointed him out as they walked over the cobbles, and watched Marsha race towards the table and stop, suddenly shy; she watched them all greet each other, following slowly, suddenly shy herself.

'Hello.'

'*Dobry den*, Harriet.' He had risen, he kissed her hand. 'My mother sends her greetings: she has gone to Mass. So – you are well, this morning? You look a little tired.'

'I'm fine, thanks, I expect it's just the travelling catching up with me. I'm sorry we're a bit late.'

'Not at all. We are well occupied, as you can see.' He gestured at the papers, the cups of coffee. Harriet greeted Gabrielle; they all sat in the sun, waiting for a waitress, and she looked at what he'd been reading.

'It feels like a lifetime since I read an English paper.'

'I am sure. For me, the papers are like a drug, you know; the day at the office has not begun until I have looked through them all. After so many years of propaganda it is a blood transfusion.'

What a pleasure, what relief, to talk of something neutral. Harriet sat looking through the Czech *Lidove Noviny* and *Telegraf*, the English *Prague News*. Amongst the news, advertisements for brothels and clubs – 'all erotic services in very luxurious surroundings' – were brazen. Karel followed her gaze as she raised her eyebrows, and laughed.

'A growth industry.'

'I'm sure.'

'*After forty years of being told what they couldn't have, people should be given what they want. And if that's trash and pornography, too bad –* '

She turned the page.

A waitress came, they ordered more coffee, and Coke for the girls. She looked at another Czech paper, *Železni*.

'What's this?'

'Ah, that is *Green*,' said Karel, pushing his glasses up his nose. 'I was telling you yesterday, I think, of my involvement. *Železni* comes out twice a week, but I have time for it only on Sundays. Today I have the pleasure of your company – I have hardly looked at it.'

'I'm sorry – '

'Please. I brought it because I thought it might interest you. I prefer the pleasure of your company, I am just explaining. Sometimes it is a little dry, but there is generally something worth reading. Recently there has been much about restoration – ' He gestured at the richly decorated medieval houses round the square. 'You understand that behind these nice façades is rot in many places. On Wenceslas Square they are ripping out the backs of buildings and putting in concrete and glass offices, and sometimes they are managing this without protest, without a finger lifted. After so many years of being unable to make decisions, we have forgotten how to. This is something of Danielle's field – tomorrow, if you have time, perhaps you will come to our offices and meet her. She can tell you more, if you are interested.'

'Yes,' said Harriet, ' I should like that.' She looked through the pages of the journal, at photographs of demolition sites, hydroelectric power stations, sulphurous clouds of burning lignite, cooling towers. She listened to Karel, soothed, after yesterday's distress, by this reference to issues in the public domain.

I seemed to hold two lives: the life of thought, and that of reality . . .

'It is possible that your brother sees this journal,' Karel was saying. 'We must talk again about the visit you wish to make. I must make a day free.' He smiled, anticipating her demur. 'And that is not a problem. So.' He looked at his watch. 'In a few moments you will hear the clock strike twelve.' He nodded towards the Old Town Hall, where people were gathering.

'We heard it yesterday,' said Marsha.

He bowed. 'My apologies. You are a seasoned traveller.'

She blushed. 'I didn't mean to be rude.'

'You were not rude. But it is something rather special, don't you think?'

'Yes. My mother went on and on about it.'

'Ah. To have a history teacher for a mother – this is a great burden.'

They all laughed, and then the clock began to strike, and, as yesterday, a hush fell over the square. The chimes rang out and the tourists beneath the tower looked up at the steady procession of figures, passing the open windows, passing the angel's wings. Eleven – twelve – silence. The doors of the windows closed. And then, far above them, Death: warning, waiting.

Harriet covered her face.

'Mum?'

'Harriet?' Karel, beside her, was all concern. 'You are unwell?'

'No, no.' She shook her head, lowered her hands, reached for her coffee cup. It was empty.

'You would like a glass of water?'

'No, no, thank you. I'm fine, I expect it's the heat – '

The midday sun shone brightly; bells were ringing all over the city.

Karel gathered up his newspapers; he signalled to a waitress for the menu.

'Perhaps you will be better with something to eat.'

263

Perhaps she would.

'And this afternoon? What would you like to do?'

The steps up to the castle at Hradcany were broad and shallow, patterned in a herringbone of grey and dusty blue, following the course of a high stone wall dripping with vines and creeper. In late August, the leaves were changing colour: rich and gleaming crimson trailed down pale stone between wrought-iron lamps; the steps were dappled with shade from trees in the gardens alongside.

Harriet and Karel climbed slowly, followed by the children. They had eaten lunch, and Harriet had felt better, and then, as the square had begun to fill with tourists looking for a second sitting beneath the parasols, they had wandered away, down to Wenceslas Square again. Walking in the shade of the plane trees all along the pavement, Karel indicated buildings under wraps of heavy plastic sheeting, and they listened to the intermittent sound of hammering. Puffs of brick dust rose into the air, cranes swung over the rooftops.

At Harriet's request, he pointed out the place near the National Museum fountains, below the statue of Wenceslas, where Palach had stood with a can of petrol.

'It is something of a shrine – there are usually candles and flowers.' They looked. There were.

She said: 'I had a poster of him above my desk. I must still have it somewhere.' They walked on, feeling the heat grow more intense; the pavements grew more crowded. The girls were flagging; she said, 'Perhaps we shouldn't try to do too much. I made that mistake in Berlin.'

'You have told me almost nothing of your time in Berlin.'

'No.'

Couples were wandering hand in hand beneath the trees ahead of them, stopping every now and then for a drink, a kiss, a cigarette. Everyone smoked in Prague.

She said: 'It may sound silly, but this is a kind of pilgrimage for me – to come here and see all the places we saw on television.'

'To make a piece of history come alive. It does not sound silly.'

'Yes, but it's more than that. I looked for you, amongst all those crowds in the snow – '

'Of course. If London had been on the television here, I also should look for you. It is natural to look for someone you know.' He smiled at her. 'Naturally, you never see them.'

Harriet smiled back. They came to a wooden bench; they all sank on to it, watching the traffic go by. Harriet thought: he makes it sound as if I could be anyone – 'It is natural to look for someone you know.' Was I just 'someone' in those distant, happy days? Am I just 'someone' now?

A few dry leaves fell from the trees, spinning slowly in the dusty air.

'What are we going to do now?' asked Marsha, swinging her legs.

'I want to see where you stay,' said Gaby.

'Oh, yes!'

'We could have tea there,' said Harriet. 'We could visit the castle. And the cathedral.'

'That is a lot to do,' said Karel, and Marsha looked at him gratefully. 'And it will be crowded. But still – ' he got to his feet. 'We can go up and look at the view.'

They caught the 22 tram across the river to Neruda Street and walked up the hill to the foot of the Castle walls. Now they were making the steep climb up the steps, going more and more slowly in the heat. But still. They were not on a route march, they could stop and rest, as others were doing, holding on to the handrail, listening to the birds, and it was, after all, ancient and beautiful, with this view over the city, this delicious combination of blues and greys and crimson and stone and shady green. And for Harriet it was, above all, distraction: from thoughts of Susanna and Hugh, from thoughts of Christopher, and when he might pick up her message, and what he might do when he did.

They came to the top of the steps; they walked along by the castle railings.

'I thought that was the castle,' said Marsha, pointing to the towering cathedral behind it.

'It is understandable.' Karel had taken off his jacket and carried it over his shoulder. He reached in his pocket for a handkerchief to wipe his face. 'This is more like a palace, I think. And the President has his office there – ' He pointed out a section of the long neoclassical façade behind the railings. 'You know about President Havel?'

Marsha looked mulish. 'A bit.'

'Quite enough, I am sure. He was in prison and now he is in a castle. It is a fairytale.'

In the baking heat, they turned to look down over the hill and the city. The orange rooftops of the Little Quarter tumbled away below them; beyond were trees, and the hazy afternoon blue of the river. On the other side were shimmering turrets and spires, chalky green domes and golden weather vanes. And cranes, everywhere.

'Have I been up here before?' asked Gaby.

'Not for a long while. When you were little, I think.'

'When Mama was living with us.'

'Yes.'

They walked on, seeking the shade of trees again, and Harriet looked at Gaby, who seemed to mind so little that her mother was not with them, while Marsha cared so passionately about her fatherless state. Well. Gabrielle saw her mother, relations between her and Karel were good, it was different. But still, but even so. Did Gabrielle never have outbursts? Did she and Karel never quarrel?

Tourists were walking through tall iron gates. 'We could visit the apartments,' said Karel. 'Now we are here. We could walk through and visit the cathedral, as you suggested, Harriet. It will be cool in there, and the Chapel of St Wenceslas is particularly fine.'

There was a silence.

'Or,' he continued, turning to look down over the hillside again, 'we could walk down to the orchards of Petrin – you see over there, to your right? Beyond the dome of St Nicholas? It's very pleasant there, almost like the countryside.' He looked at them all. 'What do you think?'

Marsha looked back at him. 'What do you think?'

Apples and plums were ripening; the grass was waving and tall, and wild flowers grew amongst it. The air was balmy, and a breeze like the one which had accompanied Harriet's walk through the cemeteries in Žižkov yesterday – was it only yesterday? – was stirring now, a gentle rustle in the leaves of the fruit trees, a caress on the grass, on their faces. Birds sang, there was the hum of bees. The city stretched out before them, but on this quiet slope of the hill it was, as Karel had told them, like being in the country. Marsha and Gaby were picking flowers. Their voices floated through the afternoon heat, to where Harriet and Karel were sitting, under an apple tree.

Harriet lifted her face to the sun, and closed her eyes. She let the warmth seep into her, and the sadness, unease and tension she had been carrying with her since yesterday evening all began, just a little, to dissipate. She was sitting on a hillside above Prague; it was summer; her daughter was happy. Beside her was someone she had thought she might never see again, who had given her the sweetest and most poignant moments of her youth. She opened her eyes and turned to look at him.

He was watching the children; he felt her gaze upon him.

'So. How is Harriet?'

'Well, thank you.' She stretched and yawned and smiled at him. 'I feel, for the first time since we set out, as if I were on holiday.'

Was it true? It was true.

He said: 'A great deal has happened to you on this journey.'

'Yes.'

'And some of these things have distressed you, I think.'

She clasped her knees; she looked down at the uncut grass, where insects were clambering.

'You mentioned this yesterday – you said that the cemeteries had made you unhappy. Or made you think of someone else who was unhappy, is that correct?' He was tugging at a long tough stem, bending it this way and that. 'Do you want to talk to me about this, or is it something private?'

'I – ' She wanted to tell him; she knew that to talk here, on this flowery hillside, of the darkness and despair which Susanna carried within her, and what it had led her to do, would help to dispel some of her own grief and confusion. But it also felt like betrayal: to tell someone to whom Susanna meant nothing, before she had told someone who understood her, to whom she had once been everything. And also: to tell Karel about Susanna would mean telling him about Christopher, and that she could not do. Not yet. Perhaps never. Nothing had happened, and yet, and yet –

Karel had broken off the stem of grass, and was running it between his fingers. The air was full of birdsong, the summery drone of bees, and children's voices. A couple of feet away a grasshopper leapt, suddenly, and vanished – such a joyous, spontaneous sight.

She said: 'It's perfect here. I don't want to spoil it.' It was true. 'And anyway – I'm feeling better.' That was also true. How, in such company, in such a place, could she not feel better?

He smiled at her. 'Good. But even so – if you feel you would like to tell me . . .' He ran finger and thumb along the grass stem, a graceful, repeated movement. 'I will listen.'

'Thank you.'

The children were coming towards them, bare legs brushed by the long thick grass. They carried bunches of wild, unfamiliar flowers, yellow and white and mauvey-pink, and more grasses, heavy with seeds.

'Happy?' asked Harriet, as Marsha drew near.

She nodded. 'It's the best day of the holiday. Here.' She held out her flowers; the stems in Harriet's hands felt warm and damp and crushed. She buried her face, brushing insects away.

'Lovely; thank you.'

'You have picked the whole hillside,' Karel said to Gaby.

'No, we haven't.' She flopped down beside him and leaned against his shoulder.

'Gaby wants to see our room,' Marsha told Harriet.

'Yes. Well – we can do that. Let's just stay for a little while, shall we?'

And so, for a little while, they went on sitting there, under the apple trees, watching the sun begin to sink over the city once more, and the air grow rich and golden and still. A little funicular railway ran up and down the hillside. Bees murmured; invisible grasshoppers scraped and rasped and occasionally leapt into view and were gone again. The bells of St Nicholas began to ring.

Marsha said: 'I'll always remember this.'

And then, after a while, they got up from the grass, and began the walk back down the hill, and into the shady streets of Mala Strana.

Harriet and Marsha, guides for once, led the others through to their own particular street, to the blue-painted door in the wall which opened into their cramped little courtyard.

'But you have found the nicest place in Prague,' said Karel, as Harriet closed it behind them.

'Is that true?' She led them up the winding back stairs to their bedroom, turning the key in the lock. The door swung open: the room, as it had been on the afternoon of their arrival, was very warm, smelling of dust and wood. She crossed to open the window, and a pigeon on the tiled roof below flew away, startled, and came back at once. Behind her were murmurs in English and Czech as others looked round.

Harriet leaned for a moment on the worn and rotting wood of the window frame, looking out across the orange tiles, hearing the Sunday evening bells. She thought of the star-filled night which had passed, of how she had stood here shivering, filled with sadness, and how the afternoon, and Karel's company – his solid engagement with the world, his gentle humour, easy kindness to Marsha, and sensitivity towards her own state of mind – had warmed and helped to calm her.

She turned. Marsha had sunk on to her bed in exhaustion; Gaby, perched beside her, was looking at the unread English children's books on the bedside table.

Karel was leaning against the door, looking round him. She watched him take in the high iron beds, rush chair, suitcases, chest of drawers. The setting sun streamed in and touched, as it had touched on the afternoon of their arrival, the small wooden box she had placed there.

She said: 'Those are your letters.'

'In here?' He crossed the bare floorboards, bleached by the sun; he picked up the box, looked at her questioningly, lifted the lid. He took out the bundle of thin, airmail envelopes, with their hesitant, Biroed capitals, and stood looking at it, shaking his head. And as on the afternoon of their arrival, Harriet thought again of the film she had seen once, in another lifetime, down at the NFT on a winter's evening: an old man in a clean white shirt, taking off his wedding ring, putting it side by side with his wife's, in a little open box on a chest of drawers. A whole life together.

The room was full of quietness.

Karel put the letters back in the box, and with long graceful fingers closed the lid. He crossed the room and lifted her hand to his lips.

5

On Mondays the tourist attractions of museums and galleries were closed.

'Thank God for that,' said Marsha, as they breakfasted out in the courtyard. Pigeons cooed on the gables above them, walking back and forth, and a feather or two drifted down, landing on the table. She blew them softly away again, reaching for a roll. 'So today we're visiting Karel's office. Good.'

'And meeting Danielle, perhaps,' Harriet leaned back in her chair, slowly drinking her coffee.

'I wonder what she's like.'

'So do I.' She was filled, all at once, with apprehension.

After breakfast, they walked through the streets towards Malostranske Square again. The shops were not long open, and shopkeepers were pulling down the awnings, setting out baskets of vegetables and fruit on the pavements. The air was still cool, the streets were not yet crowded; they walked companionably down the hill towards the great gateways at the entrance to the Charles Bridge.

The river gleamed and sparkled in the early morning sun. They leaned on the parapet between two stone saints, and looked down at the swans, at the barges. Men were throwing ropes, and calling; when they crossed to the other side they could hear building work: banging and hammering, the clang of scaffolding poles coming down, and whistling.

Karel's office was in a street not far from Charles Square, in the heart of Nove Mesto, the New Town. Harriet took out her map.

'It's such a beautiful morning. Why don't we walk? We carry on along the river, and then cut through, after a couple of bridges.'

'Okay.'

The houses along the waterfront were tall and gabled with decorated façades. Havel's family apartment was somewhere near here, not far from an old bomb site, ripe for redevelopment. They passed long islands, thickly planted, and a low white 1930s art gallery, straddling the water. They stopped to look up at the golden finials piercing the sky on the roof of the National Theatre, at the foot of the Leglí Bridge. They were on a long riverside road once named after Marx and Engels: their names had vanished, and Harriet was taken back to graffiti-covered statues in windswept concrete plazas in Berlin, the bitter scrawling out of the past.

She looked at her map again, checking how far they had gone. 'Here we are.' At the end of Jiráskuv Bridge they crossed into Resslova, walking towards the long narrow park which was Charles Square, once a cattle market.

Nove Mesto was business Prague, commercial and administrative Prague, a medieval city with a modern city added, during the industrial revolution, on to its original plan. The broad boulevards, streets and open squares had been built by Charles IV: to link the Old Town with the fortress of Vysehrad, further south; to cater for the monks and merchants pouring into the new capital of the Holy Roman Empire, and to house workers and craftsmen away from the peaceful university atmosphere of the Old Town. But the workers and craftsmen went to hear radical Jan Hus, preaching passionate sermons in the Bethelem Chapel in Czech, not Latin. The area became a hotbed of reformist discontent; it became rundown, neglected. Many of the churches remained, but in the nineteenth century a great swathe of slum clearance cut through the houses. Now, the district was bustling, full of office blocks, bars, department stores and cinemas.

Harriet and Marsha walked along the filling pavements, and up through the park. Karel's street was off Vodičkova, running to the north; they stopped to look at the shops, and a vast McDonald's.

'Can we have lunch there?'

'Certainly not.' They came to his corner. 'Here we are.'

Karel might live in a tenement, but his office was modern and smart, an open-plan floor on the fourth storey of a block through whose large windows you could glimpse the river. Marsha and Harriet took the lift, and coming out on the landing walked through swing doors and were at once amidst a hubbub: ringing phones, a chattering fax and printer, desks piled high with documents. They stood looking around them, at red filing cabinets, maps and posters, computer screens. A busy lawyers' office, where people came and went and ignored them. There was a reception desk, but no receptionist. A phone on the desk rang and rang.

'Gosh,' said Marsha. 'Where is he?'

He was over in a far corner by a window overlooking the street. He was on the phone, wearing his glasses, leaning on his elbow, listening, playing with a pencil. Harriet had the impression of complete concentration, of someone who knew exactly what he was doing, as he nodded and answered, and made notes. Like Hugh, a little, but speedier, more driven.

'Who do you think's Danielle?' asked Marsha.

'Ssh. I don't know.'

'I do. Bet you anything. Look over there.'

Harriet looked. A woman about her own age, perhaps a bit younger, was perched half on, half off a desk, laughing with a man at the next one. Glossy fair hair, cut in a swinging bob, scarlet lipstick, a linen suit with a short skirt which could have come from Paris. Perhaps it had. A woman of charm and vitality and self-possession: you could see it at a glance. Someone who could go anywhere, who knew what she wanted and made sure she got it: you could see that, too. And Harriet, taking all this in, had two thoughts assail her. The first that there was something of the *Zeitgeist* of the new Europe: confident, energetic, catching up, racing towards the future. And, simultaneously, on quite another track: if Karel and I – if we continue – if we – It is possible I might know this woman all my life.

'See?' said Marsha, beside her. 'Don't you think?'

'Sssh. Yes, think you're right.'

'I'm always right.'

The woman became aware of being watched. She glanced round, saw Harriet and Marsha, and gave them a look both direct and curious. With a sudden gesture of understanding, she slid off the edge of her desk and crossed the room, her hand outstretched.

'You are Harriet! Karel's friend, yes? And Marsha? I am Danielle. How do you do.'

'How do you do.' They shook hands, and she called across the office. 'Karel! What are you doing? Look who is here.'

He looked, lowering his glasses; Marsha laughed. He raised a finger; he finished his conversation, and came over. There were greetings, a kiss on the hand for each of them. Marsha blushed.

'You must excuse me – I did not realise – So. You have met.' He was looking from one to the other.

'We have,' said Harriet, and did not know what else to say for a minute. She waved a hand at the office and its activity. 'This is all very – '

'It is all very boring, perhaps,' said Danielle.

'No, not at all – '

They followed her across to her desk.

'You would like coffee? Tea? For you, Marsha? I am so pleased to meet you – Gaby has been telling me all about you. Now – ' She had taken charge, she had taken over. Drinks appeared, and she questioned them with animation: about their journey, the place where they were staying, how long it was since Harriet and Karel had met. In 1968? So long ago! *Then!* Even before she and Karel themselves had known each other. She listened to their responses and glanced, now and then, at her watch.

'You must be very busy,' said Harriet. Karel had returned to his desk, to take another call – 'Excuse me, one moment – ' She felt the intimacy they had begun to establish slip away. She was a visitor from England. Prague was full of visitors.

'There must be many beautiful girls in Czechoslovakia – '

She buried her face in his neck; thinking of them all.

'But none of them called Harriet – '

Had such moments ever taken place? Did they mean anything now?

They talked, they finished their coffee and Coke. Danielle hoped they would join them for lunch – Hannah was bringing Gaby down, they could eat at the Café Slavia, a few blocks away on Narodni. She was sure they would like it, most tourists did.

Yes, said Harriet, she had seen pictures.

'You can't tell my mother anything,' said Marsha.

Danielle laughed. All mothers were the same. And then, after lunch, if they were really interested, she could show them something of a project she was working on, for one of her clients.

She picked up her jacket and bag.

They followed in her wake.

The Café Slavia was a dream, an art nouveau coffee house not far from the river, opposite the National Theatre, all cream and chocolate and brass interior, with opaque glass lamps on curving stems, a grand piano, round tables, ladies in hats. Havel used to come here, Karel told them: it had long been a writers' haunt, a place for talking, smoking, exchanging ideas. He did not seem to be here today. Hannah arrived – looking, in a skirt and blouse, as if she had made an effort but still felt out of place. Gaby, accompanying her, wore a dress.

'I wish you had told us,' said Harriet, as they all sat down.

Karel shrugged. 'I did not know. This is Danielle's idea.'

Danielle laughed. It had been a spur of the moment thought, when she had heard they were coming. She passed the menu. So. What would they have?

They had chicken in paprika sauce, a cucumber salad, fruit *compote*. They had coffee in tiny black and gold cups and Danielle paid the bill. And then she led them all outside again.

Karel had to return to the office for a meeting.

'My apologies. I shall see you soon.'

They spent an hour or longer with Danielle, in a street behind the waterfront, looking at the restoration work being done on a fine baroque building. Plastic sheeting shrouded the upper floors, a skip stood on the pavement, there was dust everywhere. Danielle talked and talked. Her clients, a new property company, were running out of money; she was advising them about a loan, but suggesting that perhaps they might consider turning the ground floor into a restaurant. This was the kind of thing Karel had mentioned as helping to destroy a local community. Harriet, carefully, mentioned this, and rather wished she hadn't. Danielle produced papers from her briefcase; she quoted statistics detailing growth in the economy, the healthy effect of foreign tourism on restaurants of just such character. They followed her from room to empty room, smelling new plaster, picturing it all. Marsha and Gaby picked up workmen's tools and put them down again.

'You will get filthy,' said Danielle.

And then, at last, the tour stopped, they were out in the street again, saying goodbye. Hannah and Gaby were accompanying Danielle back to the office, where they would wait for her to finish work. This evening, she was taking Gaby home to her own apartment, on the other side of Nove Mesto. Harriet and Marsha must come and see her there one evening, before their return to London: that would be a pleasure.

Perhaps, Hannah suggested, Marsha could come and see Gaby tomorrow? Harriet could have a little time to herself, if she wished.

They shook hands, they thanked Danielle; she gave them, both, the lightest kiss on each cheek. And then she was gone, turning the corner, down towards Charles Square, and Harriet and Marsha drew breath, and made for the river again, where they found a wooden bench and sat looking out at the water in an exhausted silence.

Harriet, in the pension bathroom, washing away the heat and fatigue of the afternoon in cloudy tap water, heard the low, single, continental note of the telephone sound through the house. She dried her hands and came out, wondering. Pani Maria was calling her, from the foot of the stairs. An English gentleman, in a phone box.

Harriet came down slowly to the dark little hall overlooking the courtyard. Outside, it was still very hot, though the sun was sinking. A few dry leaves fell from the tree, on to the cracked flagstones.

'Hello?'

'Harriet.'

'Christopher.' Her stomach turned over. 'How nice to hear you.'

'And you.' He went straight to the point. 'You said you had news of Susanna.'

'Yes.' She drew a breath, leaning against the wall by the telephone table, seeing herself, very pale, in the mildewed mirror above. Pani Maria, in slippers, had gone out into the courtyard, she was sweeping the ground, as she did every evening, brushing up the day's accumulation of city dust, bread dropped from the table, fallen leaves.

She said: 'It's not very good – ' and told him, listening to the steady sweep sweep of the long rush broom, over and over the flags.

She found she was shaking again.

'Christopher?'

'Yes. Jesus.' He had gone white, she could feel it.

'I want to see you.'

'Yes.' He was thinking. 'Tomorrow?' A pause. 'I'll meet you in the saddest place in Prague.'

'I know where that is,' she said, thinking of Kafka, of dandelions in uncut grass, clouds passing over the empty plots of land, but she didn't know.

Dark elder grew within the perimeter walls; birches and lime trees shaded raised, uneven ground, bare earth. In the Old Jewish Cemetery in Josefov, the gravestones stood so close together that in many places it was difficult to walk between them: they leaned against one another at angles, broken and grey, crammed into the ground. Lichen covered the worn reliefs of hands giving benediction, of jugs anointing; it crept into the crevices of Hebrew lettering: dates, verses, names of the dead.

Beyond the walls, the sound of traffic on the northern, art nouveau boulevard of Parizska was a distant hum. It was mid-afternoon.

Harriet, who had left Marsha with Gaby and Hannah, walked in the heat past leafy Jan Palach Square, and along to the crossroads of Listo Padu and Brehova. She came to the cemetery entrance – a synagogue on one side, the Memorial Hall on the other – and went through.

Christopher was waiting beneath the trees, amidst the gravestones.

He was wearing his creased linen jacket, his hands in the pockets. He looked as he had looked the last time she saw him, in the hall of the Hotel Scheiber: heavy and tired and ill at ease, his face puffy, though the bruise had faded, had almost gone.

'Hello.' He came towards her, unsmiling; he did not give her a kiss in greeting.

'Hello.' Harriet looked up at him, nervous and uncertain.

'Where's your daughter?'

'With friends. Down in Žižkov.' She looked away.

'Well – ' he said abruptly, and turned, moving towards a narrow path.

Here we are again –

She did not say it. She moved alongside him; they walked where they could, amidst the stones. For over three hundred years, since the fifteenth century, this cramped plot had been the only burial ground for the Jews of Prague. As they died within the overcrowded ghetto, where four or five families shared a house, they were brought here, the earth reopened, another coffin dropped down on to those below. The ground was raised, as more bodies came; some of the stones, shifting, now marked the graves of the wrong family. The bodies lay eight, ten, twelve deep; Harriet and Christopher, two of the afternoon's visitors, were walking amongst ten or twelve thousand stones, above a hundred thousand bodies. In death, as in life, the Jews were crammed together.

In 1781, when the Emperor Josef granted an Edict of Toleration, the gates came off the walled ghetto. The district was given his name – Josefov – and a community was effectively destroyed: no separate schools, no Hebrew or Yiddish. Six years later the cemetery was closed: from that time, burials were in the New Jewish Cemetery which Harriet had visited.

In the war, yellow stars replaced medieval yellow cloaks. Then came the Holocaust, and the burial plots lay empty. And now, the cemetery where Harriet and Christopher were walking in a difficult silence was almost all that remained of the old Jewish Quarter. In a sweep-clean, expansionist mood at the end of the nineteenth century, when Prague had looked to Paris for an elegant, bourgeois city on which to model itself, every tenement, every little shop had been razed to the ground. Now there were only synagogues, a town hall, a museum; this densely populated graveyard, evoking the vanished lives of centuries.

And what of Susanna's life, which she had so nearly ended? What of Christopher, walking beside Harriet in silence, his hands in his pockets, looking straight ahead?

'Not the best circumstances in which to meet,' he said at last.

'No. I'm sorry.'

'What for?'

'I don't know. For Susanna, about Susanna – I've been thinking of her so much since we arrived. When I spoke to Hugh it was – I don't know – almost like a confirmation. I could feel something building up in me – it's hard to explain.'

Footsteps were passing the perimeter walls; the afternoon heat was intense. Birds rustled the leaves in the branches above them.

She said: 'I visited Kafka's grave,' and she told him – or tried to tell him – of her feelings then: unease, desolation, her sense of Susanna's broken spirit.

She said, with great hesitation, 'And I thought of you, too. In that way, in that context . . .'

He did not answer. They walked on, coming back to the entrance, continuing. Harriet was looking at the ground, at the caked earth, dappled with shade.

He said: 'We should be here in winter. Let me show you something I find unbearably sad, and poetic.'

She lifted her head: he was indicating a gravestone with something resting on its worn flat rim: a pebble, and beneath it a piece of paper.

'What's that?' She moved towards it.

'A wish. A message. From someone to someone else, from lovers, from descendants to the Lord Jehovah – who knows? They leave them here all the time.' He crossed to the pebble, and lifted it; he unfolded the paper. They looked at a few Hebrew words, a signature. 'Sometimes they're in Hebrew, but mostly in Czech. And visitors leave them. Like prayers in churches, you know?'

'Yes.'

He refolded the paper. 'Keep looking, there'll be more.'

'What happens to them?'

'No doubt they're collected. Mostly they're blown away by the wind.

Then more come. People have been leaving them here for centuries. Tradition dates it back to the Exodus – nothing but stones to mark desert graves. There.' He replaced the pebble; she noticed, again, the tremor in his hands. 'A little piece of history for you.'

'Thank you.'

They walked on. He said: 'For all I know, they could be shopping lists. But I don't think they are. And I do find the idea moving – all that hope, all that longing, left for the wind to blow across a graveyard.'

She could not speak. This was the man she had once dismissed? This was the loud, intrusive guest?

At length she said, again with infinite caution, 'Susanna left a message, too. I do not begin to understand it – '

'No.' He felt in his pocket, then lit a cigarette, dropping the lighter back. 'I'm sorry, I suppose I shouldn't.'

'Everyone smokes in Prague.'

'But not here.' He inhaled deeply.

She said, remembering the starry sky above Malá Strana, leaning out of the window, the night of the telephone call, 'Since Berlin – since what has happened – sometimes I've wondered if you're the person Susanna needs, in spite of everything – you're the one who understands her, and can help her – '

'On the contrary.' He drew in smoke again, almost violently; he let it out again in a great stream. 'I am the last person to help Susanna.'

'Because – '

'Because I can't even help myself. Because I ruin every bloody thing I touch, that's why.'

'Christopher – '

'What?' He was smoking, pacing, looking at the ground. 'Here we are again,' he said bitterly. 'Because somebody tried to kill herself.'

'Not just because – '

'Isn't it? Listen.' He threw the cigarette to the ground, crushed it with his foot, kicked over a covering of earth. 'Listen. I want to talk to you. I wanted to see you, I've seen you. I'm going to talk, if you will be kind enough to listen, and then we shall say goodbye.'

She said bleakly: 'Go on.'

He said: 'I'm divorced. You're divorced. The whole fucking world is divorced, these days.'

Karel, also. She thought of the box on the chest of drawers, the two rings, side by side.

'And your parents?'

'My parents are happy,' she said. 'They have a good marriage, I think.'

'How reassuring. Perhaps that explains your fundamental good sense. My parents hated each other. They split up when I was four, then they tried again, then it didn't work. I was sent off to boarding school, out of the way of the rows. That's where I met your nice brother.'

'Yes.'

Pritchard was a bit of a bully in those days – we kept an eye on him –

Did he ever do anything to harm you?

No, never, he just had a reputation –

'Most of the rest of my life I've told you about – an edited version, anyway. In Berlin. But that's where it all began, I think. I was abandoned. Bring on the violins. It almost killed me.'

There were others in the cemetery: middle-aged women were talking quietly, a man in a skull-cap was leading a child, pointing things out on the gravestones. Christopher walked away from them all; Harriet followed.

He said: 'I did various unpleasant things to people at school. That's not so uncommon. Bullying in distant places, coming home in the holidays to listen to your parents tear each other apart. All term I wanted to go home, all holidays I wanted to go back to school. Jesus. You can't talk about yourself to your teachers, you can't talk to your parents – it all gets sat on, and buried. That's how I understand Susanna – not her particular brand of self-hatred, it's true, but the fact of its existence, the feelings that go with it. That doesn't mean I can help her. We almost destroyed each other, I told you.'

He lit another cigarette; disapproving glances came across the cemetery.

'They're right, they're right, everyone's right except me.'

'Christopher – I care so much for you . . .'

It was true, it was true.

He shook his head. 'You wouldn't, Harriet, not if you got to know me.'

That's what Susanna had said, weeping in the little garden behind the Grand Place, rubbing her foot in the gravel, over and over, a bear in a cage –

'Christopher, please – '

'What? Too much self-pity? It's true – you wouldn't like me. I thought in Berlin – when we were talking – I thought perhaps – It's hopeless. I'm eaten away. All the feelings you sit on come out in the end: all that fucking misery has to get out somehow. With me it was risks, and dangerous money. I fell foul, I told you, I'm still paying for it, literally. I do things you wouldn't believe – '

'That's enough,' said Harriet, her hands to her face. 'Stop. Please. I don't want to hear any more.'

He stopped, dead in his tracks. 'You see? What did I tell you?'

'No, no, I mean just for now – it's too much, after hearing about Susanna, I'm too upset – perhaps all this touches a chord in myself, I don't know. But for now – I think you should stop. I think we should go somewhere else, and sit quietly, and try to be calm – '

He walked towards the wall, he leaned against it, smoking. He ground the cigarette underfoot.

'A desecration.'

'It is, rather.'

He nodded. 'I'm sorry. I've alarmed you, I've upset you, I shouldn't have come to meet you.'

'It was I who asked to meet you.'

'Yes, so it was. But even so – ' He rubbed at his cheek. 'You're right: that's enough, now.' He looked at her, full in the face, as she stood before him. 'How is your reunion? How is your friend?'

She looked back at him. She swallowed. 'He's terribly nice.'

'I'm sure.'

'But – '

'But nothing.' He held out his hand; she took it. They went on standing there, just a foot or two apart, holding hands, looking in each other's eyes, exploring each other's faces. Around them were the sounds of departing footsteps, and birds, and distant traffic. Then he drew her to him, and turned her round, and held her against his chest, his arms round her, his chin resting on her head.

They stood for a while without speaking, quiet and close.

'There's another message,' he said at last.

'Where?'

'Just there, to your right, see?'

She looked. It was there: a torn scrap of paper, a smooth white stone.

'Where do they come from, all these stones and pebbles?'

'I don't know. People bring them, I suppose. Perhaps I should have

280

brought one. Perhaps I should leave you a message. Yes? What do you think?' He buried his face in her hair; she leaned back, brushing her face against his.

'What would it say? Your message.'

He was silent. 'Who knows? *Dear Harriet, I have fallen in love with you, but I wouldn't make you happy.* Something like that. Bring on the violins.'

She turned in his arms, her mouth met his. There came oblivion, the taste of cigarettes.

'Christopher – '

Across the cemetery, somebody coughed. They drew apart.

'A desecration.'

'Yes.'

'Come on.' He took her hand; they walked in the deepest silence back towards the gate. Harriet looked down at the caked earth. The first dry leaves of late summer, or early autumn, were falling, now and then, to the ground, brushing the stones. She was trembling.

She said, as they came to the gate, not looking at him, speaking unsteadily, 'I don't want to say goodbye.'

'I thought I should be saying that to you,' he said slowly.

'But – '

'But I wouldn't make you happy. I know it. I know myself. I'm very sorry.'

They were standing outside on the street again. Passers-by came and went.

Harriet looked at Christopher, heavy and tall and sombre. She thought: I want to lie naked before this man in a shuttered room, and have him stand naked before me –

She closed her eyes.

'Goodbye.' He kissed her hair: the gentlest, most tender touch. And then he walked away from her.

So. This was love. So complex, so full of pain.

Harriet stood at the entrance: a synagogue on one side, a Memorial Hall on the other. She thought: I must distract myself. I am not used to feelings like this. I don't know what to do when I feel like this.

People walked past her; somebody said, 'You okay?'

It was the young American, the boy she had met by Jan Palach's grave.

'Hey -- you again.'

She looked at him blankly.

He came towards her. 'Listen, you don't look too good – '

'Go away, go away.' She was incoherent. She turned aside: she was by the open door of the Memorial Hall; she walked inside: swiftly, blindly.

The Memorial Hall housed the poems and paintings done by the children of Terezín, the model concentration camp outside Prague. They were hung on bare walls; strands of barbed wire evoked the camp perimeter. The children had painted gardens, flowers, butterflies. They had painted hangings, dark skies, grimacing faces; children, herded away. And then they had been herded away, to the death camps over the border.

Harriet walked round the two rooms, looking at these harrowing images from the past.

The past is more real to me than my own life –

That was no longer true.

After a while, she came out again. The young American boy had gone. She walked past the cemetery walls, looking straight ahead, and rapidly beneath the trees alongside, down to Jan Palach Square, along Kaprova, and into the Old Town Square. The clock was striking five. She did not stop to look up at the procession of saints, or listen to Death ring out his warning. She walked rapidly over the cobbles, and into Celetna, catching the tram to Žižkov, where Marsha – to whom, all afternoon, she had not given a thought – was waiting for her.

6

In the early 1880s, towards the end of his life, Marx took the water at Karlovy Vary. Better known to the world as Karlsbad, the spa town in western Bohemia, set on the steep wooded banks of the River Tepla, was a belle époque dream, all pastel coloured houses with façades like iced cakes, and shops as fine as Vienna's. A little funicular railway ran up and down the hillside: at the top, you could walk amongst oak and beech trees and admire the view. In the town, after rising at six to take the waters, you might indulge yourself with coffee and rich *Torten*, dance flirtatious afternoons away to a string quartet, visit the theatre with frescoes and swishing curtain by Gustav Klimt.

Everyone, celebrated and obscure, came to Karlsbad. Goethe enjoyed romantic assignments, Schiller drank eighteen cure cups of the sparkling salty waters. Gushing from deep springs and geysers, they were reputed to cure almost everything.

But even then, mine workings were encroaching on the mineral-rich land beneath the Krušne Hory mountains, along the German–Czech border of northern Bohemia. Mining companies dug for porcelain clay, and for lignite, which fuelled the factories being built alongside. Northeast of Karlsbad, some ninety kilometres from Prague, stood the lovely spa town of Teplice – concerts, swans on the lakes, a château, the drawing room of Europe – visited by Wagner, Liszt and Beethoven. Nearby, mine workings breached an underwater lake, flooding the natural springs.

Already, here and there, the smell of burning lignite hung in the air. Already sulphurous yellow fumes rose from the factory chimneys, drifting in and out of the clouds.

'The alternative,' said Karel, overtaking a lorry, 'is nuclear power. The issue of nuclear power is dividing Bohemia in two.' He glanced in the rear-view mirror. 'Marsha? I am alarming you with my driving? Gaby is used to me, but you must say if I drive too fast.'

'I'm fine,' said Marsha, squashed up next to Gaby and Hanna. 'It's fun.'

'Harriet?' He turned towards her. 'You are quiet this morning. Perhaps I am talking too much?'

'No, no. I'm listening.'

She looked away, gazing at the countryside. They were travelling in Karel's bright red Skoda, towards the German border, on the road from Prague to Berlin. Yesterday had been a blur, Karel too busy to see them and Harriet too filled with emotion to know what to do – with herself, or with Marsha. In the end, after wandering among stalls and markets, she had looked in an English-language entertainments guide and taken her to a puppet theatre in a street off the Old Town Square. They sat in the darkness watching Czech fairytales unfold on a tiny stage. Black paper silhouettes made forests and castles; pinpricks of stars illuminated the progress of clicking wooden feet down paths full of danger; goblin voices croaked from beneath the footlights. Marsha was entranced.

'Didn't you like it?' she asked, as they came out into the crowded little foyer. 'You're not *saying* anything.'

'Sorry. Perhaps I'm under a spell.'

They walked back to Mala Strana over the Charles Bridge, stopping, as usual, to look at the stalls of painted eggs and cheap wooden toys, and listen to buskers' Mozart float across the water.

'I feel really at home here now,' said Marsha.

Back in the pension, Harriet telephoned Hugh, letting Marsha speak first this time.

'We're going out to the country tomorrow,' she told him. 'With Karel. We're going to visit your power station place. Love to Susanna. Here's Mum.'

She handed the receiver to Harriet and wandered out to the courtyard.

'Hugh? How is she?'

'She's low, but she's coming home tomorrow. We seem to have found someone she can talk to – a priest turned therapist. He seems okay, the clinic found him – ' He sounded drained, exhausted. 'This isn't exactly my territory . . .'

'Oh, Hugh – I'm so sorry. Would you not like me to come?'

'No, no – we'll be all right. What about you, how are you? I hope all this hasn't clouded – '

She could not speak.

'Harriet?'

'It's okay – ' She felt tears well up, and put her hand to her mouth.
'Darling – '
'Don't, don't, it's okay, I'm fine. Talk to you soon.'
She put down the receiver and leaned against the wall by the mirror, feeling grief and pain make war within her, looking out over the darkening courtyard. Marsha was sitting at the table.
'You coming out, Mum?'
'Yes, in a minute.'
'It's nice out here.'
Harriet drew a breath. She went to sit beside her. The pigeons on the rooftop were murmuring contentedly, settling for the night.

The camp at Terezín stood on the road from Prague to Berlin, but Harriet, in the end, had been unable to contemplate a visit. To read of it was enough; to see the children's pictures in Josefov had been enough. And Marsha and Gaby were too young to be taken through gates bearing the slogan ARBEIT MACHT FREI, to follow a tour of the barracks, the railway tracks, the scaffold. They drove past the turn-off without mentioning it to the children; only to Hannah, squeezed on the back seat between them, did Karel give a nod as they passed the sign, and she made no comment.

They drove on, through gently undulating countryside, farmland, fed by the river Labe. To the east, towards Karlovy Vary, lay the great hop-growing regions. Here, Harriet looked out of the window at harvested fields full of stubble and stooks, at tractors moving along the skyline, cattle swishing away flies beneath the trees.

It was mid-morning, the sun climbing the sky, but the air through the open car windows felt cooler than in the city streets. She leaned back in her seat, adjusting the worn belt and listening to the girls singing pop songs they both knew from the radio; to Hannah's good-humoured reproaches when they grew too shrill; and to Karel, rehearsing the issues of the day as they made their way towards the old spa town of Teplice, near to where Hugh had made his investment.

She was trying not to think of Hugh in any other context. She was trying not to think of Susanna, the morning they had visited his office in the immaculately clean street near the Parliament building in Brussels: her back to the window, fingering her wristwatch, observing them all, set apart.

'*Susanna?*'

'Yes?'

'I should so like to get to know you better.'

'Now is not the moment.'

'It never is.'

'No.' She lifted her hands to her head and clasped it – briefly, but as if she couldn't help herself, as if she were trying to hold everything in place –

Harriet, trying to concentrate on what Karel was saying, put her hands to her own head for a moment. She was trying not to think of Susanna; she was trying to banish the continual reliving of a more recent conversation, held amongst gravestones, walking alongside someone heavy and tall and sombre.

'You see this is something of a real dilemma,' Karel was saying. 'There is this very serious pollution of a whole region from power stations on which the rest of us are quite dependent: for energy, for heavy industry. So. We look for an alternative. In the past there was the possibility of gas from our friends in the Soviet Union, and naturally we have resisted this idea, because such dependence could mean we are held to ransom.' He pulled out, passing a car piled high with hay bales. 'The other alternative is nuclear power, and here is the split. In the north, where our children are wearing gas masks as they walk to school in the winter, nuclear power seems clean and safe – so long as it comes from somewhere else. In the south, perhaps you know of this, we have such a reactor, on the Vltava, near Temelin. It is close to the Austrian border. It is designed to be the largest nuclear power station in the world. And naturally, no one near Temelin wishes to live in the shadow of something that is untested, that is resembling Chernobyl. There is a report on the possible dangers even before this disaster, which they try to keep a secret. Since Chernobyl, Greenpeace have been kind enough to draw attention by dropping a banner down the side of one of the cooling towers – perhaps, in the British press, you have seen pictures?'

'Yes,' said Harriet, welcoming distraction. 'And I thought of you – '

He turned to smile at her. 'As you looked on the television in Wenceslas Square, I think, in 1989 – '

'Yes.' She returned the smile. Cool air blew back her hair, they were driving fast, and the landscape was changing: undulating arable fields became rolling hills of pasture, dotted with sheep. 'On every hill a castle, in every woods a château; rivers and forests and soaring skies – '

Travel-guide, picture-book Bohemia, with no sign, yet, of the ravages both Hugh and Karel had talked about.

'You okay in the back?' she asked Marsha.

'How long till we get there?'

She looked at Karel.

'Until Teplice? Perhaps a half-hour, forty minutes? It is a place to remember: somewhere once so lovely but ruined now.'

'Yes,' said Marsha, 'you said.'

Karel raised an eyebrow at her in the mirror.

Harriet felt Marsha go red. 'She didn't mean to sound rude.'

'No,' said Marsha. 'I didn't.' And then, in a rush, 'It's because I feel okay with you. I feel I can say what I want. Sometimes it comes out wrong.'

'Yes,' said Karel. 'We all have such moments.' He gave her an almost imperceptible wink; he spoke to his mother and Gaby in Czech: they were enjoying this day out of the city? They needed to stop, to stretch their legs? Harriet, aware that this was roughly what he must be asking, thought once again: he's kind, he's generous and sensitive. And although their recent encounter with Danielle had been eclipsed by what had felt like a much more important meeting since, she did now wonder, as they drove on: what happened between them? How could anyone wish to leave him?

She wondered, but she did not enquire. Now was not the moment.

'So?' she asked, seeking refuge, once again, in issues of the public domain, as he turned back to her. 'You were saying. What is the answer to this dilemma?'

'Your brother is helping to find it,' he said seriously. 'It is very important, this kind of investment from the western banks. But perhaps it is something of a stopgap. In the end, it will not be only a question of curbing pollution, but of finding a real alternative. When that happens, it will bring another problem: at present there are many people employed in these power stations. Unemployment is something new to us, as in East Germany. In places like Teplice there are already unpleasant meetings between the skinheads and the workers from other countries. And with the gypsies, too.'

'Are there? As in East Germany?'

'It is not yet so serious, I think, but certainly there is an element – ' He pulled out to overtake a tourist caravan, then swung back sharply as a speeding car approached. 'Excuse me.' He looked at her, drumming his hands on the wheel.

'You know something of the situation in Germany? Perhaps in Berlin – '

'Berlin was horrible,' said Marsha, from the back.

He looked in the mirror. 'I am sorry to hear it.'

'We got caught up in an unpleasant incident,' said Harriet flatly.

'You mean we nearly got killed.' Marsha leaned forward. 'We went to visit this factory, and on the way back Mum had to stop and look at a sort of refugee place, and there were skinheads there, and – '

'Marsha – '

'What?'

'I really don't want to talk about that now.'

'Why?'

'Please.' Harriet could hear herself sound sharp. 'I just don't, okay?'

Karel reached back for Marsha's hand. 'Leave it, little one, yes? For now.'

Marsha sat back. Karel said something in Czech. There was a rustle of sweet papers from Hannah's bag.

'Thank you,' said Harriet, as they drove on.

He glanced at her. 'It is the memory of this incident which has been distressing you?'

She looked away again. 'Not entirely, no.'

They were close to the German border now: much of the traffic heading towards them bore D numberplates; touring families in Volkswagen estate cars crammed with holiday luggage sped towards Prague; heavy articulated lorries climbed the hills, turning off to Usti nad Labem, and Litvinov, returning to Dresden and Leipzig. Hitchhikers with backpacks stood on the other side of the road, holding up cards.

'Everyone wants to go to Prague,' said Marsha.

'And Czechs wish to go to Dresden.' Karel indicated young girls stationed at intervals on the near side. 'They are hoping for German clients,' he said to Harriet, and from the back of the car came a disapproving murmur of Czech from his mother.

Distant mountains came into view; they reached the brow of a hill and Karel drew into the roadside. There was a worn flat area on the verge: he pulled over, and stopped the car.

'And so,' he said drily, opening his door and gesturing to them all, 'behold the view.'

They clambered out, stood on the hilltop and beheld. Ahead was the Krušne Hory range: dark, forested with conifers. Below, stretching for mile upon mile, were the devastated foothills. Mineworkings, filthy factory buildings, sprawling prefabricated estates: they lay in the shadow of the mountains on a sea of mud. Bulldozers crawled from site to site, towering chimneys belched vaporous smoke, black and evil yellow, into hazy sky.

'Dear God,' said Harriet, half to herself.

'Look,' said Karel. 'Let me show you.' He pointed to the north, where dense low cloud hung above the outskirts of a town. 'The chemical plant at Litvinov. When the emissions are too high, red lights flash on the road, and you must switch off your engine.' He had his hands on Harriet's shoulders; he turned her so that she was looking west. 'See those cooling towers? Those are the power stations of Tusmice and Prunerov.'

He released her; he spread his arms. 'You see the mud? There used to be small villages – they have all been flattened, to make way for these developments. You see the forests on the mountainside? Marsha – you see where I am pointing? All through, the trees are dying. It is not possible to see from here, but I assure you that if we were to drive up into those mountains you would see not trees but skeletons. And the silence – ' He shook his head. 'All such forests are quiet and still, but there . . . it is something eerie.'

Marsha was frowning, looking from side to side. 'It's horrible. It's *real* pollution.'

'Yes. Because they are mining the brown coal and also they are burning it: in these power stations, in the factories, the heavy industry plant, the chemical plant . . . It is an onslaught. If it were winter I should not bring you here. In winter all this makes a great smog: it can make you ill.'

'It smells even now,' she said. 'Where's Hugh's power station?'

'If it is near Teplice, it is probably the one you can see to your right.' He turned her round, and pointed. They all looked towards a squat, ugly line of buildings beyond a distant town. 'There, the sulphur is filtered out, it is not so dangerous.'

'Can we go and see it?'

'Go right up to it? No. There are high fences all round such places, Marsha, there are many restrictions. But we can drive to the town. Perhaps, if anyone still wishes to eat, we can have lunch.'

There were swans, still, on the lake, but the château was now a museum. The blocks of nineteenth-century houses along the main street were still standing, but the paint was peeling, like the bark on the lime trees, whose blackened leaves lay here and there on the pavements. There was a park, there was a sky-blue swimming pool, but the air, even on a summer's day, was faintly acrid, and a haze that had nothing to do with the weather hung over the park, the shuttered houses, the empty school playground and ill-stocked shops. There were few people about. It was not quite a ghost town, but it had that quality, and when they had parked the car and were walking through the quiet streets looking for somewhere to eat they fell into silence themselves. as if they, too, had to live here, amidst a desolate landscape, dreading the winter.

But the place had to survive, and there were two or three hotel restaurants. They chose one on the corner of a fading square – cobbles, a bicycle propped against a tree, a child going home with a loaf of bread. Leaves fell with a papery rustle. A dull-coated cat sat on the steps of the hotel, blinking in the sun.

'He's nice, this cat,' said Marsha, and she and Gaby stopped to stroke him. 'It's like Berlin, seeing a hotel cat again.'

'You said you did not like Berlin.' Gaby was rubbing his ears.

'The cat was the only nice thing. She had kittens, I wanted to bring one, but Mum wouldn't let me. This one looks so old and ill. Poor puss.'

'You're blocking the way,' said Harriet, drawing the children aside as a young couple came out of the doorway. 'Come on.' They followed Karel into the hall, and into a shadowy dining room.

'In fact, it's a bit like the Hotel Scheiber, isn't it, Mum?' said Marsha, looking about her at half-closed shutters, white linen on empty tables, a beaten brass gong.

'It is a bit. Come on,' said Harriet again, shepherding the girls forward. She was conscious of a rising tension as she did so – as if, in urging and ushering, she could push away the hour ahead, when she must sit in this room and eat and talk like an ordinary human being.

Dust in a narrow beam of sunlight, a heavy face across the table, a stillness, a silence, a moment you might look back on all your life, thinking –

Then. That's when it was.

Karel was talking to the waitress. He was showing his mother to a pleasant table overlooking the square, holding out a chair for her, and for Harriet; motioning the girls to their places. He took the menu from the waitress with a smile, then read out the dishes in Czech, translating into English with some difficulty.

'*Houskovy knedliky* – these are a dumpling as big as your fist, sliced up . . . There are also potato dumplings, potato soup, a roasted pork, a roasted hen . . .'

'Cluck cluck, cluck,' said Marsha, laughing.

He looked at her over his glasses. 'What should I say?'

'I don't know – if you say hen, it sounds as if it's still got its feathers on.'

'It has.'

The waitress, her straight brown hair held back with a slide, stood chewing a fingernail. Karel consulted Hannah, and ordered. Wine came, and syrupy squash for the girls, and a basket of bread. They ate, they talked, they looked out at the square, where old men sat smoking beneath the trees. The food, when it eventually arrived, was overcooked and heavy, but Karel could not have made the hour or so they sat there more enjoyable. He concentrated on being a host as he did upon his work: he was attentive and charming and funny, and Harriet, finishing, put down her knife and fork and raised her glass.

'Thank you. You have given us a lovely time.' She looked across at Marsha. 'Hasn't he?'

Marsha nodded. 'It's been great. It's been brilliant ever since we got here.' She chinked her glass with his; she got up, went round the table and hugged him, resting her cheek against his. 'Thanks. Thanks a lot.'

Karel patted her face. 'It is my pleasure, little one.'

They had coffee and cake, and Harriet insisted on paying the bill.

'Please. We must do something for you.'

'No, no – '

'Let her,' said Marsha, and Karel bowed.

They left – Gaby and Marsha sounding the gong, very quietly, as they went past. Outside, the cat had fallen asleep on the steps, and the square was almost empty. Hannah made a suggestion; Karel translated.

'My mother wonders if we would like to go for a drive in the mountains, before we return to Prague. That is – ' he turned to the girls. 'You two may go to the park, with Granny, yes? And we – ' He looked at Harriet ' – we might have a little time together. Would that suit you?'

'I – yes, yes, I think so. Marsha? Is that okay?'

Marsha hesitated. '*I'd* like to go up to the mountains.'

Karel put his hand on her shoulder. 'I understand. But your mother and I have not seen each other for twenty-five years, you know, and soon you will be going back to England. We have not had time to talk to each other. I mean, like boring grown-ups.'

It was true.

She nodded. 'Okay.'

'Good girl.'

They arranged to meet, back here in the square, for tea in the hotel if it grew too hot and they were delayed. They walked back to the car; Hannah took the girls across to the park. There were swings, there was a view of the lake, the château.

Harriet and Marsha kissed goodbye.

The road wound upwards, between dense conifers. They passed signs to Dresden and Berlin, they passed a few other cars, a lorry or two. On either side of them the forest stretched dark and still, the ground carpeted thickly with needles, fir cones, brushwood. Here and there were clearings; once, the sound of an axe.

'You see,' said Karel, nodding towards the window.

Harriet looked, and saw, here and there, trees bleached of colour, the needles fallen, the branches bare. They were, indeed, like skeletons, and when other cars had disappeared the silence was, as Karel had said it would be, eerie and oppressive.

She thought: I have come to a place of death –

'You are quiet,' he said, changing gear. 'You are finding this unpleasant?'

'Well – '

'I am sorry. When we reach the top it is better. I know some people who dislike the forest, but it is such a long time since I have been here, and it is important to me. Not just to write about, but to see these things. For your brother, too. You will be able to describe to him – or perhaps he will come one day to see for himself.'

'Perhaps.' Then, unable to stop herself, she said, 'At the moment he has other things on his mind.'

'Yes?' Karel turned to look at her. 'And you, also, I think.'

She did not answer.

'Harriet?'

She closed her eyes, fighting back tears.

He said gravely, 'You are very sad, I know it. I should like very much to help you.'

'Don't, don't – ' She covered her face.

'I should stop the car?'

'No, no. I'm sorry – ' she felt in her bag, and found a packet of tissues. She blew her nose as they drove on in silence, climbing higher and higher.

They reached the top. It was better. Karel parked the car at the side of the road.

'Shall we walk a little?'

They got out, locking the doors. A path ran alongside the road. He put his arm round her; they walked. Every now and then a car or lorry went past, this way, that way, coming to Prague, going to Berlin. They were on a ridge, Germany on one side, the new Czech Republic on the other. Somewhere to the south was Austria; somewhere to the north the Polish border.

Karel said: 'We have talked of many things since your arrival. Perhaps I should say I have talked. Of public, political things. Yes?'

'Yes.'

'Harriet has talked little. She has asked a lot of questions.'

'I am sorry.'

'No, no. Sometimes it is easier to talk about public, political issues.'

She said, thinking, 'I thought you preferred it.'

'I enjoy it, that is true. I am deeply engaged. But prefer it? I am not sure. There is another side to life, after all.'

'Yes.' They walked on in silence.

She said carefully: 'May I ask you, then? About you and Danielle?'

'Danielle and I are friends, now, I have told you.'

'Yes, but – '

'But it was not always so. She left me for someone else. Well – ' he smiled wryly. 'For several someone elses. Danielle does not find it easy to be faithful. I found that difficult. But still – ' he made a gesture. 'In the end I had to accept it. In the end we said goodbye and we have made great efforts, since; she too has made this effort.'

'For Gabrielle – '

'For Gabrielle, and also for ourselves. It is not pleasant to be on bad terms. There has to be an ... accommodation. Yes? That is the right expression?'

'I think so.'

They walked on; she said, thinking of everything she had observed in

293

him, everything she knew about him: 'It's hard to imagine how anyone could wish to leave you.'

'That is a very nice thing to say.'

'It's true.'

They stopped on the path; looked at each other; he turned her to face him, his hands on her shoulders. On either side of them the forest stretched away, sloping to east and west.

He said: 'But still we are talking about me, and my life. What about Harriet? You come on a journey to look for a friend from the past. Yes? And something happens. Perhaps a great deal happens. I try to work it out, I make guesses, I do not like to press you, but I wish to know you better.' He looked at her with great seriousness and affection. 'You are going to tell me?'

From some distance behind her a lorry was approaching, on the other side of the road, coming from Germany.

She said slowly, 'I do not know where to begin. I told you: I am a political person, too. I have always been active, and . . . and so on. There was an expression in Britain which had great currency, for a while: the personal is political. I think that's true. I've always thought it was true. But on this journey I have met – what can I say? A darkness? In other people, perhaps in myself. Perhaps it has changed me. It is something which until now I have not had time for, or been really aware of. But in Brussels – in Berlin – '

The lorry was drawing closer, its heavy rumble the only sound on the road. Karel, for a moment, glanced towards it.

'In Berlin,' she said, 'I spent a long time talking to someone I thought I despised. I no longer despise him. He is here in Prague, but – '

'Harriet.' Karel raised a finger to stop her. 'One moment.' He was looking over her shoulder, as the lorry drew near.

She turned, she saw it. A container lorry, driving at speed on the flat, a lorry she had seen – had she? – somewhere before, or something like it. She looked, shading her eyes from the sun. It drew near, it was level: she saw, just for a moment, German words on the side. She had noticed those words somewhere else.

INDUSTRIELLE MATERIELEN FÜR WEITERE WERARBEITUNG –

RÜCKSTAND WIEDERVERWERTEN –

NICHT SPEZIFIKATIONGERECHTES MATERIAL –

Where had she seen them before?

A lorry was pulling out of a gate –

Approaching the gate was a group of people, shouting, holding up banners. A skull and crossbones? What were they shouting? The lorry went out of the gate, and a barrier came down swiftly –

Wilkendorf & Scheiber.

The lorry roared past them, disturbing the air, and she and Karel stepped back from the roadside.

He was frowning; he said: 'Harriet, you must forgive me – ' and he turned and began to run, back towards the car.

'What is it!' She followed him, panting. 'What is it?'

They reached the red Skoda, he unlocked the doors. 'Quick! I am sorry, but quick!'

She fell into the passenger seat and he started the engine.

'What?' she said, as they squealed away from the roadside. 'What's in that lorry?'

'Something that comes across the border too often, that's dumped here where we are already – ' His face was grim, he changed gear and banged his foot down. 'Waste. They are dumping toxic waste.' He glanced at her. 'Put on your belt, I am going to follow them.'

The road through the forest wound down, down, and the trees were dark and still. Ahead of them, the lorry had slowed, and they were keeping their distance. They rounded a bend; a narrower road ran off to the left, following the line of the mountains. The lorry took it. They waited, and followed, keeping it in sight.

INDUSTRIELLE MATERIELEN –

RÜCKSTAND WIEDERVERWERTEN –

NICHT SPEZIFIKATIONGERECHTES MATERIAL –

The words were painted on the back, as well as the sides.

'What's in there?' asked Harriet bleakly. 'What do they mean?'

'I do not know the English exactly.' He was frowning again, intent on the road. 'Residues for recycling? Off-specification materials. That is clumsy. Industrial goods for further use. Something like this. It is a blind, it is making it all sound respectable. Recycling – it even sounds good, correct.'

'But in fact – '

'In fact there are drums of chemicals in there which no one is going to recycle. Solvents. Paint wastes with metals. Mercury, perhaps. Old pesticides, DDT, chemicals from the laboratory – who knows? All we know is that it is dangerous. More than dangerous, deadly. No one wants it in their own country. It is very expensive to burn. It is illegal to take it across borders without notifying the country of destination. Naturally, the country of destination does not want it. Someone is paid to take it away, and dump it. Over the border, naturally.'

The road grew narrower and twisting, the trees alongside were dense and sunless. The lorry rounded a bend; they followed. Harriet could no longer bear to look.

She leaned back in her seat, she closed her eyes, but the images followed her –

A tram, humming across East Berlin; an argument. She had overstated her case. And yet –

A gut reaction was a gut reaction, and it told you who you were. What was the point at which you might say that somebody's politics mattered a lot, and more than anything else?

On the far side of the industrial estate, a building, bolted and barred –

'*What's in there?*'

'*I've no idea.*' *He was hurrying her away across the compound –*

She had thought the people shouting at the gate were thugs, skinheads, the young neo-Nazis who had followed them later, across the estate to the refugee hostel –

'*Scheiber!*' *A dog leapt on his chain.* '*Scheiber!*'

But no – that was another thread in the political tapestry. The group at the gate had been shouting about something else; the skull and crossbones on banners had been not about Fascism, or racism, or unemployment, but criminal dumping.

A graveyard, an overcrowded burial ground; pieces of paper held down by pebbles, messages left for the wind, unbearably sad and poetic.

'*All that fucking misery has to come out somewhere – You wouldn't care for me if you knew me, Harriet – I still do things you wouldn't believe –*'

Smoking, smoking, smoking.

Cigarettes kill you. Who cares?

Christopher, Christopher – I don't want to say goodbye –

'They dump it over the border, naturally,' Karel was saying beside her. 'They dump it here, and I see them, we go to the International Court of Justice.'

Then he slowed right down, and she opened her eyes. The lorry ahead of them bumped over an unmade track and they bumped after it, slowly, slowly, seeing the driver look in his mirror, aware of them, no doubt about it, but going on because there was nowhere to stop and turn back, only the ruts and the mud, a clearing, a barn, and somebody waiting.

Even before they all stopped and got out, even before the driver turned to Karel and shouted, she knew who they would see at the entrance to that rotting barn, coming towards them, heavy and tall and smoking, greyer than grey when he saw her –

'Christopher!' She heard herself wailing.

'Harriet – '

He took a few steps, inhaled on the cigarette, flicked it away.

And stopped, suddenly, clutching his chest.

He staggered, as if he had been hit –

And doubled up, groaning and crumpled, and fell.

'*Christopher!*' She raced towards him, weeping, weeping, flung herself down beside him, cradled his head in her arms.

7

There are those who embrace life, and those for whom death is always a shadow, walking alongside.

Was that true?

Harriet was not used to thinking like this. She had grown used to thinking like this. She leaned on the sill of the pension bedroom window and looked out: at the moon, at the star-filled sky, at one or two lights in other windows. Someone was walking down the hill, through gaslit streets, towards the river. It was very late.

Not far from here, one winter, Kafka had written all night in a rented house, feverish fingers racing across the page, drawing his coat about him as the fire sank low, coughing and coughing. His sister, asleep in another room, woke and heard him.

'Franz?'

He spat into his handkerchief, his pen scratched the page, writing, writing . . .

I have scarcely anything in common with myself –

Harriet put her head in her hands. She listened to Marsha, breathing unsteadily, restless. She listened to the footsteps, walking away down the hill, growing fainter. A church clock chimed, then, almost at once, another: single, sombre notes. One o'clock. Again, in another part of the city. Again. Like the sound of a funeral bell, tolling the years of a life.

Was that how Christopher would be buried? Would wish to be buried?

They had left him there in the barn, on sacking –

Somebody else would have to –

Papers, an inquest, a flight back to London –

'Mummy?'

Prickles rose on the back of her neck; she turned round, shivering.

'I thought you were asleep.'

'I can't.' Marsha was sitting up in bed. 'I can't, I can't.' She held out her arms.

'No,' said Harriet, 'neither can I.'

She climbed into bed beside her; they lay with their arms wrapped rond each other. Harriet heard herself murmuring, comforting, trying to make everything right.

The moon rose, and light fell through the window, touching the end of the bed, the chest of drawers, the wooden box of letters which had brought them here.

8

They were walking along the waterfront. Behind them, the children were following slowly, keeping their distance. Barges went past, going north, going south; black-headed gulls cried above them.

Harriet said: 'And now I have told you everything.'

'Thank you.'

She said: 'Do you understand? How it is possible to care so much? Even when – '

'I think so. I am not sure, but I think so.'

'I don't,' said Harriet.

They stopped, and the girls caught up with them. For a while they walked on together, the Charles Bridge behind them, the islands ahead. The sun was sinking, the air was tranquil and still. They leaned on a railing, watching the swans.

Marsha said: 'I feel a bit better, now.'

'Good. Why don't you and Gaby walk on? You lead the way for a bit.'

'Okay.'

They left the railing; the sun sank lower; the river shone.

Harriet and Karel followed the children, walking slowly.

She said: 'You have never been troubled by doubt, or self-dislike – '

'Not in the way you have spoken of, no.'

'You know who you are.'

'I think so. Yes. I think that is true.'

'I used to be like that. I think that is how I used to be – '

'And now?

'Now I'm not certain. Nothing seems certain. I have to pick up my life again – '

How was that possible? What should she do?

They came to the stretch of gabled houses, ochre and cream beneath tiled roofs. Havel and his family lived near here. She remembered something.

'Karel? I read – I think I read somewhere that since the Revolution something has gone from politics now. The existential kick, I think that's what I read. Is that true?'

He thought about it. 'Yes, in a way. But still – I feel I have plenty to do.' He looked at her, walking so slowly beside him. 'We are talking again about the public arena – '

'What happened – in the mountains – for you that was very much in the public arena.'

'But not for you.'

'No. I'm in different territory, now.'

The children were tiring. Time to go back.

He said: 'I feel we still have a great deal to talk about. Not now. Now you are too distressed. But I should like to – to keep in touch. Yes? May I come to London? To visit you and Marsha?'

'Yes. Yes, of course. We should love it. You have been wonderful.'

'Thank you. You also, I think.'

They stopped; he turned her towards him, his hands on her shoulders.

'And perhaps – one day, perhaps you will come back here. When you are calmer. When you are ready.'

'Yes. Yes, I should like that.'

He drew her towards him; he kissed her forehead. The children were calling. He held her away again.

'Shall we see?' he asked gravely.

She looked at the face which had haunted her, for months after his departure, twenty-five years ago, when she was young. Clever and vital and loving. And now she had found him again.

A bell was ringing, a single note, sounding across the water. She felt herself on the threshold of a journey, which began here, now, in this moment of grief and consolation, and ended – where would it end?

THE LAST GUESTS OF THE SEASON

After years out of contact, Claire and Frances, once fellow-students, meet again by chance. Both are married now, with children: impulsively, the families agree to go on holiday together.

The house in Portugal is set in a garden of lemon trees. Inside, it is cool and dark; outside, the valley shimmers in the heat and cicadas sing. In an atmosphere of watchfulness and longing, secrets are revealed whose intensity threatens to tear both families apart, and the night is full of terrors. As events move inexorably toward tragedy, no one sees who is to be the real victim.

Haunting and beautifully crafted, this is a novel which illuminates the darker side of family life and the salvation that is found in it.

'A subtle and revealing look at human interaction . . . three stars' NEW WOMAN

'Careful, evocative writing full of touching observation' WOMAN'S JOURNAL

BREAKING THE CHAIN

Maggie Makepeace

When Phoebe married Duncan Moon, she imagined they would get around to loving one another. But she hadn't bargained on the stifling effect on her husband of his alarming family, nor the many ways in which the family would contrive to exclude her from their affluent but hollow lives. It is only when Phoebe reads the hidden diaries of her father-in-law's ex-mistress that she learns the truth about the Moons – and discovers love where she'd never thought she'd find it.

In this wickedly funny first novel Maggie Makepeace paints a devastating portrait of upper middle class family life. By turns hilarious, painful, tragic and unexpectedly poignant, this is black comedy at its startling best.

A PRICE FOR EVERYTHING

Mary Sheepshanks

Sonia, Lady Duntan, loves the family seat rather more than she does her husband. Archie, however, is adamant: their lifestyle must be preserved and the house must go.

When Archie embarks on an affair with the pneumatic Rosie Bartlett, Sonia is even more determined to thwart his plans. But as her conspiracy widens to include her glamorous but unreliable mother-in-law, a rather sinister bogus monk and the urbane Simon Hadleigh from the company Heritage at Risk, things begin to spiral out of control . . .

In turns hilariously funny and genuinely sad, *A Price for Everything* is a bittersweet novel of love, loss and the art of compromise.

OTHER TITLES
AVAILABLE IN ARROW

☐	The Last Guests of the Season	Sue Gee	£4.99
☐	Queen of the Witches	Jessica Berens	£4.99
☐	Damage	Josephine Hart	£5.99
☐	Sin	Josephine Hart	£5.99
☐	Magic Flutes	Eva Ibbotson	£4.99
☐	The Morning Gift	Eva Ibbotson	£5.99
☐	A Countess Below Stairs	Eva Ibbotson	£5.99
☐	Breaking the Chain	Maggie Makepeace	£5.99
☐	Telling Only Lies	Jessica Mann	£5.99
☐	Plucking the Apple	Elizabeth Palmer	£5.99
☐	The Stainless Angel	Elizabeth Palmer	£4.99
☐	Old Money	Elizabeth Palmer	£5.99
☐	The Young Italians	Amanda Prantera	£5.99
☐	A Price For Everything	Mary Sheepshanks	£5.99
☐	My Life as a Whale	Dyan Sheldon	£4.99

Prices and other details are liable to change

**ARROW BOOKS, BOOKSERVICE BY POST, PO BOX 29,
DOUGLAS, ISLE OF MAN, BRITISH ISLES**

NAME ....

ADDRESS ....

....

....

Please enclose a cheque or postal order made out to Arrow Books
Ltd, for the amount due and allow for the following for postage and
packing.

U.K. CUSTOMERS: Please allow 75p per book to a maximum of
£7.50

B.F.P.O. & EIRE: Please allow 75p per book to a maximum of £7.50

OVERSEAS CUSTOMERS: Please allow £1.00 per book.

Whilst every effort is made to keep prices low it is sometimes necessary
to increase cover prices at short notice. Arrow Books reserve the right
to show new retail prices on covers which may differ from those
previously advertised in the text or elsewhere.